veiled rose

veiled rose

TALES OF GOLDSTONE WOOD

✦✦

ANNE ELISABETH STENGL

BETHANY HOUSE PUBLISHERS
Minneapolis, Minnesota

Veiled Rose
Copyright © 2011
Anne Elisabeth Stengl

Book design by Paul Higdon
Cover illustration by William Graf

Published by Bethany House Publishers
11400 Hampshire Avenue South
Bloomington, Minnesota 55438

Bethany House Publishers is a division of
Baker Publishing Group, Grand Rapids, Michigan.

Printed in the United States of America

**Library of Congress Cataloging-in-Publication Data
is available for this title.**

To my David Rohan

Tales of Goldstone Wood

Heartless
Veiled Rose
Moonblood

PROLOGUE

HILL HOUSE, though abandoned, had remained unscathed during the years of the Dragon's occupation. This pleased the young man as he climbed the forlorn path to that place where he had spent many happy months. He had feared that Hill House, despite its remote location, would have been one of the Dragon's primary targets. But as he passed various shepherding villages and proceeded up the mountain road to the house itself, he felt his spirits lifting. And when he saw the house still standing and its sloping gardens yet unburned, something close to a smile touched his too serious face.

Of all the familiar haunts he had passed since returning to his homeland, this was the only one that bore no visible scars of the Dragon's work.

His progress up into the mountains had been solitary. Companions had journeyed with him to the foot of the mountain road, but he had requested that they let him make the climb alone. This meant a long day of rough going with only a shaggy pony for company. But the young man was used to this kind of loneliness by now.

Lately, he felt far lonelier in a crowd than when left to himself.

The mountain air was clean compared to the stench that lingered behind every breath in the low country. The sturdy pony enjoyed it as well, wuffling to itself and shaking its mane with renewed vigor. The young man tethered his mount at the house gate and entered the overgrown gardens.

Hill House's empty windows, like mourning eyes, gazed down on him. He sought the big windows framed by heavy curtains that belonged to the library; the smaller, set up a story higher, opened from his old bedroom. The glass panes were dusty with time and neglect, but at least they were not filmed over with ash, and the curtains did not reek with poison.

The young man did not enter the house, though a part of him longed to walk those corridors again, to feel a comfort that he had not yet felt since returning to his native land. No, he had made the climb to Hill House for a purpose, and he dared not linger.

He had a monster to hunt.

He found the garden shed, which was locked just as old Mousehand, the gardener, had always left it. The young man knew he would never get those complicated locks undone. When Mousehand died, his replacement had been unable to work them either and had been obliged to build a whole new shed. But the tools in that new shed would be insufficient, the young man knew. Some traditions must be maintained if one hoped to hunt a monster successfully.

The wooden door was soft in places. He kicked at it and pulled out several panels until he could force his way inside. He did not look around too carefully in that gloom, feeling as unwilling to disturb the old gardener's secrets as he would be to desecrate a sacred tomb. He sought only one thing: the weapon of a warrior.

Which he found in the form of a beanpole.

Not just any beanpole. He recognized it the moment his fingers wrapped around the thin wooden rod. This was the beanpole of all beanpoles, mighty in purpose and fell with use. Another smile tugged at the young man's mouth as he climbed back out of the shed, his weapon in hand. In the daylight, one could see the rough carvings that ran up and down the pole's length, jagged and unlovely but made with care. And at the tip of the pole was tied a faded red scarf.

So armed, the young man made his way to the far garden gate, which these days was encrusted with rust. It squeaked in lazy protest when he opened it to step onto the trail that led farther up the mountain.

It wouldn't be much of a hunt. He had a fair notion where his monster was to be found. This was by no means the first time he had pursued this quarry.

The first time, he had been no more than eleven years old.

PART ONE

1

They said a monster lived in the mountains.

They couldn't say where it hid. They couldn't say when it had come. They certainly couldn't say what it looked like, though they had plenty of conflicting ideas on that subject. But they all agreed that it was there. Somewhere.

They being no one in particular and everyone in general who lived and worked at Hill House, where Leo spent the summer of his eleventh year. At first, Leo assumed it was simply another one of those sayings that grown-ups liked to bandy about, such as swearing "Silent Lady!" when frightened, or "Dragon's teeth!" when angry.

"Best come in, it's almost dark," his nursemaid would call from his bedroom window when he was playing out on the sloping lawns and gardens of Hill House. "You don't want the mountain monster to carry you off."

This wasn't true. Leo wouldn't have minded much if the monster did carry him off, or at least made the attempt. He put off coming in until the very last minute, just before his nursemaid would feel obliged to sally forth and fetch him. But no matter how long the shadows in the mountainside garden grew, he saw neither hide nor hair of anything monsterlike.

Then one day he took the servants' stairway down from his rooms, for it was a quicker route to the gardens. He overheard furtive voices and could not have stopped himself from eavesdropping for the world.

"I swear on my hand, I saw it!" said the voice Leo recognized as belonging to Leanbear, the carriage man. "I was on my way up the mountain trail to my old granna's house, and I saw it clear as day!"

Leanbear was a strong man, used to working with the tough mountain ponies that pulled the carriages in this rough part of the country. But his voice quavered and remained low as he spoke.

"What did it look like?" Mistress Redbird, the cook, asked in a tone rather too dry to be sympathetic. "Was it big and shaggy? Did you see the Wolf Lord's ghost? He was said to prowl these parts back in the day."

"This was no wolf, Redbird, I'll tell you that straight," said the carriage man. "I've hunted down my share of wolves, and I'm proud to say I've yet to feel even a twinge when they set up their howling on winter's nights. But this was no wolf."

"What, then?" demanded Redbird. "A troll? A goblin? A sylph?"

"More like . . . a demon."

Leo shuddered in his dark stairway, a delightful shudder of terror such as only boys of a particular spirit may experience. But Mistress Redbird laughed outright. "I'd have sooner you said *dragon*, Leanbear."

"You know as well as I that it's out there," the carriage man growled.

For a moment, Mistress Redbird's voice became more serious. "I know what I know, and the rest I don't pretend to understand. But I say it's best you keep such fool talk to yourself, especially while the little mister is running about the place."

Leanbear grunted, and both of them moved on without seeing Leo where he stood in the dark stairway.

Leo did not move for a long moment. He'd made plans for his day already, packing up the fine library chess pieces into a leather sack to sneak them out to the garden, where he intended to dig a dirt fortress and wage a battle that had nothing whatsoever to do with chess. But such paltry games were as nothing to the inspiration that now filled his soul.

His chess pieces rattling in their sack, Leo turned and raced back up the stairs and on to the Hill House library, where he could be certain to find his cousin, Foxbrush.

Foxbrush was a pale, sickly, self-styled cherub, and a favorite of Leo's mother. She thought him a good influence on Leo, so she insisted the two of them be the best of friends. Leo wouldn't have minded this so much—not even his mother's constant nagging of "Why can't you be more like your cousin?"—if once in a while Foxbrush could have been convinced to put down his books and get out of his overstuffed chair.

"Foxbrush!" Leo cried, bursting into the library. His cousin looked up from behind the cover of his book. It was one of his "improving reads," something like *Economic Concerns of the Trade Merchant's Status,* full of numbers and dates and other hideous things of that nature. Foxbrush pretended to enjoy them and was so good at the pretense that Leo sometimes believed him. He'd even picked up one or two of these books himself but had found them to be rubbish.

"Foxbrush!" he cried. "There's a monster in the mountains!"

"No there isn't," said Foxbrush.

Hill House belonged to Foxbrush's widowed mother, which meant that when any disagreement arose between the boys, Foxbrush could usually win with a final swipe of, "This is *my* mother's house, so you have to do what *I* say!" However, Leo's was by far the stronger personality, so if he made the effort he could sometimes barrage Foxbrush with so much enthusiasm that his cousin forgot to employ that dreaded line.

Foxbrush took one look at Leo's face, flushed and bright-eyed with the prospect of adventure, and ducked behind his book as though sheltering from a siege.

"Yes there is!" Leo said. "The carriage man saw it!"

"He also sees pixies dancing when he's been into last year's cider."

"We must hunt it!"

"No, we mustn't." Foxbrush nestled more solidly into his comfortable chair. "Aunt Starflower wouldn't like it."

"Mother's not here!"

"She'd find out."

"And praise us for catching a demon that's been terrorizing the countryside!"

"There isn't any demon."

"How do you know?"

Foxbrush's face emerged from behind the book, this time wearing his patient expression, the one that made Leo want to poke him in the eye, and said, "I've lived here all my life. I've heard people babble nonsense for years. But I've not seen it. I've not heard it. It doesn't exist." Back behind the book again, he added, "Go away."

Leo stared at the thick red cover for several fuming seconds. Then he took the sack of chess pieces from his belt and tossed it so that it came down on Foxbrush's head, eliciting a satisfactory "Ow!"

"You're no better than a girl, Foxbrush," Leo declared, storming from the library. It was much too fine a day to waste on his cousin.

Out in the gardens, Leo stood for some time a few steps from the door, gazing about. Hill House was so named because it rested high in the mountains in the southern part of the country. It commanded a fine prospect, looking north toward the spreading landscape of Leo's homeland. The weather was pleasant here, a little cool due to the altitude, but fresh and invigorating . . . the right air for an adventurous heart.

On regular days, the mountainside gardens of Hill House were interesting enough to occupy the boy. But now that he knew there was more to this monster talk than a mere nursemaid's warning, the gardens were suddenly much too small and cramped. No monster would come within the bounds of Hill House's gardens. Leo would have to venture out after it himself.

But first he must be properly armed.

"I need a weapon," he told Mousehand, the gardener. Mousehand was probably the oldest, creaking-est man in the world, and his face was a mass of beard. At Leo's words, the beard wrinkled into something that was probably a smile underneath, and the gardener's little eyes winked.

"A weapon, eh?" said Mousehand.

"Yes. A sword, if you have one."

Mousehand grunted, pausing to contemplate the row of parsnips he was weeding. "I think I know what you need."

With a splendid cacophony of crackling, the old man rose from his knees and hobbled to his toolshed with Leo close behind. In moments, Mousehand undid the various chains and latches that had baffled Leo every time he'd tried to get into the shed on his own, and the door swung open with almost as much creaking as Mousehand's joints. The gardener stepped inside and emerged with his selected weapon, which he handed to Leo with great ceremony.

Leo took it and frowned. "A beanpole?"

"A mighty sword, good sir knight, if you look at it right."

Leo wrinkled his nose. "You mean, use my imagination?"

"I might. Or I might not," said the gardener.

If there was one thing Leo disliked about grown-ups, it was their tendency to treat him like a child. "I'm going to hunt a monster. Is this really going to help?"

Here the gardener seemed to really look at Leo for the first time. He put his gnarled hand on the doorpost, leaning against it as his eyes traveled up and down the boy's slight frame. He took in the fine clothing, slightly mussed from play. He took in the scrapes on the hands that indicated a willingness to plunge into any activity with a will. He noted the spark that shone behind the sulkiness in a pair of large black eyes.

"What monster do you hunt?"

"The monster up the mountain," Leo replied. "Have you heard of it?"

The gardener nodded. "I have."

"Have you seen it?"

The gardener's beard shifted as the mouth somewhere in its depths worked back and forth in thought. "What I've seen and what others've seen ain't likely to be the same thing."

Leo shouldered his beanpole. "What have you seen?"

Mousehand shook his head. "You must see for yourself, lad, and decide for yourself. So, you're setting off up the mountain, are you?"

"I am."

"Does your nursemaid know?"

Dragon's teeth! He hadn't thought of that detail. "Um . . ."

"I'll just tell her you'll be home by nightfall when she asks, eh?"

Here Leo gave the old man a real smile; a smile that Mousehand, who had been a spirited boy himself ages ago, returned. Then the gardener escorted the boy up the mountainside to the edge of the garden and saluted solemnly as Leo stepped through the gate.

"Which way is quickest to the monster?"

"Never be in too much of a hurry to catch your quarry, young master," the gardener responded. "The adventure is the hunt, not the catch, remember." Then he pointed an arthritic finger up the beaten trail. "Follow that a good hundred yards, then look for the deer path on your left, beginning just under the silver-branched sapling tied with a red scarf. Follow that path, and you'll make a wide loop around that side of the mountain and end back where you started. Be careful you don't stray, now."

"I won't find a monster while following a path."

"If you're meant to meet with the monster, you'll meet it on that path. I swear to you. Do you believe me?" His eyes met Leo's and held the boy's gaze for much longer than Leo was comfortable. But Leo was not one to look away, so he studied the old man and considered what he'd said.

Oddly enough, he found that he believed Mousehand.

"All right," he said. "I'll follow the path."

With those words, he adjusted his grip on the beanpole, squared his shoulders, and started at a trot up the mountain.

"Hey!" the gardener called.

Leo looked back over his shoulder.

"Try not to get eaten whilst you're about. Might be kinda hard for me to explain to your folks, eh?"

Leo nodded, saluted the gardener, and continued up the path.

At first, it was a fantastic feeling. The forest at that time of year was a heavy dark green that breathed mystery. The birds sang tempting tunes like sirens, not so cheerful as to destroy the ambiance. Leo felt that surge of manliness common to all young adventurers and tried the mettle of his beanpole on an offending sapling or two. Perhaps it was a little lonely sallying forth on his own. Perhaps he would have preferred a brave comrade-in-arms. But there's a certain spirit that follows the solitary adventurer and prevents any real loneliness from setting in.

The path was broad, for many lived in the higher reaches of the mountain and trekked down to the lower village once or twice a week. It was hardly the right location to hunt monsters, but to Leo it was nonetheless exciting. He'd never before been so far away from home on his own. In fact, he had never before been so completely *alone*.

This thought struck him just as he came upon the silver-branched sapling tied with a red scarf. It was a threadbare scarf looped around the thin trunk. The red dye was so faded with age that it was lucky it caught Leo's eye. Obviously, someone had placed it there as an unobtrusive marker, not for the whole world to see. Leo might have stopped to wonder how the gardener knew about it or why he had decided to point it out to Leo . . . but he didn't. His mind was much too caught up in the sudden decision presented him.

The deer trail led around the mountain rather than up, and it led deep into the forest. The dark forest. Like a pathway into the blackness of a mine, the light dimmed and then vanished only a few paces in.

Leo had to make the choice. Did he truly desire the adventure he had come seeking? Did he truly wish to make that plunge and hunt the monster? Or would he rather turn around and call it a day after a brisk and relatively interesting walk? No one would blame him, after all.

For a terrible moment, he stood undecided, doubting his own courage, excusing his fear.

Then from the depths of the mountain forest, so distant as to sound like an echo, he heard a trill of silver notes from a bird that might almost have been singing words had Leo known the language.

And something about that song told him, *It's all right. Make the plunge. Hunt your monster and see what you find.*

With a mighty cry to prove to himself how unafraid he was, Leo smacked his beanpole against the sapling as hard as he could, making it sway and tremble. Then he pushed through low growth and on down the narrow trail.

The going was slower now, since he had to watch the ground for roots and duck to avoid branches that swung at his eyes. His heart raced, but it felt good to let it race, and his grip on the beanpole tightened until his knuckles were white. In his mind he pictured the monster again and again, remembering the bits and pieces he'd overheard.

A demon, Leanbear had said. Leo imagined a towering, lurching, spine-shouldered fiend with dripping jowls and red eyes. He imagined his beanpole really was a sword, slashing away grasping claws and driving home to rid the world of this abomination.

A dragon, Redbird had remarked. Leo saw in his mind scaly wings, smoke-fuming nostrils, and a long, sinuous tail. Of course, it would be difficult for a dragon to crawl about in this overgrown forest without making a terrible racket.

Perhaps a sylph, a creature of the wind, wafting and horrible, with sharp white claws. Leo liked this idea better. Immaterial monsters were frightening, but they were less likely to cause physical harm . . . and when one was venturing out with only a beanpole for protection, this was just as well.

Monster after monster flitted across Leo's imagination. The day lengthened, and the path beneath him did as well. He could not guess how long he had been traveling; it seemed like forever. All that tramping around, even sheltered as he was from the hot sun, made Leo hungry, and the monsters in his mind swiftly grew less interesting.

"Bah!"

His beanpole out at an awkward angle to push aside a clump of nettles, Leo froze. Then his heart started to pound wildly, yet still he could not move. Other than the birds' random twittering and the crunch and crash of his own feet on the uneven terrain, he hadn't heard a sound that deep in the forest. Not until this moment.

"Baaaah!"

It was closer now, he thought. Was it moving his way? He'd never pictured seven-foot spine-backed fiends making noises quite like that, but who was to say what monsters sound like? He brandished his beanpole, leaving the nettles to swing back and bite him in the leg. "Dragon's teeth!" he yelped.

"BAAAAH!"

Leo whirled around, for the sound had come from behind him.

Peering into the brambles through which he had just come, he saw fur and an inhuman body. And for a second, he saw the glint of an evil yellow eye.

Then the goat pushed her nose through. "Bah!" she said.

Leo only just stopped himself from swinging his pole. He stared at the goat, which stared back at him, and the accusatory gleam in her eyes made him feel very stupid.

"Dragon-eaten beast," he growled. "What are you doing out here all alone? You're not even wearing a bell. Did you wander away from your flock?"

"Bah," said the goat, stamping a cloven hoof.

It was embarrassing how fast his heart was still drumming. Leo bent down to rub his leg where the nettles had caught him, muttering to himself about goat stew. What a waste this afternoon was turning out to be! He'd have been better off with chess pieces in the dirt like a stupid little boy rather than all this adventuring nonsense. Monster indeed! Nothing but a stupid goat.

Something cracked behind him.

Leo turned.

There it stood, not ten feet away. Swathed in veils, white and incorporeal and horrifying in the shadows cast by the tallest trees.

Leo did not wait for a second look. Pushing past the goat, he crashed headlong back through the forest as fast as his feet could carry him, leaving his beanpole behind.

2

Heroes did not abandon their weapons.

The following morning was a mess of drizzle. A fine excuse to huddle inside all day, Leo told himself. But excuses were for cowards and children.

His nursemaid was busy, and Foxbrush was amusing himself by solving long algebraic equations and hadn't time for a game of chess or a romp up and down the stairs. Nothing suggested itself as a distraction from his nagging conscience, so Leo sat in turmoil before the library fire, rolling marbles back and forth without ever settling on a game. His thoughts plagued him.

What had he seen on the hillside? When he thought back, he could not even give it a specific form. He remembered being terrified, but what had terrified him exactly? It certainly hadn't been a monster in the traditional seven-foot, slavering-jaws sense. Which left him feeling silly. What excuse had he to run?

And to leave his weapon.

He thought of the heroes that peppered his history textbooks. Most of the stories were complete nonsense, he knew, but even so! Had not King Shadow Hand bargained away his own two hands to a powerful Faerie queen for the sake of protecting his kingdom? Had not the child Sight-of-Day stood up in the face of the Dragonwitch even when those around her surrendered? Had not Maid Starflower—the nation's most famous and beloved heroine, for whom half the girls were named to this day—had she not done battle with the dreadful Wolf Lord and, well, if not lived to tell the tale, at the very least lived on in reverent memory?

And those last two were girls, no less!

Leo felt ashamed. Faerie queens, witches, and giant wolves were about as terrible as they came. He couldn't pretend that whatever he had seen in the forest was anything so frightening as they. Especially when he couldn't even say *what* he had seen. How could he ever hope to number himself among heroes if . . .

It was more than he could stand.

Leo got up. Foxbrush did not raise his eyes from his equations, so there was no need to offer an explanation. Leo found an oiled coat and a hat, both a little large for him, and slipped out the back door. No one saw him save that bush-bearded gardener, who was still about his work on the lawn, even in the drizzle. Leo waved to the old man but did not address him as he made his way to the garden gate and out to the path beyond.

Yesterday that initial hundred yards had been easy enough to walk, for the sun had been shining and the birds singing. Today the path was gloomy, and when he came to that turn into the deeper forest, his heart nearly gave out. His memory conjured up images of that wafting, shrouded thing, and he thought for a longing moment of his marbles by the fire, and even of Foxbrush and his wretched algebra.

But real heroes don't leave their weapons behind. Perhaps he'd not hunt a monster, but if nothing else, Leo would retrieve his beanpole.

Pushing through the thicker growth caused dollops of accumulated water to splash on his hat and roll from the brim. Some went down the back of his coat, ice-cold. His boots were clumped with mud and wet leaves, and his adventurous spirit was long since dampened to death.

Nothing but pure stubbornness propelled him forward. At least his misery distracted him from his fright. It was difficult to be scared of a supposed monster when suffering the agonies of cold water down one's collar.

He vaguely recognized bits of the trail. There was that spot where the trees opened up and he could glimpse the sweep of the mountain down to the valleys below. There was that odd tree that bent at a right angle three feet up, then grew straight to its topmost branches. There was that boulder that looked like a goblin's ugly face, either leering or smiling; it was hard to say which.

And there was his beanpole.

It was leaning up against a tree, not lying in the trail where he had left it. As Leo drew nearer on tentative feet, he saw a red scarf tied near its top end, like a flag to attract his attention.

The sight of that scarf made his stomach lurch. Foolish, he knew, but he couldn't help it. Who had tied it there? It was the same fabric as the scarf signaling the turn in the path, though the dye was brighter. Someone knew he would come searching for his pole. But no one had seen him come this way.

No one but the goat and . . . and whatever that apparition was.

He could be pretty certain the goat hadn't tied the scarf to his pole. But why would that . . . thing? If it was that thing. Who else, though?

He stood dithering, staring at his beanpole, which, for all that it lacked features, stared accusingly back. As though it were saying, "How could you leave me behind like that? *Anything* could have happened to me! Anything at all!"

Leo's mouth twisted. Then he put out a hand and took his weapon, nearly expecting to be struck by lightning the moment his fingers touched the wood. Nothing happened. He stood in the damp and the drizzle of the mountain forest, alone with a beanpole in his hands. He felt silly.

"Monsters," he growled. "Dragons eat them!"

And he turned to find himself face-to-face with the veiled apparition.

"Dragon's teeth!" Leo bellowed.

"Silent Lady!" the apparition screamed at the same time, and each leapt back from the other, Leo landing in a damp patch of moss and slipping so that he came down hard on his rump. The apparition disappeared behind a thick tree trunk.

Leo sat on the moss, clutching his pole, his hat tilted back on his head, mouth open so that drizzle fell into it. His heart was racing so fast that he could scarcely breathe.

But the apparition did not come out.

It was still there. He could see the end of its white veil caught on a branch and also the edge of one sleeve. After a moment, he could have sworn he heard it breathing.

Did apparitions breathe?

"I'm not scared of you!" he said at length.

"Me neither" came a small voice from behind the tree.

"I've got a weapon!"

"Um . . . I don't."

Leo frowned. "You're not supposed to have a weapon."

"I don't."

"No, I mean, ghosts don't carry weapons."

"I ain't no ghost."

Well, that put things in a new light. Leo wiggled on the moss and noticed the dampness seeping into his britches. Using the beanpole for support, he got back to his feet. "If you aren't a ghost, what are you?"

"I don't know."

Leo saw a hand reach out and take hold of the bit of veil caught on the branch. It was a tiny hand covered in a thick glove. After a moment's struggle, it freed the bit of dirty linen, and now the apparition disappeared entirely behind the tree. But he could still hear it breathing.

"Are you a monster?" Leo asked.

"I don't think so. Are you?"

"No." Leo frowned. There was nothing horrible about the apparition's voice. It sounded too much like a child's. Did monsters take the shape of children to lure unsuspecting prey?

Then a terrible thought came to him, and he knew that he was right as soon as he thought it. He sighed and rolled his eyes, in that moment more irritated than even Foxbrush could make him.

"Wait a minute. You're nothing but a girl!"

The apparition looked around the tree trunk. "Yup," she said. And she was.

The last thing, the very last thing Leo needed was some girl trailing after him. Not if he was going to seriously hunt this monster.

And hunt it he would. Now that the fright of the shrouded something was so prosaically explained, all his vigor renewed with driving force. The world *had* to be more exciting than marbles and algebra and sniveling girls, and he would discover the source of that excitement if it took him until suppertime! Leo would walk—soggily, to be sure, but walk no less—in the footsteps of his heroic predecessors.

Just not with an odd little girl following him.

"Go away," he told the girl after squelching a few yards farther up the deer trail.

"Why?" she asked.

The drizzle had changed to full-fledged rain now, and Leo's patience was as flattened as the hair on his forehead. Was it really so much to ask for a little somber ambiance without her snuffling three steps back?

"Because. You'll get in the way."

"Of what?"

This Leo did not like to answer. It was bad enough when Foxbrush laughed at his ideas. But Foxbrush was his cousin and a boy, so there was nothing to stop Leo from taking a swing at his offensive face if necessary. If this strange girl—all wrapped up in her veils and scarves against the rain so that he couldn't see even a bit of her face—made fun of his heroism, he didn't know what he would do. Leo picked up his pace, pushing quickly through a sweeping pine bough, which splattered him with soggy needles. But the girl kept pace behind.

"Of what?" she repeated.

"Nothing," Leo growled.

"Then why cain't I come?"

"It's dangerous, that's why." He brandished his beanpole as he spoke, glaring over his shoulder at the girl. She stood there, rainwater dripping from the edge of her veils, unmoved.

"I ain't scared," she said.

"You should be."

"I ain't."

Leo had no younger brothers or sisters. He was friends with Foxbrush and knew a handful of other children close to his own age that his mother deemed "acceptable" playmates. They were easy enough to bend to his will, except Foxbrush, who didn't count. Leo and his cousin could hit each other a few times and usually come to a quick solution. But rational argument with irrational children was not a skill Leo had ever seen the need to develop.

He tried an age-old approach. "Your mum wouldn't like it."

"I don't have a mum."

Leo paused in midstride, his beanpole upraised to hold a branch out of his face. A pang of sympathy shot through him before he could stop it. He found himself looking down on her with new eyes. "No mother?" he said.

"Nope," said she.

"What about your father?"

She put her head to one side. "What about him?"

"Do you have one of those?"

"Just me old dad."

"He will mind if you're doing something dangerous."

The girl shrugged. "Dad don't care. He knows nothin' can happen to me."

She was a strange-looking child. Her clothing was ragged, but it covered every inch of her body, from the top of her head, to her fingertips, to the soles of her feet. She wore a dull red outer dress over a dirty white shift, and a frayed red belt, the same color as that tied to his beanpole. And over all she wore a tattered veil that, in the rain, clung to the sides of her face. Even then, Leo could get no clear impression of her features.

"Why are you wearing that fool thing?" he demanded, gesturing at the veil.

She crossed her scrawny arms. "Why are you wearin' *that* fool thing?" she snapped, indicating his floppy hat.

Leo put a hand to his head and straightened the brim, causing water to gush down his cuff and sleeve. "It keeps the rain off," he said.

"Not well, it don't."

"Better than those silly wrappings of yours!"

"I ain't wet."

Leo rolled his eyes and turned to continue his exploration of the trail. "*Somebody* is going to mind you being out with me, so you had better run off," he called over his shoulder.

"Nobody's goin' to mind," she insisted. "Except Beana."

"Who's Beana?"

"My nanny."

Leo made a face back at her. There was no chance this mountain urchin could possibly have a nanny. Not even the son of the village elder in the valley had a nanny. Nannies were for rich people's children, and this girl was not within dreaming distance of that kind of wealth.

"Now you're making up stories."

"I ain't!"

"Yes you are."

"*You're* makin' up stories!"

He shrugged and rolled his eyes and continued tromping up the narrow trail. She followed. A few times as they went, he tried turning on her, baring his teeth and threatening with his beanpole. Every time, she stood there still as stone, all but yawning with boredom. When he gave up and continued on his way, she followed as close as a shadow.

The rain let up after a while, and not long after that Leo saw sunlight struggling through the canopy of leaves overhead and the canopy of clouds still higher up. The trail was longer than he had expected. The old gardener had told him it would loop back to Hill House eventually, hadn't he? Not that Leo cared about that; he was hunting a monster, not taking a stroll. But the sun was crossing the sky, and he might be missed if he wasn't home for supper.

These weren't the thoughts of a warrior. He scouted ahead and saw a gnarled tree trunk that had almost the look of a troll. Taking his pole in both hands like a club, he charged that old trunk and hit it a few times, feeling better about himself and his mission immediately thereafter.

The girl behind him put her hands on her hips, shaking her head. "You're silly," she declared. "Why'd you beat on that poor tree?"

"I'm practicing," said Leo, rolling his arms and shoulders like he'd seen the guardsmen in his father's yard do when getting ready to spar.

"What for?"

"For when I catch the monster."

They marched on up the mountain for almost five minutes before she spoke again. "You huntin' for the monster?"

Her voice was meek, nothing like the devil-may-care tone Leo was growing accustomed to. He had determined to not look at her anymore, thinking lack of attention might drive her away. But something in the way she spoke the question made him look around once more.

She stood several yards behind him now, huddling into herself so that she seemed even smaller than before. Though he could not see her face, something in her stance suggested . . . fear? Or maybe nothing that strong. Maybe just worry.

Leo licked his lips and frowned. She looked like she was about to run away, and inexplicably he realized he disliked that idea. Annoying as she was, she was company. Not the stalwart cohort he had always envisioned, but company even so. It was only right for an adventurer to have a companion.

Leo motioned sharply with his arm. "Come on, keep up! You're going to slow me down."

She remained still several moments, then shook her head.

"Come on," Leo repeated. "There's nothing to be scared of. I'm good at fighting monsters! That is, I beat my cousin at wrestling all the time, and I know how to take care of myself."

Still no response.

"If I leave you behind, it might come eat you," Leo threatened. Threatening seemed like a good idea; someone that small was bound to be scared into submission. "You need to stay close."

Her gloved hands reached up to touch the edge of her long veil, wringing it nervously so that water dripped to the dirt. "It's not . . .

You shouldn't look for the monster," she said in such a quiet voice that Leo had to step closer, and she was obliged to repeat herself a few times before he understood.

"Why not?" he asked.

"Folks say it's bad luck. Bad luck to even see it."

"Not if I defeat it in battle!"

"The monster won't fight."

Leo's frown deepened. "How do you know?"

"I just . . . know."

Then the girl vanished.

3

I T HAPPENED IN A BLINK. One moment she was there, the next . . .
gone. Leo stood openmouthed, staring at the empty place where she
should have been.

"I say." He gulped. "That is . . . I *say*! Where are you?"

The wind stirred the leaves, which dropped their burdens of water
on Leo's head almost spitefully. But he didn't notice. He turned this way
and that, casting about for the girl. Then he cursed, "Iubdan's beard! Why
didn't I think of it sooner?"

This high-country bumpkin was much more likely to know about
the mountain monster than Foxbrush or the Hill House servants. She
lived out in this wild country after all, didn't she? And she'd probably
heard stories that even Leanbear hadn't.

Leo shook his beanpole with frustration, then plunged into the foliage
off the path, scrambling uphill as fast as he could go. He hadn't the faintest
idea which way the girl had gone, so thorough was her disappearance,
but she couldn't have gone far.

The vegetation thinned the higher up he scrambled, and soon even the trees were little more than scraggly bushes. Leo climbed nearly straight uphill as far as the terrain permitted, still without catching a single glimpse of the girl. He called out now and again as he went, "I say! Girl, where are you?"

She didn't respond. Leo had left the path far behind. Not that he cared; nor did he care that he hadn't the first idea how to get home, so intent was he upon his quarry.

But thin air and soggy clothing soon took their toll. Leo used his beanpole as a walking stick, clambering up the mountainous terrain, still calling out to the girl without response. He thought perhaps he hated girls. Little ones anyway. He'd always figured they were all like the girls who visited his father's house, all the pretty little Starflowers and Day-lilies and Dewdrops, so dolled up in flounces that he couldn't have told them apart for the world, filling the air with their silly giggles and games.

This girl was nothing like any of them, which made her even stranger. He didn't pretend to understand the girls back home, but at least he was used to them. They wouldn't go disappearing on a chap on a mountain-side in the rain!

Huffing and puffing, Leo was both too hot and too cold out on that mountain. He sweated under the coat, but his wet face and hands stung every time the wind blew. At last he stood on top of a lichen-covered boulder that looked very much like an old man's head with either bad hair or a still worse wig. He stopped to catch his breath and looked about himself for the first time.

He had come much farther than he'd thought.

The forest was far down the mountainside, and he stood exposed among the rocks of the higher slopes. This mountain was not the highest in the range, but Leo was certainly higher now than he had ever before climbed. Not high enough to see anything beyond the tree line, however, save more trees. The sister mountains loomed menacingly above him, like giants with disapproving faces. Out here in the open, Leo felt very small indeed. The sun was starting its downward dip, and he realized that he would likely be out after dark.

If he made it home at all.

"Iubdan's beard!" he growled, turning to look down the way he had come. Or the way he thought he had come. It all looked the same from here.

"Oi!"

He whirled about, clutching his beanpole, and saw the little girl appear in the rocks overhead. The wind caught at her veil, but she grabbed it and held it in place. "There you are! I thought maybe you'd gotten lost."

Leo growled and lowered his beanpole quickly so she wouldn't think he was scared. "Why did you disappear on me?"

She shrugged. "I led you up the mountain."

"No you didn't!"

"Did."

"I didn't see you."

She shrugged again. "Ain't you comin' up?"

"Coming up?" Leo looked at the climb between him and her. He felt elevated enough as it was, perhaps even a little dizzy with altitude. But the girl shouted down to him from a good twenty feet higher still, up what looked to him like a sheer rock face. Besides, now that he'd stopped to catch his breath, he was getting cold. "What for?"

"I got somethin' to show you."

"I don't want to see it."

"Ain't you huntin' the monster?"

Leo stared up at her. He knew as sure as he breathed that he was being manipulated. He also knew that it was working.

Not liking to lay down his beanpole, he clutched it tightly in his left hand while using his right for climbing. The rocks were cold under his fingers and felt like knives as he gripped them. He made it perhaps two feet up before his foot slipped and he skidded back down, panting with fear. The ground was solid beneath him, but a few false steps and he had a long fall behind him.

"What're you doin'?"

Leo glared at her, with her head tilted to one side. "I'm coming up, like you said!"

"Why don't you use the Path?"

"What path?"

Then, much to his surprise, she came skittering down the rocks, fast as a beetle down a wall. Before he quite knew what was happening, she had taken his hand in one of her grimy gloves and was leading him up that sheer wall, following a path that, even while he stood upon it, he could scarcely see. But it was there; he felt it under his feet, real as anything. And if his head spun while he climbed and his eyes felt fuzzy and strange, well, that must be due to the height.

They reached the top, and once more Leo looked out across the way he had come. But now, only twenty feet higher, his perspective changed.

The whole world seemed to spread beneath his feet. From here he could see beyond the mountain range to the southern ocean. The forest spread like a thick rug across the mountain's lap, smoke rising from the villages in the valleys. He could see the low country, where the Baron of Blackrock's grounds, shrouded now in heavy rain clouds, began at the base of the mountains and stretched all the way to a marble-white bridge. To his left and his right, the mountains continued in a vast ring all around the kingdom, the largest mountain range on the entire known Continent. The Circle of Faces, it was called, for legend had it that giants once dwelt here and, because of a great sin, were turned into stone and had at last crumbled into mere mountains. Now only their faces, on certain spellbound nights, could be seen in the rocks.

But most important, Leo could see the higher gables of Hill House peeking through the trees below, and the twirling smoke ascending from its many chimneys.

"Silent Lady," he breathed, in awe rather than fear.

The little girl let go of his hand, and though Leo hated to admit it, he felt momentarily lost without her grip. Disoriented, as if suddenly plunged into the middle of a maze. He turned to her, and though her face remained covered, he could almost feel her smiling.

"A fine sight, what?"

He gulped. "So where is this monster?"

She turned and led the way. For while they had come a long way, there were yet higher slopes to this mountain and still more sheer climbs than they had already traversed. But she didn't lead him toward these. Rather, she picked her way among the stones around the side of the mountain, veering to the right rather than continuing the ascent. Leo followed slowly, for he was not surefooted among the rocks. So focused was he upon his feet that he nearly ran into her when she stopped abruptly.

"Do you see?"

His heart pounding, Leo looked where she pointed. At first he didn't see it; then his eyes seemed to squint and adjust on their own, and he saw the monster's mouth.

He sucked in a sharp breath and held it for several seconds before he realized that what he saw was only a cave. The rocks around it formed the shape of a great beast, perhaps a wolf, but unlike any wolf Leo had ever seen brought back by hunters, slung on a pole. This stone wolf was also frighteningly like a man.

But it was still just a cave. Leo sagely stated as much.

The girl tilted her head at him. "Shows what you know."

Leo shifted his beanpole from hand to hand, squaring his shoulders. "It's just a cave," he repeated as he took several steps forward. And it was. But it wasn't as well. His imagination worked powerfully on his mind, and he could almost swear he felt the pulse of air flowing to and from that gaping maw. And were those merely trails of moss and stone, or were they teeth?

He stood at the threshold and peered inside. There were signs that a stream had once issued from the cave mouth down the mountainside, but it had long since dried up. The light ended only a few feet in, leaving a blackness so absolute that, just by looking at it, one could almost forget what daylight meant.

Something tugged at his memory. "I know this place," he whispered.

"Not likely," the girl snorted. "No one finds this place who don't know the Paths."

Leo shook his head. "I don't mean I've *been* here. I just know what this is."

"It's called the Monster Cave by folks round here," the girl said. "Though none of them knows how to find it no more." She crossed her arms and stuck out her skinny chest with pride. "I'm the only one what does."

But Leo wasn't listening. His mind was furiously at work, struggling to recall tutorials and lessons he'd spent the last several summer weeks trying to forget. *"Ashiun!"* he declared at last.

"Bless you," said the girl.

"No!" Leo glared at her. "No, the Legend of Ashiun. That's what this is . . . or could be right out of. It's the cave from the Legend of Ashiun!"

She shook her head, bewildered.

"You don't know the legend?" Leo grinned, self-importance momentarily eclipsing his fear as he stood at the mouth of the cave. "The Brothers Ashiun were sent from the Far World to help the mortals of our world when it was new."

"What's the Far World?" the girl asked.

"The Faerie Realm," said Leo. "It's not real. At least, I don't think it is. The Legend of Ashiun is one of the oldest Faerie stories there is. I have it in a text back home. One of the engravings shows the older brother approaching the gateway to Death's Path. It was a cave that looked exactly like this. . . ."

Leo's voice trailed off, and he shivered. When he backed away from the cave mouth, the girl said nothing, only followed him quietly. It was just a cave, of course. Dark, dank, mysterious . . . but just a cave. Leo took a seat on an obliging boulder. The girl sat beside him, folding her knees up to her chest and wrapping her twiglike arms around them. "There's a stream inside," she said.

"A stream?"

"Yup. Deep down, but I think you can hear it if you listen close."

Leo strained his ears but heard nothing from that distance. He felt no desire to draw closer to the cave's mouth again. "You went in there?" he asked, his respect for the girl rising despite himself.

"Yup."

"Isn't it . . . dark?"

"Yup. But not too bad."

Leo made a face. If that wasn't too dark, what by all the dragon's teeth was? He shivered again and hoped the girl would think he was merely cold.

"So what did they do?" the girl asked.

"Who?"

"The brothers you were talkin' about. What did they do what made them story folk?"

Leo thought back over his lessons. The Brothers Ashiun featured in many of the oldest stories in the history of the Near World. The earliest ballads attributed to the famous Bard Eanrin were about the brothers and their great gifts. Leo preferred the legends of his own kingdom, in which the heroes had names he could pronounce and the locations were familiar landmarks. But he recalled what he could of the Legend of Ashiun.

"They were two Faerie warriors," he said. "The great Prince over all the Faerie folk sent them to aid mortals when the Near World was newly created. You see, there was this Dragon . . . not just any dragon, mind you, but the King of all dragons, and he hated the people of the Near World. So these two warriors, two brothers, were sent by the Prince to rescue mortal men and to teach them to fight the Dragon. And the Prince gave each brother a gift to use on his mission.

"The younger brother was given a sword. Let me think, what was the name? Hasli . . . no, Halisa, maybe? Something foreign. It translates as *Fireword*, though. And the older brother was given the Asha Lantern, which means hope, or life, or something like that."

Leo saw he was losing his audience's interest. The girl began to fidget, her veiled face tilting to one side as though she was ready to fall asleep. This would not do. Leo narrowed his eyes. Perhaps he wasn't the greatest hero in the world, nor the most successful monster hunter. But by Iubdan's beard, he was a masterful entertainer!

He leapt to his feet, brandishing his beanpole as though he bore the famed Fireword itself.

"The younger brother became a great hero in the Near World, and he trained other heroes like him. He fought back the monsters of the Far World that tried to cross over and devour the weak mortals." Leo stabbed at the air and twirled about, drawing the girl's attention once more. She ducked to avoid a blow, but Leo heard her laugh as well.

Stopping for breath, Leo continued. "Together, the brothers built great houses over all the Continent. These were enormous halls with doors opening east and west. And when the older brother shone the light of his lantern inside them, the glow remained for years afterward."

"Was it pretty?" the girl asked.

Leo nodded. He indicated the orange sun, which was beginning to set heavily, casting saffron light upon the clouds. "Do you see that sunset? Imagine that, only a hundred times prettier! That was what the Asha Lantern was like."

"Coo," breathed the girl.

"The Near World became prosperous under the brothers' care. People felt safe and happy." Leo crouched down suddenly, his beanpole behind him, and jabbed a finger at the girl's veil, startling her. "But it couldn't last."

"What happened?" she asked.

"The Dragonwitch."

"I heard of her. She lived in these here parts once, didn't she?"

"I think so. Not really, of course. Only in stories. But they say she came to this land. Twice, actually. But that's not part of this story. In this story, she came bursting from the Far World in a great *POOF*!"

"Poof?" The girl looked unimpressed.

"You know what I mean," Leo said. "The sound fire makes." Then he roared, his very best dragon imitation . . . which was pretty good considering he had never heard a dragon. "She was the firstborn child of the Dragon King, a Faerie queen herself once upon a time. And she hated mortal men! So she set upon the Great Houses built by the brothers, tore down the doors, and burned the rooftops. She lit them up like so many bonfires across the Continent!"

"Sad."

"Not just sad," Leo declared. "Terrifying! Of course, the brothers set out to stop her. It was the older brother who tracked her down, using the light of his lantern. And then the younger brother—I believe his name was Etanun. It means *strength*. Anyway, he fought her." With more roars and an appropriate amount of spitting, Leo struck the air with his beanpole. "Fireword plunged into the Dragonwitch's heart, and she fell down dead.

"The older brother found Etanun nearly killed from the wounds the Dragonwitch gave him in battle. A dragon's claws are poisonous, you know, even more poisonous than its breath. Some of the dragon poison got into the younger brother, and though the older brother—his name was Akilun—though he tried to heal him, a trace of poison remained in Etanun's veins."

"So what about my cave?" asked the girl. "How does it fit into this story?"

"Just listen!" Leo sprawled out on the stone, pretending to be badly wounded, gasping for breath and pressing a hand to his neck. "Etanun was weak, but he would recover. He said to his brother, 'I have killed the Dragonwitch!' " Then Leo changed his tone to be the deeper voice of the other brother. " 'No, Etanun,' said Akilun. 'You have only destroyed her first life.' "

"Her what?"

"Her first life. According to stories, all the kings and queens of the Far World have three lives. That's why they live so much longer than mortals do. They get three lives before they have to cross the Final Water. Sometimes they live all three lives at once in three different bodies. Most of the time, they save them."

"That's very odd," said the girl.

"It's normal for Faeries," Leo replied. "Now listen. Etanun did not want to believe his brother. He determined that the Dragonwitch had to be dead because he had killed her with his magic sword. He was angry at Akilun for even suggesting that she would come back. But that anger was just the dragon poison in his veins.

"Generations passed. And the Dragonwitch returned. This time, she was more powerful, more dreadful than ever, and her destruction was greater. Once more, Akilun and Etanun set out to hunt her down. They found her on a beautiful plain known as Corrilond Green. But after their battle, the fertile green fields were wasted into dry desert. That's why the old kings and queens of Corrilond were called the Desert Monarchs. And now that Corrilond is gone, we call it the Red Desert."

"I ain't never heard of Corry-land."

Leo shrugged. "It doesn't matter. That's not part of this story anyway. The important thing is, Etanun killed the Dragonwitch a second time. But before he did, she cut him with her claw, into the shoulder. Akilun tended to him again, but when the wound healed over, there was still poison inside."

"That don't sound good," said the girl.

"It wasn't. When Etanun recovered, he once more declared, 'I have killed the Dragonwitch!' " Leo bellowed this in his best heroic voice. Then he changed his tone to be deep and wise. " 'No, my brother,' said Akilun. 'You have merely killed her the second time. The Dragonwitch will return once more.'

"Etanun flew into a rage, inspired by the poison inside him. He flung Fireword far from him, saying, 'Who can trust such a sword, when it could not even kill the Dragonwitch?' Then he fled from Akilun, far, far away. But Akilun knew where he was going."

"Where?"

"The younger brother was determined to find the Dragon who fathered the Dragonwitch. He wanted the power of the Dragonwitch for himself."

Leo pointed toward the mouth of the cave. In the deepening twilight, it looked even more like a wolf's head to him. But it was just a cave. And this was just a story. "In my book," he said, "there is an engraving of the Gateway to Death. It looks like that. Like a wolf's head."

"Folks say it's the face of the Wolf Lord," said the girl.

"This all happened long before the Wolf Lord," Leo replied dismissively. He continued his narrative. "Etanun walked through the gate as he sought out the Dragon. What he did not know was that Akilun, following the light of the Asha Lantern, pursued him.

"The path to the Dragon's Kingdom is long and perilous. But Akilun caught up with his brother at last and held him tight. 'I won't let you do this,' he said. 'I won't let you destroy yourself.'

" 'Ha!' said Etanun. 'My Prince abandoned me when he gave me that faulty sword of his! You will soon abandon me too! I will offer myself to the Dragon as his servant, for his power is the only power that lasts!' Then he wrestled against Akilun's grasp. His strength was much greater than that of his brother, but Akilun's love was greater still."

Leo rolled his eyes, suddenly embarrassed. "I know that sounds silly. That's the way it was in the book."

"It don't sound silly. It sounds pretty," said the girl, exactly like a girl.

Leo rolled his eyes again and continued. "They battled a long time on that dark pathway. The book said their battle lasted through generations of mortal men, but that is probably just book talk. At last, Akilun forced his brother to gaze into the light of the Asha Lantern. 'Look at it!' he cried. 'Look at it and know the truth once more!' The light nearly blinded Etanun. But it was so pure and so bright that it drove the dragon poison right out of his veins. He stopped struggling, and both brothers collapsed.

"When Etanun came to himself once more, he was no longer poisoned. He realized that he'd been wrong to doubt the power and strength of his Prince, to throw away his gift so quickly. And he realized what a narrow escape he had had, thanks to his brother. But when he turned to him, he found that Akilun was dead."

"Oh!" The girl shook her head. "Not really dead?"

"Yes. Really dead. As the book said, 'His spirit was flown across the Final Water.' "

"That's sad."

"I never said it was a happy story."

"What's the good of a story that ain't got a happy endin'?" the girl demanded, crossing her arms.

Leo considered. "Maybe it does have a happy ending. At least, when it's actually complete. I mean, this part of it is sad. But maybe something good will come from it still? I suppose you have to read all the legends together to know for sure, but I don't know all of them. This one is sad, but there might be a story out there somewhere to make it happy."

The girl nodded. "I'd like to know that story someday."

Leo didn't answer. He leaned against his beanpole, eyeing the mouth of the cave once more.

"What happened to the younger brother?" the girl asked at length.

"Oh, he buried Akilun right there on the path's side. Put a stone marker on the grave and set the lantern on top. It's supposed to shine for those who walk Death's Path, offering hope. Something like that." Leo's hand moved up and down the beanpole, knuckles whitening intermittently. "So . . . there isn't really a monster in this cave, is there?"

The girl didn't answer for a long moment. Then she said, "You'd have to go in to find out."

Leo nodded. "It's getting dark now," he said. "I . . . I should probably retire and plan my assault first. Come back again tomorrow when I'm better prepared, right?"

To his great relief, she nodded. "That's good. But you won't find the cave by yourself."

"I won't?"

"Nobody finds this place on their own."

This thought didn't bother Leo as much as she seemed to think it would.

"You'll need me," she went on. "I can lead you here in a snap, any time you like! Just so long as Beana don't catch on. Beana don't like me to come up here without her."

"Who's Beana again?"

"My nanny."

Oh, that's right! Leo breathed with sudden relief as he stepped away from the cave mouth and followed her back through the rocks. This girl made up wild stories. And that's all this cave was too . . . one of her fantasies, one of his legends. The stuff of Faerie tales and nothing else. There wasn't really a monster either, just like Foxbrush said. It was a folktale, and right now, Leo thought that was just fine. But he could pretend. The farther he got from that cave, the better this idea sounded. He could pretend to be fierce and brave, pretend there was a monster, and let all those pretends stay in the realm of imagination where they belonged.

The girl took his hand again at the cliff and guided him safely to the lower ground, but only after he made certain he knew the direction of Hill House's chimneys. "It's easy enough to find," she told him, though he did not mention where he was from or where he was going. She seemed to know without being told. "That big old house is hard to miss, and you'll see the path again soon enough. If you have any trouble, sing out, and I'll come get you."

She may have been nothing but an odd child, but somehow this offer comforted Leo more than he would have admitted. He responded with a curt nod and started on his way.

"You'll come back, won't you?" the girl called after him.

He looked about and saw her standing small again in that manner of hers, huddling into herself as though she could huddle away into nothing.

He shrugged. "I'll come back."

"What's your name?"

"I'm Leo."

"Do you want to know my name?"

"I suppose."

"I'm called Rose Red," she said. Then she was gone, vanished into the rocks and woods.

Leo descended the mountain, crashing through the underbrush as fast as he could go. Sure enough, he found the path; sure enough, he reached the garden gate not long after the sun set; sure enough, he was late to supper, scolded, and not given any pudding.

4

R OSE RED HAD THREE PEOPLE in her life who loved her: the old man she called father, her pet nanny goat, and her Imaginary Friend.

And of course, there was her Dream. But Rose Red did not like to think of her Dream during waking hours.

She found the boy's hat as she climbed back down the mountainside. Such an odd contraption, ill fitting and useless in the rain. But she picked it up and smiled. Perhaps he would come back tomorrow. He'd said he would. He would come for his hat at least. She took it with her, plopping it on her own head, over the veils.

Life was lonely in the high country, and Rose Red lived a lonelier life than most. Every morning before dawn, she woke and fixed a lumpy porridge for the man she called father. Just as the sky began to lighten, he would wake, eat what she fed him, and make his way down the narrow, almost nonexistent path from their cottage to Hill House, where he worked until after the sun set. During the time between, Rose Red kept the cottage in repair, tended their meager garden, found food for her nanny goat, and kept to herself.

Away from the main road.

Deep in the forest.

"Why do I have to wear these things?" she had asked her Imaginary Friend once, plucking at her veils.

You don't, said he. He was a prince, of course. Rose Red, being a romantic child at heart, would hardly imagine anything less. But he always appeared to her in the form of a wood thrush. *You never do with me.*

"Me dad says I do. If I go out and about, he says I've got to wear them."

Your father loves you. Trust him. Obey him.

"I do, but . . ." Rose Red plucked at the veils again and huffed loudly. "Gets awful hot sometimes!"

Her Imaginary Friend sang gently in his silvery voice. *You needn't wear them with me.*

He really was a wonderful friend. But unfortunately he remained imaginary. And sometimes—such as when she dreamed—she couldn't conjure him up at all.

Rose Red never saw other children. Once in a while she would climb a certain tree that grew high on the mountain slopes, and from its topmost branches she could see the shepherding valleys, where young boys and girls tended the family flocks. She could also see the main road that wound down the mountain to the village of Torfoot far below, and on still days in autumn or winter she could hear the town bells ringing, announcing fetes and feast days, weddings and funerals.

"I wish I could see them up close," she had told her Imaginary Friend one spring. He sat in a branch by her cheek. "I wish I could dance with the other little girls round the Maypole."

You will, sang the thrush. *In good time.*

"But not today?"

No, my child. Not today.

She scowled at the bird through her veils. "I want a real friend," she told him.

I am a real friend.

"No you ain't."

Why say you this? Being a prince, albeit a bird, he had a pretty way of speaking. Very different from the man she called father.

"Because you ain't really here!" she said. "You come and go as I picture you, but you're only in my head. I'm the only one what sees you. I want a friend that everyone knows and everyone sees is my friend."

I am more real than you know.

"No you ain't," she said again, turning away from him. When at last she looked for him again, he was gone. But that may have been because she wanted him to go. She climbed back down from her tree, returned to her goat and the cottage, and prepared a meal for the man she called father. For those things at least were real.

But now, maybe things could be different.

Rose Red climbed the familiar branches of the old tree as swiftly as she climbed the ladder to her loft room in the cottage. The limbs extended almost like hands to help her, and she scaled all that dizzying way to the top, only stopping here and there to disentangle her long veils when they caught on stray twigs. She climbed until she nestled high above the rest of the world and could watch the garden gate of Hill House farther down the mountain. She saw when the boy arrived and crept quietly through the gate and across the yard. Despite the folds of her veil, she saw with eagle-eyed clarity as a red-faced woman met the boy at the kitchen door and shook a finger at his nose. She saw him propelled inside and the door shut.

"I wonder if he'll come back," she whispered to the tree. It swayed gently, soothingly. Rose Red sighed, adjusted her veil once more, and descended to the forest floor. At the base of the tree, where she had dropped it, lay the boy's broad-brimmed floppy hat. She plucked it up again and carried it home.

Her nanny goat waited in the cottage yard and let out a great bellowing bleat the moment Rose Red emerged from the wood. She was an ornery creature and disliked above anything being staked in the yard all day. But Rose Red had not wanted her pet tagging along behind her today and, despite the goat's irate protests, had left her in a patch of clover before venturing into the wood that morning.

The goat gave the girl evil glares and stamped her hooves. She'd demolished the patch of clover and grown bored with chewing her cud, and now strained at her tether, shaking her ears. "Bah!"

"Right, right, I'm comin'," Rose Red said, picking up her pace. Despite the heavy gloves she wore, she undid the lead with nimble fingers and set the goat loose. The old nanny bounded away like a kid, kicking her back feet and shivering her shaggy coat.

"Baaah!"

"Don't give me that," Rose Red said, looping the tether into a neat pile and hitching it on the stake. "It's not like you're goin' to starve. Looks like you've eaten down half the lawn just this afternoon."

"Baaaah!" said the goat, prancing over to a patch of thistles and dandelions that she set to demolishing with a will. Rose Red left her grazing and began building a small fire in the yard, over which she would boil her porridge, as it was much too stuffy inside to cook. She did not speak as she worked, for her mind was taken up with the day's adventures.

This was unacceptable.

The goat trotted over to where Rose Red crouched before her fire pit and gave her a nip on the shoulder.

"Hen's teeth, Beana!" Rose Red exclaimed, lost her balance, and sat down hard. She pushed the goat's long nose away angrily. "Hen's teeth! I know you don't like it when I leave you but . . . but honestly, cain't a girl take a walk by herself once in a while? Fool goat! What's eatin' you?"

"Bah!" said the goat. She stamped and shook her little horns. "What's eating me, she asks? Cruel, cruel girl! Running off like that without so much as a by-your-leave, and leaving me tied to a stake all day! In the rain! Like some *animal*!"

"Beana, you are an animal."

"You do that again, and you'll just have to find yourself some other goat to talk to, so help me!"

"I weren't in no trouble."

"Whoever taught you to speak?" The goat snorted. " '*Wasn't* in *any* trouble.' You sound like you were raised by a bunch of sheep!"

Rose Red shrugged and clambered up from the dirt, brushing off the back of her skirt. The goat followed her to the cottage door and stood on the threshold bleating while Rose Red found a safe place for the boy's floppy hat and started rooting around for her cooking pot and materials for a meal. "Where did you go, Rosie?"

"Up the mountain."

"*Up* the mountain, did you say?"

"Yes, *up* the mountain, Beana!" She found a small bundle of dried leaves and took them down from their nail on the wall. "I know better than to go *down*; you've told me often enough."

"Well, if you were going up the mountain, why didn't you take me with you?" Beana's eyes narrowed and her slitted nostrils flared. "Did you go up to the cave by yourself?"

"No."

"Where *did* you go, then?"

The girl took a few more herbs, slipped them into a raggedy pocket, then carried her pot and foodstuffs back out to the fire, which was starting to blaze to life. She took a moment to tie the long ends of her veil back behind her head, out of her way. Now she wore not so much a veil as a mask. Tiny slits in the fabric at eye level provided her only line of sight, yet she moved gracefully enough for a country bumpkin. She tied the knot of fabric carefully, stalling for time as she chose her words. But she hadn't been brought up to lie.

"I did go to the cave," she said. "But not by myself."

Beana stared with all the potency of a goat's gaze. Then she *baaah*ed again and tossed her head. "You know I don't like you to use those Paths, Rosie! Who, by Lumé's crown, did you go with?"

"Leo."

"And who is Leo? Another imaginary friend?"

"A boy."

"What, the boy who gave us such a fright in the wood yesterday?"

"Yup."

Beana snorted. "Now you're making up stories."

The girl took a stick and moved the ashes in the fire pit to smother the fire, leaving behind glowing coals, over which she placed her pot.

"Why does everybody think I make up stories? I went up the mountain to the cave, and I took Leo with me! He wants to hunt the monster, and now he thinks it lives in there, and now he's my friend, and I'm goin' to help him."

"Hunt the monster?"

Rose Red nodded.

Beana backed away from the fire pit and walked out to a far corner of the yard. She fell to nibbling the grass in a thoughtful way, her tail to the cottage. And still the scents of the mountain drifted to her, the smell of Hill House's kitchen fires and the sloping gardens where the old man worked.

And far down the hill, away in the low country, she could smell that Other unlike all others, could feel it with senses beyond the five natural ones. She muttered soft goaty noises to herself as she grazed. She'd been a goat as long as the girl had been alive, and ten years of eating anything that would fit in her stomach had wiped out any dietary scruples with which she might have been born.

The girl slipped up beside her and placed a hand on her back. "He's goin' to be my friend, Beana."

"Bah."

"I'll take you with us next time, right?"

"Baaah."

"I will! And you'll like him. He's not much good at climbin' and he's loud as anythin' in the forest. But he's nice. He tells good stories and makes funny faces."

"And that's the real measure of a friend, isn't it?"

The girl chewed her lip beneath her veil, biting a bit of the linen along with it. "I want a friend, Beana. A real friend. Who really talks."

The goat raised her nose and gazed up at the girl with as much tenderness as a goat's face can express. "Times are changing, Rosie," she said. "You're growing up faster than I can blink! And I'm sad to say, there's nothing I can do to stop it." She nuzzled the girl's hand, lipping at the ragged glove. "Promise me, girl, that you'll not take the boy back to the cave."

Rose Red licked her lips. "He wants to, Beana."

"But he shouldn't."

Rose Red shrugged.

"We both know what it would mean should he see the monster, Rosie."

"Maybe he won't see it?" The girl whispered this hope as though afraid to even acknowledge it. "Maybe he won't see anythin'?"

"Sweetest girl," said the goat, "you'll only hurt yourself if you become attached to this boy. Let him go. Let us keep to our simple life the way we always have. Quiet, to ourselves, watching over that man you call father. Yes?"

Rose Red shook her head. "Leo's goin' to be my friend, Beana." Tears pricked her eyes and dampened the cloth of her veil. "He's goin' to."

The goat huffed. "We'll see, then, won't we? But you're not to go to the cave again. And you're *not* to stake me out in the yard, Lord Lumé help you if you do! Agreed?"

Rose Red nodded. "All right, Beana."

The man she called father came home well after dark.

"Did you have a good day, Rose Red?" he asked her.

"I did, Dad," she replied, then fed him porridge for supper.

He did not ask if she had seen the boy or not. He himself had watched the young mister enter the wood in a raincoat and hat and emerge again without the hat but carrying his beanpole. And the old gardener thought his own thoughts on the matter, ate his lumpy gruel, and creaked his way to bed.

Rose Red checked to be certain her goat was bedded down for the night. Beana gave her a slobbery kiss on the cheek through the veil, and Rose Red patted her nanny between the horns. Then she returned to the cottage, banked the fire, and climbed to her little loft bedroom up above. She fell asleep to the sound of the old man's snores as though they were soothing lullabies.

And then she dreamed.

Rose Red steps down the ladder like a spider descending its thread, then glides from the cottage on a breath of wind. No one, not even Beana, notices her passing, for she is dreaming and invisible. She glides into the wood and climbs the mountain, higher and higher, to where the rocks are dagger sharp. But they cannot hurt her, for she has no substance.

She approaches the cave at last.

In the odd, moonless light of dreams, it looks more like a wolf's head than ever. But Rose Red enters without fear or hesitation, and now she sees as well in that close darkness as she does in broad daylight. The cave leads downward, and soon she comes to a subterranean stream. The water flows silently, not even a trickle disturbing the quiet. It pools in a hollow before continuing its long journey through the mountains. The water in this pool swirls and steams.

She approaches. Till this moment, she has felt neither hot nor cold in this dreamland, but the steam rising from the pool is scalding. Nevertheless, she kneels at its edge, removes her veil, and looks into the turning water.

A face not her own looks back at her.

"Princess," speaks a voice as smooth as the night sky, "you come again to visit me."

"Silly," says she. "I always come."

"And always it is such a pleasure to me. How fares your lonely life?"

She shakes her head and shrugs. "Right enough. Nothin' much different."

But he gazes at her from his pool and sees many things in her face. "What secret are you keeping from me?"

She licks her lips and shrugs again.

"I see that you are hiding something. Tell me, my princess. Why should we have secrets from each other?"

"You knows that you hadn't ought to call me 'princess,' don't you?" she says.

"That is what you are," speaks the one in the pool.

"That's a silly game from when I was a bit of a girl! I'm grown up now; I'm nearly ten! I don't need to play games no more. No pretend."

The one in the pool looks upon her with narrowing eyes. Then he says, "You will always be a princess to me."

"Hogwash," she snaps. "Beana wouldn't approve of such things, not even in dreams, if she was to know."

"Beana doesn't need to know."

"I don't keep secrets from Beana. I even told her about the boy."

"What boy?"

Rose Red gets to her feet and backs away from the pool, not wanting to look in his face anymore. The steam rises like thin hands beckoning her back, but she crosses her arms and turns away, moving all the way to the cave's entrance. Standing in this spot, she looks out on the vast spread of the kingdom below her, its detail impossible outside her dreams. She sees the twelve baronies separated by deep gorges. She sees all the shining white bridges—built by Faerie hands, the legends say—that span the gorges so that no one ever need enter the dark woods that grow below. She sees the beautiful houses of the barons, more beautiful even than Hill House, which, in her mind, is very fine.

But her gaze lingers longest on the Eldest's House, with its tall minarets and gleaming gates, and its gardens and parks extending over more than thirty acres. How she longs to see that place up close, especially to see the magnificent garden of roses about which the man she calls father has told her so much.

Yet even in her dreams Rose Red dares not travel down from the mountain. She has promised Beana that she won't. Besides, the Eldest's House is no place for the likes of her.

"What boy?"

She shivers at the voice, the only sound besides her own voice that she can hear. Even the wind touching her bare face is silent.

"Just a boy."

"A friend?"

"I think so."

The voice says nothing for some time. Then it says in a whisper that could carry across miles, "You will forget me."

"No!" Rose Red cries. She marches back to the pool, her hands on her hips as she glares down at the face in the water. "That ain't fair, and you shouldn't say such things! I ain't goin' to forget you. But remember, you're just a dream. Cain't I have any real friends?"

"I am your only friend."

She shakes a finger at the pool. "I have Beana, and she's the best friend I *could ever have." She opens her mouth to speak of her Imaginary Friend but finds she does not like to. Instead she finishes with, "And I have old Dad."*

"They are not the friends to you that I could be, princess. They do not know who you truly are."

"Ah. And who am I, truly?"

He does not answer.

"See? You say things what sound nice in dreams. I want to think that I'm more than I am. That I was meant for more than this hidin' away all the time. That somewhere I can walk without wearin' . . ." She stops and shakes her head violently. "But I know the difference! I know the difference between this world and the other. I'm a big girl, and I know."

"They will never see you," says her Dream, and his eyes are sad as he gazes up from the pool. "None of these others you call your friends. They will never look upon your true face."

Her scowl deepens. "You say one more word against my dad or my Beana, and I'll spit in your pool, so help me!"

"Very well," says he in a voice most gentle. "We'll have no more of that. Let me kiss you and end our differences, princess."

She wrinkles her nose. "Ain't kissin' you, that's sure. I'm mad at you now."

"Don't be mad." The speaker's voice is as kind as his face. He puts out a hand, though it does not break the surface of the churning water. "You know how I care for you."

"A likely story."

"You know how I long for your visits. You would not leave me alone up here, would you?"

Rose Red sighs and slowly shakes her head as her irritation fades away. She feels too sorry for the speaker in the pool to stay angry. "You know I'll come back. I always do."

"And you'll not tell anyone else about this place?"

She thinks of the boy and their trek up to the cave, and the Dream in the pool watches her face. But that was in the waking world, so she nods and says, "I won't. In any case, Beana don't like me to come up here when I'm awake."

"Beana doesn't know about me."

"No. Beana don't know."

"And you're not angry with me anymore, are you?"

"No." She kneels down again and puts a hand out to the water. The steam curls through her fingers, and she feels the heat rising through her glove. The Dream extends his hand as well, but their palms do not meet. Then Rose Red rises again. "I'm goin' home now."

"Won't you let me kiss you good-night?"

She snorts. "I ain't forgiven you that much."

With those words Rose Red leaves the cave and drifts back down the mountain. Back down the steep rock face, down through the forest and back around to the places most familiar to her in waking life. Back to the cottage nestled in its clearing, and onto her straw pallet in the loft above the place where the man she calls father snores.

Back to dreams less vivid.

5

"WHY DID YOU BRING a beanpole to breakfast?"

Leo and his cousin sat in the breakfast room with only themselves for company. Dame Willowfair, Foxbrush's mother, considered herself too delicate to rise before noon and rarely showed her face (and then, only carefully powdered and pinched) before suppertime. It was not uncommon for Foxbrush and Leo to go through an entire day without catching a glimpse of the good dame, or she of them, which suited all parties admirably. Dame Willowfair was a little frightened of boys.

So Foxbrush sat at one end of the breakfast table, eyeing his cousin, who slouched at the other. Leo, who was not a boy Foxbrush would accuse of being overly couth, had come to breakfast with the beanpole in hand and propped it against his chair while he ate. Leo had not spoken two words together, which normally would suit Foxbrush fine. His chatter tended to unbalance Foxbrush's daily mental exercises, and it was a mercy when his cousin started the day in a silent sulk.

But today, Leo wasn't sulking. He was merely quiet.

Foxbrush sipped his coffee (he drank it black and had done so since he was five years old, considering sugar and milk to be signs of a weak mind. Leo, by contrast, liked a little coffee flavoring in his milky sugar-water) and waited for Leo to answer. But Leo was staring out the window and chewing his toast in a distinctly thoughtful manner. "I say." Foxbrush set his coffee cup down with perhaps a little more force than necessary. "I say, why did you bring a beanpole to breakfast?"

"A what?" Leo gave him a stupid look. But then, Foxbrush thought all Leo's looks were stupid, so that was no surprise.

"A *beanpole*."

"What beanpole?"

"The one propped against your chair."

Leo looked at it, still chewing, then took another bite and answered with his mouth full. "That's my sword."

"Your what?"

Leo swallowed. "My sword."

"You're an idiot," said Foxbrush, or at least he thought about saying it. The fact stood that—beanpole or sword—Leo's stick was the only weapon in the room, and it was just long enough to reach across the breakfast table for a good smack on the head, which Foxbrush did not doubt Leo would be willing to give. So Foxbrush instead smiled in a superior manner and was annoyed to see his cousin smile back.

When Leo rose from his meal, took up his beanpole, and headed for the door, Foxbrush called after him, "Where are you going?"

"Out," Leo said with scarcely a glance over his shoulder.

Without thinking (which *never* happened to him) Foxbrush said, "Can I come with you?"

Dragon's teeth! What was this? Could his slouching cousin's secret enthusiasm for who-knows-what truly be that catching? What about algebra? What about the economic patterns of the last three decades? What about that enormous history of the second-class farmers' tax records, which he had only just begun? What about—

"No."

And Leo was gone.

Foxbrush stared as the breakfast room door swung shut.

He rose and, telling himself he wasn't really interested, stepped to the window, which overlooked part of the garden. Craning his neck, he saw his cousin, beanpole in hand, march resolutely across the lawn before he disappeared from sight.

A boy climbed one path and a girl, some distance off, descended another, each hoping to meet again and neither certain whether or not to expect such a meeting. The mountain was quiet, but it observed them with an interested, even eager gaze.

All the eyes of the wood, both visible and invisible, both friendly and not so friendly, watched the children's progress. Some watchers trembled. Some merely wondered. Neither Leo nor Rose Red was aware of this, however, and each pursued his or her path with blissful ignorance and hope. The morning grew bright around them.

Rose Red, the boy's floppy hat jammed on her head, her veils draped beneath, carried two pails as she made for a mountain stream a short ways from the cottage. Her large pails had iron handles and were heavy even when empty. Yet they did not encumber Rose Red, despite her tiny frame. If her gait was awkward as she hauled them along, it was no more so than at any other time.

As she reached the stream, a wood thrush sang in the branches above her. Looking up briefly, she half smiled, though none could tell behind her grimy veil. She waded out to the middle of the creek, where it was deep enough to quickly fill her pails. Her soft shoes, stockings, and skirt were soaked up to the knees, but she made no attempt to remove them to keep them dry. She filled both pails and, with no apparent strain, carried them back to the bank. But instead of returning home, she set her pails aside and settled herself down on a moss-covered stone to wait.

And to listen.

Beana, back in the cottage yard, dozed contentedly most of the morning but came suddenly awake when she realized the girl had been gone much longer than necessary. Grumbling, she trotted into the forest, following the unmarked trail down to the creek, and there found Rose Red sitting on her stone, twirling the floppy-brimmed hat about one finger.

The goat bleated in relief. "Going to take all day, are you, Rosie?"

Rose Red spared her not a glance. "I'm waitin' for Leo."

"That boy you met yesterday?"

"Yup."

"He's not coming to visit you. Is he?"

Rose Red shrugged and continued as she was, doing nothing with all that was in her. Beana grumbled again and went to browse the underbrush along the streambed, flicking her tail and shaking her ears to ward off mosquitoes. "Fool girl will daydream her life away!"

But Rose Red wasn't daydreaming.

She was listening.

Rose Red did not listen like other children her age. For one thing, she was significantly better at it. She heard all the regular sounds of the forest around her. She heard the babbling creek, the hum of a million mosquitoes. Beana's hooves squelched in the muddy bank and clicked against pebbles. The wind blew in the trees, rustling the leaves in soft shushing, and the birds chattered to each other back and forth in their many bright voices.

But Rose Red heard more.

While she sat still as the stone beneath her, her eyes closed behind her long veil, she listened to the songs.

There were hundreds of songs all over the mountainside, playing constantly for anyone who had the ears to hear them. When the birds sang, Rose Red did not hear sweet chirpings and chatters; rather, she could understand the melody and complex harmonies of an entire chorus. When the trees sighed, she heard them whispering songs of longing, songs of love, songs of sorrow for bygone days.

And this morning, when the sun broke through the canopy of the forest and fell upon the creek in blinding, sparkling light too bright for her to gaze upon, the wood thrush began to sing, and Rose Red recognized the voice of her Imaginary Friend. His song blended with the sound of water in a harmony beyond description, and she understood the words without quite realizing that she did.

> *Beyond the Final Water falling,*
> *The Songs of Spheres recalling.*
> *Will you answer me?*

She did not answer. She only listened. But Rose Red listened so hard that soon the other sounds faded away, Beana's grumbles, the creek's trickle, the birds' caroling, and even the mosquitoes' whining. The gold and silver music filled her ears and warmed her heart so that even her loneliness backed into the far corners of her mind.

Until a loud voice cut through the song, chasing it from her thoughts and bringing her scrambling to her feet.

"Dragons eat these dragon-kissed flies! Die, blood-sucking fiends, *die*!"

Beana *baah*ed, but Rose Red leapt from her rock and splashed across the creek, crashing through the underbrush on the far side. The slope of the mountain was steep here, and she caught hold of a tree to keep herself from falling. The deer trail that led from the main road wound down below her and, sure enough, she saw the boy hacking his way through the thicker growth with his beanpole, smacking at bugs as he went. His face was sour and his hair stood up in black tufts all over his head.

Rose Red wondered if she should call out to him. But her natural inclination to hide held her tongue, so she stood there clutching the tree with one hand and removing the floppy hat from her head with the other, watching his progress up the path. He must have felt her eyes on him, for just as he passed underneath her, he looked up.

"Iubdan's beard!" he exclaimed, immediately smacking at another fly. He missed and succeeded only in reddening his own cheek. "There you are. You do creep about, don't you?"

Rose Red shrugged. Then she held up his hat. "I found this for you."

"Oh, right," said he. "Wait a minute; I'll come up." Using various tufts of growth for leverage, he scrambled up the slope to her. The top of the rise was bare and steep, however, and Rose Red could see the boy dithering over how best to scale it.

"Pass me your stick," she said.

"What?"

"Pass me the end of your stick. I'll pull you up."

Leo gave her a once-over. He wasn't certain of her age but didn't think she was nearly as old as he, and beneath all her wrappings she was hardly thicker at the wrist than his beanpole. And she was standing precariously on the edge of the slope.

"Unlikely," Leo said. "I'd pull *you* down."

"No you won't," she insisted. "I'm much stronger than I look."

"That's not saying much."

"Come on. Pass it to me."

He wished he could see her face under that veil, could read whether or not she was teasing him. But she kept beckoning with her extended hand, so at last he, still gripping a clump of long grass with one hand, lifted the beanpole with the other. She took it, and the next thing Leo knew, he was being dragged up the rise and onto her level, his ribcage scraping rather painfully on the exposed roots of an old tree as he went. It was over before he had a chance to think, so he lay there a moment, letting his thoughts catch up with himself.

"Lumé's crown," he said at last. "You are strong!"

Rose Red let go of his beanpole and backed up. "Told you."

"I mean," said Leo, getting to his feet, "I mean, you're *really* strong! How much can you lift?"

"I don't know."

"Do you think you could move a boulder?"

She shrugged again and started moving back toward the creek and Beana. Leo followed behind, crashing through the underbrush like an avalanche and talking all the while.

"Because I was thinking, if we could figure out a system of pulleys and levers—and, seriously, how hard can that be?—we could pile up a bunch of boulders. But I wasn't sure how we'd move the boulders, unless we stole one of Leanbear's carriage horses, and they have a lot of teeth, so I thought maybe we'd have to steal some carrots to tempt them, or maybe some sugar, but that means raiding Mistress Redbird's larder, and she's got a lot of teeth too. But we won't need horses at all if you're as strong as all that! I bet you could move a boulder, at least a small one, and a bunch of small boulders would work just as well as a big one, don't you think?"

They came to the creek, and Beana raised her nose from her browsing and flapped her ears at them, giving Rose Red a look that said, "What *is* he going on about?" Once more, Rose Red shrugged.

"We could tie them up in a net—can't be that hard to make a net. We could weave it with grasses or something. It doesn't have to be strong since it's got to break when the trigger is pulled, and— I didn't know this stream was here!"

Leo stopped prattling long enough to look up and down the creek. Then he stepped onto a rock in its middle, planting his beanpole for balance. Running water suggested all kinds of possibilities to his active mind, possibilities of a nautical nature that would inevitably lead to muddy stockings. His eyes sparkled as he gazed about. He turned to Rose Red and said eagerly, "As soon as we've caught the monster, we should come back here and build a dam!"

Rose Red stared at him for a moment. Then she folded her arms across her chest and turned away. "We ain't goin' to hunt the monster."

"We're not?" Leo stared at her hunched back. It was uncanny, but somehow she almost vanished even as she stood there in plain sight. If he focused, he could still see her standing there, but if he let his attention wander at all, she simply disappeared. "Why not?"

She didn't answer as she continued to vanish from his vision more and more. Afraid he'd lose her altogether, Leo stepped back onto the bank and hurried over to the spot where he was fairly certain she still stood. Even standing right beside her, he had to force his mind to believe that she remained present. "Why aren't we going to hunt the monster?" he asked, putting out a hand to grab her shoulder.

He never touched her. Instead, he found himself lying flat on his back, the wind knocked out of him.

By the time Leo was able to sit upright and look about, Rose Red was gone. The goat was standing in the same place, however, roundly chewing leaves and blinking complacent eyes at him.

"Rose Red?" Leo called, putting a hand to his chest as he labored to breathe again. "Rose Red? Where'd you go?"

She was standing right next to him and perhaps had been there the whole time. Her head was bowed between her shoulders. "You oughtn't to have nabbed at me," she said.

He shook his head and puffed, "Now you tell me!" The world still spun a little, but he closed his eyes and shook his head, and things began to reorient themselves. "Why aren't we going to hunt the monster?" he asked again as he got carefully back to his feet.

"Beana don't want us to."

"Beana?"

"Yup."

"Who's Beana again?"

"My nanny, like I tells you!"

"Your—" Leo broke off and turned with a laugh to look at the old nanny goat. "Oh! Your nanny! That explains a lot." Then he made a face. "Why does your nanny care?"

"She just does."

"Oh." Leo licked his lips. The fact was, after all that tramping through the woods, the idea of climbing up to the cave lacked its former appeal. Besides, most of his ideas for monster hunting were not the stuff of legends. And the creek really was too full of possibilities to pass up.

"You don't want to play with me no more, do you?" said the tiny voice of Rose Red, and he realized that she'd almost disappeared again.

Stopping himself from reaching out to her, since that had proven disastrous, Leo quickly said, "Yes, I still want to play! Monsters are silly; besides, they don't exist. We should build a dam, like I said. Make a lake over in that hollow down there. Do you think you could lift some of those bigger stones if I helped you?"

Rose Red nodded, and though Leo couldn't see it, she smiled underneath her veil.

So began a friendship such as neither child had ever before experienced. And that first day, as they rolled stones and sticks into the creek despite Beana's disapproving bleats, all thoughts of monsters and algebra forgotten in the pleasures of mud and running water, they could never have predicted how far that new friendship would take them.

6

"YOU HAVE FORGOTTEN ME."

"You're pretty hard to forget."

Rose Red kneels at the mouth of the cave, her back to the dark pool. She does not want to meet the gaze of the one in the pool. Her eyes drift across the high mountains, across the landscape of the kingdom that, in her dreams, is visible from here all the way to Bald Mountain in the north.

"Shall I take that as a compliment, princess?"

"You take everythin' as a compliment." She spares him no more than a quick glance over her shoulder before returning her focus to the landscape. Although she can see to any corner of the kingdom at any moment she wishes, it is a particular gabled room at Hill House that draws her eyes. A room in which the lamplight has long since been extinguished, and a boy dreams certain dreams that do not connect with hers.

The one in the pool sighs, and his eyes are full of longing as he looks upon her unveiled face, so pensive in the silver light.

"Am I no longer your friend?"

Her shoulders heave as she draws and releases a great breath. "Of course you're important to me. You've been here all my life. But you're nothin' but a dream!"

"I care for you as no one else does."

Rose Red wraps her arms about herself as if cold, yet still she avoids his gaze. She feels him reading her face, however, and without her veils she feels vulnerable. "Stop it."

"Stop what?"

"Stop lookin' at me uncovered like this. I don't like it."

"Your face is so beautiful, princess."

She grinds her teeth and presses the heels of her hands over her eyes. "You're a liar."

"Never. Never, my lovely—"

"Shut up!" Rocks scatter and fall silently down the side of the mountain as Rose Red leaps to her feet. "Shut up! I cain't bear it no more. I'm a big girl, and I don't need your pretty stories! I have a real friend now."

The one in the pool smiles sadly, or perhaps it is more an expression of pain. "He has not seen your true face."

"He's still my friend. He comes to play with me every day that he can. And we have fun! We don't just sit and talk; we have real adventures."

"What kind of adventures, princess?"

"We sail ships on the Lake of Endless Blackness. We storm the strongholds of evil magicians. Today there was this Dragonwitch what kidnapped Beana and turned her into a goat, and we rescued her, though we couldn't undo the goat spell, so we found her a good home and cared for her to the end of our days. And we—"

"And you hunt the monster, don't you?"

Rose Red feels him trying to draw her back into the cave, back to the pool. But she won't move.

"Princess, have you told him?"

She shakes her head.

"You should bring him to me."

"Hen's teeth!" she growls. "Why would I want to do that?"

"You must let me meet this boy. This so-called friend of yours."

She leans a shoulder against one of the jagged stones, her face lifted to the moonless, starless sky. "You never wanted to meet Beana."

"Why would I want to meet a goat? She is no rival to me."

"He ain't no rival neither."

"You flatter me."

"You ain't real," whispers Rose Red. "So there ain't no rivalry."

"Princess—"

"Stop callin' me that!"

"You know he will never care for you when he truly knows you. But I know you better than you know yourself. And I long for nothing so much as to kiss you. Do you hear me?"

She looks over her shoulder and sticks her tongue out at the pool. "Ain't never goin' to let you kiss me."

Then she begins to make her way back across the dreamscape. Yet the one in the pool calls after her. "You'll come see me again, won't you?"

"Maybe."

"And you shall bring the boy to me," says the Dream.

As far as Leo was concerned, it was the best summer of his life. His mother had sent express orders with his nursemaid to make certain he "applied himself admirably to his studies" throughout the holiday months, but his nursemaid was so caught up with writing love notes back and forth to her young man at home that she paid no attention to Leo's lack of academic pursuits. His aunt could scarcely care less what he did with his time, and since for the first two weeks of the summer the household staff had found him annoyingly underfoot, they were happy to see him traipse off into the woods every day. He returned in relatively decent shape (except the holes he kept wearing through his stockings, which his nursemaid grumbled over mending each night), so they let the boy have his fun.

Perhaps Foxbrush appreciated the time to himself, without Leo's constant nagging for attention. Perhaps he didn't. Foxbrush was a quiet lad and had little to say on the subject.

Leo was bursting with life and excitement. Rose Red was not exactly the type of person he would have picked for a companion, and he certainly never referred to her even in his thoughts as a "friend." But she was a jolly good sport, he'd give her that for sure, and was always brimming with new ideas.

One of those lazy summer afternoons, he and Rose Red were both down by the pool they had made by damming part of the creek. Rose Red had wanted to call it the Lake of Shining Dreams, but Leo had vetoed that notion and rechristened it the Lake of Endless Blackness, which was far superior. They amused themselves for hours on end building stick-and-leaf boats, sailing them to the middle of their lake, and sinking them with well-aimed acorns.

But this particular day they had already sunk an entire armada, and both were feeling too sluggish and comfortable to think up a more exciting game. Leo used his beanpole to stir the hulks of sunken ships around the pool's bottom. Over the course of the summer, he had dubbed the beanpole Bloodbiter's Wrath and covered it with carvings of monsters (which tended to look like stick-bugs with teeth) and heroes (which tended to look like stick-bugs with swords). It had indeed become a weapon worthy of his boyhood heroism.

Rose Red sat a little farther upstream, her back against a tree. For once she had not brought her nanny goat along but left her in the cottage yard, though only after swearing that she and Leo would venture nowhere near the cave up the mountain slope. Satisfied that the children would while their time away safely in the woods, Beana was more than happy to take an afternoon off.

Leo contemplated the swirling skeletons of ships, and Rose Red contemplated Leo, thinking of nothing other than perhaps a secret desire to remove her veil in that heat. She always removed it for her Imaginary Friend. She always removed it for her Dream too. And Beana saw her unveiled nearly every day.

But it was different with Leo.

So Rose Red sat covered, despite the summer heat. She tried not to hear the voice of the wood thrush, singing in the branches above her in a voice she recognized as her Imaginary Friend's.

Won't you answer me?

She didn't want to answer. She had a real friend now.

Leo looked up suddenly. "What do you think you'll be when you grow up?"

Rose Red blinked. "What's that?"

"What do you think you'll be?" Leo hooked a piece of a broken ship on the end of Bloodbiter's Wrath and lifted it, dripping, from the water. "If you could be anything at all."

She didn't know what to say. Such a question had never suggested itself to her. So she folded her hands and waited quietly, knowing that Leo could never let a silence go unfilled. Sure enough, he dropped the broken ship back into the Lake of Endless Blackness and went on.

"I'm going to be a jester."

"What's a jester?"

"What's a jester?" Leo repeated, making a face at her. "How can you not know that? It's only the very best occupation in the world! You get to travel all over and wear loose, comfortable clothing of whatever colors you want. No itchy collars and *no lace.* You write songs too, lots of them, and you sing them for kings and dukes."

Rose Red considered this. "Like the songs of Eanrin?"

"Dragon's teeth!" Leo stuck out his tongue and closed one eye, making choking noises. "*Nothing* like those."

"But the songs of Eanrin are the best ones, ain't they? That's what me dad says. Ain't he the spiffiest poet of all?"

Leo shivered and stuck his beanpole into the mud, then got to his feet. "Sir Eanrin of Rudiobus is the most celebrated bard in the history of the world. And I solemnly swear to you, here and now, before the shores of this dread lake, when I am a jester, I will *never* sing a single song written by Iubdan's chief poet. Not if my life depends upon it!"

"Why not?"

"They're lovey-mushy songs; dragons eat them."

Rose Red shrugged. She was only going on ten years old, but she was a girl all the way through. "I like lovey songs."

Leo made another face to better express his feelings, sticking his tongue out even farther this time. Then he said, "When I'm a jester, I'm going to write my own songs. Better ones than Sir Eanrin's. Just wait. And I'll sing them for all the kings of the Continent."

"All of them?"

"And the emperors of the East!"

Rose Red couldn't help but be impressed. "Maybe," she said shyly, "maybe I'll come with you?"

But Leo shook his head at that. He was searching around now, gathering stones, testing their weights, discarding some and keeping others. "Jesters always travel alone. It's part of the job. We are a solitary lot. Watch this!"

Using the stones he'd deemed acceptable, he started to juggle, first with just two, then adding a third, then a fourth and a fifth. They whirled around, faster and faster, and Rose Red's head whirled as well, like a cat watching birds in flight. Leo began to pace back and forth, still keeping track of the stones, stepping high as a prancing pony. Then he flung up his hands, and all five stones flew out and landed in a nearly perfect circle around him.

Rose Red applauded, and Leo took a bow. "I've been practicing that," he said. "I saw a man do it once. He was a jester indentured to the Duke of Shippening, and the duke sent him down from Capaneus City to perform for my fa—to perform at the Eldest's House. But when he did it, the stones burst into flame as they landed. All colors of fire! He swallowed fire too."

"Swallowed fire?"

"Like a dragon! I knew then that I wanted to be a jester, just like the Duke of Shippening's man."

He gathered the stones and tossed them one at a time into the Lake of Endless Blackness. But the expression on his face was no longer the bright and eager one Rose Red had seen while he was juggling. Instead, as each stone splashed and sank, Leo looked as though he were watching his dreams plummet. He whispered so that she could not hear, "As if that were possible."

Then he put another smile on his face and turned to Rose Red once more. "What about you? What do you want to be?"

She shrugged, the safest answer she knew to questions she didn't quite understand.

"You want to be something, don't you?" Leo insisted, grabbing Bloodbiter's Wrath and stirring the lake again.

"I'll probably just be me," she said, hugging her knees to her chest. "It's all I ever thought to be."

"That's boring!" Leo stirred with more vigor, tossing the broken ships in a whirlpool of wreckage. "You've got to have a dream of some kind. Something you want to become. Maybe a duchess? Or a princess?"

To Leo's surprise, Rose Red leapt to her feet. Her rag-covered body shivered, and her gloved hands formed little fists at her sides. But her voice was firm and the loudest he had ever heard when she said, "I won't *never* be a princess. Never. Do you hear me?"

And the next moment she vanished like a puff of vapor.

"Rosie!" Leo jumped up, turning this way and that. He searched the whole Lake of Endless Blackness, but she was nowhere to be found. "Rosie! Rose Red!" he called, to no avail.

Leo did not see Rose Red again the next day or the day after, though he came out to the lake and waited for many long hours.

Five days later he found her again, sitting beside their lake as though nothing had happened, weaving grasses and twigs into a fine ship. He knelt beside her and started work on his own without a word. They sailed their vessels and sank them with skill, then started on another set.

"I missed you," Leo said.

"Me too," said Rose Red. And that was all.

"The post is due today," said Foxbrush one morning.

It was late in the summer by then, and he had yet to discover what Leo did with himself in the woods every day. The only time he saw his cousin was at breakfast and supper, and all efforts to wheedle information from him had proven useless. "Mother says she's expecting a letter from Aunt Starflower."

"Iubdan's beard!" muttered Leo, downing his milky coffee in a gulp before fleeing the table. Foxbrush was left blinking, a piece of toast in his hand. He'd long since decided that his cousin was a few turrets short of a castle, but this was erratic behavior even for Leo.

"What did I say?" he inquired of the salt shaker. But the salt shaker would venture no opinion.

Everyone in Hill House and the lower village of Torfoot looked forward to the advent of the postmaster every second week of each month. All, that is, except young Leo, for whom the occasion meant a certain amount of hassle. Stopping only to grab Bloodbiter's Wrath from his room, he bolted out the back door, across the garden, and off into the woods as fast as he could go.

The deer trail he had followed at the beginning of the summer now led off into other trails at intervals, according to his and Rose Red's various games. The most noticeable of these trails was that which led to the Lake of Endless Blackness. Leo found Rose Red beside the lake, working on a stick ship, this one double the size of previous efforts. Beana browsed the underbrush nearby and did not even raise her head as Leo approached.

"Hurry, Rose Red!" Leo cried as he burst upon the scene. "Danger!"

"What?" Rose Red was on her feet in a moment, her stick ship crumpling to pieces as it fell from her hands and down her skirt. "What danger?"

"The postmaster is due today!" Leo panted for breath, supporting himself on Bloodbiter's Wrath as he spoke.

Rose Red's tense body relaxed, and she placed her hands on her skinny hips. "Well, ain't that cause for fear and tremblin'?"

"Oh, but it is!" Leo struggled to get the words out fast enough. "He'll send a boy up to Hill House with our letters. There . . . there might be one from my *mother*!"

"Bah," said Beana, twitching her ears, several long grasses sticking from the corners of her mouth.

Rose Red nodded. "I agree. Bah! You scared me, Leo, and now look at my—"

Leo flung up his free hand and brandished his beanpole with the other. Without thinking, he reached out and grabbed Rose Red's arm, exclaiming, "Dragon's teeth, Rosie, you've got to—"

And the next moment he lay staring up at the leaf-edged sky.

His head spun so hard at first that Leo didn't notice how badly it hurt. But that sensation didn't last long, and he cursed the pain and shut his eyes, waiting for the spinning world to settle back into place. When at last he sat up and looked around again, Rose Red was gone.

Growling to himself, he got to his feet. Beana gave him a mild look, as if to say, "You asked for it."

"Did not," Leo snapped at her as though she'd really spoken. "You girls are all such . . . girls!" Then he called to the wood in general, "Fine, Rosie! I was just going to say that if Mother writes to my nursemaid and tells her to force me back into algebra and history and economics again, it'll be the end of our fun. But obviously you don't care!" He rubbed the place on the side of his head where he felt a lump rising. Iubdan's beard, that girl had a right swing like a club!

Back through the wood he stalked, more slowly now because of his whirling head. He avoided Hill House on the way down, taking a long circle around it to the road that led up from Torfoot Village. The same road any village boy the postmaster hired must take to deliver his bundle of messages.

Still gingerly feeling the side of his head, Leo settled into a hollow off the road from which he could see anybody coming and going. Blood-biter's Wrath lay ready at his side, and he thought himself something of a bandit prince, ready to do or die for the cause of freedom, or at least for an academics-free summer.

"What's alger-bruh?"

Leo yelped and tried to grab Bloodbiter's Wrath, but Rose Red stood on the end of it, her arms folded and shoulders hunched, the picture of contrition. "So you're back, are you?" Leo growled. "You've got to stop hitting me like that!"

"You hadn't ought to—"

"I know, I know, I hadn't ought to grab at you! Get down before he sees you."

"Who sees me? The alger-bruh?"

"No, the postmaster's boy."

Rose Red knelt beside Leo, peering through the branches, which caught and snagged on her veil. "And he's bringin' the alger-bruh?"

"More likely a letter from my mother telling my nursemaid to get me back to work, and by Lumé's crown, that's the last thing we want!"

"Is it a kind o' snake?"

"What?"

"The alger-bruh."

Leo gave her a look. "Don't you know anything?"

Before she could answer, their attention was arrested by a high, tuneless whistling. Leo crouched a little lower. "That'll be him now. Here's what we'll do: I'll jump down in front and distract his attention; then you sneak down behind and nab his sack. Find the letter from my mother while I keep him busy, then make for the Lake of Endless Blackness as fast as you can!"

"Leo, I—"

"There he is!"

A scruffy boy a size or two smaller than Leo came up the road, whistling like a tone-deaf cicada, a satchel over his shoulder. His face was blissfully ignorant of his impending doom.

"On the count of three," said Leo.

"I cain't—"

"One, two . . ."

"Leo, I cain't—"

"THREE!"

Leo burst from his hollow, tripped on his beanpole, and rolled down into the road with much scraping of hands and knees, but was on his feet in a trice and bolting after the boy . . . who by now was making good time up the hill as fast as his skinny legs could carry him. But Leo had the threat of academics to motivate him, and he overtook the lad and barred his way with Bloodbiter's Wrath. Leo looked quite the sight with his hair all on end and adorned with sticks and leaves. The boy gave a squawk, froze in place for a moment, then suddenly darted to the left.

"No you don't!" Leo cried, blocking the path with Bloodbiter's Wrath. "Where do you think you're going?"

"Oi gots me some mez'ges ter deliver!" the mountain boy declared, his face a mask of outraged dignity. "Oi weres promised a coin fer me troubles."

"Not until I see them first," Leo said. "All right, Rose Red! Come on out!"

Nothing happened.

The boy's eyes narrowed. "Oi's goin' ter be late. And Oi ain't suppose ter let nobody sees 'em save Mistress Redbird."

"Now's the time, Rose Red!" Leo didn't take his eyes from the boy as he kept his beanpole up and ready. They sidled back and forth, but the mountain lad didn't dare make a break. "Like we planned!"

Rose Red didn't appear.

"Oi ain't s'pose ter stop fer bandits nor bears nor nobody," said the boy, and Leo could see him gathering his bony person together for another burst.

"Rosie!" he called.

The boy broke into a run, and Leo was hard-pressed to catch him, though he still couldn't wrest away the satchel. The best he could manage was to keep the boy from progressing up the hill, and once more they stood facing each other. Leo panted, his sore head throbbing, and the other boy's face hardened into something like war.

And still no Rose Red.

Leo puffed, exasperated, and planted his beanpole in the dirt. "I say, look here, let's come to an agreement. Why don't you let me just look through your bag and take what I need?"

"Not fer bandits, nor fer bears, nor even fer the mountain monster!"

Leo rubbed a hand down his face, hating himself for what he was about to say next. "Look, boy, don't you recognize me?" And he smoothed down his hair, straightened his shirt, and struck a profile pose with his beanpole extended.

The mountain boy gasped. "Oi! Oi! Silent Lady save us, Oi dern't recogg-er-nize yer, Yer High—"

"Yes, yes, I know." Leo shook his hair back out and extended a hand to the boy. "Pass them over."

The satchel strap was looped over the boy's palm, and Leo hastily dug inside. He found the envelope sealed with a panther and starflower, his mother's emblem. It was addressed to him, so he did not feel quite as guilty as he might when he slipped it from the sack and into his pocket. No other missives with the panther and starflower symbol were inside, and he handed the lot back to the mountain urchin. The boy bowed several times, then scurried on up the hill and out of sight.

Rose Red appeared at Leo's side. "Why didn't you ask him for it from the start?"

Leo glared at her. "Some help you are. You wouldn't mind if I got swallowed by studies the whole rest of this summer, would you?"

She bowed her head. "I cain't read in no case."

"Excuses."

"And I cain't . . ."

She shivered and went silent for so long that Leo guessed she was done saying her piece and started marching up the hill again. He was too busy anyway, opening the letter from his mother, finding the passages that would certainly have led to trouble had his nursemaid come across them, and carefully tearing the whole into pieces.

He passed the mountain boy already on his way back down, now richer by one bright coin, and Leo did his best to ignore the sniveling reverence the boy made as he went. All Leo's adventurous spirit was sapped, and he figured he'd spend the rest of the day at chess or something just to show Rose Red what was what and who was whom. Friends didn't leave other friends in a lurch while ambushing unsuspecting strangers! That sort of thing wasn't—

A high scream ran up the road to Hill House like a cold chill up a spine. Leo startled and whirled around, brandishing his beanpole and staring down the way he'd just seen the mountain boy go. He told himself to move, to run, but that scream was too terrible, and he remained frozen in place even as Leanbear and old Mousehand barreled past him down the hill, armed with clubs and knives.

They found the mountain boy curled up in a ball in the middle of the road. When at last they could get him to speak, all he would say was, "The monster! The monster!"

7

SO THE MONSTER DID EXIST. There was no denying it now. Leo had seen the messenger boy's face when Leanbear and Mousehand carried him back up to the kitchen. He had heard his babbling terror, and Leo knew beyond doubt that nobody could invent that kind of fear.

So the monster was real, and much closer than he would have imagined.

Leo was not allowed outside for a week following that event. The weather turned sour in any case, but this did not help Leo's feelings of pent-up frustration. He worried about Rose Red and her fool goat, somewhere out there in the wilds in the almost constant downpour, with that creature on the loose.

"What did you see?" Mistress Redbird had asked the messenger boy.

"The eyes!" the boy had babbled. "The big, turr-ble eyes! And teeth, so many teeth!"

Leo shivered as he remembered. He'd stood in the kitchen doorway, looking in on the scene as Leanbear and Mousehand stood on either side of the dirty child and Mistress Redbird tried to force something strong down his throat with a spoon. Leanbear knelt before the boy just as he spat out what Redbird had given him, right into the carriage man's eye. Leanbear backed away, cursing, and Mousehand stepped in to take his place.

"Listen carefully, boy," said the old gardener. "I need you to answer a few questions. You say you saw big eyes and big teeth. But don't you think it might have been a fox you saw? Maybe a wolf? They say there's been somethin' preyin' on the flocks these days, and maybe—"

"It were the monster!" The boy's face went red as he screamed at Mousehand. "Oi knows what Oi seen! It weren't no wolf, an' it weren't no fox neither. It were like nothin' else ever there was, and it's goin' to eat me!" With that, he succumbed to a fit of hysterics that, Leo thought, disgraced the whole race of boys.

But then again, Leo admitted to himself now as he sat in the library and watched the rain beating down on the windowpane, he hadn't seen the monster for himself. How would he have reacted in the messenger boy's place?

"Silly, isn't it?" said Foxbrush from his desk. Leo had done his best to ignore his cousin while cooped up in the house with him these past several days. But Foxbrush, for all his studious ways, was not always one to be ignored. "All this fuss over the monster, I mean. I've never seen Leanbear in such a jumpy state, and Mistress Redbird won't even put the cat out at night."

Leo leaned his forehead against the window frame, watching droplets chase each other down the far side of the glass. "It's been raining. That's why."

"Huh," said Foxbrush. "Mistress Redbird would toss that cat out in a cyclone." He scratched away at the long essay he was composing on how the literary norms of olden days might have affected historical documentation of such infamous figures as the last Queen of Corrilond. Foxbrush found it fascinating, but it was the kind of stuff that gave Leo a strong urge to push his cousin out the window.

Nevertheless, after penning a few more lines, Foxbrush turned to

Leo once more, a small smile on his face. "So is it the rain that's keeping you from your silly games in the woods?"

Leo shrugged.

"A little bad weather has never stopped you before."

Leo shrugged again. Old Mousehand was out in the garden working away despite the rain, his narrow shoulders covered only with a short cloak, which, as far as Leo could tell from the library window, was not waterproof.

"They're scared you'll get eaten by the monster, aren't they?"

Still Leo made no answer. He watched the gardener moving arthritically about the garden, covering certain blooms with protective sacking, tying back trailing vines, replanting fallen beanpoles.

"Are you scared of being eaten, Leo?"

Leo whirled on his cousin then, his fists clenched. "Dragons eat you, Foxbrush!" he growled and stormed from the room. Foxbrush's laughter trailed behind him as he went.

He was *not* scared of the monster, Lumé help him! Neither was Leo scared of bad weather, or even of his nursemaid's wrath. He pounded up a flight of stairs to his bedroom, retrieved Bloodbiter and his rain hat, then galloped all the way back down to the lower floors. Sneaking like a ghost so as not to be caught by the household staff, he slipped out into the wet of the garden. The brim of his hat immediately flopped to his ears under the heavy torrents.

He slogged across the wet garden until he found Mousehand tying up some drooping starflower vines. The gardener did not notice the boy until Leo burst out with, "Is there really a monster?"

Mousehand cast a sideways glance Leo's way but continued his work. His gnarled fingers didn't want to twist the twine the way they once had, and he had to be methodical to accomplish his tasks. So he let the boy stand there, breathing hard and getting more drenched by the moment, until Mousehand was quite done. Then he brushed his hands on his trousers and turned his sopping beard to look down into Leo's pale but determined face.

"What do you think, young master?"

"I think you know," said Leo, clutching his beanpole with both hands.

"I think you've always known. I think you know more than anyone else on this mountain."

Mousehand stuck out his chin, and rainwater dripped heavily from the end of his beard. "I don't know 'bout that. What I know is just different from what everybody else knows."

"There is a monster, isn't there."

Suddenly the gardener's face went dark, as though all the storm clouds flowing in from the ocean were gathering just above his face. His eyes flashed like lightning, and he glared down at Leo.

"Boy," he said, "if you ain't figured out by now that there ain't no monster on this mountain save that which you brought yourself, you're a greater fool than you look."

Leo took a step back. Mousehand's face was so dark, so angry, so . . . disappointed. Leo gripped Bloodbiter's Wrath and backed away, unable to break his gaze from those eyes.

Then Leo turned and pelted across the yard, his boots slurping in the mud. He was through the garden gate and up the beaten path in a matter of minutes, still running. He broke into the forest where the red-scarfed sapling indicated, the ground slick with wet leaves beneath him. But he climbed the deer trail leading up, past the place where he had first met Rose Red and her goat, past the turn that led to the Lake of Endless Blackness (*which must be overflowing by now*, he thought, *with all this rain*). He climbed through the gloom and the rumble of thunder until at last the trees began to give way and he reached the higher slopes of the mountain.

They're all lying to me, he thought. *There is a monster. I know that boy didn't make it up. There is a monster, and I'm going to find it.*

He wondered about Rose Red as he climbed. He hadn't seen her in a week, had not come across her in the woods all afternoon. Perhaps the monster had taken her, or taken that dragon-eaten goat. All because those who admitted it existed were too afraid! Like Rose Red, always thinking up excuses not to hunt it. And the rest pretended it never was.

Well, Leo was not to be put off any longer. He would find that cave again, and when he did, he knew he would also find that monster.

But the first flush of determination wore off as the rain continued to pour and he continued to get nowhere. Out in the open above the forest, there was no protection from the gales, and he started to shiver. The stones were slippery too, and several times he fell and hit his knees or elbows hard.

"All right," he muttered as he used Bloodbiter's Wrath to support himself. "All right, this wasn't the best idea I've ever had. *Oof!*" He fell again, and this time he remained where he landed for a long moment. The rain was beginning to lessen, and when he looked up, Leo thought he glimpsed the sun shining through in patches, low on the horizon. The afternoon was wearing out and evening drawing on. The rocks loomed lonely and dark around him, and the forest waited below.

"I'm lost," Leo whispered. Somehow, it was better to admit it out loud than to sit there pretending otherwise. He'd climbed all over this part of the mountain, and still there was no sign of the cave or even of the impossible rock face up which Rose Red had led him that day so many weeks ago. Nothing, as though it had all been a dream.

The rain beat in one final rush like the last roll of a drum. Then it stopped. Thick clouds churned overhead, but the mountain was silent without the sounds of the storm.

Leo pushed himself back up on his feet. No point, as far as he could see, in wandering about the mountaintop searching for a cave that he must have imagined. He huffed a few irate curses between his teeth and made his way carefully back down the rocks and into the shelter of the forest.

But it wasn't the same forest.

The difference was subtle. One would hardly notice it at first. Leo was several paces in before he realized the smell was wrong. It didn't smell like rain. And though he could see the underbrush growing thick beneath the spreading trees, wherever he walked, there was none.

Leo's heart beat in his throat as he passed between the sentinel trunks. Rain dripped all around, rolling down branches and leaves. But no droplets landed on him. The ground where he walked did not squish with mud, and wet leaves did not cling to his boots, for all was dry beneath his feet.

His mind hurt as it struggled to comprehend the impossible strangeness surrounding him . . . then suddenly stopped hurting as it refused to try. Instead, tapping the ground with Bloodbiter's Wrath, Leo set off at a quick pace through the forest. So what if the underbrush grew in a thick snarl all around him but somehow just *wasn't* where he walked? Why should he care? He could make good time this way, take a brisk pace back to Hill House and be home in time for supper.

But the Wood laughed at him.

He could feel the laughter if not hear it. Laughter as old as the world that had begun long before he was born and would continue long after he was gone. And Leo started to glimpse shapes that flickered on the edge of his vision, deep in the forest shadows. His heart beat faster and his pace increased. The laughter around him continued, and more and more often he kept almost glimpsing things not there. Or things he hoped were not there.

He saw a wolf.

It was as big as a horse, loping between the trunks. Faster and faster it approached, and Leo could not see its face, for it was nothing but a shadow, but he could feel eyes like daggers fixed upon him. Predator and prey. Yet Leo could not run. He came to a standstill and watched as the shadowed horror drew nearer. He could almost hear the panting of hot breath, could almost smell the musk of the hunter, until it was but a few feet away and leaping. . . .

It passed through Leo's chest. Then it vanished.

Leo stood gasping, turning to search before and behind, desperately trying to comprehend what had just happened. But the forest continued to darken, and he couldn't stand there forever. Besides, he must have imagined it. It would be easy to do in these shadows as the sun set farther behind the mountains. He must get home.

Leo walked on. Though the sun vanished and left the forest in blackness, still, like magic, his eyes could discern just far enough in front to allow him to keep moving.

He saw fire.

It was only for a moment. First he saw a tall figure running ahead of him, graceful as a dancer in that strange half-light. A woman, he thought, but not quite a woman.

In a flash, what he had thought was her long, streaming hair was a tongue of flame, lashing through the forest, catching branches and leaves and devouring them. The whole world was swallowed in heat and smoke.

In a moment it was gone.

There was no fire, no smell of burning, no blinding light before his eyes.

Leo started to run.

Running did not help. The trees continued to part before him, and that was terrible. The shadows continued to deepen everywhere but where he walked, and that was terrible too. And everywhere there were those wisps of nothing or something, little half whispers pleading to be heeded that he must ignore at all costs. Leo ran uphill and downhill simultaneously, and no matter how fast he went, he made no progress.

At last he collapsed, too exhausted to draw a full breath. The strange light that should not exist huddled him into a world of his own, surrounded by the darkness and the voices that were not quite there. Leo wrapped his hands over his head, willing himself to wake from this nightmare; for surely, he kept telling himself, he must be dreaming.

Out of the darkness, one voice spoke without language, and yet he understood. It sang a song of liquid light that fell softly through the dark branches and touched his ears.

Won't you remember me?

It came back to him then, a faint memory.

He recalled the beginning of summer, climbing behind Rose Red up to the mountain cave. She had given him directions back to Hill House then, hadn't she? And she had said, *"If you have any trouble, sing out, and I'll come get you."*

Leo sat up on his knees but kept his eyes closed, for he did not like to see the looming black around him. His voice trembled, yet he called as loud as he dared, "Rose Red! I . . . I'm kind of lost, I think!"

"Right you are, Leo. What are you doin' all the way out here?"

She was standing beside him. Of all the frights Leo had experienced that evening, this one just about took the prize.

"Dragon's teeth!" he cried, leaping to his feet. "How did you get here?"

Rose Red backed up a few steps, her shoulders hunched and the edge of her veil swishing. "You called me, didn't you?"

The smell was right again, Leo noticed. The forest smelled like wet earth and new rain, just the way it was supposed to. The light was almost gone, but it was not so impossibly dark and impossibly light simultaneously as it had been. It was simply the dimness of twilight. And the underbrush was back, for he stood in the midst of a bramble patch and struggled to extract himself. "Yes, I called you," he said as he stuck his fingers on thorns. "How did you even hear me?"

Rose Red helped pull brambles from his sleeves, for the thorns couldn't pierce through her thick gloves. "I'm always listenin' for you, Leo," she whispered.

"But how could you get here that fast?" His fright and the darkness and a long tramp through the rain left him exhausted and, worse than that, angry. He found himself wanting to break Bloodbiter's Wrath over his knee. Instead he gave a last tug and pulled free of the thorns, then squeezed his beanpole hard in both hands as though he could somehow wring all the anger out of himself. "Were you following me all along?" That idea made him angrier still.

Rose Red shook her head. "I used one of the Paths. Looks like you got on one of them too, and not a nice one. How'd you manage that?"

"Manage what?"

"To get on one of the Paths?"

"What are you talking about?"

Rose Red tossed up her hands, exasperated. "I'm talkin' about the Paths what run through the forest, but what you cain't see when you're on this side of the worlds. Beana showed them to me."

"Your goat?"

"But she don't like me to use them. Says they're dangerous, though I ain't never seen nothin' so wrong with them. Usually other folks cain't find them, though. I'm surprised you did."

Leo rubbed the side of his head, which was hurting almost as bad as if she'd smacked him again. Worlds and paths and shadows and whispers . . . it was too much. He didn't like it. "There aren't any paths this deep in the forest."

"There's more Paths than you can count, Leo."

His knuckles whitened. "I can count a lot better than you can. You don't even know what algebra is!" He sounded like a little boy, he realized with embarrassment, not the great lad of eleven that he was. Licking his lips and drawing in a deep breath, he forced himself to calm down. After all, he wasn't alone anymore. And he wasn't dreaming either. It had been many days since he'd seen Rose Red, and here they were, back out in the forest on one of their adventures, just like always. Everything else that had happened this evening was all silliness brought on by his overtired imagination. He licked his lips again. He couldn't see her anymore and wasn't certain if this was because of the twilight or if she was doing her vanishing trick again. His hand started to reach out for her, but he stopped himself. Past experience had taught him that this wasn't a brilliant idea.

"I'm sorry, Rosie," he whispered. "I'm just . . . I'm sorry."

"It's all right, Leo," she said, and her form became visible again. "I'll take you home now, shall I?"

He nodded. Rose Red took hold of the end of his beanpole and started walking, and Leo, thus linked to her, followed. They said nothing as they went, but even in the midst of their silence, Leo couldn't help but be glad to have found her again. To find her safe and whole, despite all the rumors of the monster.

"What were you doin' out here late like this?" Rose Red asked him after a while. She proceeded quickly considering how dark it had become. Leo could scarcely make out the ground beneath his feet, but Rose Red led him straight and true, and if he walked in her footsteps he rarely stumbled.

"I was hunting for the monster," he said.

Rose Red stopped, and he almost walked into her, dropping his end of Bloodbiter's Wrath as he did so. "Careful, Rosie!" He knelt to find his end of the pole and realized with a flash of irritation that she had disappeared again. "Rosie! Come on, I don't need this." He found the beanpole, but the girl, for all intents and purposes, was gone.

Swearing under his breath, he hacked his way a couple of steps but lost his footing in the dark and rolled down an incline. Sticks and stones bit through his clothing, and he lost his floppy hat. When Leo stopped rolling, he heard running water nearby and guessed that he must be somewhere near the Lake of Endless Blackness. But that didn't help in the dark. Bruises were cropping up all over his body faster than weeds in a rose garden. He crawled to a nearby tree and pressed his back against the trunk, tucking his knees up.

Somewhere far away a wolf howled. Leo swore again.

"You hadn't ought to hunt the monster."

"Silent Lady!" He swung about and could just make out the contours of her veil near his face. "Why do you keep doing that to me?"

"Please, Leo," she said, and he felt her gloved hand gripping his shoulder. "Please, don't hunt the monster no more."

He drew several long breaths. "Why won't you take me back to the cave, Rosie?"

She was so still that only the hand on his shoulder told him she remained beside him. At last she whispered, "Please don't ask me to."

Leo ground his teeth. Using Bloodbiter for support, he pushed himself back onto his feet. Her hand slipped away from his shoulder, but he felt her standing near. "I want to see this monster, Rose Red. I know it exists. And I'm not afraid. I want to face it, like a real hero, and . . . and see what happens."

"You won't like what you see," said the girl, her voice atremble.

But Leo, his heart in his throat, said, "Show me."

8

THEY WALKED IN SILENCE through the wood, Rose Red clutching one end of Bloodbiter's Wrath, Leo clinging to the other. He smelled rain and dampness and all the scents of night, and he shielded his face with his free hand as sticks and branches went for his eyes.

Then they emerged into the open high country, and here Leo used his free hand to support himself in the upward climb. Rose Red moved without hesitation, never stumbling on the wet rocks, never turning to check Leo's progress as he followed.

When they came to the sheer rock face and Rose Red began to climb a path Leo could not see, he felt the change in the air. The smells of the night vanished, replaced with nothing, and the darkness was acute. Leo's head went fuzzy. He wanted to support himself on the rocks, but when he reached for them, they weren't there. Instead, he clung to the end of his beanpole with both hands and all but shut his eyes as Rose Red led him up and up.

At night, the cave's mouth looked so like a wolf that Leo had to bite his own tongue to keep from crying out. His feet stopped moving, and his grip on Bloodbiter's Wrath tightened so that Rose Red, who kept on walking, dropped her end. Only then did she turn around.

"What?"

Leo shook his head, staring at the cave's mouth and telling himself not to be a fool. He'd seen it by daylight and knew it was only a cave.

"You want to see the monster, don't you?" said Rose Red. Her voice was tight and thin as a bowstring.

Leo nodded.

"Then come." She turned and marched right to the cave's mouth. Hating every step he made, but hating himself still more for being afraid, Leo followed. He raised his beanpole and muttered, "I am a warrior. I am a hero. I am going to face the monster."

What a tale this would be at breakfast tomorrow. Foxbrush would drop his teeth! This thought comforted Leo, and he followed Rose Red all the way to the cave's mouth.

She vanished inside.

He couldn't say how long he stood there, his courage twisting and writhing in his heart. At length he heard Rose Red calling from the blackness. "Ain't you comin'?"

"I . . . I can't see anything."

"It's not that dark."

Leo gulped. "I can't see anything," he repeated.

He felt her hand, so tiny in its glove, reach out and take hold of his. Then her veil wafted against his cheek as she spoke softly in his ear: "Come along, Leo. I'll take you."

He followed her into the darkness, and it was dank and stale and close. His feet gingerly felt out each step before he trusted his weight to them. Rose Red was kind and waited for him as he made his hesitant way, and she kept a tight grip on his hand. Bloodbiter's Wrath scraped against the low ceiling, and Leo was obliged to angle it forward as he went.

He heard running water, and the sound brought his heart hammering to his throat. "Is that the stream you mentioned before?" he asked, amazed at how loud his whisper sounded.

"Yup," she said. "We're close now."

"To the monster?"

"Very close."

"How . . . how will I see it?"

She did not answer. They proceeded several more paces; then she pulled him to a stop. From the sound of it, the water was near. "Kneel here," she said.

Leo obeyed, keeping hold of his beanpole in his right hand, but Rose Red dropped his left. He put it out, feeling for her in the dark, but found instead the edge of the water. He gasped and pulled back, for it was scalding hot.

"Careful," Rose Red whispered.

He had to work to find a voice again. "So where is it?" he managed at last, speaking all in a rush.

"Look in the pool."

"I can't see in here."

"Lean forward, then, and keep your eyes open."

He obeyed. A rustling sound, like fabric moving, startled him, and he wondered for a split second if Rose Red had removed her veil.

"Look in the pool," the girl repeated. Leo, straining his eyes against blindness, looked.

A light.

At first faint and distant, glowing from deep, deep down, no more than a pinprick but impossible to miss in that darkness. It grew, and now Leo could see ripples moving on the surface of the water. The light continued to grow, and he thought it might be fire, but that was impossible, so deep underwater. Strange too, for this pool by which he knelt couldn't be more than a few feet deep, and that light seemed to shine from leagues away. And still it grew, drawing nearer and nearer.

Suddenly it was blinding. Leo put up his arm to shield his face as the light burned away the shadows in a brilliant flash. Then it was gone, replaced by a glow that gleamed out of the water to illuminate the walls of the cavern. Leo lowered his arm and looked in the pool.

He saw the monster.

The next moment, Leo was on his feet and storming from the cave as fast as he could in that semidarkness. It wasn't fear that drove him, breathless, out through the cave mouth and into the biting cold of the mountain air. It was anger. Blinding, unreasonable anger.

He stood panting with his back to the cave, grinding his teeth and twisting his beanpole in both hands. He heard Rose Red's soft footsteps behind him but wouldn't turn to look at her. His hands strained as though he would like to break the pole in half.

"Leo?" Rose Red spoke softly.

He smashed his beanpole against the nearest rock, and it rang through the bones of his hand. "Dragon's teeth!" he swore and smacked the rock again. "Dragon's teeth! Dragon's teeth and fire and tail! Why did you do that to me, Rosie?"

"You wanted to see—"

"A reflection. That's all there was! After all that, dragging me all over this dragon-kissed mountain, scaring me to death with caves and spooky voices . . . Just a reflection!"

"Leo, I—"

"This was the rottenest idea you ever had, Rosie, and it's not funny! You should have told me there was nothing to see, not run me ragged just for a glimpse of . . . of my own fool face!" He started walking then, hardly caring where he went, scraping his beanpole on the rocks behind him as he went. "That was rotten, and now I'm going to be in more trouble than you can imagine, being out so late. They're probably worried sick, and they'll never let me out of their sights again. And for nothing! Nothing, you hear?"

"I hear you, Leo," Rose Red whispered.

Without a word, she guided him back down the mountain, listening to his rants all the way. Then she led him through the forest, seeing him all the way to the road, for it was too dark for him to make his own way. He did not say good-bye to her, only waved an arm angrily and burst into a run, as though the Black Dogs themselves pursued him, all the way to Hill House's gardens.

He was scolded soundly and sent to bed with threats of all kinds hanging over him. Yet Leo didn't care. He was too furious as he crawled under his covers that night. But as soon as his head touched the pillow and he'd pulled his quilts up over his face, he became angrier still.

For he started to cry.

"Dragons eat her," he growled and dashed the tears away. "Dragons eat her to pieces!"

They did not let him out of their sight, just as Leo predicted.

He didn't care. His aunt wrote a letter to his mother and sent it off posthaste, and even that didn't bother him. Foxbrush dropped snide remark after snide remark, impressing himself with his own witticisms. Yet Leo couldn't even work up the ambition to knock his cousin over the head. He remained in his room most of the time, practicing juggling and headstands, sometimes even working on the bits of reading he had been told to accomplish over the course of the summer but that he had not even looked at yet. There were several essays he was supposed to have begun as well, and he was irked to find that his nursemaid had used up most of his parchment and ink on love letters to her young man . . . irked enough to threaten reporting her to his mother, but not irked enough to follow through.

The reply arrived from his mother. Just as expected, that fine lady was shocked to discover that her son had run off against orders and caroused all over the dangerous mountain well after dark, scaring everybody in Hill House out of their minds. He was to return home immediately.

The packing began. Dame Willowfair dithered over whether or not to send her son along with Leo. Foxbrush usually spent his autumns with Leo's family down in the tablelands, but it was early for him to go away, and what if Leo's corrupting influence began to get the better of her angel boy?

And still Leo kept to himself. He sat at his bedroom window, gazing out at the mountain country that had become so familiar to him. One tree in particular rose above the rest, a lordly grandfather oak, and he wondered idly what it would be like to sit in its topmost branches and survey all the world below.

He'd be leaving Hill House the following day. Likely never to return.

Leo pressed his forehead against the window glass, warring with himself. He was still angrier than he liked to admit. How could Rose Red do that to him? After a whole summer together, knowing as well as she did how much he wanted to hunt the monster, how could she show him . . . that?

Suddenly he got to his feet and swept up Bloodbiter's Wrath from where it had lain untouched since that night at the cave. He had to pass the library door, which was cracked open, but he didn't stop to see if his cousin was inside. Everybody was busy in Hill House, packing and making arrangements for his journey back home, and nobody noticed him as he made his way to the back garden. Nobody except perhaps old Mousehand, who was trimming the starflower vines and said not a word to anybody when he saw Leo pass through the garden gate and up the mountain path.

Leo's anger cooled as he walked that familiar way and took the turn at the sapling tied with a red scarf. The deer trail was more comfortable even than the hallways of Hill House, the trees friendlier than the household inhabitants. Even the air was easier to breathe.

He climbed to the Lake of Endless Blackness. The dam had fallen into disrepair, and the lake was mostly gone, leaving behind the litter of dozens of broken ships. Leo knelt beside the little dam wall, inspecting the places where the mud and pebbles had broken free, but he did not try to repair them.

"Bah."

He looked up. The goat stood on the other side of the stream. She blinked her yellow eyes at him, twitching her long ears.

"Hullo, Beana," he said.

She put her nose down to drink. When she raised it again, droplets falling from her snout, she solemnly said, "Bah."

"Where's Rose Red?"

The goat shook her head and stamped her hind hoof.

Leo stood up, leaning against Bloodbiter's Wrath like an old man weary from a long journey. "I was hoping she'd be here today. But she probably doesn't want to see me anymore, does she?"

"Baaaaah!" said the goat.

"I was pretty mad. I was . . . it was so . . ." He couldn't finish, for he didn't know what he was trying to say exactly. It was difficult to think with the old nanny giving him that no-nonsense stare of hers. "You shouldn't be so far from home, Beana," he growled. "Liable to get picked off by wolves or something. Shoo now, girl, shoo!"

"She ain't alone."

Of course, he thought as Rose Red emerged. She had been standing beside the goat all along; he had simply not seen her.

Leo hung his head in shame or sorrow; he wasn't certain which. "Hullo, Rose Red," he whispered.

"Hullo, Leo."

"I'm leaving tomorrow. Back to the tablelands."

"So me old dad told me."

They looked at each other shyly, and Leo rubbed his toe against the back of the other leg. "I don't think my mother will let me come back," he said at length. "She was pretty angry in her letter. About me staying out after hours, that is."

"Beana wasn't too pleased with me neither." Rose Red patted her goat's back and shrugged. "So it's probably for the best."

Leo's face wrinkled and he suddenly found it difficult to breathe, to think even. He didn't know what emotion it was that clutched at his heart, but it was something like fear. Fear of nothing he could name, but fear as potent as poison. Dragons eat them, why were there tears in his eyes?

"Rosie," he said, speaking louder and all in a rush, "I don't want to leave without you knowing that . . . without you understanding that . . . what we saw in the cave . . . What I saw—what you saw—it wasn't what you think—"

"Leo, what are you *doing*?"

The shout shot through Leo's head like an arrow. He whirled about, brandishing his beanpole, just in time to see Foxbrush scrambling over the rise, his fine clothes disheveled and a few strands of his perfect hair blown out of place.

"Foxbrush!" Leo cried, only just keeping from smacking his cousin across the face. "Foxbrush, why are you here?"

"Do you see?" Foxbrush was pointing, gesturing wildly behind him. Leo whirled again, just in time to catch a last evil-eyed glare from the goat. Then she turned tail and ran into the brush, the sounds of her passage crashing back to his ears long after she left his sight. There was no sign of Rose Red.

"Leo, did you see? Did you *see* that?"

Leo's face was red with fury when he turned to his cousin again. Foxbrush, however, was white as a ghost and babbling. "You saw it, didn't you? That thing? It's just like they all said! Leanbear and Redbird and the rest. It's just like—"

"You idiot!" Leo shouted, nearly spitting in his anger. "That was nothing at all! She's just a little girl with a dumb goat, and now you scared her away! I might never see her again, and you scared her away!"

"A little girl?" Foxbrush was trembling so hard he had to reach out and support himself against a nearby tree. "So *this* is what you've been doing all summer! *This* is why you never give anyone a straight answer about anything and run off at cursed hours of the night! You're bewitched, Leo, that's what you are. Don't you know who she is? Don't you realize that she's—"

He didn't have a chance to finish. Leo grabbed Foxbrush by the shirtfront and pinned him up against the tree so that his daintily shod feet kicked several inches above the ground. All the muscles in Leo's scrawny arms strained to keep his cousin in place, but he was too furious in that moment to care. He spoke through grinding teeth.

"Shut your mouth, Foxbrush. Shut it now, and don't ever open it on this subject again, or by the Silent Lady's Guide, I swear I'll choke you with your own tongue."

Foxbrush couldn't speak. His collar was pulled up too tightly under his jaw to allow for it. And by the time Leo let go of him and he slid into a messy heap at the foot of the tree, he'd had just enough time to consider his cousin's words and decide it best to abide by them. Leo careened wildly down the steep incline back to the deer trail, and Foxbrush was hard-pressed (he'd spent the whole summer over books, after all) to keep up with him. No amount of huffing and puffing convinced his cousin to slow down.

He did not hear Leo's muttered curses. And he did not see Leo's tears.

The following day, young Master Leo was piled into a carriage along with his nursemaid and all his belongings (save for a certain beanpole, which was placed in the care of old Mousehand, who was told to guard it until such time as its owner might return for it). Leanbear clucked to the mountain ponies, which started down the road at an easy pace. No one in Hill House stood at the door to wave good-bye. Dame Willowfair had not yet risen, and her fine young son was hiding away in the library, hoping that nobody would decide at the last minute to send him with his cousin.

Leo pressed his nose to the carriage window and looked back, gazing into the higher forest as though somehow he thought he might see something in those deep shadows. But he did not think to look in the topmost branches of the great grandfather tree, so he did not notice the veiled figure clinging there, seeing him off until he was long out of sight.

9

"DID HE SEE?"

"I ain't sure what he saw."

"You are withholding something from me, princess."

She sinks her chin down to her chest, but she cannot disappear in this place. "I told you, I don't know what he saw."

"He did not see me."

"No, I don't think he did."

"But I saw him. This handsome young friend of yours. This Leo, who makes you forget me."

She turns away from the pool, and her Dream puts out a hand as though to tilt her face back to him. "Would that I had a corporeal body, sweet princess. Then I should be your playfellow, and I would make you forget him as swiftly as he made you forget me."

She shivers and refuses to look at him.

"Now," says he, "things will return to what they were. Your Leo left you, just as you knew he must. But I am here still, and though I may not be so *fine to look upon, I will care for you just as I have always done. We will talk together, here in your dreams, and you will know that I am the only friend you need. And someday, sweet princess, you will let me kiss you."*

Here Rose Red straightens her shoulders and draws her head up, for a moment as imperious as the princess he says she is. She looks him in the eye when she speaks in a clear, even tone:

"You ain't never goin' to kiss me."

The Dream watches her rise and slip her veil back over her face. Without another word, she leaves his presence, and though his eyes are full of longing, he does not try to stop her. He watches until her tiny frame disappears through the mouth of the cave.

Then he too leaves.

He steps from one dream to another, then another, spreading his shadow far and caring nothing for the sleepers he disturbs. They moan in their sleep as they watch their dreams burn, then wake up in cold sweats, afraid to close their eyes again.

On he progresses, through the realm of the sleeping, until he crosses into the world where dreams come true. There they cease to be dreams and dissolve into nothingness. No color exists in this land, only shades. Even nightmares dare not venture past its borders for fear of losing themselves. It is a solitary world, wherein only one being can dwell.

She is the Lady of Dreams Realized.

The Lady Life-in-Death.

Her brother rarely visits her. He finds her company rather cold and prefers the fiery fervor of worlds where he can move and breathe and work with equal passion. But every so often, he finds it necessary to remember the Lady and to pay her a visit, as he does now.

"Greetings, sister," he hails her, and his voice carries across the colorless expanse of her kingdom to the center, where she sits upon her throne.

"Greetings, brother," she replies. At a word from her, the world about her alters, reorienting its boundaries and bearings so that her brother is suddenly before her and she need not raise her voice. "Have you come to play our game?"

He raises his hand. In the palm are two dice. "Only one game this time,"
he says.

"One is enough."

"There is a boy."

"Boy, girl. Man, woman. I care not which."

"I want him for one of mine."

"Roll the dice."

He smiles. His smile is strangely hot in that land, and the heat of it
sizzles the air before freezing into nothing. "You know, dear sister, they all
must be mine in the end." His teeth are blackened from the fire that burns
inside him, and his skin is white as leprosy. He rattles the dice in his hand.

She does not return his smile. Beneath the ghostly white mantle of her
hair, her face is as black and still as a petrified tree. "Roll the dice," she repeats.

"It will avail you nothing," he says as he continues to jangle the dice.
"Eventually all of yours come to me."

She speaks without moving her mouth. "And yet, you have not found
the last child for which we played. The princess, Beloved of your Enemy."

"I believe I have found her," says he, though the smile turns to a snarl. "The
child of Arpiar, hidden in the mountains, guarded by one of his knights . . .
she must be the one. My Enemy may protect her from Arpiar, but he cannot
keep her hidden from me. Besides, I won our game. I have my rights."

"Then kiss her and be done."

"Patience!" he replies, then licks a forked tongue across the jagged cage
of his teeth. "These things take time. But give me the life of this boy, and I
shall find it far easier to convince her that my kiss is her desire."

Her eyes narrow, and they are cold eyes indeed. "Roll the dice."

He casts the lot, and they watch them fly across the floor, his eyes empty
blackness edged with fire, hers empty whiteness edged with more emptiness.
Under their fervid gazes the twin dice roll, a light chipping clatter on the
stone, and the mists swirl in their wake.

At last they are still.

He steps forward to inspect the result, and fire flicks across his eyes. The
Lady reads what those eyes say. Now it is her turn to smile.

"The game is done. I've won."

Her brother turns on her with a snarl, and for a moment the fire in his throat shines red before the airless chill dissolves its color and heat. "He's yours, then, sister," he says. "I'll not touch him. Yet. But he will be mine. All of yours come to me in the end!"

The Lady makes no reply. But the smile remains fixed upon her face.

PART TWO

1

The Baron of Middlecrescent had only one child, a girl, which many would have considered an inconvenience as far as family inheritances went. But the Baron of Middlecrescent was a far-seeing man, and from the time his daughter was two years old he hatched what he fondly called The Plan.

For his daughter was already beginning to display certain talents.

She sported a mass of curly red hair and a pair of enormous blue eyes, unusual coloring in a country given to darker complexions. Young Daylily of Middlecrescent was, in fact, remarkably fetching.

She also possessed a willful nature that her nursemaids thought dreadful but which, the baron soon recognized, could be found charming when she came of age. So the baron took Daylily and her willfulness in hand and began the work of shaping her into the right sort of person to fulfill The Plan.

"You see, my dear," he said to his wife, "we are just distant enough of relations."

His wife, a simple woman with huge doe eyes, smiled at him. "Are we, husband?"

"We are."

"In what respect?"

The baron had long since given up hope of his wife's developing anything like a cunning mind. At one time this had bothered him. But as he aged he came around to appreciating her. In the scheming world where he moved and breathed, it was a relief to know that at least one person in his inner circle couldn't begin to plot.

He took a patient tone with her. "We are one of the noblest families in the kingdom. Your pedigree is beyond reproach."

"Oh, go on!" His wife giggled. "You flatterer!"

"Yes, dear. As I was saying, your pedigree is beyond reproach, and not a speck of foreign blood runs in my veins. Our estate is rich enough to support our title, thanks in large part to your dowry, my love."

She giggled again.

"And our daughter is without peer among the daughters of any lord in the Eldest's court."

"She is a sweet ducky, isn't she?"

She certainly was not a sweet ducky, in the baron's opinion, but she was everything necessary to fulfill every wish of his fatherly heart. Nevertheless, he bided his time and did not inform Daylily of The Plan until the evening of her sixteenth birthday.

"You like the boy, don't you?" he asked her when he had finished laying out the details.

Daylily considered in that thoughtful way she had. "He's a blessed idiot, Father."

"But a handsome enough young man, you must admit."

"Last time I saw him, he tried to stand on his head and play the lute at the same time."

"Yes," said the baron, trying not to be exasperated, "but he was no more than ten years old. He has since matured."

Daylily raised an eyebrow. It was a fine, delicate eyebrow, and more expressive than words.

"Think of the title," said her father.

She did think of the title. She even said it out loud, trying her own name with it.

"It sounds well, does it not?" said the baron.

"It would require me to marry him."

"Yes. Yes, it would."

"I could never love him."

"Did I ask you to love him?"

Daylily regarded her father a long moment, during which time several responses crossed her mind. But she managed to stifle them before they reached her lips. To the fiery temper of her childhood had been added a measure of discretion. And the look on her father's face told her that she would need to choose her battles carefully in the following months, perhaps years.

"Very well, Father. Invite him if you must."

"Of course, my darling," said Middlecrescent with a smile.

So the baron wrote a missive and sent it by a fast horseman to the Eldest's House, where Leo's mother, Starflower, received it with interest. She spoke of the matter to her husband, for it was he who must make the final decision. He asked a few questions but expressed little interest in the subject, deferring to his wife's opinion.

What Starflower did not know was that Leo talked to his father too, though regarding a different matter.

Starflower sent for her son. He came to her favorite sitting room (she had three) and knocked politely, but when she bade him enter, he leaned against the doorpost and crossed his arms. She sat at an enormous desk that was all cupboards and drawers, writing at an important-looking document without a glance to spare for her son. "Are you well?" she asked in a tone that implied she could not care less.

Leo shrugged. "Well enough." Somehow he knew that this conversation was bound to turn into a confrontation. His mother ignored him for several long moments, as though he were nothing more than a mildly annoying bug on the wall. Yet he must go on lingering, waiting for her to speak, his hackles rising all the while.

At last she continued. "I am composing a letter."

"So I see," Leo replied.

"To the Baron of Middlecrescent, my second cousin. You will be spending your summer with him."

Leo licked his lips and continued glaring at his feet. He had known this conversation was coming. Each year, as spring ran into summer, he and his mother had the same annual argument with slight variations. Last year it had been Upperwold, the year before, Idlewild. This time, Middlecrescent, but Leo was determined that the outcome should be different.

"I don't want to spend the summer in Middlecrescent," he said, his voice low but firm.

His mother continued without pause. "Middlecrescent is fine country with clean air, conducive to the studies you are pursuing."

Here came the tricky part. Leo knew his mother would never forgive him for what he was about to say.

"I spoke to Father."

The temperature in the room dropped. Leo's mouth went dry. He cleared his throat, however, and forced himself to go on, despite the dreadful *scritch-scratch*ing from his mother's pen, which never stopped. "He agrees that I'm old enough to choose how to spend my summers."

Mother never crossed Father, at least as far as Leo knew. But her shoulders set a little more firmly than before. "I see," she said. "And where have you and your father agreed upon for this year's jaunt? Will you sojourn to Shippening? Sail to Parumvir and pass your time gallivanting with those northerners? Or maybe the Far East better suits you?" Her voice was like ice. "Tell me, son. I am eager to learn of your plans."

How she could manage to half convince him to give in to her pleasure without so much as an argument was beyond Leo. He had to force himself not to exclaim, "Never mind! Middlecrescent is the place for me after all. Finish your letter and send me on my way."

But he had come too far now to retreat. "I want to visit Hill House."

No answer.

Not once had he dared touch on this subject in the years since he'd visited his aunt Willowfair. Upon returning to his father's house after that disastrous summer, he had been forbidden to speak upon the subject. His "behavior" at Hill House was dubbed "reprehensible" and he was never to be given the opportunity for repetition. A lad of his station shouldn't dream of such tomfoolery, running about the countryside unattended, disregarding his studies, bullying his cousin (a part Leo didn't remember but couldn't argue), and fraternizing with the locals. What would people think?

So five years had passed, and Foxbrush had come to visit Leo's home, but Leo had never returned the favor. He and his cousin got along about as well as they always had, which is to say, not at all.

And yet, there Leo stood (his mother could see him from the corner of her eye), bold as brass, requesting to spend the summer months in a remote mountain household, shut away with a cousin he despised.

Starflower narrowed her eyes at the parchment before her and at her own elegant handwriting. What had gone on that summer so many years ago? She knew that Leo thought about his time at Hill House frequently, though they never spoke of it. What had he found up in those lonely forests that so captivated him? She had asked young Foxbrush many questions on the subject (for Foxbrush was always his aunt's special pet), but even he had proven reticent. The last thing she wanted was to send her son back to that place where, at least that once, her control over him had slipped.

But his father had agreed. And Starflower never crossed Leo's father.

Yet even now she could turn this situation to her advantage. A smile touched the corner of her mouth. Starflower made certain it was the corner Leo could not see.

"Very well," she said, her voice as smooth as silk. "You may visit your aunt at Hill House this summer."

"Really?" The clouds on Leo's face cleared, though his expression was far more surprised than pleased. "Really, you don't mind?"

"Of course not! Why should I mind?" She lifted her half-complete letter so that Leo could watch as she tore it into three long pieces. "I shall not send this letter to Middlecrescent after all, but shall inform the baron that you have regretfully declined his kind offer." Then she turned, and Leo saw the heretofore hidden smile, and his heart sank.

Starflower handed her quill to him, along with a fresh sheet of parchment. "You may write and invite Baron Middlecrescent's daughter to join you. Have a pleasant summer, darling."

So that was her game, was it?

Leo should have known this was coming. After all, he was sixteen. Lads in his position always started having eligible girls forced down their throats right about this time. He shouldn't be surprised; he should have seen it coming a mile off!

But this knowledge did nothing to improve Leo's mood as he stormed down the passage from his mother's sitting room, up a flight of stairs, and on to his own set of rooms in a nearby wing. He slammed the wall with his fist as he went, rattling the gilt-edged frames and mirrors, and knocking a few candles from their sconces. Servants took one look at his face and quickly bowed their heads, pretending not to see him as he passed.

Which one was Middlecrescent's daughter anyway?

Leo entered the first in his series of five connected rooms, slammed the door, realized there was someone cleaning his hearth, and barked for that person to get out, all without really noticing. His mind was caught up in trying to recall Daylily of Middlecrescent's face. But memory escaped him. She blended in with all the other girls around his age who'd come and gone from the house throughout the last several years. Of course, he had always known that he would be matched up with one of them eventually, but this thought had never encouraged any particular effort to differentiate among the lot. They were all pretty, flouncy, chattery things as far as he was concerned.

There was no avoiding writing the required letter, however. He knew better than to take up arms against his mother twice in one day. Standing up to her about his summer destination had depleted his supply of courage. There could be no further rebellion on this score.

Dragon's teeth, she would poke, prod, and pry him into the shape she wanted, and Lumé help him if he resisted!

Leo wrote the letter. Everything polite and well expressed, just as expected, not a single word misspelled, not a single sentiment sincere. Any girl with half a brain reading that missive would immediately write a similarly polite refusal . . . but no chance Daylily would be so perceptive.

No, no, she'd probably consider herself highly complimented and set out for Hill House posthaste.

Leo growled wordlessly as he placed the letter in the gold tray on the end of his desk. Then, because his mood was too black for anything else, he went to his fireplace and took an old urn down from the mantel. Supposedly this urn, carved in a relief of Maid Starflower on one side, the Wolf Lord on the other, and a motif of wood thrushes around the lip and lid, contained the ashes of some venerable ancestor. What it really contained was a set of juggling sacks.

Leo started to juggle. First one sack, then two, then three, finally five sacks altogether. He moved about the room as he went, first at a slow, sedate pace, then adding little hop-steps, then moving into a silly jig, all the while keeping his eyes fixed on the rotation of his sacks. He orbited the room, avoiding furniture and corners, still jigging, still juggling, and as his concentration increased, his anger faded away.

This was a world that had room for no one else, just him and his sacks, and the energy it took to keep them moving in time to his dancing feet. No one could touch him here, in his element, just so long as Leo kept his eyes steady and his hands flashing, and those sacks flying. He was no prince in this realm of existence; he was king.

He added a sixth sack. Six was the most he'd ever managed to juggle at one time, and then only for a precious few rounds. But today they flowed almost effortlessly, and he started to jig again, softly singing as he went:

> "With dicacity pawky, the Geestly Knout
> Would foiter his noggle and try
> To becket the Bywoner with his snout
> And louche the filiferous—"

It was too much. He missed a step and the sacks flew wild. One hit a window, two landed in the hearth ashes, one knocked the gold tray with its letter clattering to the floor, and two more rolled out of sight beneath furniture. Leo stood empty-handed, feeling a bit of a fool.

No, not a fool. A jester.

He remembered dreams of boyhood days. Dreams of travel and

laughter and tomfoolery. *"I'm going to be a jester,"* he'd boasted once. A jester, traveling the world, performing for kings but answering to no one. For jesters were wild, madcap, and best of all . . . free.

Which Leo was not.

Gritting his teeth, he collapsed into a chair before the fire, contemplating the empty grate. He should have known how his power struggle with Mother would turn out. She'd take even the freedom he'd known at Hill House and turn it into means for her own ends.

Hill House.

Leo grimaced. Memories of that summer were indistinct. Over the last five years, many things had slipped away, leaving only vague impressions in their wake. But those impressions weren't unpleasant . . . he remembered games in the forest, and building a dam. He remembered laughing and running and feeling more himself than he ever had before or since. He remembered breathing freedom in that wild mountain air.

He remembered Rose Red. His friend.

Nothing had been the same after leaving Hill House. Perhaps nothing would be the same again, but—dragons eat Foxbrush, Daylily, his mother, the whole fire-blazed world—he was going to find out this summer if it killed him!

Leo closed his eyes, and his head rested on the back of his chair. Soon his breathing relaxed into a snore. But when the snoring ceased, he dreamed.

"Tell me what you want."

The Lady steps into his dream as if through parting curtains, and they stand face-to-face. He does not want to look into the vast emptiness of her eyes. But she holds his gaze.

"Tell me what you want."

Slowly, the Lady takes him by the shoulder and turns him to the right. There he sees a vista open up before him. He sees a road leading off into the horizon. He sees beyond the horizon, beyond the edge of the world he knows, and the path leads all the way to the sea. Then he speeds across that blue expanse, riding the wind, following the path over land, over water, over mountains, on and on. His soul thrills at the freedom of it, and he laughs and somersaults and leaps just because he can, as light as a wind-tossed leaf.

"Tell me what you want."

The Lady takes his other shoulder and turns him to the left. He wrenches his gaze unwillingly, but as his eyes adjust to the new scene, the smile dies on his lips, replaced with a stern line.

He sees a prince . . . no, a king. Noble and bearded and strong, he sits upon the Seat of the Eldest in a great hall of sweeping alabaster arches. The king sits with a golden sword upon his knee, and people flock to his feet, pleading their causes, looking to him for justice, protection, wisdom. At this king's right hand stands a lady of great beauty, her red hair circled in gold. All those assembled are amazed at the sight of her.

"Tell me what you want."

The Lady cups his face in her hands and forces Leo to look at her, though he strains to catch a last glimpse of that brilliant hall and noble king. But her white eyes fill his vision.

"Tell me."

"I don't know," he says, trying to ward off her hands, which latch onto his face like roots gripping soil. "I don't know. How can I?"

"I can make you a king," she says. "A king like no other in the history of the world. This power I possess."

"I don't know what I want!" Leo repeats. "Why must everyone pressure me? It's always push, push, push . . . but I don't know who I am yet."

The Lady continues as though he has not spoken. "I can set you free. I can send you down a path without cares or expectations, where you may become whomever you will."

He tries to close his eyes and shield himself from her gaze but cannot. "I don't know," he whispers.

"Tell me what you want." Her white hair surrounds him like a cloud, but the ends of it strike his face like tiny, biting snakes. "The time is near. You must make your choice and let me fulfill your dreams for you."

"I'll make my choice when I'm jolly well ready!"

"Soon."

Blood oozes from the stinging cuts on his cheeks.

"Tell me what you want, and I will make it so."

"When I know what I want, I'll tell you. Agreed?"

The stinging stops. Leo opens his eyes and sees her hair, still in a billow about him, but soft and gentle now as droplets of mist. And the Lady's eyes smile.

"Agreed."

2

Daylily received a letter sealed in red wax and stamped with the image of a seated panther. She rolled her eyes heavenward when she saw that seal, then braced herself, broke it open, and read the letter's contents in a quick glance.

"Dragon's teeth," she murmured, though it was not a ladylike phrase.

"What have you there, my lovely?" asked Baron Middlecrescent. He appeared at her elbow like some bad fairy, and she had no choice but to hand over the letter.

"Light of Lumé!" said the Baron. "This is better than I'd hoped."

"I thought he was to come here, Father," said Daylily. Not a trace of rebellion could be found in her voice, but her eyes may have flashed beneath those long lashes.

"And now you'll go there instead. A fine thing indeed, and his invitation is a sure sign of favor."

But for all her pretty arrangement of curls, Daylily was no fool. She had read between the lines and knew that young Leo's real sentiments were quite different from those expressed in ink. Her face remained calm, however, and she went about the necessary preparations for her journey to Hill House.

It was the most forsaken and loathsome location imaginable for a summer holiday, she concluded before her father's carriage had carried her even halfway. She was used to spending her holidays with friends in Middlecrescent City, enjoying the society there, the balls and assemblies and theatrical performances. There was more than one young man of certain birth who had proven himself most ardent in his admiration of the baron's daughter. And while Daylily bestowed favors on no one, she was not opposed to receiving favors herself.

Yet here she found herself trundling across bridge after bridge, passing towns of excellent societal repute, even bypassing the Eldest's City itself, on her way to some remote house in remote mountains where no one in her right mind would want to pass half a day. And under strict orders to beguile, bewitch, and otherwise entrance a boy for whom she had no use whatsoever.

Life was cruel.

But nobody who saw her passing would have guessed at the thunderous thoughts behind Daylily's face. She kept herself in excellent order (though her pillow, had it possessed a voice, may have complained of a few vicious poundings in the small hours of the night).

The carriage rolled through the Barony of Idlewild, and now the road led increasingly upward. Soon enough, Daylily found herself gazing back down on the world, and she had to admit, it was a thrilling view. Then the woods grew tall all around her, and villages were few and far between.

One night, while resting herself before the great fire of a mountain inn, she heard a sound such as she had never heard before. She raised her face from a cup of steaming cider and inquired of her goodwoman what it was.

"A wolf, m'lady," said her goodwoman.

"Ah," said Lady Daylily, taking another sip. The sound came again, and it gave her a delightful shiver. "Are there many wolves in this part of the country?"

"More than anywhere else, they say," her goodwoman replied. "Once upon a time, 'tis said the Wolf Lord himself hunted in these mountains. But that was long ago."

"A legend," said Daylily with the tiniest shrug. "A Faerie story." But she was pleased to hear that lone wolf cry a third time. A smile touched the corner of her mouth.

Her goodwoman shuddered, however, and her movements were hurried as she laid out her lady's clothing for tomorrow's journey. "They say that a monster lives in these parts to this day," she said in a low voice.

"A monster?" Daylily's smile vanished. "What sort of monster? The Wolf Lord's ghost?"

"Not a ghost, m'lady," said her goodwoman. "No one can say what it is exactly, but all agree that it is no ghost."

Daylily shook her head and finished off her cider. "Silly country talk," she said, setting aside her mug. "I don't know why you listen to it."

But the wolf's cry had awakened in her something she had not known existed: the same spirit of adventure that had touched young Leo many years before. Perhaps—and she scarcely allowed herself to think this—perhaps a summer away from dances and assemblies might not be so horrible? The mountain air was crisp and fresh like no air she had ever before breathed. Perhaps she had fallen on her feet after all.

Then Daylily met Leo, and all such thoughts vanished.

The baron's carriage rumbled into the yard of Hill House, and Dame Willowfair, her son, Foxbrush, and young Leo stood on the doorstep to meet it. The house was grand enough, Daylily admitted to herself as she gazed out the carriage window and waited for the footman to open the door. Rather a strange sight so far out in the wild, but handsome. She need not fear passing the summer in want.

The footman handed her out, and she curtsied before those at the doorstep. Dame Willowfair said something unmemorable, but when Daylily rose again she fixed her attention solely on the boy she was to win for her husband.

What a gawky clown!

True, he was dressed up well enough in velvets and lace (much too hot for a summer day), and these were tailored so as to disguise as much of his scrawniness as possible. But it would take miracles to hide it all.

And he wouldn't even meet her eyes as he bowed stiffly. He stood there like a ridiculous schoolboy, shuffling his feet.

Daylily scarcely spared a glance for his cousin, who was, as far as that one glance could tell her, an oiled and stuffed mimic of Leo.

But her father had given her orders, and Daylily was not one to shirk a duty. She extended a gloved hand to Leo, giving him no choice but to take it. "Thank you for inviting me to join you this summer," she said.

Leo accepted her hand and was obliged to really look at her for the first time. He found himself gazing into the face of the prettiest girl he had ever met.

"Um. Glad you came," he said.

Two weeks passed at Hill House, and still Leo could not catch a moment for himself.

He sat in the library with Foxbrush and Daylily a few days after that lady's arrival. She remained aloof as ever, working at stitching. Leo and Foxbrush sat in armchairs opposite each other in the library, each pretending to concentrate on his summer studies and neither succeeding. Leo's mind kept running among three distinct subjects: first, how much he disliked his cousin's hair oil; second, how surprisingly good-looking Lady Daylily was; third, how much longer it might be before he found a chance to slip out on his own.

He knew if he dared attempt an escape out the garden gate, his cousin was sure to follow. Neither he nor Foxbrush had breathed a word about their confrontation in the forest years ago, but neither had forgotten. Leo felt Foxbrush's squint-eyed stare upon him far more often than he liked. *Don't even think about leaving,* that stare said. But Leo thought about it.

Something had changed at Hill House, though Leo couldn't quite put his finger on what. Perhaps it was merely the difference between an eleven-year-old boy's perspective and that of a lad of sixteen. Leo suspected not, however. No one in the house itself had changed significantly: Leanbear still drove the horses, Redbird still cooked and baked, Dame Willowfair still rose at noon to powder her nose.

But this time, everyone watched him. And once Daylily arrived, they watched him even more closely, as though expecting him to explode with professions of love and poetry and nonsense at any moment. He glanced at Daylily again, seated with ramrod-straight back, her delicate hands working away at a bit of stitching. She really was a fine-looking girl, he had to admit. Somehow, he couldn't picture her climbing boulders or building dams or waging war upon invisible enemies. Which was acceptable, he supposed. Pretty girls weren't intended for such activities. But he could not see her as a friend.

Leo set aside his textbook and moved to the window, gazing out upon the garden. Funny, he thought as he looked at all the starflower vines tumbling over the garden walls. They'd really let those vines get out of control in the last few years. Where was old Mousehand to prune them back? There wasn't a sign of the bush-bearded gardener's creaking form as far as Leo could see. He frowned.

All the while he stood there, Daylily watched him over her stitchery. And Foxbrush watched Daylily watching him and thought many thoughts, most of them unkind. The day drifted by at an interminable rate.

At length, Daylily set aside her work. "I hear tell there is a monster in these parts."

Leo startled at her words, then turned to glare furiously at his cousin. "What did you tell her?" he growled.

Foxbrush raised his textbook like a shield. "I didn't breathe a word! You're the one with the obsession."

"Mind your own business!"

"I will, as I always have," Foxbrush retorted. They continued to glare at each other, though perhaps Foxbrush sank a little behind his tome.

Daylily eyed the two with a quizzically raised brow. In that moment, how she missed the elegant young men with whom she was accustomed to passing her days. What *had* her father's fool Plan brought her to?

"Well," she said, tapping a finger on the arm of her chair, "is there or isn't there?"

"What?" Leo asked.

"A monster?"

"No," said Leo.

"No," said Foxbrush.

But their tones implied otherwise.

Daylily sighed. This was going to be the longest summer of her existence, but at least she could make the most of it. She rose from her chair, arranged her skirts, and gave the lads a deceptively placid look. "Shall we, then?"

Leo narrowed his eyes. "Shall we what?"

"Hunt the monster?" She stepped from the room.

Leo and his cousin stared at the door through which she'd just gone, stared at each other, then broke and bolted at the same time, calling after her as they went. "Lady Daylily, wait!" She was halfway down the stairway when they caught up with her, both of them out of breath, and Foxbrush's oiled hair standing up in a most unnatural manner.

"Lady Daylily," said Foxbrush, leaping ahead of her and putting an arm on the stair rail to bar her way, "you really mustn't."

"Why mustn't I?"

"It's not right for a lady of your station to wander in the forest alone," said Leo.

"I don't intend to go alone," she replied. "I intend for you to accompany me."

"But we told you," Foxbrush insisted, "there is no monster. And you shouldn't hunt it."

"I have hunted foxes many a time," said she with a quick dart from her eyes that sent Foxbrush down an extra step or two. She was very beautiful indeed when angry, and her eyes were very blue. "I think I can hunt an imaginary monster without mishap."

"You'll dirty your dress," said Leo.

The look she gave him was withering. "I am not some dainty flower. I can suffer a little dirt."

She pushed past them both, heedless of their cries, grabbed a bonnet from its place near the door, and paused a moment to tie it on. Here, Foxbrush gave Leo a last desperate glance, then blurted, "They're under orders to not let Leo out of their sight."

So the secret was out. Leo felt his heart sink before leaping back into place, racing double time. He was a prisoner, was he? No wonder the atmosphere at Hill House was altered! This was his mother's doing, no doubt. Starflower wasn't about to let her young colt kick up his heels without ramming a bit of some sort between his teeth. Leo swore under his breath.

Daylily's face remained calm as ever. She finished tying her bonnet, then swept down a side passage, the two lads trailing behind her to the kitchens, where Redbird worked and Leanbear took his ease with a cup of tea. They both looked up in surprise when Daylily entered the room. The beautiful baron's daughter had scarcely given any of the household staff a glance since arriving; even her servant considered herself too good for those who lived at Hill House.

Yet there Daylily stood, her hair very red, her gown very green, and Redbird had to agree that she was far too fine a lady to be standing in Hill House's kitchen.

"I am going for a walk up the mountain," Daylily declared before Leanbear had the chance to scramble to his feet. "These two will accompany me."

There could be no gainsaying her wishes. Redbird curtsied and said that dinner was at six, but that was all the say she had in the matter. Daylily was gone and the two boys with her.

So maybe pretty girls were worth more than he had first thought, Leo considered as he followed Daylily through the gardens and out the garden gate. The path up the mountain was exactly as he remembered it, but it took on a whole new aura with Daylily marching up it, as purposeful as a queen; not to mention Foxbrush, perspiring a few steps after her.

It would be all right, Leo told himself as he lagged a little behind them both. Daylily knew nothing about this mountain. She would lead them on a long march up the path, eventually realize that she wasn't going to find anything, and turn around once more. This thought brought him comfort, for despite his pleasure at being at last beyond the garden wall, Leo found that he had no desire to pursue that old monster-hunting game of his.

He did not want anyone else to hunt it either.

"We should turn around now," Foxbrush said before they'd gone even ten minutes up the road.

Daylily graced him with no answer. Her red curls escaped from beneath her hat and trailed down her back like some battle standard, and her eyes were sharp as they gazed about the forest. She was no fool; her years in the cunning social circles at the baron's court had taught her a good deal about reading people, and she could read Leo and his cousin without difficulty. They were both frightened when she mentioned the monster, though for different reasons . . . and the conflict in their emotions led her to believe she had nothing to fear as she progressed up the mountain, while it simultaneously whetted her curiosity. Dancing and receiving attentions from admiring young men were all well and good, but here was a mystery like none she had ever before encountered. Daylily was not one to shy away from a mystery.

She saw the red scarf tied to the silver tree. And she saw the trail, almost hidden, leading deeper into the forest.

Gathering up her skirts still more firmly in each hand, she made the plunge into the wood. Foxbrush and Leo gave each other horrified looks, then darted in after her. "Wait, wait!" they both cried. "You can't go in there!"

"I see no reason why not," she replied. "Though if you two keep making that racket, we'll not find so much as a squirrel, much less a monster."

How strange it was to walk this path again, far stranger in this company. It was something terrible to watch Daylily in her finery marching through the underbrush like she owned it and, notwithstanding her long skirts, making less noise than Foxbrush, who muttered and cursed and stepped on every crackly stick as he went.

The landmarks were familiar, despite the passage of years. Things change slowly in the forest, and Leo felt as does a man returning home after a long absence. His eyes, when they weren't following Foxbrush and Daylily, sought out those little haunts and hollows that he had missed without realizing he missed them.

And everywhere he looked, he expected to see Rose Red. But she was not there.

They came to the place where the narrow path passed near the creek, and Leo, who was listening for it, heard the water flowing up above. He paused, watching Daylily and Foxbrush continue on ahead until they had disappeared into the greenery. Even Daylily's bright hair had vanished from sight.

Still he debated with himself. Did he want to make that climb? Did he truly want to see the lonely spot where he had spent so many happy hours? Did he dare hope to find . . .

"Iubdan's beard," he muttered, "be a man, Leo! There's nothing to be scared of."

He scrambled up the steep incline, pushing through the thick mountain growth.

He found the creek flowing as it had for countless generations. The water was ice-cold and high enough to flow over the tops of his shoes and wet his stockings thoroughly. He splashed on through it anyway, not bothering to step from stone to stone, for they were too slippery to trust.

All signs of the dam that once created the Lake of Endless Blackness were gone, the sticks of sunken ships long since washed away, and the stones blended in with all the others on the creek bottom. But Leo recognized the spot at once. And his gaze sought those familiar places where a little girl should be sitting, swathed in her veils, hard at work weaving sticks together to form a seaworthy hull, or those spots in the foliage where a goat might forage with irritable bleats.

But they were gone. Only their memories, like ghosts, remained.

Leo sat beside the creek, his wet shoes still in the flowing water, his shoulders slumped. "I'm sorry, Rose Red," he whispered, and the babbling water drowned his voice. "I'm sorry for what I saw in the cave."

An awful silence fell.

It was as though deafness struck him, and all the sounds of the mountain went still, even the stream's murmuring. He felt the strange tension of the forest. For a moment, he sensed the anger that flowed across the mountain, indefinable but undeniable. He drew his feet up from the water, which was suddenly warm, almost hot. The air trembled, and Leo, just in that instant, was afraid.

The moment passed. The silence broke to the sound of birdsong far away. Birdsong that nearly, but not quite, held words:

Beyond the Final Water falling
The Songs of Spheres recalling . . .

"Rose Red," Leo whispered, bowing his head, "won't you return to—"

"What are you doing?"

He startled. Daylily stood across the creek, her hands holding her skirts, which were more than a little mussed by now, and her bonnet was crooked on her head. But her face, though flushed from the climb, was as quiet and inscrutable as ever.

"What are *you* doing?" Leo asked back, and though he knew it was terribly impolite, he did not rise. After all, it wasn't ladylike for Daylily to be tramping about the forest; why should he follow all the social niceties?

Daylily put out a daintily shod foot to one of the creek stones, felt it to make certain she would not slip, then stepped onto it. In this way she crossed over the creek, only wetting the edge of her skirt. Then, to Leo's surprise, she took a seat on the dirty bank beside him.

"You are hunting something out here, aren't you?" she said, and he felt her penetrating gaze on the side of his face. He shrugged. "Not a monster?" she guessed.

"No," said Leo. "Not a monster."

Daylily's eyes narrowed as she studied him. His features were soft, more a boy's than a man's as yet. But she could see where maturity might make him handsome. He was, she thought, one who would need to succeed at something. Not merely succeed to the position to which he was born; no, much more than that. He would need a quest, a purpose, some deed to fulfill before he could hope to become the man he should be.

A pity, really, for a boy like Leo was rarely given such an opportunity.

Daylily pursed her lips, surprised how, for the briefest moment, her heart went out to this boy who, though the same age as she, seemed so much younger. "Why are you sad?" she asked.

"I'm not sad."

"You are."

"Where did you leave Foxbrush?"

"Don't change the subject."

Leo hung his head lower, his black hair flopping over his forehead.

But Daylily persisted. "You're searching for someone. Whom?"

"My best friend."

"Ha!"

Leo looked up in time to see her brief smile. It was the first he'd seen on her face since she came to Hill House, and it was, he thought, rather nice, if not altogether comfortable on her face.

"Not Foxbrush, then."

"No! Definitely not Foxbrush."

"Someone you met when you came here before?" She reached out and put a hand on top of one of his. He flinched but did not pull away. Her hand was soft. "Someone *they* don't want you to associate with?"

Leo nodded. Her eyes were so blue. He had never seen eyes like hers before.

"What was his name?" she asked in a gentle voice.

"Rose Red," Leo blurted, though he'd not intended to share. Something in those eyes of hers made him want to tell her his secrets, even as he blushed. "Her name was Rose Red. She was a girl who kept a goat around here."

"Oh."

Daylily's hand withdrew from his, and he found that he rather missed it. Her whole body stiffened beside him, and she wrapped her hands very firmly about her knees. "I see. They would frown upon you associating with one of the country goat girls, wouldn't they?"

"Well, you know, they—"

"Young love is always quickly squelched in a boy of your position, and I understand why you would resent it."

"I wasn't really—"

"But no fear," continued Daylily, rising and brushing off her skirts in a most businesslike manner. "I'm sure you will find your—what was her name?—your little goat girl again. These things have a way of coming out right."

"Daylily, I—"

"We'd best be on our way." She was already halfway across the creek, and Leo hastened to rise and follow her. "I left Foxbrush in a bramble somewhere, and I doubt that he's extracted himself. I don't suppose you brought a pair of gloves with you?"

Daylily descended the incline with surprising grace in all those skirts, and again Leo thought, as he followed her, that perhaps pretty girls had more uses than he'd ever given them credit for.

3

I FEARED YOU'D NEVER COME BACK TO ME."

Rose Red enters the cave as though drawn against her will. Steam rises and swirls about her uncovered face like caressing hands as she kneels before the dark pool. She turns away. But she cannot escape the voice.

"I thought you would forget me again, now that he's returned."

"I want to forget you."

"But you always come back to me."

She shudders in the dark of that nightmare and clenches her hands into fists. "You never let me go!"

"You never leave."

"How can I leave? You plague my dreams."

Her Dream smiles up from the water, and his face is horrible to see. "If you wanted to, you could leave the mountain. Yet you choose to stay. You cannot be parted from me, my sweet princess."

Her head bows to her chest. Tears burn in her eyes. "Beana don't want me to leave the mountain."

"Beana does not love you as I do."

"Shut up."

"Leo does not love you as I do."

"Shut up!" She leaps up and grabs the nearest loose stone she can reach, flinging it at the face in the water with all her strength. The splash shatters the image, and for a moment Rose Red is free of his gaze.

But the rock sinks. The waters settle. And the face returns.

"Someday, princess, you will understand that no one can be so constant a friend as I."

Then his eyes burn hers, and she cannot look away.

"If you choose him over me, make no mistake . . . I will make him pay."

Rose Red woke up. She was covered in sweat yet very cold.

Those dreams! They grew more horrible with each passing night, and sometimes she could not shake them even as day drew on. "Just a dream," she whispered, trying to force her heart to slow its racing. "Just a dream, nothin' more."

She put up a hand, realized that her face was bare, and hastily felt around for her veil. Not that there was anybody near besides Beana, but she did not like to take chances.

It was chilly in the cottage. She had not lit a fire in the hearth for many months now, nor had she attempted to mend the thatch. It was more like a shed these days than a home, an empty, inhospitable shed. Beana slept in the center of the one room, and Rose Red lay with her head pillowed on the goat's shaggy back. She sat up now and drew her veil over her head, listening for the familiar sound she knew she would not hear.

The old man's snoring.

How long had it been now since . . . since everything?

Rose Red got up carefully so as not to disturb Beana and stepped through the sagging cottage door. How long had it been since she'd had a proper meal? Much too long ago to calculate! How long since she'd had a proper night's sleep? Several weeks now at least. Not since the boy had returned to Hill House.

She made her way into the yard. It was a shambles these days, and the kitchen garden was overgrown with weeds save where Beana had nibbled them down. Though the night was dark, Rose Red could see it all clearly through the slit in her veil, but she turned her gaze away and passed into the forest.

The watching and unhappy wood.

She did not know how intently it watched her, though she felt the tension running through the very bones of the mountain. Was the wood's unhappiness connected with her own?

The shadows fell deep and solemn where she walked. She caught a gleam of white in the darkness and recognized at once her Imaginary Friend. But she turned away, shaking her head. She did not want to imagine anything right now.

A thrush sang in the darkness. Then she heard the soft rustle of wings and a light weight pressed into her shoulder.

My child, said the thrush in the voice of her Prince. *Why do you scorn me?*

"I don't want you," said Rose Red, trying to shrug the little bird away. "Scat."

You are weary with sorrow. Allow me to comfort you.

"Some comfort you are."

Have I not promised never to abandon you?

"Is that so?" She took hold of the gently gripping claws with her gloved fingers and wrenched the bird from her shoulder. It fluttered from her grasp and settled on the ground before her, the white of its breast luminous in the darkness. But Rose Red turned away and continued down the mountain. "Make me some more promises, why don't you? Promise imaginary food to keep off starvation. Promise imaginary shelter to keep me warm. Promise a whole town full of imaginary folks what will pretend they don't hate the very sight of me. Promise to give me work so that I might pretend to live again!"

The thrush took to the air and followed her. She did not see it, for her head was bowed. "Promise imaginary medicine what can pretend to heal," she whispered, "even after hope of healin' is long gone."

My child—

"Stupid fancies!" she growled. "Why do you trouble me so? You when I'm awake, *him* when I'm sleeping! Cain't you just let me alone?"

The bird spoke no more, at least not that she heard. The silence of the wood fell heavily around her. How long, she wondered, since she'd spoken a word to another person? Beana didn't count. She was only a goat, after all, and so couldn't really talk, for all she was the best friend Rose Red had.

Leo had been her best friend once. But that was years ago. He wouldn't remember her. Not the way she remembered him.

She'd seen the carriage climbing the hill from her perch in the topmost boughs of the grandfather tree. Somehow she'd known it must be he. But the thought gave her no joy.

She emerged from the forest onto the path and continued on down. "I ain't goin' to the house for him," she muttered to herself as her feet padded softly on the hard dirt. Her quick eyes darted about, for even at this darkest hour of the night it wouldn't be impossible to meet one of the mountain folk coming or going. That was the last thing she wanted. And as she approached Hill House, she must watch all the windows for any sign of a candle, any indication that some member of the staff might yet be awake or even rising early for some odd duty.

There was none, so she climbed the garden gate into the yard.

The gardens held no interest for her, not even the starflower vines that bloomed white at night. She passed over the lawns to a quiet corner in the back. A corner where marble stones were planted in the earth, some elegantly carved, some not. The founder of Hill House had a most impressive statue, a white panther seated with its mouth open. A spider had, indecorously, built a web among those carved fangs.

In a smaller, simpler nook were wooden markers carved with nothing save names. Rose Red, like a ghost in her rags and veils, passed between the graves until she came to one of those wood markers on which the name *Mousehand* was written, though she could not read it.

She knelt there and wept behind her veil.

"What did you have to go and die for, Dad?" she demanded, putting a hand on the marker. "What did you have to go and die for and leave me all alone? I told you, didn't I? I told you not to!"

She pressed her forehead to the marker, and her veil grew damp with her tears.

He had died on a cold autumn night, many months ago now. She had known he would but had lied to herself that he would not. In retrospect, she could not deny that she had known all along that it was his final night when he crawled onto his pallet and called her to him.

"Rosie, com'ere a moment, will you?"

"Yeah, Dad?" She'd knelt by his side and put out a hand for him to find and grasp. When his fingers closed about hers, she noticed how weak they were.

His fingers squeezed hers until the blue veins stood out. "Rosie," he said, "did I ever tell you about the first time I laid eyes on you?"

" 'Course you did," she whispered, but he wanted to tell it again, and she did not stop him.

"It was late one moonlit night," he said, "and you know I cain't sleep in the full moon. It works on my joints a right awful magic! So I took myself for a little walk. Now that was back when I worked for the Eldest, our good King Hawkeye. He'd asked me to plant the red roses along the Swan Bridge path. A sad thing that, for now all the roses are gone. Aye, within a year of that very night, some strange blight struck every bush in Southlands, and not a single blossom grew, not so much as a pink-edged bud.

"But that night, I was mighty proud of the landscaping I'd done, and there is nothing like the scent of roses in the moonlight to fill a man with all sorts of goodness, swollen joints be dashed!"

Rose Red smiled, running her thumb up and down the man's bony wrist.

"I strolled down that path, enjoying my roses, then on out across Swan Bridge. I walked a long way out there under the moon, and looked down into the dark wood below. All the trees rippled like water, their leaves reflecting back the white light so's I could have thought I stood above the ocean. It was a sight, Rosie!"

"Sure, Dad. Sure it was."

"But it was cold too, so I had to start making my way back homeward. I was nearin' the end of the bridge and just getting a whiff of them roses of mine when I heard in my ear the prettiest sound I ever did hear. It was a bird's song, one I didn't know, prettier than a nightingale, prettier than a mourning dove's coo."

"A wood thrush," Rose Red murmured.

"That's what it was, girl, right enough. A wood thrush, and at that hour, singing as though his heart would break for the pure joy of singin'! And I saw him, sittin' all proud and mighty like a little prince in the throne of my grandest, reddest rosebush, not two steps from Swan Bridge."

The old man's voice trailed off, and Rose Red thought perhaps he had gone to sleep. But when she tried to lay his hand aside, his grip tightened. A deep chuckle rumbled in his chest, though it ended with a wheezy cough. "Ah, Rosie," he said, "I'll not forget my surprise when suddenly this awful commotion under the bush started up! But then I saw this white bundle and realized it was that bitty thing makin' all the racket. So I made my way to the bush, and that's when I found you."

He smiled a toothless smile, and his dim eyes circled about, as though wanting to meet her gaze. "You were somethin' different, Rosie," he said. "Like no other baby I'd seen."

"I'm sure I was that," she said.

"Now, Rosie, there ain't no call for soundin' so down in the mouth! When I say you were like no other baby, I mean because it was obvious to me that you were a miracle, brought to me by the moon and that bird, and born right under my reddest bush, with three great red petals fallen on your forehead."

She could tell he was close to dozing off by now. His eyelids slid slowly over his bleary eyes, and he rubbed them with his free hand like a toddler insistent on staying up.

"My Rose Red," he said, "you are a Faerie child. Born different from everyone else, and that's why you look the way you do. It takes special eyes, Faerie eyes, to see you as you really are.

"You've never seen them, my girl, but listen to me now: Not in all the world was there a flower that can excel the rose. The fairest of the fair is she, with a smell as sweet as spring and summer combined. But when I looked at you there in the moonlight, you were more beautiful even than my reddest rosebush. You listenin' to me, girl?"

"I'm listenin', Dad."

In that last moment before sleep claimed him, his eyes became very bright. "Rosie," he said, "keep yourself safe, d'you hear me? Keep your face covered, for they won't know what to make of a face like yours. And never forget, you were the greatest gift to me."

With that, he let go of her hand and fell asleep, filling their hovel with his thunderous snores. And when the sun crested the mountain and Rose Red went to shake him awake before the porridge went cold, she found he'd gone and died on her without so much as a by-your-leave.

She'd had to carry his body down to Hill House. Those who served in Hill House were honored to be buried among their predecessors, and Mousehand deserved that honor more than anyone. Down the deer trail and the mountain path Rose Red had borne him, to the gates of Hill House . . . then the most horrible part. She could not call out to those in the house. She could not ask for their aid. No, she must leave the man she called father there by the gate to be discovered later that day, for the household to suppose that he had died on his way to work.

For if the household saw him with her, even in death, they would shun him and refuse to lay him to rest in the house graveyard.

He was found, he was buried, his name carved on a wooden marker.

She did not realize until he was gone just how greatly she had depended on the old gardener. Of course she had loved him and been cared for by him. Though they had lived simply, she had never had to worry about where the food would come from. Mousehand would venture down to the village to buy the meal and barley. Mousehand had purchased seeds as needed for the kitchen garden, and when the garden was insufficient, Mousehand had provided supplements.

Rose Red, covered in her veils, dared not venture to town. So she remained in the forest, and winter set in, and she rationed out her meager supplies. Those supplies failed, and Rose Red starved.

Eventually, things became so bad that hunger drove her from her safe cottage yard and into the more remote mountainfolk homesteads. She stole for the first time in her life. Only little bits and pieces, things she was almost certain would not be missed. But that did not make it any easier on her, and she hated herself for having come to this state.

"Don't blame yourself, Rosie," Beana told her. "If these folks were as good and kind as they like to think themselves, all you'd have to do is ask, and they'd give you as much or more."

There could be no asking, however. So Rose Red stole from storage houses and took no comfort in Beana's words. After all, Beana was only a goat. What did she know?

The only relief in all this terrible time was that when she fell asleep at night, she never dreamed.

When spring and summer returned, survival became a little easier. Rose Red could find roots and wild vegetables, and her body was tougher than anyone looking at her small form might suppose. Beana was always there with her to comfort her. She busied herself making plans for the coming winter, attempting to salvage what she could of the kitchen garden despite the lack of new seeds.

But then Leo had returned to Hill House. And with him came the dreams.

Angry dreams born, Rose Red was sure, out of her hurt and fear. Dreams that grew angrier with each passing day, until even in waking hours she still felt that anger surging along beside her. Beana sensed it too, but they never spoke of it, nor of Leo. But what work Rose Red had managed on the kitchen garden failed, and ruin took the cottage yard in a hold that would never be broken. The summer was passing; winter would soon be upon them.

As she knelt that night before Mousehand's grave, her back to the house and her veiled face streaked with drying tears, Rose Red knew that she would not survive another such winter.

"Bah."

A gentle nose nuzzled the back of her neck. Rose Red startled only a little before turning to put an arm over Beana's neck. "What you doin' here, fool goat?"

"I could ask the same of you," Beana replied.

"How'd you get through the gate?"

"You left it open."

Rose Red frowned. "I didn't."

The goat tossed her horns. "You're not supposed to come down here. It isn't safe; you know that."

Rose Red turned back to the grave and rested one hand on the mound of earth under which the old gardener rested. "I miss him sometimes."

"Doesn't make it any less dangerous," said Beana, but she knelt down beside the girl anyway, and they remained awhile in silence, listening to the sounds of the night.

"Beana," Rose Red said, her gloved fingers twining in the goat's hair, "what becomes of a person when they die?"

The goat gave her a sidelong glance. "How should I know? I'm just an old goat."

"He cain't be gone. Not completely," Rose Red persisted. "His body wore out, but *he* wouldn't just be gone." Tears dampened the veil where it rested on her cheeks. "Don't goats have notions of what happens afterward?"

Beana sighed, tilting her head as she thought. "Mind you," she said at last, "I couldn't tell you for sure, but . . . but what I heard is that when a body dies, the spirit leaves this world and passes into the Netherworld, where one must walk Death's Path. This path looks different to different folks. For some, it is a hard and lonely way . . . and they walk it alone, in darkness."

Rose Red breathed a shuddering sob and bowed her head over the grave once more.

"No, no, listen!" the goat hastened to say. "It isn't that way for everybody! Some, once they've passed through the gate, see a light shining on top of an old stone by the pathway. An old gravestone." Her voice became faraway, as though she were recalling something from her own past, not merely recounting a story she'd once heard. "The stone is white, but you hardly see that for the brightness that shines upon it. A silver lantern of delicate work, older than you can imagine. And within that lantern shines a wonder. Like a star, yet unlike as well."

Rose Red whispered, "The Asha Lantern." She remembered the legend of the Brothers Ashiun that Leo had related to her years ago.

"This lantern," said Beana, "is full of Hope. Not hope as you and

I think of it, an emotion or a dream. I mean true, brilliant Hope. That you see and smell and feel through your whole body.

"The folks who see the lantern take it with them as they walk the path. And the light guides them through the darkness, keeping at bay all the terrors of the Netherworld. At long last it leads them to the Final Water, and there . . ."

"And there, what?"

The goat shook her horns and snorted. "I don't know exactly from that point. It's not as though I've crossed the Final Water myself!" Then she reached up and nuzzled her girl. "But you may be sure the man you call father has. He found that lantern beyond the gate, and it guided him true. And when the time comes for you to cross the Final Water yourself, he'll be waiting for you on the Farthestshore. And that's a place you'll want to see, for it's a land where no lantern is needed. Darkness has no room in that country where Hope is finally satisfied."

Rose Red ran a hand down her goat's neck and sighed. "I don't know what you're talkin' about exactly," she said. "But it sounds pretty. Thank you."

"Bah." Beana shivered the fur down her spine, a goat's shrug. "Like I said, it's what I've heard. Being an old nanny, I don't pretend to be an expert on these things."

Rose Red was silent a long moment as she continued to stroke Beana's neck. "Beana," she said at last, "what would you say to . . . us two makin' our way off?"

"What do you mean?"

"I mean . . ." She hesitated, then continued in a rush. "I mean leavin' the mountain."

"*What?*"

"It's too dangerous for us up here, Beana! Folks are scared of us . . . of me. I'm not a fool, Beana, I know what they say. They ain't never goin' to give us a chance to make it. But down there, down in the low country, they don't have no mountain monster to . . . to make them nervous. They don't have no reason to hate us like these folks do, and I could find work maybe, and—"

"Rose Red," said Beana with a bleat that sounded much too loud in that quiet graveyard, "if I've said it once, I've said it a thousand times: You must *not* go down the mountain!" She bleated again but calmed herself with an effort and went on in a softer tone, "Why do you think the old man left his place at the Eldest's House?"

Rose Red shrugged.

"For you, girlie. He understood more than you think; he understood that he had to get you away, into the high country, where you could not hear . . . where you would be safe. Lonely, yes. Shunned, yes. But safe, my Rosie, as you can never be down in the tablelands."

"But I don't—"

The goat nuzzled the girl's hand and lipped at her sleeve. "Please don't ask why. It's best you know as little as possible. Someday, perhaps, I'll be able to explain. But in the meanwhile, you must trust your old Beana."

"Trust my goat," said Rose Red, "who cain't really talk. You know what you are, Beana? You are my own mind makin' up excuses not to face my fears, that's what you are."

"My, my," said the goat, "aren't we the little philosopher?" She chewed her cud at a furious rate. Then she said, "You should talk to the boy."

"What's that you say?"

"Tell him your father died. Ask him for help."

Rose Red shook her head and removed her hand from the goat's neck, wrapping both arms around her middle instead. "I ain't askin' him for nothin'." She tilted her head to one side, trying to keep more tears from falling, though the goat could not see them. "He don't remember me."

"Bah!" said the goat. "Sure he does. Give him more credit than that!"

"Now you're just my own mind tellin' me what I want to hear. I ain't listenin', Beana!"

The goat bleated angrily. "Stop talking foolishness, girl! You know as well as I that we won't pull through this next winter without a little help. Ask the boy. He can do something for us, I have no—"

"I ain't askin'," Rose Red said in a voice that was quiet but absolute. They were silent again for some time, pressing into each other. But Rose Red's mind was not still; it was full of a voice from a dream that burned in her memory no matter how often she told herself it was not real.

"I will make him pay."

"I ain't askin' him," she said to herself in a voice too low for the goat to hear. "I'll keep Leo safe from the monster if it kills me."

A few hours later, dawn crept up to the mountaintops and spilled at last into the Hill House gardens. It touched the markers of humble graves, but the girl and her goat had long since gone, leaving Mousehand, and all those of the house, to sleep.

"Make him pay, will you?"

"Don't take on so! I've got to keep the girl in check, haven't I? What business is it of yours what I tell her?"

"He's mine, brother," says the Lady, and her empty eyes bore into the Dragon's with a force greater than fire. *"Don't forget who won our game. Touch him, and I'll take that girl from you!"*

"You wouldn't dare," snarls the Dragon. *"I've worked too hard. My Enemy's Beloved will become my child, and I will finally have my vengeance for those centuries of binding. Don't you dare take her from me."*

"Then don't touch the boy. His dreams are mine."

The Dragon flashes his long teeth. *"I'll use him as I can to win that kiss,"* he snarls, yet the rules of the game hold fast. *"I'll not touch his dreams, sister. But I'll use him as I can. And the girl had better not leave the mountain."*

4

THE SUMMER WAS NOT TURNING INTO anything like Leo had expected, but that didn't mean it was worse. After all, childhood memories rarely matched up with reality. He would not have enjoyed a summer traipsing about the mountainside as he once had, carrying a silly beanpole and building dams. Quiet afternoons of playing cards or chess with Daylily were a fine substitute, and this way he didn't have to worry about the household staff watching him wherever he went.

Foxbrush gave him the evil eye more often than not, but that was nothing new, so Leo ignored him.

He slept well at night for the most part, with his window open to admit the fresh mountain air, so different from the stifling atmosphere of the tablelands in the summer. Sometimes, if he half awoke, he would think the drifting curtains looked like a spectral woman's robes and billowing hair, but after a few blinks, the illusion would fade, and Leo could sleep again.

One night, sleep did not come to him as easily, nor did that daft image of the specter fade like it should. So he got out of bed and marched right to the window, grabbing the curtains in both hands just to prove to himself that they were, in fact, curtains.

They were, which was something of a relief.

Before returning to bed, he gazed out on the moonlit lawns, admiring how the starflower vines blossomed white at night. During that lonely moment, he remembered Rose Red more clearly than he had since the day he last climbed to the creek. But she was gone, he was certain. It was foolish to think he would find her again.

And foolish to try to make sense of what he had seen in the cave that night so many years ago. He'd probably dreamt it.

Leo went back to bed and fell asleep immediately.

The next day, Daylily noticed a damper on Leo's mood. He had, over the last several weeks, been in remarkably good spirits. She hadn't once heard him mention that goat girl of his, which was encouraging. And he certainly was, in his boyish way, paying her attention. He could hardly compare with the more sophisticated gentlemen from whom she'd enjoyed similar attentions in the past, but she wasn't under orders to marry any of them, so she mustn't complain.

Besides, Daylily had to admit, there was a certain pleasure in having a chance to play little girl again. Over the last few years she had found herself flung into the dizzying society of Middlecrescent, learning the flirtation game and dancing until her feet were sore. Here at Hill House, the most exciting pastime was a rousing game of chess, or if they were feeling particularly sophisticated, Daylily might play an instrument and sing some ballad of Eanrin the Bard . . . which never failed to put Leo to sleep, though Foxbrush always listened with rapt attention. A unique summer, to be sure, but not altogether unpleasant.

She would win him over before the holiday was out.

Yet today, between moves across the chessboard, Daylily watched her prospective husband and noticed a distinct lack of vim. He slouched more than usual, and his attention was not on the game. She saw his gaze wandering to the window.

Daylily took his queen, and Leo didn't notice.

"Why don't you inquire after her?" she asked, perhaps more sharply than necessary.

Leo pulled his attention from the window and examined the chessboard. "Oh. I guess you killed her, huh?"

"Not the queen," said Daylily as she added the white piece to her collection of pawns, knights, and rooks on one side of the board. "Your goat girl."

Leo gave her a darting glance and slouched farther than Daylily would have thought humanly possible.

"You're thinking of her, aren't you?" Her voice was calm and even. No one could have guessed at Lady Daylily's true feelings on the subject, least of all Leo . . . who wasn't paying attention in any case.

He shrugged. "She's probably left the mountain. It doesn't matter."

Daylily's eyes narrowed. "Are you going to play?"

He moved a bishop, and she killed it with her knight. Iubdan's beard! It wasn't even a strategic pleasure to destroy him today. Leo fixed his eyes on the board and appeared to be making a real effort to study what was happening. But he didn't move a piece.

"You should inquire in the village."

Leo's hand, resting quietly beside the board heretofore, formed a fist, and he smacked the tabletop. "Dragon's teeth, Daylily!" Then he took a breath, and she braced herself for his apology. She hated apologies. They implied weakness.

"I'm sorry," he said.

She nodded and folded her hands.

"I'm just tired today," he continued. "Not feeling too well."

Excuses were worse than apologies. Daylily rose. "This game is not what it might be. I shall retire and see you at dinner."

Leo watched her exit the room and cursed himself several times over. It didn't help at all.

Daylily swept from the sitting room where she and Leo had been playing and made straight for the library. She usually avoided Foxbrush, who spent far too much time gazing at her with long-suffering adoration to be agreeable, but she sought him out now and found him madly scribbling away at something.

He blushed when he saw her and quickly hid whatever he was writing beneath several stray papers and a couple of large textbooks. Brilliant. He was probably composing love letters that she could only hope he would lack the courage to give her. She pretended not to have noticed.

"Lady Daylily," Foxbrush said, trying to assume a courtly manner. He rose and bowed and held a chair for her. His face was still crimson. "To what do I owe this pleasure?"

"Tell me about Leo," she said, taking the seat, "and this goat girl of his."

Foxbrush's blush drained away, leaving him surprisingly pale. "I . . . I beg your pardon, my lady. I don't know what you're—"

"Oh, don't try that with me," she said as lightly as though remarking on some concert or dance. "I know very well that you are as knowledgeable of this situation as anyone here. I suspect you know more even than his good mother and father—long life to them—so I suggest that you be straightforward now." She allowed her eyes to stray, however briefly, to the pile of texts and papers on the desk. Foxbrush saw that glance and went from pale, to red, to a horrible gray. Daylily smiled. "Besides, we are friends, aren't we?"

"Of course," he managed.

"Then tell me what you know."

He said nothing.

"They had some sweet little childhood romance, yes?" Daylily tilted her head fetchingly to one side. "Adorable, I'm sure. But inappropriate for a lad of Leo's position. His parents brought him back home and had her sent away, am I right? Is he still pining for her?"

Foxbrush drew a long breath, his hand running nervously back and forth along the edge of his desk. "Lady Daylily, I . . . I really know nothing of this matter. Leo liked to play out in the woods that summer, which Aunt Starflower did not like when she heard. That's all I—"

"Why are you lying to me, Foxbrush?"

"I'm not, I—" He made the mistake of looking into her eyes, which were very wide and very blue and very much fixed on his. All the manly resolve with which he'd been blessed fled him in that moment, and he bowed his head. "She wasn't a goat girl," he whispered.

Daylily opened her mouth to speak, then closed it and frowned as she considered his words. "What was she, then?"

"She was . . . it was . . ." Foxbrush licked his lips and dropped his voice to a whisper. "Leo was bewitched."

"How intriguing," Daylily said dryly. She shook her head. "Don't bandy words about, my dear Foxbrush. All I ask of you is—"

"It's true!"

No one ever interrupted Daylily. Her eyes flashed. But she saw the expression on Foxbrush's face before he turned his back on her and stood with his head bowed and a hand pressed into the desk for support. So she said nothing and waited for him to continue.

"It's true," he repeated in a lower voice. "But we don't speak of such things here. We all know it, and we all pretend not to. The monster does not exist according to us here at Hill House. But the whole mountain knows the truth of the matter." He was, Daylily noticed, trembling. "Leo was bewitched, and it wasn't by a goat girl. I know this as sure as I'm standing here. I . . . I saw her myself."

Not a feature moved on Daylily's face, and she was silent for some time. At last she said in a cool voice, "I have no doubt that you believe everything you have told me." She got to her feet but did not grace Foxbrush with a glance when he turned back to her. Instead she gathered her skirts and started toward the door, saying to herself as she went and not caring who heard, "I'll get to the truth of this matter yet. Whatever it may be."

Tell me what you want.

Leo stirred fitfully, somewhere between the waking world and the world of dreams, comfortable in neither. Over and over, the phrase circled through his mind. Sometimes he thought he dreamt it; others, he believed he heard the voice in his ear.

Tell me.

He startled awake at last and sat up in bed. The moon was bright and shining through those dragon-eaten curtains, which again looked so much like a tall woman to him. Leo forced himself to stare at them, and they devolved back into drapes of velvet edged in moonlight. But his heart continued pounding.

"What do I want?" he muttered to himself, picking at his bedclothes and finally pushing them back altogether and swinging his legs over the side of the bed. His feet sought across the cold floorboards until they found slippers, and he shrugged himself into a dressing gown. Hardly knowing what he was doing, he left his room without a candle and made his way down the passageway, down the stairs.

"What do I want?" A midnight snack, perhaps? He rubbed his eyes as though he could somehow rub the sleep right out of them, but his head remained woolly. He crept into the kitchen, which seemed so ghostly and abandoned with the fire banked and Redbird not at her post. No one to guard the larder. But food was definitely not what Leo desired just then.

The back kitchen door creaked when he opened it, and he cringed at the sound. He left it cracked open for fear it might latch behind him, then stepped out into the gardens. "What do I want?" he murmured as he went. He had gone a good ten paces before he stopped and scratched the top of his head. "And what, by Bebo's crown, am I *doing* out here?"

Tut, tut, tut, o-lay o-leeeee!

The silver birdcall sang from the forest, unlike all the other sounds of the night. It was a song of morning, of dawn, and strange in the moonlight. Leo followed it across the lawn. They would all think him mad if they caught him at this. Could he pass it off as sleepwalking? Or should he turn around and go back to bed like a sensible person?

O-lay o-leee!

There were words, almost. But not quite. Leo thought that if he had slightly different ears he might be able to understand them. As it was, the song was lovely, if eerie in the semidarkness.

He saw the marble stones of the graveyard and shivered. Not once, in all his boyish imaginings, had he thought to explore the Hill House graveyard after dark. Not that he believed in ghosts, of course, but . . . well, maybe he did.

Tut, tut, tut!

"Dragons eat that bird," Leo muttered. But somehow he felt compelled to follow the song. He crossed the lawn and passed through the low gate that marked the edge of the graveyard. The white panther statue of Hill House's founder snarled at him in the moonlight. But that wasn't half so bad as the shadows cast by all the markers and stones. For the first time since returning to Hill House, Leo wished for Bloodbiter's Wrath. For all the good a beanpole would do against shadow frights and ghosts! But he passed between the marble stones, following that birdsong as it led.

O-lay o-leee!

His heart leapt into his throat. Something had moved, back among the humble wood markers. Something shrouded rose up from one of the graves.

Leo tried to scream but had no voice.

Then he remembered.

"Rose Red!" The name came out more frightened than he liked, but his heart was still hammering so hard he could scarcely form the words. He staggered forward, tripping over a low stone, landing hard on his hands and knees but calling, "Rose Red! Rosie, wait!" By the time he'd righted himself, she'd vanished.

It was she, Leo knew it was. Just like when he'd first seen her in the woods, terrifying in all her veils, but still very much herself. "Rosie, please!" he called, hastening toward the grave by which she had knelt. He paused there to rub grass from his knees and realized with some embarrassment that he was still in his nightshirt and dressing gown. Drawing the gown more tightly about himself and feeling rather silly, he said in a lower voice, "Rosie, I know you're here. I know how you are, disappearing when you're angry at me. Please don't be angry, though! I didn't mean to be gone for so long, but the people back home wouldn't let me come, and then I came and you were gone! I thought you had—"

He stopped, for his eyes, adjusting to the moonlight, were just able to make out the word carved across the grave marker: *Mousehand.*

Realization sank in, and his shoulders bowed at the weight of it. Of course, that made sense. Her "old dad" was the gardener; what an idiot he had been not to realize it! The gardener who did not see what other people saw. The gardener who had set Leo on the path to meet Rose Red.

The gardener who had chided Leo because, after a summer with her, he had still wanted to find the monster.

"I'm sorry, Rosie," he said in a whisper, not expecting her to hear. "You've been all alone up here, haven't you? No wonder you're mad at me."

"I ain't mad at you, Leo."

She appeared at his side. He'd forgotten how strange she was, all wrapped up in rags and her face covered; or perhaps when he was younger he simply hadn't noticed. He couldn't suppress the shudder that ran through him at first sight of her. Then he put out a quick hand and took hers. He half expected to find himself on his back the next instant, with the breath knocked out of him. Instead, her tiny gloved fingers wrapped around his and gave a gentle squeeze. "I ain't mad," she repeated.

He turned and looked at her. She was scarcely any taller than when he'd last seen her, and seemed smaller still compared to the great height to which he had grown. Her body, which had always been thin, was wasted beneath its wrappings and rags. He shuddered again but said, "I'm glad. I'm glad I found you."

"I'm glad you did too." Her veiled head bowed and her fingers tightened before releasing his. "But I ain't supposed to see you."

"What? Why not?"

"It's dangerous."

"Dangerous for you?"

"Dangerous for you, Leo."

His mouth went dry, but he forced himself to speak. "You couldn't hurt me, Rosie."

"Oh no, not me!" she exclaimed quickly. "I couldn't hurt nobody. But, Leo, the monster—"

"There is no monster." Leo's voice was hard when he spoke, and he took a step away from her, folding his arms over his chest. "There is no monster, Rose Red. I saw the cave. I saw the reflection, and I know."

"Then . . . then you didn't see—"

"There is no monster, and that's that!" His tone softened. "You're living alone now, aren't you?"

"I have Beana."

"You're starving."

"I'm a little hungry."

"You can't stay up here, living like this."

She shrugged. The wind blew down the mountain, tugging at her rags and veils, and she looked quite terrible standing there in the moonlight. Terrible yet frail. "I'll get by."

"You'll die."

"Maybe."

Leo shook his head, grinding his teeth. An idea came to him in a flash, and he knew it was a bad one. But he couldn't shake it and, the more he thought about it, the more he knew he must say it. "You need to come with me," he said.

She did not answer but tilted her head at him.

"Back home, I mean," he continued all in a rush, afraid that common sense would stop him if he didn't say his piece now. "You need to leave the mountain and come back to my home, where I can make sure you don't starve."

"Oh, Leo!" she gasped.

"What?" he demanded irritably. "It's not such a bad idea, and what do you have to keep you here now? I know how it is for you, Rosie. I know these people and their dragon-eaten superstitions. It won't be like that for you where I live, and—"

"I cain't come stay with you! I ain't fit for that!"

"You can be my servant," he said. "There's nothing wrong with that, and I'm sure you'd be good at it. You can sweep and clean, and who's to complain if I want to hire a chambermaid? It will all be perfectly appropriate, I promise you, and then I can keep an eye on you." He warmed to this idea, and his voice was eager, despite the resistance he read all over her rigid body. "It would be a new start for you, Rosie. A new life. Look, you've got to get away from this place and—"

She shook her head violently. "Beana won't let me leave the mountain."

"Iubdan's beard!" Leo barked. "She's a *goat*! You are going to die up here."

"I cain't leave. He . . . she . . . they won't let me."

"There is no one to stop you," Leo said. "No one, you understand? Beana is a goat. Who else can tell you what to do?"

"The monster," she whispered.

"No!" said Leo. "I told you, there is no monster, and I know it! I'll protect you; I won't let anyone hurt you. You're not . . ." He didn't finish but gnashed his teeth and drew a deep breath as he tried to compose his thoughts. "There's nothing to keep you here, Rosie. Nothing but your own fears. Now, listen, I am leaving in just two weeks, and I don't know when I'll be able to return. I can't just abandon you up here, knowing they'll drive you out the moment you enter town, knowing they'll leave you to starve in the forest." He stepped forward, putting out his hands to her, though he dared not touch her. "Rosie, please. Let me help."

He stood there with his hands in empty air, talking to no one.

Leo sighed and bowed his head. She was gone. Perhaps she had never been there, and he had dreamt it all out of his loneliness? The moonlight can play strange tricks on a fellow's eyes, and he was tired. Very tired. The wind was cold on his neck, and Leo shivered as he left the graveyard and made his way back across the lawn. At the kitchen door he paused a moment and looked back out into the half-lit landscape, up to the forests above.

"Think about it, Rose Red," he whispered. "That's all I ask."

5

S HE HAD NEVER FELT so trapped before. Not once, in all her years
hiding away from the world, secluded and outcast, had Rose Red
felt such a horrible sense of imprisonment. It ate at her for the next two
weeks, like a cancer becoming ever more unbearable.

You had better not leave me, princess.

It was all in her mind, of course. Dreams couldn't hurt her. But they
could plague her day and night . . . and what if they were to come true?

She sat in the top of the grandfather tree, looking out across the
sweep of her mountains, down to the tablelands far below. They looked
so big. They looked so foreign. They looked like freedom.

"I cain't go," she whispered to herself.

I will make him pay.

"What if Leo were to suffer for helpin' me? Folks up here are scared
of me; why should folks down there be any different? I cain't go with
him. I cain't!"

Stay with me, princess.

"Or can I?"

Stay with me.

She clung to the high branches, swaying there above the world. And the voice in her head spoke with such venom, it was almost real. Rose Red closed her eyes and forced her mind to quiet, driving away all thoughts except the smell of the forest, the bite of the mountain wind through her rags and veils, the feel of sap running through her grasp. The dream voice slowly faded from her mind, and calm descended. Rose Red found herself able to climb down the tree, though her limbs trembled. Lack of food made her weaker every day.

Beana met her at the base of the tree, her yellow eyes full of worry. "You shouldn't climb up there, Rosie girl," she said. "One of these days you—"

"We're goin', Beana," Rose Red said.

"What? Going where?"

"We're leavin' the mountain."

Rose Red set off through the trees without a backward glance even when Beana's "Baaaah!" rattled the air behind her. Her shoulders were set and her pace was firm as she began the descent to Hill House. She could only hope she wasn't too late, that Leo hadn't changed his mind.

Princess, stop!

"Rose Red, stop!"

She wouldn't. If she did, she might never start again. But the goat trotted around in front of her, bleating and tearing at the earth with her sharp hooves. "What are you thinking, girl? I've told you countless times, you can't leave the mountain!"

"I've got to, Beana." The goat tried to block her path, but Rose Red pushed past her through the underbrush. Branches tore at her clothing as though the forest itself would restrain her if it could. "I've got to get away!"

"Get away to where?" Beana was nearly frantic. Rose Red had never heard her voice tremble so. But she kept on her way as fast as she could in her weakness, afraid her resolve would falter.

"Leo asked me," she said, "to come to his house."

"Iubdan's beard!" the goat exclaimed, and this time when she blocked

Rose Red, she was like a wall, forcing the girl to come to a halt. "You can't go to the tablelands! I don't care if the Eldest himself invited you."

Rose Red's heart was racing now, and she stood there breathing hard and twisting the end of her veil in her hands. The Dream's voice roared in her head. The words it shouted were horrible, but she could hardly understand them for the roaring. But Beana was still standing before her, and she must speak.

"He . . . he wants me to be his servant," she panted. "It's good work, Beana."

"I don't care if he wants you to be a knight of the realm! You're not going."

You will stay with me!

She thought her head would explode. Pressing her fists to her temples, she shouted in her goat's face, "Beana, I've *got* to get away. I've *got* to leave this mountain, to leave the monster."

"Rosie, you know there is no monster. The folks up here are cruel and foolish, that's all. You're no—"

"You don't understand!"

How could she understand? Beana couldn't hear that fiery voice.

But she's right, princess. You cannot leave the mountain. You cannot—

"You're trying to trap me here," Rose Red cried to the goat, to the Dream, to the whole mountain if it would listen. "You've got me so scared I can hardly think! Leo wants me to come away, to . . . to *live*. If I stay up here any longer, I'll die."

"I won't let you die."

The goat's voice still trembled, but it was gentler. She put out her slender nose and nuzzled Rose Red's hand. "I know you don't trust me, my girl, but I wish you would. I can protect you. I can keep you safe, and I won't let you die."

I can keep you safe.

"But you must trust me. And you must stay up here in the mountains. Down lower . . ." Beana's trembling increased and she twitched her nose as she considered her words. "Down lower, you will be much closer to the Wilderlands. And they are dangerous for you! This forest may seem frightening sometimes. It may seem wild and lonely."

I won't let you die.

"But it is as nothing to the Wilderlands," the goat continued.

"I don't know what you're talkin' about," Rose Red sighed. Her head throbbed with the ferocious voice of her Dream, and sweat slid down her neck beneath the veils. She was exhausted and couldn't make herself think of things or places beyond her experience. All she knew was the mountain, the fear and hatred, and that Dream. Those things she knew with a certainty that could drive her wild . . . but she also knew Leo. She shook her head, and her breath came with difficulty.

"And it's well that you don't know," Beana said. "I can keep you safe up here, but I don't know that I can should we descend to the low country. Not that I wouldn't try. I would try with all the grace and power granted me! I would die for you, my Rosie."

I won't let you die.

"But if I were dead, what good could I do you then? You'd be unprotected." The goat nuzzled her again, the long lashes over her eyes fluttering delicately on her scruffy face. "So let's not talk any more of going with Leo, of leaving the mountain. We'll find a way to get by up here. We've done well enough up to now."

Stay with me.

Rose Red gazed through the slit in her veil down at her friend.

Stay with me, princess.

Leo wanted her to come.

Rose Red put out her hands and, with strength that she did not know remained to her, shoved the goat out of her way. On down the mountain she continued, now at a run, though sticks and brambles lashed out at her and several times she nearly lost her footing. She could hear Beana right behind her, but she continued running as though pursued by hounds, making for Hill House.

A low branch snagged her veil and dragged it from her face.

Rose Red crumpled to the ground, her arms over her head, hiding herself from the forest and all its watching eyes. She curled up, tighter and tighter, making herself disappear.

See, princess? You cannot leave.

The Dream's voice was softer now. Soothing and kind.

You were not meant to live in the world of mortals, of men. You are different. You are special.

She could feel him reaching out to her, could almost feel his hot breath blowing upon her neck, though she knew it was all in her mind.

You were always meant to be mine.

"Rosie!" Beana bleated, drawing up behind her.

Don't leave the mountain.

This last came in the faintest whisper; then Beana trotted around and stood before her, the ragged veil dangling from her mouth. She dropped it in Rose Red's lap and stood there watching as the girl carefully slid it back into place. "You're quite determined, aren't you?" Beana said, and her voice was heavy.

Rose Red checked the edges of the veil to be sure everything was as it should be. Then she nodded. "I've got to leave, Beana," she whispered. "I've got to get off this mountain or . . . I know I will die."

"It's impossible!" Beana bleated. "It's dragon-eaten foolishness, girl, and you don't understand! It's—"

Her voice trailed off suddenly amid a flood of silver music flowing down from the tree above.

Both goat and girl looked up, unable to see for the blinding sunlight through the branches. But they heard the lyric voice of the wood thrush throwing his heart to the sky in the joy of his song. And both their hearts lifted at the sound, though what else they may have heard—what words perhaps may have emerged out of the trilling tune—they could not have told each other for the world. It affected each of them differently. For Rose Red, that song drove out all the fire of the voice in her head, leaving her calm, allowing her to breathe fully again.

To Beana, the song gave peace. Peace she did not altogether want, but peace nonetheless. She bowed her head and drew a long breath. "If you must go, I cannot stop you," she said. "I would if I could, but such is not my place. Let me give you something, though, child. Because I might be unable to protect you once we've gone to the low country, let me give you something with which you may protect yourself. As long as I know you have it, I won't be so afraid every time you're out of my sight."

Rose Red gave her goat a puzzled shrug. "What could you possibly have to give me?"

"It's a name."

"I've got a name. I've got the name my old dad gave me."

"This isn't your name. But it's a powerful name, and one I want you to hold on to. Give me your ear, Rosie!"

The girl leaned forward, and the nanny goat whispered through the veil, "Keep it in your heart, my love, and treasure it down deep. And when you have need . . . it doesn't matter when, or how, or what . . . if you have need of any kind, call on this name, and you will have help. I'll give it to you in your own tongue, darling, though you may not understand it."

Then she spoke a word, harsh and soft at the same time, which sounded odd coming from her goat mouth. The sound of it sank through the girl's mind and flowed down to her heart, where it rested, strangely comforting.

Eshkhan.

Rose Red stood up, shaking her head. "Don't be daft, Beana. I don't need anythin' silly like that to help me. I've got you, and I've got a strong constitution that has served me right enough so far. And I've got Leo. He promised he'd watch out for me, and I know he means it." If there was a trace of desperation in her voice, only the goat heard it. She continued on down the mountain, Beana trailing behind her. "So you needn't be tellin' me Faerie stories to make me feel better. I'm a big girl and I can handle myself."

"Suit yourself, child," said the goat softly. "But you know it, and that's all I care about for now."

They progressed through the forest in silence, passing by the creek, neither one looking at the trail that led back to their cottage. They would not walk that path again. After all, Rose Red owned nothing that she might take with her. All that remained were memories, many of them painful now. So they said nothing but continued across the creek and down to the deer trail, neither speaking.

Beana's thoughts were consumed with that Other, that one unlike all others, whom she sensed with such terror. They would draw nearer to it, the farther down the mountain they journeyed. It would know they were coming. And it would call to Rose Red. Her skin trembled with terror at the thought, and many times she was tempted to stand upright, to shed all pretenses, to force the girl to remain in hiding.

She would not. No, by grace and good courage, Beana would continue as she had been all these years, and perhaps by some miracle she would succeed.

Rose Red's thoughts were full of Leo. He would protect her. Had he not promised? He would take her in and give her work, and she would become his servant. Leo, her best friend, now her best master. What a good and true servant she would be, as faithful as a . . . as a goat. She would bless him with her service in every way, and eventually she would win over the people of his household. They would see with what a true heart she poured herself into her tasks. They would see.

And they would know that she could not be a monster.

It'll never work.

"Shut up," she hissed low enough that Beana, trotting behind her, could not hear. "Shut up, shut up!"

They'll never trust you behind that veil, and you dare not show your face to them. Not as you may show it to me, my beautiful prin—

"I won't hear another word of yours!" She dared not speak the words out loud, so she mouthed them silently behind the veil. "I won't hear you anymore. I'm leavin', and there's nothin' you can do to stop me, 'cause you're only a nightmare! I'll follow Leo down this mountain, and in that fresh air down lower, I won't dream no more. I'll sleep like a little baby, I will, and I'll never see you again!"

You will see me again.

She increased her pace and would not answer.

You were meant to be mine.

She came to the end of the deer trail and stepped out upon the path leading down the mountain. Beana emerged behind her, and the two of them picked their way down.

Leave the mountain if you dare. See how the dogs below will bark and worry your bones. See how Leo, his good deed done, will forget all about you save when he remembers the nuisance you cause him.

"I won't hear you no more," she muttered.

"What's that, child?"

"Nothin'."

See how they will abuse you. And then, you will return to me.

Rose Red shook her head. She would die before she came back.

If you do not, said her Dream in a whisper like seeping poisons, *if I do not see you at my doorstep within a year and a day, I swear to you . . . I swear by that cursed stone of gold upon which I slept those long centuries . . . I will come for you myself. And you will not like that. No, you will not like that at all.*

The gates of Hill House gleamed below her as the sun touched their polished hinges, and Rose Red was suddenly terrified almost beyond bearing. But Beana pressed up beside her, and Rose Red touched the goat's forehead between her horns and drew comfort from her. "I'm leavin' with Leo," she said in a firm voice. "And there ain't nothin' nobody can do to stop me."

"I won't try to stop you, girl," Beana said. "Though I'm against it. Well, shall we knock or just barge inside? Perhaps we could leave a calling card and let them get back to us at their leisure."

The girl and the goat approached the gate, leaving the forest behind them. And Rose Red did not hear the whisper that blew among the shadows of the trees, then vanished like a puff of smoke.

A year and a day, princess.

6

In some ways, it had been the longest summer of her existence. In others, Daylily had to admit, it had been a singularly pleasant one, and she was rather sorry to see it drawing to a close. There was something so fresh and, simultaneously, so ancient about the air of the mountains. An out-of-this-world sensation such as she had never experienced in the social hubbub of Middlecrescent.

She sat in her bedroom, gazing out the window. Daylily could not put a name to her present feelings. She was not one to be anxious, but was she, perhaps, a little concerned at the prospect of leaving Hill House? Here she had enjoyed peace; peace edged with that hint of danger that the country folks' rumors and superstitions delightfully fed. It was a danger like the fears children experience in the night, when they know beyond doubt that something lurks under the bed, though their parents may not believe.

Nothing like the dangers of conspiracy. Nothing like the dangers of failure.

If anything, this thought caused Daylily's brow to smooth even more perfectly into a beautiful mask. "I am a child no longer," she whispered to the window, to the dark green forest of the mountain. "And this is not a child's game." No, her father's Plan was certainly no game, but there would be a winning and a losing side nonetheless. She must be certain of her position.

Dragons eat that goat girl, whoever she might be!

Her goodwoman entered the room, dragging an empty trunk behind her. She curtsied to her mistress. "Am I disturbing you, m'lady?"

"No, do continue," Daylily said with a wave of her hand. Her servant set the trunk in the middle of the room and started gathering Daylily's belongings.

They were leaving Hill House on the morrow. Daylily was struck now by how quickly the summer had flown. And she would return to her father's house with . . . with what?

She rose, straightening her skirts and touching her hair to be sure each curl was properly in place. Properly in place, up here in the mountains, meant just the slightest bit out of place, a few tendrils escaping here and there as would appeal to a boy of Leo's nature. Too much perfection might frighten him. "Lay out my green for tomorrow's journey, good-woman," Daylily said as she passed from the room. Her maid, who knew the baron's daughter perhaps better than anyone in this world, could not have told a soul what Daylily's thoughts were from what she could see on her lady's face. If someone had asked, she would have curtsied and said, "M'lady is herself, and her thoughts are her own. Pardon me, I have work to which I must attend."

Daylily avoided the library. She always avoided the chance of meeting Foxbrush, particularly since that conversation they'd shared a few weeks back. She'd known from the moment she set eyes on him that he was no more than a stuffed shirt, but a superstitious stuffed shirt was even worse. He was too well educated, had spent too much time at court to hide behind the excuse of a rustic country upbringing. It was silly for a lad of his station, who could boast the lineage he did, to believe in Faerie stories and monsters. Daylily made it a point to shun him.

The house was busy, though she passed no one in the corridors. She could hear the bustle of packing and travel arrangements being made. Tomorrow, she and the two young sirs would set out from Hill House and journey together to the low country and across Baron Blackstone's land. Then they would part ways, Daylily for Middlecrescent, the boys for the Eldest's City. Or at least, this was the plan.

But it would not be much longer, if Daylily had any say in the matter.

She found Leo in the Blue Room. This was one of the many pointless rooms to be found in houses such as Hill House. Its sole purpose for existence was to be decorated, painted, and otherwise fitted out in shades of blue, many shades of which did not blend happily together. A lord or lady knew they had truly arrived when they could afford to have a Blue Room in their household, and Dame Willowfair was proud of hers. People seldom sat in it of course, for it was difficult to think anything but blue thoughts within its walls. But it provided a solitary spot in the house, and Leo liked it for that reason.

He sat in an overstuffed chair of blue velvet, to all apparent purposes studying a large textbook, but in reality, staring into the fireplace. His face was as empty as a face could be when he looked up to meet Daylily's eyes. But he offered her a smile. "Hullo. How's the packing going?"

"Well enough," said Daylily, and her voice was sweet, but not nearly so sweet as her face when she settled into a low chair across from Leo's. She was wearing a rich sienna-hued gown that contrasted starkly with the hues of that room, giving her skin a glow and her hair a fine sheen. It would be impossible not to admire her, even if she had not arranged herself to look so very fetching while seated.

Leo noticed. He even admired. He simply didn't care.

They looked at each other, then looked away, then looked at each other again. This little exercise continued for about three rounds, and still Leo neither spoke nor seemed to notice the faraway sorrow that Daylily was so carefully painting on her face. She sighed and almost gave up then and there. But her father's voice still spoke in her memory: *"Did I ask you to love him?"*

"I have enjoyed these last few months, Leo," she said, her eyes gently veiled with long lashes. She waited a few poignant moments before softly adding, "Have you?"

"Have I what?"

"Have you enjoyed these last few months?"

He shrugged. This summer had not been what he had hoped, and his sleep had been less than restful. When the sun rose, Leo's spirits failed to rise with it, and no amount of strong coffee had enabled him to clear his fuzzy head. That blasted dream returned every night, always with the same demand: *Tell me what you want.*

All he really wanted right now was an answer from Rose Red, but he'd not seen her since that night in the graveyard. And perhaps he'd dreamt that too. Moonlight and graveyards and beings that disappeared in a waft of rags . . . definitely not the stuff of waking hours.

He closed his eyes and sank his head into his hand. "It's been right enough, I suppose," he answered. "For summer, you know. Better than last year at Upperwold, where they made me attend an entire concert devoted to Poet Eanrin's work. A misery."

Daylily licked her lips. "Perhaps next year will be better still?" she suggested. "You might consider visiting Middlecrescent."

"Maybe." He shrugged again. Why did she have to come and talk at him just now? Why did girls talk so much anyway? He wanted to be alone, and he wanted a quiet snooze, a chance to catch up on sleep before beginning tomorrow's long journey. A chance to—

Suddenly Daylily stood beside him, one soft hand removing his from his head, the other gently stroking his cheek. Leo came wide awake, blinking up at her, and noticed now how pretty all that red hair of hers was. Almost as pretty as it had been out in the forest with the light shining through the leaves and landing on it in bursts. What a brave creature she had looked that day, so beautiful and strong as she led the way up the mountain. A woman fit to be queen if ever there was one. And she was gazing deep into his eyes.

"Um." Leo licked his lips.

"Yes?" said she, her mouth just hinting at a smile.

"Maybe . . . maybe you'd like to come stay at my house this winter?" He spoke the words in a bit of a rush, and his tongue tangled around several of them. "I'm sure my mother would love to have you."

"Your mother?"

"Yes, I know she would."

"What about you, Leo?"

His mouth opened, but his brain could not form any words. Her smile was growing, and he found it difficult to think. "Um," he tried, and it was not a propitious beginning. "I think . . . well, I think—"

He heard the sound as though he'd been listening for it all along. It was faint through the closed window, but unmistakable.

"Baaaah!"

Leo was on his feet in an instant, sliding past Daylily, who remained blinking where she stood for a moment before following him to the window. Leo opened the casement and leaned out, and a gust of mountain air caught his hair and tossed it back from his face. He saw the garden gate open, and he saw who entered.

"*Rose Red!*" he shouted.

She heard him, all the way out there by the gate. He saw her hesitate as she gazed about, looking for him. Beana, that shaggy old nanny, walked in her footsteps. Leo leaned farther out the window, waving an arm. "Rose Red! Rosie!"

She saw him. One gloved hand raised in a hesitant wave.

Leo cupped his hands around his mouth. "Wait there! I'll be right down!"

"What is it?" Daylily demanded, pressing up behind him and trying to see through the window herself. She received an elbow in the stomach for her pains, and then a string of hasty apologies as Leo excused himself around her. All trace of a smile vanished from her face.

"She's coming!" Leo cried, disappearing out the door. Daylily looked out the open window. She saw the girl, covered in rags from head to toe, making tentative progress into the yard. She saw the veils, and her teeth set on edge.

Perhaps Foxbrush wasn't such a blessed fool after all.

Leo pounded down the stairs and was out the kitchen door within moments, running across the garden to meet his friend. "Rosie!" he cried as he approached. She had stopped in her tracks, as though afraid to progress any farther, but the set of her shoulders relaxed as he neared. "Rosie, have you decided?"

She nodded. "I think I'd like to be your servant, Leo. I think I'd like that very well."

"Lumé's crown!" Leo could not stop his smiles. "I knew you would; I knew it! Just wait and see what a difference it'll make to you, getting off this mountain."

"Bah," Beana said.

"You can bring Beana too, of course," Leo added with another smile for the goat. He reached out to stroke her ears, but Beana gave him a look like death, and he retrieved his hand. "There's plenty of room in my father's stables for her, especially if she gives good milk."

But Rose Red no longer saw Leo. She watched over his shoulder as person after person stepped through Hill House's various doors and approached up the lawn. It took all her willpower to keep from vanishing right then, fleeing back into the forest. Redbird came from the kitchen, her face pale as a sheet, her meaty hand gripping an iron ladle. Leanbear appeared soon after, and he held fire irons in both fists. Foxbrush followed, his eyes huge beneath his oiled hair, and behind him came several footmen and servants, clustering together for the comfort of numbers.

Rose Red saw this cluster of servants part as Daylily marched between them. Her face was like that of some queen of old. She moved ahead of the others, but Leanbear, Redbird, and Foxbrush fell into step just behind, and the others followed after. She was so beautiful that Rose Red's heart leapt with terror at the sight.

Leo, turning around and seeing what Rose Red saw, reached out and quickly squeezed her hand. "Don't worry," he said, and his voice was not like that of the Leo she knew. It was, in that moment, older. And harder. "Don't disappear."

Beana stepped in front of her like a forbidding fortress, and Leo faced the oncoming folk, his arms crossed over his chest.

"So, Leo," said Daylily, and the smile on her face as she neared was very lovely indeed. "You found your goat girl again, did you?"

Leo smiled back, but his shoulders were tense. "This is Rose Red," he said. "She grew up in the mountains, but her parents are dead. I've offered her a position as my servant, and she will be joining us tomorrow when we leave." He turned to Redbird and the other servants. "You will make sure she is fitted out properly for the journey."

"By the Sleeper's waking snort," Leanbear growled. "That we certainly won't." He was trembling in every limb as he clutched his fire irons. "She ain't welcome in these parts. Ain't welcome in the village, nor on this mountain neither."

"Then it's just as well she's coming with me, isn't it?" said Leo.

Redbird whispered, "Silent Lady!" and Leanbear spat. "You don't know what she is, do you? Have you taken a moment to look at her?"

Leo stood with his feet planted. "Look at what?" he demanded. "There's nothing to look at."

Leanbear bared his teeth like a dog. "Look at how she covers herself. Look how she hides."

"So what?" Leo shrugged but did not relax. His hands balled into fists. "She's got a right to wear what she likes. It's her business."

"You know what she is, same as the rest of us," Leanbear said. "That, or you're blinded. Or bewitched."

Daylily caught Leo's eye. *"Bewitched,"* Foxbrush had told her, just as Leanbear said now. She searched now for signs of that bewitchment but saw none. Perhaps the enchantment was too powerful to be detected, but all she saw in Leo's eyes was a rising, boiling anger.

"You all are dragon-eaten idiots," he declared, advancing aggressively. The servants backed up, save for Leanbear, who also stepped forward. "What nonsense are you all talking? Bewitchment? Spells? *Magic?* You're as backward as first-year schoolboys! Your mountain superstitions have blinded you."

"Careful what you say about the mountain folk," Leanbear growled. "We know more of the goings-on in these parts than you, with all your pretty city ways. We've lived in these forests, breathed this air, dug our hands deep into the roots and dirt and rock. Call us superstitious if you must, but don't insult our ways. We've survived up here for centuries while the rest of you fled to the lowlands. And we've survived by not lettin' the likes of her poison our lives." Leanbear raised his fire irons threateningly and took yet another step forward. "She's not welcome among us."

"Baah!" said the goat.

Leo uncrossed his arms and held his fists tense at his sides. "I'm not scared of your nursery stories." He turned to Foxbrush then. "You're as bad as the rest of them, aren't you? My own fool cousin—why don't you speak up? You've studied science; you've studied logic. Tell them they're being idiots, and let's all move on. Or do you believe in this *magic* as well?"

Foxbrush hung his head, too ashamed to speak. For Daylily had turned her gaze upon him, and he found he had no courage under that blue-eyed stare.

Leo snorted and returned his attention to Leanbear. "Stand aside."

"For your own sake, I will not," said he.

Suddenly, to the surprise of everyone watching, Daylily stepped forward. With a sneer on her face for the carriage man and Foxbrush, she passed between them and approached the veiled girl. Rose Red had remained silent and trembling throughout the encounter, her goat pressed up against her legs. Daylily stood more than a head taller than she and looked like some ancient goddess to Rose Red, crowned by all that russet hair shining in the setting sun's light. Daylily's face alone in that crowd showed neither fear nor anger.

Which made her still more terrible.

Rose Red had been taught social niceties only in the vaguest theory. So when she tried to curtsy, it was not a pretty sight, and her scrawny limbs stuck out at awkward angles. But Daylily's keen eyes noticed a certain natural grace behind the awkwardness, and her mouth set in a thin line.

"So you are the goat girl," she said quietly.

Rose Red, still crouched in her curtsy, whispered, "And it please m'lady."

"Leo has spoken of you," Daylily said. "Several times, in fact. He is, I believe, fond of you."

"And it please you," Rose Red repeated.

Daylily studied the slit in the veil. It revealed nothing of the girl's face, not even a glimpse of her eyes. "Why are you veiled?" Daylily asked. Her voice was too soft to be heard by any save Rose Red and her goat.

Rose Red gulped. "That is my secret," she said.

"Does he know your secret?"

Rose Red hesitated before she shook her head.

Daylily did not believe her. She knew very well what those gathered in the yard thought of the goat girl, what they believed she hid beneath all those rags. But Daylily was not one to believe simply because everyone else said it was so. Her own idea began to form then and there, an idea she did not altogether like.

She turned to Leo. "You have asked this girl to become your servant?" she said.

"I have," Leo replied. His tone was defensive.

"Then why is she not inside being prepared for the journey?"

Leo flung up his hands. "Don't you hear what they're saying? They think she's . . . they think there's something wrong with her, and they're scared. It doesn't take half a brain to see she's as harmless as a butterfly, but they're scared out of their minds, the dragon-eaten fools!"

Daylily did not budge in the face of his bluster, but let him talk until he'd quite run down. All the while the household staff watched and the goat girl cringed behind her goat. When at last he had finished, Daylily took a step closer to him.

"Are you the prince?" she asked. "Or aren't you?"

Leo's face drained of color.

For a long moment, he did not breathe. Then he turned to those assembled. If his voice cracked when he spoke, it was still deep and full of force.

"I declare to you all, by the blood in my veins, by the sign of the panther, and the blessing of the Silent Lady on the house of my forefathers: This girl is my servant and under my protection. You will treat her as such. I, Lionheart, son of Hawkeye, Crown Prince of Southlands, command it."

7

Rose Red sat in the rumble seat on the back of the carriage, looking backward up the path down which the carriage rolled. With one hand, she gripped a side bar to keep herself from being jostled out of place; the other hand she wrapped around Beana's neck as the goat knelt awkwardly beside her.

Rose Red's head hurt from gazing up the mountain, from watching those familiar peaks grow smaller and smaller, from passing out of forests she knew better than her own face into lands unknown, surrounded by strangers.

Strangers who hated her.

She closed her eyes.

The crown prince! How, by Hymlumé's light, had she missed that detail? "Hen's teeth!" she muttered. "What a fool I am."

The moment she'd understood what Leo said, panic had seized her, and she had flown up through the gate and up the mountain, using secret paths she hoped that he could not follow. But Beana could, and did. The goat had caught up to her by the creek.

"What are you thinking, fool girl?" she bleated. "Get yourself back down there at once, do you hear?"

"He's the crown prince, Beana!" Rose Red cried, burying her face in her hands. "I didn't know it! I swear."

"I know you didn't," Beana replied. "But you do now. And you've left him in an awful pickle by running off! It took some nerve on his part to stand up to all of them for you, and this is how you're going to repay him?"

"I cain't go back there."

Beana rolled her eyes to the heavens, muttering, "Lumé grant me grace! What did we just spend a whole afternoon arguing over?"

Rose Red did not have the chance to answer, for Leo stumbled through the brush and fell into the creek the next moment. Up to the elbows in muddy water, he bellowed, "Dragon's *teeth*!" then glared at Rose Red for all he was worth. "Dragons eat you, Rosie. Why did you run away?"

To Rose Red's horror, she thought she saw tears glimmering in his eyes. But only for a second.

She got to her feet and scrambled into the creek to help him upright. "I'm so sorry, Leo—Your Highness," she said, then bobbed another of her awkward curtsies. "I didn't know who you were or else I'd never ha—"

"And that's just why I didn't want you to know!" Leo exclaimed. "Don't you see, Rosie, the minute you found out, I knew you'd do just what you've done. Did you think you were the only person on this mountain who wanted a friend? A friend who could see past names and titles and . . . and veils?"

Rose Red could not answer. She bowed her head, ashamed.

"I knew you'd run off on me." His voice was tight, angry. "And I didn't think there was a chance in this world that I'd find you again." He put out a hand to her, and his voice softened as though afraid to frighten her away. "Rosie, we've both kept secrets. But I'm still Leo. You're still you. Titles and veils and all that nonsense . . . it doesn't change anything."

When she looked up, she saw no more trace of tears in his eyes. But they were large and serious when he spoke. "Please don't leave me again. Come back, and let's do as we planned."

"Leo—I mean, Your Highness . . ."

Suddenly *he* was there again, deep in her mind. The voice that she knew could not be real, but that screamed all of her fears in words of fire.

I'll make him pay!

She cringed and bowed her head. But Leo was still with her, and he put his hands on her shoulders, gently, as though half expecting her to hurl him across the creek in a second. She didn't but stood stiff as a board while he carefully held her at arm's length.

"We can't be friends anymore, of course," he said. "It's not allowed. But you can be my servant, and I can watch out for you, just like we agreed. Nobody can touch you as long as you're under my protection; it's the law. Only the Eldest himself can reverse my command. And he won't. Father's a good sport, really, if a little stiff on taxes sometimes. And Mother won't cross Father, so you're safe. Do you see?"

Don't leave me, princess.

"You're not real," she hissed.

Leo trembled at the sound of her voice, but he couldn't understand the words. "I'm sorry, Rosie, what was that?" She looked up at him. He thought, if only for an instant, that he caught a glimpse of her eyes through the slit of fabric. Then the folds settled, and he realized he must have imagined it. "Are you coming with me?" he asked.

She nodded.

And here Rose Red was now, riding on the back of that carriage, leaving the mountain far behind her.

Come back to me, princess, or I will come find you.

Rose Red glanced at her goat in the rumble seat beside her, eyes half closed, chewing her cud. She did not hear the fiery voice. No one else did.

"I must be mad," Rose Red whispered to herself.

As though to confirm that thought, her Imaginary Friend sang suddenly from the trees along the roadside.

> *Beyond the Final Water falling,*
> *The Songs of Spheres recalling.*
> *When you find you must pursue that lonely way,*
> *Won't you return to me?*

Rose Red's eyes flashed and her breathing came fast. Though she dared not speak aloud with Beana right beside her, she fairly shouted in her mind. Since her friend was only imaginary, he would hear her.

"I will never return!"

My child, sang the bird who was also a prince, *I am with you wherever you go. Even as your heart wanders from me.*

"You're worse than my Dream!" Her own voice rattled in her head. "How you plague me. I want nothin' to do with either of you! I may be mad, I may hear voices, but that don't mean I've got to stay that way."

Don't forget that I love you, sang the thrush.

"I'll forget, all right. 'Cause it's nothin' but a pretty story . . . a children's tale. Where were you when my old dad was taken and I was left to starve? Dreams and stories . . . they cain't be depended on. I've got to make my own way now. And Leo—Prince Lionheart, that is—he's goin' to help me. He's my good and kind master now."

The Prince's voice was faint, singing as though across a vast gulf.

Don't forget my name. . . .

And when that voice had faded, the Dream's remained.

I will come find you.

🙙

Behind the prince's carriage, in which both Lionheart and Foxbrush rode in stony silence, came the coach of the Baron of Middlecrescent's daughter. Daylily sat alone inside; her serving woman, at her order, had climbed out to sit in front with the driver. Thus Daylily had time to think many thoughts as she followed Prince Lionheart down the mountain.

Prince Lionheart and his little protégée.

"What secret is she hiding?" Daylily whispered. "There's something more here than meets the eye. These fools are scared to death of her, but why then is Leo so . . . so"—she bit out the word—"smitten?"

Daylily thought she knew the answer. What is more, she determined to verify her hypothesis at the first possible opportunity.

🙙

The Starflower Fountain stood in the front courtyard of the Eldest's House. It was two stories tall, a fantastic piece of workmanship carved in white marble, portraying Southlands' famous historic heroine, Maid Starflower, Panther Master's daughter, wearing very little, truth be told. A tiny stone bird sat on one shoulder, a classic icon in every depiction of the maid, the meaning of which everyone had long since forgotten. The maid herself stood with one arm raised above her head, the other flung out before her as though to ward off the monstrous wolf that stood opposite her, baring its marble teeth. Her body formed a crescent arch, and her proportions were haphazard at best. The fountain was nevertheless revered as a great depiction of that lady after whom half the girls of Southlands were named.

Queen Starflower stood beside her husband on the steps facing the fountain. She was not a beautiful woman like her namesake. But she was strong. King Hawkeye was proud to have her as his queen and depended on her in countless ways of which his subjects had no knowledge. The queen knew, however; she knew without question how indispensable she was to her husband. And she also knew how important it would be for her son to have a capable wife. Lionheart was a handsome boy but weak. Stubborn as well, which Starflower considered the most dangerous form of weakness. It would take a strong woman to manage him as he managed the kingdom.

The two carriages and several horsemen who served as escorts passed through the Eldest's gardens and on through the gates leading to the Eldest's House itself. The House was not fortified, for it was no fortress but rather a palace of tall spires and minarets and sweeping wings, the grandest house in all of Southlands. Its structure had a strong northern influence, including the great hall with doors opening east and west, but built of orange-hued stone, it was distinctly southern in effect. Many of its passages were open to the elements to keep air moving, for the atmosphere of Southlands was balmy at best, oppressive at worst. Servants stood in doorways, waving fans, and though ladies of fashion wore many petticoats, their shoulders were bare and their hair piled up to keep it off their necks.

Everything was so beautiful yet so hot after the mountain air. Even Daylily found herself momentarily longing for Hill House and the cool breezes of the high country.

King Hawkeye and Queen Starflower stood outside, surrounded by attendants, to receive their son. Prince Lionheart bowed to them both and accepted a stern kiss from his mother. Then he indicated Daylily and Foxbrush and said formally, "I have invited my cousin and Lady Daylily of Middlecrescent to stay awhile with us. At your pleasure, of course, Father."

Hawkeye nodded, and the barest hint of a smile touched the queen's face as she glanced from Lionheart to Daylily and back again. But Daylily's face was unreadable, and her son seemed distracted. This did not bode well, and Starflower's smile was replaced with a line.

Rose Red hopped down from the back of the carriage, arranging her veils as best she could and clinging to Beana's tether like a lifeline. The queen's gaze fixed upon her as an arrow to the mark. Rose Red shuddered; she felt as though that mighty lady could see right through her veils, down to the marrow of her soul. She bowed her head and curtsied deeply.

"Bah," Beana grumbled.

"Who is this person?" Starflower asked her son.

"My servant," Prince Lionheart said, his voice calm, though a trace of worry lingered on his face. "She's an orphan I met in the mountains. I've engaged her to work in my personal service."

Starflower studied her son, analyzing not only what he had said but also how he had said it. Then she turned to Foxbrush, her favorite nephew, her eyes asking him silent questions. But even faithful young Foxbrush averted his eyes and shuffled his feet, unwilling to give information.

"Why does she wear that veil?" King Hawkeye asked. His voice was kindly enough.

Lionheart licked his lips, then shrugged. "Birthmark. She's embarrassed."

Starflower looked to Daylily, whose face told her nothing. Her own eyes narrowed at her son.

Lionheart cleared his throat and said in a stronger tone, "I've given orders that she will be under my protection, and that any who disturb her will suffer my displeasure. Is this agreeable to you, Father?" His eyes flickered to his mother's.

Hawkeye nodded. "Of course, my boy, if that is your will."

That is how Rose Red was brought into the Eldest's House and officially admitted into Prince Lionheart's service.

8

So TELL ME, *is this what you want?"*

Lionheart *opens his eyes and finds that strange dark face surrounded by white hair bending over him. He gasps, but she smiles at him, and her smile eases his fear.*

"Is it?"

"What . . . what do you mean?"

"You have the girl, this little friend of yours, safely in your service. You have proven yourself able to step up to your role as Prince of Southlands and make others do your bidding. Is this then what you want? Is this the life you have chosen, the dream you desire above all others? Do you wish to be the prince you were born to be?"

He sits up, and her face pulls back. Her clothing blends into the night's shadows. All he can see is the light from her eyes and the glow of her long, long hair. She is horrible and beautiful.

"I don't know what I want," he says. "I don't want to be trapped, that's all I know."

"Trapped, my sweet one?"

"You know. Forced into a role just because it's expected of me."

Her smile grows. "You want freedom. I can give you that."

Lionheart shakes his head. "You can't make me other than I am. I am Prince of Southlands, and I need to be a prince. There's no two ways about it."

"Not when you are one of my darlings," says she. "Wait a little longer. I will set you free."

He nods and closes his eyes.

The Lady turns from him and steps out of his dreams back into her own world, seating herself upon her dark throne. Her brother is there, lurking in the shadows. She feels the heat from his eyes and it annoys her.

"What is it?"

"Don't even think about breaking the rules," says he. He steps into her line of vision, his eyes ringed in flames, his black teeth gnashing. "She is mine."

"I never said she wasn't."

"You gave her to him. My princess! My prize! You gave her to him like a gift."

The Lady shrugs. "She's not what he wants. She's only a means."

"A means to what?"

"A means to get him on the path to his own self-discovery, so that I may at last discern what his true desire is and"—she hides her smile behind a hand—"give it to him."

"But the girl is mine."

"You've not kissed her yet."

"I will!"

"Not now that she has fled the mountain, you won't."

Flames fall from between his teeth and land in sparks upon the misty floor. "She will return within a year and a day."

"Or what?"

"Or suffer my wrath."

"And tell me, brother, how will this wrath of yours manifest itself?"

He does not answer, but his sister sees everything she needs in his face, and it does not displease her.

PART THREE

1

THE BARON OF MIDDLECRESCENT eyed his daughter from across his desk. This desk was more like a throne really, a true seat of power from which the baron controlled his barony and, truth be told, the baronies of more than a few of his peers. All in the name of good King Hawkeye, of course; Middlecrescent was unbendingly loyal. If ever his views crossed the Eldest's, it would only be because Middlecrescent was best positioned to recognize benefit to his liege lord. If he pulled a few strings here and there, subtly gainsaying his master's wishes, manipulating his pawns into positions he deemed more suitable, it was only with the best interests of King Hawkeye at heart.

Hawkeye may sadly neglect the issue of his son's future marriage. He may wait until dignitaries from foreign nations arrived, offering to contaminate the royal bloodlines with strains less pure. But Middlecrescent would not be so lax.

"Why are you here, Daylily?"

"I chose to return," said she, her face a mask.

"Did the prince make you an offer?"

"He offered his parents' hospitality for the winter. That is all."

The baron swore softly, venomously. "Then tell me, my dear, what are you doing in my household now?"

"As I said, I chose to return."

"Yes, so you did say." The baron leaned forward across his desk, his elbows resting before him, his hands carefully folded. "And you had better have a good explanation for this choice. I am all ears."

Daylily neither swallowed nor blinked. But she considered her words for some moments before speaking. "Prince Lionheart is still a boy, Father. He is incapable of considering matrimony or engagements. He is foolish and headstrong, and his mind is taken up with . . ." Here she considered again. "With childhood games."

The baron was fooled by neither his daughter's mask nor her words. He'd taught her those tricks. He swore again, leaning back in his chair.

"Iubdan's beard, you've gone and fallen in love with the boy."

Daylily gave her father a contemptuous look.

The baron laughed. "Don't let these little things distract you. You know your duty to your father, to your Eldest, to Southlands. You'll not let emotions stand in your way; I brought you up better than that!"

Middlecrescent took a parchment from his desk and poised his pen. "You will return to the Eldest's House next summer. I give you until then to compose yourself properly and fix your mind upon your task. Enough of this fool flirtation, and enough sentimental nonsense."

No one else observing Daylily's cold stance would have accused her of sentimental nonsense. Her eyes narrowed ever so slightly as her father began to write. He said without looking up, "What is it? Speak your mind."

"You think you know me, Father," she said. "But you don't."

"I know you are capable of fulfilling every expectation I have of you," said he.

"And I will," said she.

The winter passed, as did the spring. Messages passed back and forth from Middlecrescent to the Eldest's House. Those from the Eldest's House were usually addressed to the baron and sealed with the starflower-and-panther crest. But the final one was different. It was addressed to Daylily and sealed with the seated panther, the crest of the prince. Middlecrescent smiled when he saw it and read it without telling his daughter. Then he informed her that she was to prepare for the journey.

Daylily sat long before her mirror the night before she and her servant were to set out for the Eldest's House. She studied what she saw there in her reflection. Not a single line marred her face, for she rarely smiled or frowned. Her eyes were solemn and wide, framed with long lashes, and her porcelain skin and red hair glowed in the candlelight. She was, she did not doubt, beautiful.

"Why then?" she whispered. "Why then does he not see?"

Her brows knit together in the most delicate line.

"What sort of beauty is she hiding?"

The Eldest's household bubbled with gossip. "Lady Daylily of Middlecrescent is coming!" "The baron's fine daughter is coming to stay!" "It can mean only one thing!"

They gave Lionheart significant looks wherever he went. He could not venture out to the stables and give his red mare a hard run without having to suffer the whispers and gazes of the whole court. Even the stableboys gossiped like schoolgirls.

He ignored it.

Let them think what they liked, the whole mad lot of them! Let his mother plot and plan with the baron. He would not be manipulated into anything. He was seventeen now, and perfectly capable of making up his own mind.

Not that he disliked Daylily. His memories of the previous summer were rather hazy. He knew that he and she had played a good amount of chess and cards. He knew that he had thought her very pretty, if a little cold.

And he knew that she had been the one to urge him to step into his role, to stand up and be the prince he was meant to be.

That was all very well, Lionheart thought as he stood in the front courtyard of his father's house, watching Middlecrescent's fine carriage approaching. A good show on Daylily's part, and he must be grateful. After all, it had achieved the desired result. Nevertheless, as the carriage drew around and came to a halt, Lionheart braced himself for battle. He would not be molded like a jelly. He would marry no one unless he wanted to.

Daylily stepped from the coach.

Lionheart gulped. He'd forgotten how beautiful she was.

"Welcome back," he said with a bright smile, masking his sudden discomfort.

Daylily smiled in return, reading a great deal more in his expression than Lionheart had intended to show. "Good afternoon, Leo," she said, choosing to use the familiar form of address. She'd debated the virtues of this during the last hour of her drive, and at last decided that Prince Lionheart would likely respond best to informal greetings. He was such a playful boy at heart. But her curtsy was nothing if not reverent.

"I trust your journey went well?" Lionheart said, bowing and offering his elbow. Her hand was so delicate as it looped through his arm, clad in a dainty velvet glove and ornamented with a silver ring shaped like her namesake.

"Everything according to plan," said she, not meeting his eyes. "I trust your parents are in health?"

"Yes, they'll see you at supper tonight." Lionheart licked his lips.

Daylily murmured something appropriate. Everything formal and just as it should be. Not a single extraordinary word spoken nor even a significant glance. Yet when Lionheart had seen her to her chambers and returned to his own, he didn't even notice the looks and smiles of those he passed in the halls. He stepped into his room, shut the door, and stood there taking long breaths. Then, muttering "Iubdan's beard!" under his breath for no explainable reason, he took the Maid Starflower urn down from the mantel and dumped out his juggling sacks.

The rhythm of the flying sacks soothed him. But he couldn't sing this time, nor attempt a jig. His concentration wasn't what it should be, and he found himself struggling to keep the circle unbroken.

A rattling across the room surprised him, and he barked and scattered half the sacks across the floor. Turning, he saw a chambermaid emerge from his study into his sitting room, carrying a dust bucket and broom.

Her hands were gloved, and her face covered in veils.

"Oh, it's you!" Lionheart grinned and ran a hand down his face. "Thought to scare me, did you, Rosie?"

"And it please Your Highness," said she, bobbing a curtsy despite the heavy pail in her hand. "Forgive my intrusion. I didn't know you was—were—here."

"Likewise." He bent to retrieve the sacks and put them back in the urn. "Don't tell anybody, eh?" His smile went lopsided as he replaced the lid. "The queen doesn't approve of her son's antics, you know."

Rose Red curtsied again and did not speak. It was not her place to speak to the prince. It was not her place to be seen by him. It was certainly not her place to have a thought on anything that went on between the prince and his royal mother.

After all, she and Prince Lionheart were not friends.

"Shall I come back to clean the hearth, Your Highness?" she asked quietly, nodding at the fireplace.

"No, by all means, go about your work," said Lionheart, backing away from the mantel. She hesitated a moment, then obeyed. Her motions were heavy, though she herself was as tiny and rail thin as ever. Lionheart stood by the window, pretending to look down upon his father's gardens but actually eyeing the girl as she worked. He did not often see her, though she worked almost exclusively in his service. The prince never associated with his cleaning staff. But he liked knowing Rose Red was about somewhere, safe under his protection.

"You're eating enough these days, aren't you?" he asked.

She looked up from her sweeping, startled. The edge of her veil was grimy with ashes. "Yes, Your Highness. Thank you."

"And your goat . . . Beana. Is she well?"

"Yes, Your Highness."

Lionheart frowned a little and indicated for her to resume her sweeping. Once more, he turned and gazed out his window. Below him spread the Eldest's Gardens as far as he could see. Rosebushes lined the nearby walkways, though they never bloomed anymore. There was some talk of uprooting them, but the idea was too heartbreaking to be taken seriously. Southlands had always been so proud of its roses. Perhaps someday they would bloom again.

Beyond those walkways stretched the park grounds, miles in each direction save north, where they ran into the Eldest's City, the greatest and proudest city in all Southlands. All these things should be Lionheart's someday. The barons would swear their vows of loyalty as they knelt at his feet. Everyone in the kingdom would pay him tribute, honor, and reverence.

And, of course, he would choose a bride to rule beside him as his mother ruled alongside his father. A strong woman, a beautiful woman. That is what the people of Southlands required.

"Rose Red," Lionheart said, without turning to look at her, "do you think I will make a good king?"

Rose Red said nothing for a long moment. Her hands froze in their work. This was not a question she should be asked, much less one she should be permitted to answer.

But Lionheart turned to her, and in that instant, as she peered through the slit in her veils, she did not see a prince. She saw Leo. She saw the boy who had once told her he would be a jester someday; the boy who had built stick-and-leaf ships and sunk them in the Lake of Endless Blackness; the boy who had brandished a beanpole like a sword and battled imaginary foes with all the vim of a legend.

The boy who had looked into the monster's pool.

"It's not my place to say, Your Highness," Rose Red whispered.

He looked hurt at this response. Rose Red wished she could take back those words.

"I give you permission to speak," Lionheart said, but his voice was harder now. He was a prince again, no longer the Leo she knew. Rose Red bowed her head and curtsied again, deeply.

"I believe you are the kindest and best master, Your Highness," she said. "Therefore, you must be the kindest and best king."

Lionheart gazed at her, searching the huddled form for some sign of the playmate he had once enjoyed. But everything was different now, down from the mountain. They were no longer a boy and a girl; they were a prince and a chambermaid. She was not his friend, not his peer, not even an upper servant with whom he could rightly exchange civilities.

"Carry on with your work," he said and stepped from the sitting room into the adjoining dressing room.

He prepared himself for dinner that night, having never liked employing a man to aid him. As befit a prince, he wore red and black, and when he sat at table with his parents and Daylily, he saw that she wore the same colors, just as though she were already a princess. But her face was demure, and she addressed herself primarily to the Eldest and Queen Starflower, only turning to Lionheart when he happened to speak to her. All politeness and poise and beneath it all, allure. No one who saw her could fail to notice what a fine queen she would make.

The meal complete, Queen Starflower turned to her son with a smile. Lionheart made an effort not to flinch under it.

"Why don't you entertain our guest, my dear?" Starflower said. "You have skill, and we would all enjoy a demonstration."

"Yes, indeed," said Daylily, turning her great eyes upon him. "I seem to remember asking you to play last summer during our stay at Hill House, but you never could be convinced."

Lionheart shrugged, an unprincely gesture.

"Won't you please now?" Daylily asked, her gaze ever so compelling.

A lute was sent for, and Lionheart accepted it and stood before those assembled. He liked the feeling of all those eyes upon him, not least of all Lady Daylily's. His father watched with mild interest, his mother like a hawk. And down the table several places, Foxbrush sat with his hair oiled, giving Lionheart dagger looks that were almost hysterical. Lionheart gave his cousin a grin before strumming the first chord. Then he sang:

"O Gleamdren fair, I love thee true.
Be the moon waxed full or new,
In all my world-enscoping view,
There shineth none so bright as you."

Daylily nodded quietly to herself as the prince performed the first few bars of the familiar song. A song of Eanrin, Chief Poet of Iubdan Rudiobus, it was one of the most renowned romantic ballads in all history. And Lionheart had chosen to play it for her. She did not smile, for that might be too obvious, but she gazed long and full at Lionheart's face.

> *"Sing of all the lovers true*
> *Beneath a sky of sapphire hue.*
> *In light o' the love I bear for you,*
> *All theirs must fade like morning dew."*

So why, she wondered, did he keep glancing at his mother that way? Lionheart sang on:

> *"This passion that I feel for you*
> *Is something rather like the flu.*
> *The flu brought on by cook's new stew*
> *That tasted like an old man's shoe.*

> *"Oh, sing me now a song of stew!*
> *A stew that's fit for lover's brew!*
> *A stew so hearty and so—"*

"Lionheart!"

Queen Starflower's voice struck like an arrow to its mark. Even King Hawkeye, who was chuckling quietly behind his hand, coughed and sat up at her words. Daylily, as those last verses poured off the prince's tongue, had grown pale and clenched her fists tightly in her lap.

The queen's eyes snapped fire. "If you cannot sing the work of Bard Eanrin with the proper reverence, I beg you will desist."

Prince Lionheart gave his mother a boyish grin. "Come on, Mother, it was just a bit of fun! Those old songs get so—"

"Have done," said Starflower, holding up her hand.

Daylily could take no more. She rose from her place and curtsied to those assembled, but did not look Lionheart's way. "Forgive me," she said in her sweetest voice, "but I am fatigued from the day's journey. May I have Your Majesties' leave to retire?"

The Eldest nodded, and Daylily swept from the room, still without a look the prince's way. As a servant opened and shut the dining hall door behind her, she heard Lionheart begin, "Now, look here, Mother, you know those songs are lousy at best. I don't see why—"

Daylily hastened on. Her expression was serene and her chin high as she made her way to her apartments, followed by her goodwoman. When she reached the doorway to her rooms, she dismissed the woman with a wave of her hand. "I will see to myself tonight," she said. "You may go."

Her goodwoman knew better than to argue and bowed herself away. Daylily stepped inside and shut the door.

She did not rage. She did not scream. She did not stamp her feet, not even once. She crossed to her fireplace and sat in the chair drawn up before it. Someone had lit a small blaze, and although it was a little too hot for comfort, Lady Daylily did not care.

"How could he treat me with such disrespect?" she whispered to the flames.

She was no fool. Nobody in that room could have failed to miss the message Prince Lionheart declared by twisting that reverenced song into a jester's ditty. What a fool he was . . . and she too for that matter! What a fool for coming here again when she knew just what he was. A rattlebrained scamp without a mature idea in his head! What a fool she was for thinking ten months would make any difference.

Daylily put a hand lightly to her temple and closed her eyes. What a fool she was for letting her heart—

A clatter from the bedchamber door. Daylily sat up straighter and folded both hands in her lap, not deigning to look around. "I thought I told you that I would look after myself tonight," she said in a crisp voice.

But it was not her maidservant who answered. "Forgive me, m'lady. I didn't realize you'd be back so soon."

Daylily turned. A chambermaid stood in the doorway between the bedroom and the sitting room, a porcelain pitcher in her hand. She curtsied and said, "I was on my way to refill this for your ladyship, but I can come back later."

The girl was covered in veils.

"Rose Red," said Daylily. "I remember you."

The chambermaid curtsied again. "Forgive me for disturbin' you, m'lady—"

"Come here," Daylily said. "Leave that pitcher, and come here."

Rose Red obeyed. If she trembled behind the veil, Daylily could not see it. Though her rags had been exchanged for a clean servant's smock and her old veils replaced with new ones of fresh linen, she still looked rather horrible, standing before the fire with its lights and shadows playing off her small frame. Daylily licked her lips.

"He cares for you a great deal, doesn't he?"

Rose Red made no answer. She did not know what to say.

"The prince, I mean," Daylily continued. "Leo."

The maid shook her head and curtsied again. "He is a good and kind master, m'lady."

"And what about me?" Daylily asked. "Do you think I might be a good and kind mistress?"

"I . . . m'lady, I—"

"That is what I will be someday," the baron's daughter continued. "Your mistress. Not just a guest in this household, but its lady. Its queen."

The maid curtsied again.

"Do you doubt me?"

"I trust you must believe what you're sayin'," Rose Red replied in a whisper, then added quickly, "m'lady."

"Will you serve me then as faithfully as you serve your prince now?"

Rose Red made no answer. She could hardly breathe, and the fire behind her was hot.

Daylily spoke again, and this time her voice was as smooth as honey. "What do you hide behind that veil, Rose Red?"

"That's my secret."

"Does Leo know your secret?"

There was something terrible in the way Daylily used the prince's boyhood nickname; something possessive. Rose Red shook her head sharply, her gloved hands clenched into fists. "The secret is mine," she said, "to tell or keep as I will."

"It is no birthmark," Daylily whispered. "Nor are you what the mountain folk claim."

"It's my secret," Rose Red repeated. She wanted to back away, but the baron's daughter held her locked in her gaze. So she closed her eyes behind her veil, hoping somehow to gain the courage to flee.

Daylily set her teeth. Then she reached out and removed the veil from Rose Red's face.

The fire crackled on its hearth. Outside, the wind pressed up against the window, rattling the glass, then moved on its way with a howl. The Lady of Middlecrescent and the prince's chambermaid stared at each other in the dimly lit chamber, and in that moment, neither wore a veil.

"I see," Daylily said at last.

Rose Red let out a shuddering breath. Then her hands were over her face, and she crouched at the lady's feet. "I see," Daylily said again, peering down at the girl. She drew her dainty slippers back. "Now I too know your secret."

The crumpled maid gave a sob. "Please, m'lady," she said. "Please, give me back my veil."

But Daylily held on to it, running the soft fabric between her fingers. "Swear to me," she said, her voice hoarse, "that you will serve me."

"Please, m'lady."

"Swear it. You will now be my servant and serve me as faithfully as you serve your master. For I know your secret as well as he." She grimaced as though she must bite out the words. "Swear it, now."

Rose Red sobbed again, but she sat upright. With unveiled face, she looked up into the face of the baron's daughter. A tear ran down her cheek. "I swear it, m'lady," she said.

Then she held out her hand. "Please give me back my veil."

2

THE GOAT PEN was a dozy place at night. All the Eldest's goats huddled on one side, their hairy haunches pressed together, long lashes lowered over yellow eyes. Some chewed their cud. Most slept the sleep of the just, for goats, on the whole, are a just lot. The atmosphere was heavy with hay and musk and sleep.

But Beana stood at the far end of the pen, her nose upraised, sniffing.

It bothered her sometimes that she could still catch a whiff of roses now and again, for she knew they were long since gone. They had once blossomed thickly in these parts, however, and perhaps the ghost of their aromas still lingered. Not even the perfumes of a hundred other flowers blossoming in the warm summer climate of Southlands could entirely disguise that memory of beauty.

Beana sought a different scent. Her senses were as tense as her body every night when the moon was new and the sky was black.

For these nights were always the worst.

"I know you're there," she muttered. "I know you're waiting."

"Waitin' for what?"

Beana turned and found her girl climbing the fence into the pen. "Rosie!" she exclaimed and trotted up to her. "What are you doing out here so late? You should have been in bed long ago—" She noticed suddenly how the girl was trembling. "Bebo's crown!" she exclaimed. "You heard it, didn't you?"

Rose Red sank to the dirty pen floor, wrapping her arms about her knees. "Heard what, Beana?" she asked in a tremulous voice.

"Why, the . . ." Beana shook her horns. "Nothing, girl, nothing. What are you shivering about?"

Then, much to the goat's surprise, Rose Red put her head down on her knees and burst into tears.

"Sweet Hymlumé! What's gotten into you?"

Beana put her nose to the girl's ear, nuzzling and bleating, but the crying ran its full course before Rose Red could gasp out any words. Then she said, "She don't love him, Beana."

"Who doesn't love whom?"

"Lady Daylily. She don't love my master, not one bit of it."

"Prince Lionheart?"

"Yes. I mean, no. I mean, yes, she don't."

Beana snorted but gently nuzzled the girl again. "Well, child, that's for them to muddle through, now, isn't it?"

Rose Red, her face still buried in her knees, shook her head. "I don't want her to marry him, Beana. She doesn't even respect him, much less love him."

"How are you to know her heart, my girl?" Beana said. "That pretty Daylily, she's an odd one, I'll grant you. Not someone I'd like to have on my bad side. But that doesn't mean she can't love your prince, doesn't mean she can't make him a good wife and a good queen."

Still Rose Red shook her head. "She don't deserve him, Beana."

"That's not for you or me to decide," said the goat. She knelt down and let the girl wrap her arms around her neck. She felt Rose Red remove her veil so that her tears could flow unchecked into Beana's rough coat. She felt the girl's mouth open several times, heard her breath catch as though she was about to speak. But she always closed it again and simply sat there, crying.

Rose Red could not bring herself to say that Daylily had seen her face. Nor could she mention the vow she had sworn at that lady's feet. So she sat there in the smelly goat pen, crying for shame and frustration.

When at last her tears began to dry, Beana said softly, "We can go back, Rosie."

"Go back where?"

"To the mountain." The goat tried to keep the eagerness from her voice but could not disguise all traces of it. "We don't have to stay here if it is so painful for you. We'd find a way to get by. Sure, you eat well here and people don't touch you, but all in all, you're as lonely here as ever you were. And I know you miss the forest."

But Rose Red began to tremble again, and this time it had nothing to do with tears. She pulled back from Beana, tugging her veil back into place. "No," she said.

"Now, Rosie, you could at least think about it. Your prince has been kind to you, for sure, but that doesn't mean—"

"No!"

So that conversation ended. They sat quietly, pressed against each other for comfort, neither speaking. Beana, though her body now relaxed, strained every sense she possessed with listening . . . listening and smelling and waiting for some sign of that Other, whom she knew must be close, but who spoke not a word. If only she could take Rose Red back up into the mountains, away from the low country, away from the Wilderlands! Up to that fresh, high air where the Other could not walk, where its voice could never penetrate. Up where Beana could be certain the girl was safe. If only, if only . . .

Rose Red's mind whirled with entirely separate thoughts. She could never return to the mountain, to the madness of that dark and terrible Dream! Starvation she could handle; loneliness she could survive. But not that Dream again. For ten months or more, she had been free. True, life was no bed of flowers, but that mattered little. She could serve her prince—her Leo—and do some good. But she could not bear to face that Dream.

Return to me in a year and a day, the voice in her memory whispered. *Or I will come for you.*

A nightmare, that's all it was. But one she must avoid.

"We ain't never goin' back to the mountain," she whispered fiercely even as she pillowed her head on Beana's warm back and closed her eyes to sleep. "Never!"

Two months slipped by. The sweltering heat of summer passed its most vicious point and slowly began to dwindle toward autumn. Rose Red's work continued as it had for the last year. She cleaned the prince's chambers. She mended his stockings and swept his hearth and ran a thousand little errands for him that he never noticed. The household staff wanted nothing to do with her, and even the head housekeeper, an imposing woman of military heritage, spoke to Rose Red only when necessary. So Rose Red kept to herself and gave herself her own assignments, and worked harder than any two maids on staff.

Only now she cleaned Lady Daylily's chambers as well as the prince's.

But she saw either of them only when she might happen to glimpse them together out on the grounds. *He ain't asked her yet,* she told herself every time she saw Prince Lionheart walking beside that tall beauty. *Not yet.*

But he would. As surely as she knew what she would have to clean from the chamber pots every morning for the rest of her life, Rose Red knew Lionheart was destined to marry the Baron of Middlecrescent's daughter. Everyone in the household knew that.

Except perhaps Prince Lionheart.

He knew what everyone expected of him. Expectations pressed in on him at every turn. Nevertheless, though already past his seventeenth birthday and beginning to look toward his eighteenth, he never made the proposal, never announced the betrothal. The Baron of Middlecrescent and his doe-eyed wife had made their annual visit to court in mid-summer, hoping for good news, but they returned to Middlecrescent with deflated hopes. Or rather, the baron left deflated, while his wife, who never did quite catch on to the Plan, was full of prattle about how well their dear ducky looked, and wasn't Prince Lionheart growing into a fine and handsome young fellow, and well, come to think of it, wouldn't it be just darling if those two were to fall in love someday?

"What would you say to that, husband?"

The baron had not answered.

Daylily herself, when questioned on the subject by her friends and attendants, merely laughed a bright laugh, saying, "Oh, Lionheart and I are such good friends!" Nothing more, nothing less. Her ladies weren't fooled for an instant.

Neither was Rose Red.

One morning, just a few weeks after the baron and his wife had departed for home, Rose Red entered Lionheart's chambers to clean as usual. She began in the main room, shoveling out the grate with practiced, methodical motions, focusing on her work and thinking of nothing. Just scrape, scoop, and dump, over and over.

Lionheart stepped from his bedchamber. She turned, surprised, not having realized that he was in there. He smiled when he saw her, giving a two-fingered salute. "Top of the morning, Rose Red."

He strode over to sit in a chair near the fireplace where she worked. She reached up quickly to adjust the veil over her face, but Lionheart was not looking at her. An attendant carrying a pair of riding boots followed him into the room. The prince held out a hand for them. "Thank you," Lionheart said. "I think I can manage to put on my own boots."

The attendant handed them over and stood back, folding his hands neatly before him.

Lionheart arched an eyebrow at him. "I mean to say, you're dismissed, Turtlebreath."

"Tortoiseshell, Your Highness."

"Yes, you. Begone. Hence to the place from whence you came!"

The attendant blinked a long, meaningful blink. Then he bowed and scuttled off, and in his scuttling managed to convey a world of disapproval.

Lionheart snorted as the door shut behind him. "The man thinks less of me because I want to put on my own boots."

Rose Red smiled behind her veil. She was uncertain whether or not to continue her work in the presence of the prince, and since he did not bid her one way or the other, she chose to stand quietly, saying nothing.

Lionheart began the process of shoving his feet into the fitted riding boots, a more arduous task than one might have expected. Rose Red began to suspect that perhaps he couldn't do it without aid, when at last something popped, and the first boot slid up over his calf. He buckled it across the top, then paused, as though tired from a great labor. Rose Red noticed, with some surprise, that his breathing was quick, and she wondered just how much exertion outfitting oneself in boots required.

Then Lionheart, taking the second boot in his hands to repeat the process, said, "You know what, Rose Red? I think I'm going to ask her today."

The shovel in her hand became unbearably heavy. She grabbed it with her other hand and just managed to keep from dropping it.

"It's as good an opportunity as any," the prince continued, grimacing in his struggle against all the laws of physics and tight leather. "Foxbrush cannot ride with us due to some meeting with Hill House's steward. It'll just be the two of us, and we're riding all the way out to Swan Bridge today, perhaps even across if the weather holds. It seems best to ask something like this in private, don't you think?"

She couldn't make a sound, couldn't even nod.

"Gah!" he gasped, and his foot at last wiggled its way into place, and he fastened the buckle. Then Lionheart stood up and stamped a few times. Wiping perspiration from his forehead, he shook out his arms and took a deep breath. "Everyone expects me to be betrothed by the time I'm eighteen. My father was. And my grandfather. And probably his grandfather before him as far back as history goes. Seems to be a tradition of some kind. Granted, I'm not one to kowtow to tradition for tradition's sake . . . but then again, a girl like Daylily isn't exactly kowtowing. She's nice enough, pretty enough, and she's a good rider. Fact is," he crossed his arms and studied the half-cleaned fireplace, "fact is, I think it's time

I did something right. Something expected of me. Just to take them unawares, know what I mean?"

Rose Red hoped to goodness he didn't expect her to answer. This was how he usually talked to her these days, the way he would talk to a mirror. As though he simply needed to hear his own thoughts out loud to make certain of their clarity, and she was as good an ear as any to hear them.

Lionheart lifted his gaze from the fireplace and smiled at her, an uneasy sort of smile. "I'm scared to death. But don't let on that I told you. Who'd have thought a girl could be so frightening? I mean, what if after all this she says no? It's not impossible . . . I mean, not everyone wants to be queen."

Rose Red tried to give an encouraging smile but suspected it came out ghastly, and was thankful yet again that he could not see it.

Lionheart reached out suddenly and, to her great surprise, patted her shoulder. "Wish me luck, Rosie. There's nothing for it now."

He turned and strode from the room, leaving her alone with her shovel and her bucket.

She dropped the shovel with a clatter and let it lie where it fell at her feet. Her hands limp at her sides, she stood there in the silence of the room until she heard outside his window the clop of hooves on the cobbles. Then, as though shot with life once more, she rushed to the window and looked out. The wind caught her veil and pulled it across her eyes, and she yanked it viciously back into place to watch the scene below.

Master Whipwind, the stable master, held the heads of the prince's red mare and Daylily's charcoal gelding, a handsome pair when next to each other. Lionheart and Daylily appeared a moment later, and Lionheart assisted the lady into her saddle. Then he swung up onto the back of his mare, let out a merry whoop, and led the way at a brisk trot from the courtyard.

Rose Red's quick eyes saw it all. She saw the significant looks the stable hands gave the guardsmen. She saw movement from a window in a wing across from her, and knew that Queen Starflower watched the goings-on with satisfaction. She even saw a forlorn figure with oiled hair standing in a darkened doorway, and though she had little use for him, her heart went out momentarily to Foxbrush.

The horses disappeared from her view.

Rose Red leapt away from that window and rushed across to the study. There she peered through a window that looked toward the Eldest's southern gardens, across the stretch of land that led at length to Swan Bridge. As she watched, she saw Lionheart and Daylily appear. They urged their horses into a gallop and thundered across the turf, Daylily's superb red hair billowing behind her like a flag, matching the flap of Lionheart's scarlet coat.

"You fool!" Rose Red growled aloud. "Oh, Leo, you fool. You're goin' to be hurt, you're goin' to be miserable, and what will I do for you then?" She shook her head hard, grinding her teeth. "Stupid girl, it's goin' to happen, as sure as I'm standin' here. Get used to it. You've known since you came how it would be. You've known all this long year. . . ."

Rose Red turned from the window. "Get back to work now," she muttered. "Get back to your tasks as you was meant to, and let the great ones do as they must. It's no concern of yours."

But she could not resist one last look out the window.

She thought she saw far up in the sky a red flame, like a falling star speeding to earth.

Beana stood on the far side of the goat pen, her ears pricked, her nose gently sniffing the breeze.

"I know you're there," she muttered.

But she heard nothing.

That was what worried her more than anything. For the first time since she and Rose Red had descended the mountain, the air was still, that trembling murmur from beyond the worlds vanished.

Beana paced. She knew she should be relieved, but she was not. For a year and a day, she had stood almost constant vigil to be certain the Other was never heard beyond its bounds. But this was not a battle to be won so easily; the Other would never give up.

"Trying to lull me into a false security," Beana muttered. "That's what you're doing."

No answer.

Beana paced up and down, looping the whole pen at last, faster and faster. Then, as the other goats watched, scandalized, she took a running start and leapt the fence, galloping awkwardly through the stable yard and the near gardens, out into the farther stretches of the Eldest's park. Her fellow goats bleated and cheered in a mixture of horror and admiration before (once she was out of sight) completely forgetting her existence. No one else witnessed her bolt for freedom.

The grass was warm and soft beneath her feet, so different from the hard mountain terrain to which she was used, full of many delectable smells. But the goat did not stop to investigate these. She slowed from a gallop to a trot, eyes focused forward on her destination.

The Eldest's grounds ended where the gorge cut across the land, sweeping sharply down into those unknown Wilderlands below.

Beana trotted to the edge of the gorge and gazed into that dark forest. The trees watched her and some beckoned gently with leaf and needle-covered hands, but she ignored these. "Bah," she muttered, searching and sniffing and becoming ever more agitated.

Suddenly she caught a new scent. It was not the one she sought.

Slowly, unwilling to believe her senses, the goat turned her eyes upward, to the sky. "Lights above, shield us," she whispered.

There, above her, appearing in a flash of fire, was a form she knew all too well. And with it came the stench that still haunted her nightmares, no matter how many centuries since last she'd smelled it! In that moment of recognition, Beana knew that descending terror and the memories it stirred in her heart better than she knew herself.

Don't be afraid, sang the wood thrush.

But Beana was running now, as fast as she could for the Eldest's House, while watching the destruction falling like lightning.

The day was overcast and rather cold for summer, with a breeze that had a sting to it.

Then the world was filled with fire.

First came the heat, an instant later the flame, and immediately afterward the sound. It was a roar that ended in a sensation of heaviness, like an enormous hand smacking down. *WHOMPH!* A sound as hot as the flames themselves. One could almost believe that the sound alone consumed the marble Starflower Fountain, that massive edifice two stories tall; consumed and destroyed it in a matter of seconds.

After that, came the Dragon.

3

THE DRAGON LANDED in the heart of the flames, atop the pile of rubble that only moments before had been Starflower and her foe. As he landed, screams rose up about him, a macabre chorus. How many died in those first few moments would be impossible to guess, but the others fled without thought, with no emotion save the overwhelming, consuming fear that gripped them by their throats and squeezed.

The Dragon raised his wings above his head, lifted his face to the sky, and sent up a fountain of flame, a ghastly parody of the pure water that had so recently flowed in the same spot. It shot to the heavens, raining sparks upon the surrounding gardens. Fire caught and spread swiftly across the grass, across the hedges, across the winding white paths. Stable hands screamed to each other as the stables caught, some rushing inside to save the horses, others taking flight through the far gate.

The people inside the Eldest's House, as the sounds outside besieged their ears, ran to various windows and looked out upon the fiery maelstrom. They saw the screaming men and women, saw the fires swiftly spreading. Most of all, filling their vision so that they could not look away no matter how dearly they might wish to, they saw the Dragon in place of the white monument that had symbolized their liberty.

Queen Starflower stood amid her attendants, many of whom were shrieking inarticulately. And as she looked out upon the destroyer standing on the ruins of her namesake's statue, fire bursting from him in a stream to the heavens, she believed she looked upon her death. In a whisper, she spoke a protective blessing: "Silent Lady, shield us!" But she spoke without hope.

Foxbrush and other men of the court hastened to the palace windows as well and, seeing what terror waited beyond the glass, formed together and hurtled toward the great front door, armed or otherwise, united in rage. Foxbrush was squeezed to the back of the crowd, though his shouts were as loud and angry as those of his fellows.

But King Hawkeye, his old bones quickened by the sights and sounds around him, ran to the same hall and raised both his arms in a commanding gesture. *"Stop!"* he cried. "The fumes—"

His voice was drowned as the foremost young men flung wide the door.

Like a tidal wave, noxious fumes poured into the hall. The men struck first by the wall of venomous heat fell as though dead to the floor. Those farther back, as the poison filled their lungs, felt their outrage melt away in a surge first of absolute terror, then of utter despair. Noble and common man alike went down on their knees with the weight of it.

The Eldest saw this effect before the fumes reached him, and his face twisted in dismay. Then he too felt the poison take hold of him in a grip that promised, like a constrictor's, to strengthen with time.

All this happened in a matter of moments, and as the following moments ticked away their small eternities, the Dragon's poison worked its way into every room, every passage, every cellar and attic chamber in all the Eldest's House, filling the lungs, then the hearts of each household member.

Save one.

Deeming his work complete, the massive beast swallowed his flame, and the world was suddenly dark as night in the cloud of his smoke.

He looked out from where he sat in the ruin of the fountain and spoke a single word.

"Out."

This command worked twofold. First, every fire that blazed in the hedgerows and across the stable roofs instantly snuffed out like a candle under glass, leaving behind only noxious smoke. Second, people of the household poured from every door and filled the yard around the Dragon. Even those who could barely stand for the poison tottered forth, servant supporting nobleman, nobleman supporting servant. They arranged themselves in groups, and the Dragon smiled.

As he smiled, his eyes scanned the crowd like a scythe cutting through a field. Those on whom his gaze fell even for an instant felt themselves collapsing inside as though the marrow of their spirits had suddenly corroded. But those awful eyes did not linger on any one person; instead they continued searching the crowd until at last the Dragon spoke again.

"Where is the princess?"

The people fell to the ground, unable to answer.

"Where is the princess?" the Dragon repeated.

Still no one could answer. If anyone thought of Lady Daylily, somewhere on the grounds riding, no one could have spoken her name even had that one wished to. The Dragon hissed, flames licking from his tongue. Then he crawled down from his perch on the rubble, like a monarch descending from his throne. The ground shook beneath him, and all the people of the Eldest's House trembled.

"Where is the princess?" he demanded yet again, fire dripping from his jaws like saliva from a mastiff's jowls. Then his attention was drawn by the sight of King Hawkeye in the middle of the throng, where his steward and several barons had tried to shield him, struggling to his feet and pushing the men aside.

"Ah, the little kingling," the Dragon said. As he drew nearer, the people scattered in screamless terror, creating an open path to the Eldest. But the aging king, despite the bitter smoke, drew himself up tall and faced the Dragon.

"Tell me, wretched *man*," the Dragon said, speaking the word like an insult, "where is the princess?"

"Terrible one," the Eldest spoke, his voice small and cold after the mountainous reverberations of the one before him, "I do not know of whom you speak."

The Dragon flared the crest on his head and turned his face so that he fixed the Eldest with a single orb. The eye was black as stone, yet fire burned deep inside, blazing so bright and hot that the stone's surface melted and roiled in the heat.

"Don't think me a fool, mortal creature," the Dragon said. "I've not made myself incarnate for nothing. I know she must be here. Don't try to shield her!"

Even before that one awful eye, Hawkeye declared, "There is no princess. Not in all of Southlands. This land has not seen a princess in many years."

The Dragon hissed again. The heat of his face so near was almost too much to bear. "I have played the game for the Beloved of my Enemy," he said. "The time is now near. I gave her a year and a day, and she did not return. But all the signs have led me to this place, all the protections surrounding your house—paltry protections though they may be. I know she is here. So I ask you again, little kingling, and I'll not waste the breath to ask further: Where is the princess?"

King Hawkeye opened his mouth to speak, knowing he invited his own doom. But the Dragon suddenly raised his head high, looking back over his black wings, back across the expanse of the Eldest's grounds. His nostrils widened and issued a great stream of black smoke as his lips drew back in a snarl that was almost a smile.

A lone rider approached, galloping hard on a bloodred mare.

In a whirl of wings and with a great slash of his long tail that sent many in the crowd tumbling, the Dragon turned to face the incomer. His crest flattened against his skull, and he snaked his long neck out, low to the ground so that he was eye level with the rider. And though both horse and rider were still some distance away, the Dragon could see his assailant's face, full of such rage that fear had not yet found a grip.

The Dragon opened wide his mouth until his lower jaw scraped along the ground. Seeing what was about to happen, Hawkeye cried, "No!" and flung himself forward, only to be snatched back by his loyal barons.

The Dragon breathed.

Rather than flames, a cloud of steam, searing hot, issued from his throat. That poison carried all fear, all terror, all the death of dreams to flood the heart and overwhelm the soul.

As the cloud engulfed her and her master, the bloodred mare screamed as though ridden to her destruction. She balked, falling hard to the dirt in her terror. When she had struggled to her feet, her eyes white in frenzied rolling, she left her master helpless on the ground.

Lionheart's mouth was wide in soundless pain, not physical, but a pain that tore down into his very spirit, ripping and shredding as the scorching steam entered his lungs. Smoke blinded him, but he clenched his teeth and felt around for a hunting knife that he knew he must have dropped nearby. His hands felt nothing, but his sight cleared as the smoke parted.

The Dragon, his neck arched like a cobra's, stood over him. The monster opened his mouth again as though to devour his victim in one bite. But instead, he laughed.

The sound was the cacophony of nightmares. Flames danced about his teeth and fell in sparks on and around his victim, who in the face of that laughter lay as one paralyzed. When at last the laughter finished and smoke roiled in coils all about them, the Dragon spoke.

"Prince Lionheart! Welcome. You wish to try your mettle on me? It's been some time since a princeling such as you took it into his head to charge into suicide! You make me feel young again."

Lionheart looked up at him, unable to turn away, gasping and with each gasp taking in more poison. He could not move for the pain that flowed through his veins, as though his blood boiled and burned him from the inside out. And the Dragon's eyes burned him from above as it studied him.

"You are a tempting morsel, little prince." He snarled another smile. Lionheart's face was red, and sweat dripped from his hair. It felt as though his clothing must shrivel away like paper held to a candle. "But alas," the Dragon continued, "I lost that game! You are my sister's prey, not mine. No, I fear I must give you up. Perhaps I should eat you instead?"

The prince tried to speak but found no voice. The poison had burned away all sound but the Dragon's hot breathing.

Then suddenly silver birdsong drowned out all else, though small as a whisper. The next moment someone was kneeling beside him, bent over him protectively. A tiny person, hardly much of a shield, and yet the furnace above Lionheart abated somewhat.

The Dragon stared down at the small veiled girl that ran under his very nose and flung herself over the prince, holding up one hand as though to push the vast monster away. He stared and then he smelled, and his eyes widened at the scent he breathed in.

"Princess!"

The growl of his voice rumbled through Rose Red's body. She thought her bones must break. The face above her was different from that of her Dream, yet she recognized it. And the sight did not so much frighten as enrage her. How dare he? How *dare* he be real?

She shook her fist at the monster, even as he blew at her veil. "Don't you hurt him!" she cried. "Don't you even try!"

The Dragon lowered his head, and Rose Red cringed away from his eyes but remained in her protective crouch over the prince. "Sweet princess," said the Dragon, "I warned you, didn't I? I warned you to return to me in a year and a day or suffer my wrath. You see now that I always keep my word." Then his voice became purring sweet behind the fire, compelling obedience. "Why do you wear that veil before me? I know your true face. You should not hide from me."

Yet Rose Red remained unaffected by his poison. She gnashed her teeth behind the veil, spitting her words as she cried, "Go away! Go back to the mountain, go back to your cave! I don't want you, you nightmare. You don't belong in this world. Get you gone, and leave us alone!"

He smiled. "I think not. Not until you let me kiss you."

"No chance of that!"

"I could kill him. What would you say then?"

Rose Red stared into those eyes, twin infernos boiling brimstone ready to burst upon her. But though the Dragon was more horrible than words, she was not afraid, not quite. "I won't let you hurt him," she said.

"And how will you stop me?" the Dragon demanded with a laugh.

"I don't know," she said. "But I will."

He snarled, spitting flames, and she threw her body across the prince's to protect him. Sparks rolled off her back and sizzled on the ground. The Dragon swung his head about. The people of the Eldest's House quailed beneath his scrutiny. He turned back to the maid, but it was to the prince sheltered beneath her that he spoke.

"Perhaps, oh you brave, lionhearted man, you are not for the snacking after all? I think you may prove more useful alive. You will help me, won't you?"

"Don't talk to him," Rose Red said.

The Dragon backed away from the two, and the swirling smoke surrounded him so that his awful size was hidden. "Get up, little prince," he spoke as he retreated. "Get up and journey into the world. I send you to your exile. But we will meet again, Prince Lionheart, and perhaps you'll find your throne after all?"

Then he vanished from sight, and all Rose Red could discern were screams beyond the wall of smoke and flashes of fire through the gloom. Lionheart, though apparently conscious, was aware of nothing, and his skin was hot to the touch. With extraordinary strength for her size, she heaved him upright, pulling his arm over her bent shoulders, and dragged him back across the poison-filled lawns of the Eldest's grounds.

4

H E DREAMED OF FIRE.

When the dreams faded, Lionheart hovered in the half-light between waking and sleeping. In that place, he thought he smelled the musk of horse, thought he heard the creak of leather and felt the touch of a supporting hand, sometimes soft and sometimes covered in ragged gloves. Then the fire would claim him again and he'd succumb to the furnace of fever and the poison that roiled in his lungs.

No, a voice repeated over and over in his mind. *No, you are mine. He may not have you.*

In desperation, he reached out to the voice, like a child lunging from a stranger's arms toward its mother, heedless of the drop beneath it, caring nothing for danger in its desire for the familiar. "Help me!" he called to the voice.

Tell me what you want, it said.

"I want to escape this fire!"

And so you shall, for you are not his lawful prey!

In an instant there flashed before his mind's eye a face, black amid the fire, white eyes full of fury.

"Thank heaven, you're safe!"

The ebony face vanished when a man's deep voice, hard-edged in relief, spoke from beyond the veil of dreams. More voices spoke, and the gloved hand took hold of him again, and he felt the shifting of the horse beneath him.

Then the fire claimed him once more.

This time the dream continued uninterrupted until Lionheart began to believe with what was left of his conscious mind that he had in fact died and, bypassing the Realm Unseen, his soul had flown straight to this hell. Despair, potent and cold amid the raging flames, slashed across his heart.

"No, no!" A new voice spoke. "No, please! Don't let him go!"

He felt, as though from a great distance, a kiss upon his forehead, and it was cool, though not cold. Then the voice, low and mellifluous, began to sing.

> *Beyond the Final Water falling,*
> *The Songs of Spheres recalling.*
> *Won't you return to me?*

When the voice became a bird's strange, inhuman song he could not guess. Or perhaps it had always been so? But as the sound washed over him like rain, the flames in his head died, the poison in his breast ebbed away. Lionheart blinked open weary eyes and for a moment saw a face he had never before seen, a beautiful one, young yet ageless, with golden skin and great silver eyes. The face of a princess.

He fell at last into a natural sleep.

2

Daylily sat beside the prince's bed in a darkened chamber. Her face was paler than usual, yet no other signs betrayed the harrowing journey she had just experienced.

Six days she had traveled without food, walking beside the fevered Lionheart slung over the back of her black gelding. They'd found little water along the way, and most of what they'd found was spoiled by the horrible smoke that filled the countryside. No one met them on the road. Everyone had fled at the Dragon's approach, and the land was as barren as an old battlefield. And always that iron-gray sky oppressed them.

Daylily may have been the darling of the royal court, but she was also the daughter of a baron. She could bear hunger and thirst and an endless trek down an empty road.

What she could not endure was the fear.

The fear of being watched. That compulsive need to look over one's shoulder or to search the heavy sky. The way one's eyes couldn't help but dart to any shadow that moved across the ground, expecting to see the spread of wings. Nearly a week of this life would drive anyone mad, and Daylily's careful mask threatened to break with tears on more than one occasion.

All that kept her going was Rose Red.

Daylily could not see behind the veil. She could not tell how the smoke, the subtle poison, or the bone-weary journey affected the maid. Perhaps she too was crumbling. Perhaps she felt nothing at all. More than once Daylily longed for a veil to hide her own weakness. She could not let this person—this goat girl—see her break.

So Daylily went on, sometimes leading the gelding, sometimes allowing Rose Red to lead while she put a hand on Lionheart's leg to support him in the saddle. He was terribly hot to the touch, and several times she thought he must die, the fever was so great.

But at last they saw a sight more welcome than angels: the dust of horsemen riding their way. The Baron of Middlecrescent, the moment word had reached him of the Dragon's coming, had set out to see that his daughter was safe.

Now at last they were hidden in Middlecrescent, many long miles from the Eldest's City and the site of all that destruction. Lionheart was tucked into a bed, where he periodically burned and froze, tossing and moaning and talking to someone unseen in his sleep. Daylily rarely left his side.

Neither did Rose Red.

❧

When Lionheart finally came to himself, the fire was mostly gone. All that remained was a dull burn in his chest, but even that seemed to fade as he returned at last to the waking world. His vision was blurred, a haze of colors and shadows. He blinked, and it cleared some; blinked again and he saw Daylily's face surrounded by her cloud of red hair. It looked like fire.

He sat up sharply with a gasp, then grimaced as his head whirled.

"Hush! Hush!" Daylily spoke softly and put her arm across his shoulders. They sat thus a moment, stiffly. Then gently, almost motheringly, she drew him to her, and he rested his head against her shoulder, his eyes closed, breathing in her scent.

"Where are we?"

"Middlecrescent. Do you recall nothing?"

He shook his head and breathed again deeply. She smelled of lilac soap, like his mother and courtly ladies. She smelled of one who had tried to scrub clean from a deeper, fouler stench.

Beneath the clean, there lingered yet a breath of smoke.

He pulled away from her, shaking his head again and opening his eyes. He looked up into her face. "Tell me."

"We traveled north," she said, her arm still about his shoulders. It felt an ineffectual weight, but he did not shake it off. "We left the House grounds and circled around the Eldest's City. He . . . he did not stop us. My father met us on the road late the sixth day and brought us back here. Lionheart." She put her other hand against his cheek, a tender gesture, but her hand was cold. Still, he did not pull away, for her sake if nothing else. "Lionheart, I thought you would die!" Her voice had never been so full of feeling. It scarcely sounded like Daylily.

Lionheart gulped, but his mouth and throat were so dry they hurt, and the muscles moved without effect. He wanted to ask for water. Instead when he spoke next, he said, "My parents?"

She bowed her head as though considering her words. "No one has word of the Eldest and his queen. The Eldest's City is abandoned, and talk is that your father, mother, your cousin, and many others are imprisoned in the House. But no one knows."

The room was stuffy and hot, although the window was open, allowing in a breeze that tugged the curtains of Lionheart's bed and struck his face without any cooling relief. The curtains themselves were red velvet, and to his tired eyes the color seemed to blend in and out of Daylily's hair.

Rose Red was present. He saw her across the room, sitting by the window, huddled deep inside her veils. Oddly, the sight of her filled him with comfort. She, at least, of all the people of his home, was safe. She was alive, and she was near, and she was familiar.

The silence had hung too long in the room. Daylily, looking to see where Lionheart's gaze rested, felt the sudden need to speak again. "The Dragon," she said, "has given commands. No one is to leave."

Lionheart dragged his eyes back to her, though they slid around as though unwilling or unable to rest upon her face. "No one is to leave the Eldest's House?"

"All of Southlands," Daylily said. "Father told me this morning. Word has it that the Dragon has created barricades of occult workings across every port and road. Those who have tried to leave have . . . they have been destroyed. Burned." She was calm as she spoke the words, a bulwark of strength in the midst of the storm. In the presence of that strength, Lionheart found himself both chilled and emboldened. Even as the residual poison in his veins sought to drag him back down, he drew himself up, determined not to be weak before this girl who could speak of her country's doom in such cool tones.

"Bridges have been set afire," she said. "They are not ruined completely; people say that because they are of Faerie make they can't be destroyed. But since the last messengers came, they have been set afire, and they burn so hot that no one can cross them anymore. We are prisoners, cut off from one another. We are at his mercy."

"Get up, little prince."

He grimaced as the words shot across his memory. He pushed away

Daylily's hands. "Rose Red," he said, and the girl by the window leapt to her feet. "Rose Red, bring me clothes, boots, a cloak."

She hastened to do his bidding, and Daylily stood back from his bedside. "Lionheart," she said, "you have been sick with fever, and we despaired of your life. You are not yet ready to—"

"Get up and journey into the world."

The fiery voice in his memory drowned out Daylily's words. Rose Red returned with the requested items and handed them to him. He sat there, looking from her to Daylily and back again. "Please," he said, "a moment of privacy?"

"What are you proposing, Lionheart?" Daylily's face sank into a deep frown.

"I send you to your exile."

"I must go."

"Go where?"

"Journey into the world."

"He told me I must journey into the world. I . . . I believe I must go, must seek help for us."

"Didn't you hear what I just told you? Those who have tried to cross have all died. Burned, Lionheart!"

"If he told me to go, then surely he must allow me to cross the borders."

"We will meet again, Prince Lionheart."

Lionheart squared his shoulders and drew as deep a breath as his damaged lungs would permit. "This is my duty, Daylily. He has commanded me to go, and I shall do so. I will cross the borders, and I will learn how to defeat this monster. And when I know, I will return."

"Perhaps you'll find your throne after all?"

"Now, are you going to let me get dressed, or shall I scandalize you both with the sight of my nightshirt?"

Though the Baron of Middlecrescent protested more vehemently than did his daughter, Lionheart was still Prince of Southlands. He was outfitted to ride before the day was out. The baron refused to give Lionheart his blessing, but at least he rode with wishes for good luck.

Middlecrescent and Daylily agreed to ride with Lionheart as far as the nearest bridge, where they both secretly believed the prince would be forced to stop. It was engulfed in a blaze of heat, though the bridge itself did not burn. Sometimes, the baron thought, young men who refuse to hear the advice of their elders simply need to find out for themselves the hard way. So be it.

Before mounting, Lionheart asked for Rose Red to be brought to him. The servant girl approached her prince, trembling, and went down on her knees before him as though to receive a benediction.

"Rosie," he said, surprised, "why do you kneel? You've never been so formal before me!"

"My prince," she said so softly that it was difficult to hear. "My good master, I must ask a boon of you."

Lionheart smiled a little, though his heart was heavy. In Rose Red's bowed figure he saw the comfort of familiarity. He found himself longing suddenly for the friendship that had once existed between them.

His voice was heavy when he spoke. "You have always been loyal to me, Rosie. More than a servant, as you well know. How can I refuse anything you ask?"

With her head still low, she said, "I ask only that you give me a cart and a goat to pull it. And I ask that you would command this good baron, your servant, to let me return to the Eldest's House."

Lionheart blinked, and the baron, standing near, after taking a moment to decipher what he thought he had heard, swore under his breath. "Rose Red," Lionheart said, "you should not return to the House."

"But if my master's family is indeed still held inside, they must be told of your plan. They must have something to hope for, or they'll . . . they'll die."

Lionheart thought of the dragon fumes to which he had nearly succumbed, the awful, heavy despair as he had watched the dearest-held dreams of his life slain before his eyes again and again. And he thought of his parents and Foxbrush and the others imprisoned with them, surrounded night and day by that poison. Could they have survived even this long?

He went down on one knee and took hold of Rose Red's hands. She tried to pull back, but he held them even so. "Such a favor is too great," he said, speaking in a whisper so that the others nearby might not hear. "I would never ask it of you. No one should be burdened with such a task."

"But you ain't askin' me, Leo," she said. Through the slit in her veil, her eyes sought his. He thought he glimpsed them shining, though it was difficult to see through the folds of fabric. "You ain't askin' me. I'm askin' you."

He shook his head, squeezing her hands between his. Then suddenly he lifted her gloved hands and kissed them. And the baron and his daughter and the attendants standing nearby gasped and didn't know which way to look. Lionheart did not notice their whispers, or if he noticed, he did not care.

"Rose Red," he said, "was there ever a better person than you? Bless you a thousand times! Yes, I will give the order. You shall have your cart and your goat and, if the Lights Above are kind, you will go to my family. Somehow, I think that if anyone could get past that monster, you could. Here." He took a ring from his finger, a gold ring carved with his seal, a seated panther. "Use this so that everyone will know you act as my servant. But tell me, while we're at this boon-granting business, is there nothing you wish for yourself?"

Her voice was so low and soft by nature that Lionheart could not discern that it struggled to speak through tears. "My only other wish, my good master," she said, "is that you would be safe, that you would return to us whole, and soon. Also that"—and here she could hardly believe her own daring, but once begun, she had to finish— "perhaps now and then you would remember your servant."

"Dearest girl," he said, "I will remember you, and I will take comfort in knowing my parents have you yet."

With those words, he kissed her hands again, then got to his feet, leaving her where she knelt, and went to his horse. He mounted stiffly, breathing hard, for he was not yet fully recovered. But his face was determined. Let all Southlands know that, scalawag though he may be, once Prince Lionheart had set his mind on something, neither time nor tides could turn him back.

He rode from Middlecrescent Manor flanked by the baron and his daughter. When they came to the northernmost bridge of the baron's land, arching across the trench-like valley below to the far tableland, they were all three surprised to see that it was not burning as they had been told, though the smell of smoke lingered in the air.

"Nothing for it, then," Lionheart said. "Good-bye, baron, Daylily. Wish me luck. I will return, if all goes well, before the year is out."

He urged his horse forward and would have ridden across the bridge without another word. But before he had gotten far, Daylily caught up with him. "Lionheart," she said, "wait."

He pulled up, and she rode up beside him. Then, to his great surprise, she leaned forward in her saddle, caught him behind the head, and kissed him, awkwardly but soundly, on the mouth.

"There," she said when she pulled back. "Remember me too, Leo. And come back to me."

He gaped. His head for a moment cleared of dragon fire and whirled with another fiery but much more pleasant sensation. Then, his face breaking into a grin, Lionheart spurred his horse onto the bridge and, without another look back, rode from Middlecrescent.

5

Rose Red sat on the steps of the baron's house and waited, her hands folded around the prince's ring. All who looked upon her through the windows were frightened, though they couldn't say why. In those dark times, with dragon smoke spreading ever more thickly across the sky, the sight of that veiled figure, still as a statue upon the doorstep, was like something from a nightmare.

"Didn't they say the prince was bewitched by a sorceress in the mountains?" someone whispered.

"Silly talk, that!" someone else snapped, not taking wary eyes from the girl.

Rose Red, oblivious to the talk, waited, watching the road down which Lionheart, the baron, and Lady Daylily had disappeared.

The baron and his daughter returned, and Rose Red breathed a sigh. This meant Lionheart had indeed crossed the bridge and gone on his way. Whether or not she was relieved, she could not say. She rose as the baron approached, curtsying when he drew his horse up before her and dismounted.

Like Daylily's, the baron's eyes were large for his face; but unlike Daylily's, his were not beautiful. They penetrated like cold daggers. Rose Red, in the moment those eyes bore down on her, was thankful for her veil.

"Get out," the baron said.

Rose Red drew a short breath. "I was promised a goat and a cart—"

"Guards." The baron's voice did not rise, and his eyes did not leave her.

Two guards approached and grabbed Rose Red by the arms. "Father!" Daylily cried, dismounting in a rush of skirts, but had no chance to say more. For Rose Red, after an instant's surprise, screamed and, with strength the guardsmen did not expect, hurled first one and then the other from her. They staggered back, surprised, and Rose Red turned upon the baron.

"I was promised a goat and a cart," she declared and held up Prince Lionheart's signet ring. "You heard the prince yourself, and you saw him give me his ring. Now do as he wished!"

The baron's mouth hardened into a thin line, his gaze fixed on her. "You will not order me about on my own land, witch," he said. "I am not under your spell."

Terror filled her, and Rose Red stepped back, turning from the baron to the guardsmen and back again. "The prince—" she began.

"He is as good as dead." The baron spoke smoothly, without emotion. His focus shifted briefly to the ring in her hand. "That will do you no good now."

Rose Red stood frozen. Then she clutched the ring tight to her chest, slumping into herself. The baron motioned, and the guards stepped forward again; this time when they grabbed her, she made no protest.

"Father," Daylily said in a voice as cold as the baron's own, "you cannot gainsay Prince Lionheart's wishes. The Eldest could be dead, for all we know, and Lionheart, your sovereign. You dare not disobey him."

The baron gave his daughter a mirthless smile. "Lionheart will not leave the country alive, my sweet child. He's a fool to try, and he will not return." He reached out and patted her cheek. Daylily stood woodenly, as though enduring some offense. The baron continued, "There is no king in Southlands now, save the Dragon. And when he eventually tires of us and leaves, there will be no king at all. Then we shall see where we are."

Daylily said nothing. Rose Red stared at her from behind her veil, desperate to read her thoughts. "M'lady," she said, trying to draw her gaze. "M'lady, help me."

But it was the baron, not his daughter, who turned at the sound of her voice. His face suddenly became vicious, and he snarled to his guards, "Take her from here and . . . get rid of her."

"Father—"

"Not a word from you, child."

"Listen to me!" Daylily's voice was sharp, a voice that would kill if it could. "I was there at the Eldest's House when . . . when *he* came. I heard what he said to the prince and to this girl. I assure you, Father, if you harm her, your new 'king' will make you pay. Depend upon it."

Her heart thudding so hard in her chest that she could scarcely think, Rose Red watched Middlecrescent and his daughter stare at each other like wildcats vying for dominance. At last, without breaking Daylily's gaze, the baron spoke. "Guards, get the creature off my land. See that she leaves Middlecrescent. Alive."

They hauled Rose Red off her feet in their haste to obey. She was bound at the wrists, placed on a horse—which was terrifying in itself, for she had never ridden before in her life—and escorted across Middlecrescent by several armed men. They passed towns and villages as silent as graveyards as the people, like so many ghosts, sequestered themselves into the recesses of their homes, hoping to escape the ever-growing stench of dragon smoke as it crept across the land. Farms were abandoned, flocks and fields left untended. Nowhere was there clean air to breathe. Rose Red watched the guardsmen gradually succumb to the poison, their faces losing color, their eyes losing light.

As the day neared its end, they had not yet reached the edge of Middlecrescent. But the men hauled her from her horse. They were under orders, so they did not kill her, but there was no gentleness in them. When she stumbled to the ground, they aimed kicks at her back, and Rose Red curled up in a ball and took the blows. She did not feel them. Those steel-toed boots would have broken the ribs of anyone else, but they could not physically harm her. Instead, humiliation slapped her with every strike.

"I think we've made our point," one of them said at last, backing up and signaling for his fellows to do the same. "Follow the road before you and leave the baron's land. If you remain anywhere within his boundaries, you will not find us merciful."

"Shouldn't we take her to the bridge?" another soldier asked.

"And be out here after nightfall?" The first man shook his head. "Be my guest."

The other did not reply. They mounted their horses again and left Rose Red where she lay, still bound at the wrists, in the dirt of the road. She did not look up until long after the hoofbeats faded away. By then, night was falling.

Rose Red sat up and snapped the thick cords on her wrists without a thought. The pieces fell into her lap, and she looked at them idly. "What am I goin' to do?" she whispered into the falling darkness. But there was no one to answer her. Not Beana, not her old dad, not even . . . not even Leo, who had promised to care for her. She was truly alone.

Her veil stank of dragon smoke. The stench of nightmares. "It's my fault," she whispered, as expressionless as stone. "I should never have left the mountain. I brought him down upon us." Then she tore the veil away, flinging it to the ground. "What have I done?"

The wood thrush sang.

Silver and lovely in that gathering gloom, its voice reached out to her. And with it, she remembered.

"Let me give you something. . . . Because I might be unable to protect you once we've gone to the low country, let me give you something with which you may protect yourself."

The Name.

The Name, which had nestled deep in near-forgotten places of her mind, slipped to her lips, resting there, ready to be spoken. Just the feel of it there gave her comfort, and her breathing eased. Then Rose Red swallowed, forcing the word back inside.

"I ain't goin' to be so foolish," she muttered, rising to her feet. She did not replace the veil but clutched it in her left hand as she began the long march down the road. All was dark by now, but still she saw well enough to avoid every rut in her path, walking smoothly, like a gliding spirit. "I ain't goin' to depend on Faerie stories. I promised Leo I'd care for his family, and that's just what I'm goin' to do . . . just as soon as I can get back to the House."

The House where the Dragon waited for her.

Well, that wasn't going to stop her either. Had Rose Red not faced that Dragon in her dreams nearly every night throughout her childhood? Granted, he'd been incorporeal. But really, if one took the time to reason with oneself, why must it be so much more frightening for one's monsters to be incarnate and huge rather than disembodied? The fear was all the same. True, disembodied frights rarely swallowed a person in one gulp . . . details like that did add up. Rose Red licked her lips but maintained her rapid pace.

And she did not speak the Name.

Rose Red walked for hours across the silent landscape, feeling as though she made no progress. Not a soul met her on that lonely road. How long would it take her to reach the Eldest's House at this rate? What would she find when she got there? She'd promised Leo to care for his family, but how could she hope to fulfill that promise? The Baron of Middlecrescent had heard the prince's orders and still disregarded them. Could she possibly convince anyone else to aid her if the baron himself would not?

The silence broke with the sound of hooves on the road behind her. Rose Red immediately slipped from the road into the still darker shadows on its edge, vanishing from any searching eyes. A horse and rider appeared, the rider sitting stiffly upright. Despite the shielding cloak and hood, Rose Red recognized her immediately.

She hesitated. For a moment, she considered letting the horse trot by without speaking a word. But she'd sworn an oath, even if under duress, and must she now add oath breaker to her crimes?

The horse passed by. Rose Red slipped her veil back over her head, stepped into the road, and called out, "M'lady!"

Daylily reined in her mount. If she was frightened by that strange voice in the night, she did not show it. She turned about, her face shadowed, and it was Rose Red who trembled.

The baron's daughter said, "I hoped to find you somewhere in these parts. My father's men are much too cowardly to have borne you any farther." She urged her gelding closer and put out her hand. "Come up."

Rose Red regarded the towering height of the horse. After her first ride today, she found herself unwilling to repeat the experience, particularly seated behind Lady Daylily. "What will your father say, you bein' out here?"

Daylily shrugged, her hand still extended.

"He'll throttle you!" Rose Red shook her head and stepped back. "You've got to go home, m'lady."

Daylily's eyes narrowed.

"It ain't safe!" Rose Red insisted. "*He* ain't safe, and I'm goin' straight to him, just like I promised Leo. But it don't matter if he burns me to a crisp. I've got to do as I promised the prince, and I will. It don't matter if I never come back. But you—"

"Do you honestly believe I have so weak a will?"

Rose Red could not breathe under Daylily's hard countenance. She curtsied deeply there in the dark before that great horse. "M'lady, what would my master do if you were taken too?" she whispered. "Think of Leo."

"I am thinking of Leo," Daylily said. "Take my hand and come up behind me. We are going to the Eldest's House to fulfill your promise."

Still Rose Red hesitated. Daylily's voice became very dark. "Remember, you are my servant as well."

Hating herself, hating the world, hating that Dragon and especially Daylily, Rose Red obeyed. With the lady's assistance, she scrambled up onto the gelding's back and clung to Daylily's belt as they continued down the road. The baron would pursue them, she suspected, might catch them before they even reached the next bridge. Or perhaps they would find themselves at a dead end at the bridge, for had not the messengers said all the bridges were burning?

Before the night was through, they approached Starling Bridge, which separated Middlecrescent from Idlewild. Like all the great bridges of Southlands, it did not span a river but a gorge. Some said that ancient rivers had once flowed throughout Southlands, cutting the ground deeply; if so, those were long since gone, replaced by younger rivers in shallower beds. But the gorges remained, and grown up inside them were the dark Wilderlands where nobody dared walk, though nobody could say why. It was an unspoken rule far stronger than mere superstition.

Be that as it may, Rose Red did not like to think what she and Daylily would do if the bridge did burn. The nearest crossing was many days' ride east, and they would not make it were the baron to give pursuit.

But they saw Starling Bridge from a distance, white and shining and free of flame. Rose Red breathed in relief at the sight. Daylily urged her horse across, though it shivered and protested. Its hooves clattered like drums on the boards and braces. Rose Red heard the whispering of the trees below them, like the sound of the sea.

Then they were across and on their way into Idlewild. Rose Red breathed deeply, perhaps in relief, and turned to look back the way they had come.

Starling Bridge burst into flames behind them.

Lionheart rode hard for many days, and when he came to the mountains in the north, he left his horse behind and crossed over on foot. He could only hope the Dragon did not spot him.

Lionheart grew ever more thankful for the time he'd spent tramping about the countryside of Hill House. It had toughened him up for this long journey through the Circle of Faces. He did wish he had brought more food and less gold. It weighed him down, and what good did it do? He met no one. The highland shepherds and miners who lived amid these mountains had all fled when the Dragon came. Lionheart wondered if any of them had escaped Southlands.

He came at last to the crest of a hill from which, when he looked south, he could see his kingdom spread before him, covered in a haze of smoke. He turned quickly from that sight to look north.

The sun was dazzling in a clear sky beyond the Dragon's canopy. It glittered upon the Bay of Chiara, the wide blue expanse that separated

Southlands from the mainland save for a narrow isthmus. Only twice before had Lionheart seen the Chiara, when his father brought him along on visits to Shippening and Beauclair. Its beauty never failed to make him catch his breath, even now in his fugitive state. His heart thrilled at the prospect before him, not only the greatness of the sea, but also the greatness of freedom.

Freedom.

He cursed himself when he realized what word he'd dared think. This was exile, not an escape! He was duty bound to find what he sought and then to return. Yet somehow he could not suppress the excitement that rose inside him, and he started on the downward path with an eager step.

A shadow passed over him.

Lionheart yelped and ducked behind a rock, crouching down with one arm flung over his head. There was precious little light beneath those thick clouds, but the Dragon's wings, swooping over him, nevertheless cast a shadow. Lionheart's throat clogged as he breathed in a gasp of poison. So this was the end of his brave venture! Here, crouched like a rat hiding from a terrier.

The Dragon landed among the crags of Bald Mountain, high above him. The Dragon held so still that, as the evening descended, he seemed to melt into the rocks, a strange formation of stone. But his eyes were red.

For an age Lionheart crouched, and he and the Dragon watched each other. At last, though his knees shook so that they scarcely supported him, Lionheart pushed himself upright. If he was to die, he decided, he would make certain his last step was forward on his quest, not retreating in defeat. He started down the track.

The Dragon did not move.

All night, without pause, Lionheart made his way down the mountain. Though exhaustion threatened to fell him, he kept going, goaded on by the brands of the Dragon's eyes. He did not dare look back to where the Dragon sat, but he felt those eyes watching him.

When morning came, Lionheart found himself stepping out onto the isthmus. The mountains were behind him, and Southlands. Only then did he turn back for a final look.

The Dragon was gone.

6

No lights winked in the windows of the Eldest's House, no life teemed behind its doors. It crouched like a rabbit in an open field, frozen in forlorn hope that the hawk would not strike, knowing that even then the talons were spread.

Its contours were the same: the familiar minarets rising like sentinels, the great iron gates, and the gardens spreading as far as the eye could see beyond. But all the colored stones were filmed over in black ash, and a great column of smoke rose from the courtyard as if a bonfire burned there.

A goat bleated at the back gate.

"Baaaah!" She rammed the gate with her hard little head until the iron rang like a bell. But it would not give. "I know you're in there! Open to me at once. I command you!"

No answer.

The netherworld boasts many furies and frights, but in that moment, none could be considered half so fearsome as that one highly irate nanny. Her yellow eyes gleamed like a devil's, her bearded chin quivered, and her cloven hooves pawed at the turf as if she were a bull preparing to charge. But the gate remained solid before her. The Dragon's spells were strong indeed.

Beana backed up a few paces to better see through the bars into the yard beyond. This gate separated her from the inner gardens, where the queen and her ladies used to stroll. Flowerless rosebushes and a hundred other plants grew here. Only now they withered into themselves, like the House itself, under the Dragon's poison.

The goat muttered, her jaw working. Then she spoke a word, or perhaps a series of words, in some language that only a goat's tongue could pronounce. She waited expectantly.

Nothing happened.

"BAH!" The gate rang again with her ramming. "Don't try these silly games with me!" she bellowed. "I'm not afraid of you."

"I know you're not," said the Dragon.

He appeared with the suddenness of a shadow across the sun, standing on the far side of the gate. He bore the appearance of a man, standing upright on two legs. Hair hung about his face like a hood, black against his leprous-white skin.

The goat stared up at him as though she would like nothing more than to ram all her fury right into his knees. But the iron bars separating them would not give.

"What you have failed to consider," said the Dragon with a hint of a smile, "is whether or not I am afraid of you."

"You should be," said the goat. "If you realized who I—"

"Oh, but I do know exactly who you are," said he, stepping closer to the gate. His thin lips curled back, revealing long fangs. "I do not forget an offense such as yours so quickly, Lady of Aiven. Thief. Trespasser."

The goat said nothing for a long moment. Then she spoke in a very different voice. "Let me in."

"Never again."

"You know your own doom. I spoke it myself all those centuries ago."

"Like yesterday."

"I'll not touch you. It is not my destiny to accomplish the words given me on the shores of the Final Water."

"Comforting as this may be," said the Dragon, "it hardly convinces me that I want you back within the borders of my realm."

Beana tensed, and her eyes flashed again. "This is not your realm."

"Yet I am king."

"Usurper! You dare not claim this land as your own. My Prince will not allow—"

The Dragon snarled, and flames dropped from his mouth, scattering about his feet. "What of your Prince, lady knight? This land is mine, and he has done nothing to stop me. Southlands and all this household are firmly in my grasp, and so shall be the heart of his Beloved. Do your worst, Lady of Aiven, you who abandoned your people, who stole from your own father! Pitiless woman, I will never allow you back within my boundaries."

A knock rang across the courtyards, across the gardens, carrying to their ears all the way from the opposite side of the Eldest's House. Incongruous and strange, like timid guests stopping in for tea.

The Dragon smiled then. "My company has arrived."

Beana lunged again at the gate, pressing her body against the bars. "Don't you *dare* admit her! Leave her alone!"

"But she's come calling, my lady," said the Dragon. "How rude would I be to leave her waiting?"

He was gone. Smoke swirled where he had stood.

Beana bleated, and her hooves tore up charred turf as she raced around the wall, desperate to reach the far side in time. "Rosie!" she called as she ran, though she knew her voice would not carry far enough. "Rosie, don't go in!"

She rounded that side of the wall in time to see the little chambermaid and the baron's tall daughter before the gate. She saw, as they could not, the Dragon standing just beyond, opening the door to admit them. They entered with hesitant steps, feeling his eyes upon them but otherwise unable to sense his immediate presence. Beana gave a last despairing bleat. "Rosie!"

The gate slammed shut, ringing and final.

※

Rose Red stood just inside the courtyard of the Eldest's House, Daylily close behind her. She gazed through her veil at the strange landscape this yard had become. The beautiful Starflower Fountain lay in a smoldering pile. Some of the marble stones still glowed red, and the faces of that lady and her wolf nemesis were melted beyond recognition. Only the stone wood thrush, which had sat upon Starflower's stone shoulder, remained recognizable.

Smoke surrounded everything in a haze, and the air was thick in their lungs. All was deathly quiet, a stark contrast to the screaming, blazing terror that yard had been when last Rose Red had seen it.

"The gate is shut," Daylily said. Neither of them had heard it slam. Other than their own voices and breathing, not a sound could be heard in that place. Daylily licked her lips. "Perhaps a breeze caught it."

"No," Rose Red whispered. "No, I think not." She took a step forward. And froze.

Something was wrong. Not just the smoke, not just the ruin. She had known it would be thus, had prepared herself for it over the course of the long journey from Middlecrescent. She had even prepared herself for the sight of the stables, decimated beyond recall and smoldering like the remains of a great bonfire. Of course the Dragon would destroy them and probably feed upon the creatures inside, poor luckless things. Not on Beana, though. No, Beana must be fine. She *must* be; Rose Red wouldn't consider any other possibility. But while dragons could, according to folklore, live entirely on their own self-sustaining fire, they notoriously craved flesh and blood to supplement that diet.

Rose Red swallowed, refusing to let her mind pursue that track. She took another step, then stopped once more.

Something was terribly, terribly off.

"We'll get nowhere dithering here," Daylily said. "Now we've come, we've come. Might as well go through with it." Gathering her heavy skirts, she began making great strides across the courtyard into the swirling smoke. Rose Red stifled a cry and instead hissed through her teeth, "M'lady, wait!"

"Wait for what?" Daylily's voice was like ice, though it trembled faintly. Rose Red wanted to draw her back from the house, from the rubble of the fountain, from that great front door which, though shut, seemed to beckon to them. A heavy presence lurked within the smoke.

The presence of the Dragon, the presence of his poison, and . . . something more.

"It's not safe," Rose Red said.

"Really? I would hardly have guessed." Daylily set her shoulders and continued across the courtyard, around the remains of the fountain, and up the front steps. And though she hated every step she took, Rose Red had no choice but to follow.

They entered the Eldest's House. They did not see the Dragon holding the door for them to pass inside. They did not hear Beana crying out to them from the gate. They entered the Eldest's House, and the door shut behind them.

The Dragon was, and always had been, King.

There was no time in this world. The shadows never shifted, never stirred. One might sit unmoving for hours, breathing in the searing scent of his poison, and it seemed like moments. His eyes, invisible, watched from every corner, for this was his house now, his kingdom, and there could be no hiding.

Queen Starflower sat before her long mirror in her private chambers, gazing upon but not seeing her own face. She was alone. She had always been alone. The others were all dead, she knew with a certainty beyond doubt. Perhaps they had never lived. Perhaps they too were nothing but a dream bound to die in this world to which she had awakened. Her husband, her son, her nephew . . . nothing but phantoms in this world, this dark, smoke-shrouded reality where dreams must die.

A voice called in some passage beyond her chambers.

"I'm lost! I'm lost!"

A young man's voice. Her son's? No, she had no son. Her nephew? No, she had dreamed him too. A ghost, then. A ghost of a wish for a life less lonely. But her life had always been lonely. This was the truth of it. Always she had shielded herself away and now she lived the life she had built with her own two hands. Alone in the darkness, in this place where the Dragon was King.

A tall man stood behind her, meeting her gaze in the mirror's reflection. His eyes were black, and red fire gleamed in their pupils.

"Breathe deep," he whispered. "Breathe in the death of dreams."

She obeyed. Poison filled her heart.

"All must come to me in the end," he said.

A hand at the door latch. The Dragon turned and bared his teeth in what might have been a snarl, but just as easily could have been a smile. Then he vanished, and Queen Starflower saw nothing but empty space reflected above her. She was alone. She had always been—

"Your Majesty!"

A strange person filled her vision; strange but no more terrible than the rest of this nightmarish reality. Starflower was unafraid. She gazed with eyes made calm with despair at the wraithlike figure covered in veils that appeared behind her in the glass.

"Your Majesty," said the little person, "please get up. We've got to get you out of here."

"I know you, don't I?" said the queen slowly, as though the words must travel across many leagues before they fell, exhausted, from her lips. "I've seen you somewhere before. In a dream, perhaps."

"I'm your son's chambermaid."

"I have no son."

"Of course you do. Don't talk such hogwash, beggin' Your Majesty's pardon." Gloved hands plucked at the queen's sleeve in the mirror, but Starflower felt nothing. She drew another long breath of dragon smoke.

"I have no son. I only dreamed him, and now the dream is dead. I must have dreamed you too, which means you too must die. Dreams cannot live here."

"Fiddle. Your son ain't no dream, and he ain't dead neither," the strange little person snapped, placing her hands on her hips. "He's alive and well, gone off to find some way to rid us of this monster. He sent me to care for you, and by Iubdan's beard, that's what I'm goin' to do! Get *up*, Your Majesty."

This time the phantom tugged so hard that the seam of her garment bit into Starflower's arm. She rose then, obediently. Why not? What did it matter one way or another in this ageless reality? Might as well humor this veiled illusion. It wouldn't make a difference.

Rose Red led the queen out of her chambers and into the hall beyond, where the baron's daughter waited. Daylily's face was as carefully expressionless as ever, but her eyes darted this way and that, up and down the long hall. A darkness like dusk had settled on the household, a gloom that was too light for candles but too dim for comfort. The rich furnishings of the household wore their shadows like mourning clothes, as though the House itself had died.

Which perhaps it had.

"Is she the last one?" Daylily asked when Rose Red emerged from the queen's chambers with Starflower in tow. They had now spent several hours combing the desolate rooms, searching for those held imprisoned. All were in a similar state to that of the queen, stunned with despair, barely living. One by one, Rose Red and Daylily had gathered them from the various rooms in which they wandered like lost spirits and led them to the kitchens, which, due to their very simplicity, seemed the least horrible of all the poison-haunted chambers. Most had come willingly enough. The Eldest, taken from his throne room, went like a lamb to the slaughter, silent tears coursing down his withered face. But some had fought, feebly, like frightened children. One man, a lesser noble, Rose Red thought, of no particular name, had fended her off with a poker and, when it became clear that she would not leave him, had tried to tear his own face with his hands. The effect of the Dragon's poison was bitter indeed.

But Rose Red, with Daylily's help, had prevailed in the end and led him to join the small cluster of prisoners sitting in the kitchen together, staring at the walls in silence.

"I think," said Rose Red, keeping her voice soft and low so as not to startle the queen, "that Sir Foxbrush is here too."

"Ah, yes," said Daylily. Her voice was vague, without interest, and she continued to look up and down the passage. Though her expression never varied, Rose Red noticed that her eyes were slowly growing rounder and rounder. Daylily's eyes had been large to begin with, but they were almost grotesque now, and ringed with black circles.

The poison was getting to her too, Rose Red thought. She'd have to get Daylily out of the house as soon as possible. She'd have to get all of them out if she could. So far there had been no sign of the Dragon himself, only of his work. Some of the windows had been torn from their frames, some of the outer walls knocked in, and the fallen stones had the appearance of having been chewed. But the Dragon was not to be found.

Maybe he was busy in some other part of the kingdom? He had given orders that no one was to leave Southlands. Did this mean he would have to patrol the borders himself?

Somehow, Rose Red suspected this wasn't the case.

"I'm lost!"

The voice called faintly from somewhere in a different passage. Rose Red turned toward the sound, still holding on to Queen Starflower's hand. It was a ghostly voice, painfully sad and alone in that gloom. A shudder ran through Rose Red's body when it came again. "I'm lost!"

"That's Foxbrush," said Daylily, her eyes wider than ever.

"He sounds close," Rose Red agreed. She glanced at the queen, standing woodenly beside her. If she tried to drag her along on a chase after that forlorn voice, they would never catch him. But she couldn't leave the queen behind.

A third time the voice cried, "I'm lost!"

"He ain't far," Rose Red said. "I think he's only one passage over. Near old Dame Fairlight's chambers. Do you know where they are, m'lady?"

Daylily nodded. Even in that half-light, with her eyes as large as a ghoul's and the poison so swiftly settling into her veins, she was beautiful. Her face was set as she struggled to keep her fear disguised.

"Can you get him?" Rose Red said.

Daylily nodded again. Without a word, she gathered her skirts and hastened ahead down the passage, disappearing around a corner. Rose Red followed more slowly, still leading the queen. Their footsteps made no sound on the thick rug. Elegant moldings decorating these walls had the strange appearance of imp faces and monsters; although if Rose Red forced herself to look closely, she saw that they were merely clusters of flowers and birds.

When they reached the end of the hall where Daylily had turned off, Rose Red pulled the queen to a gentle stop, and they waited. Rose Red counted each breath. Long, deep breaths echoing in that silent house like a banshee's sighs.

One, two, three.

Perhaps Foxbrush was farther off than she'd guessed? Beyond Dame Fairlight's passages, closer to those kept by the Baroness of Fernrise.

Seven, eight, nine.

That shadowy movement, that flicker behind them, down the passage . . . Only a curtain. Nothing more.

Twelve, thirteen, fourteen.

Once Daylily returned with Foxbrush, they would gather everyone in the kitchen. Then, out the back door and away from this place. It didn't matter that they had no supplies. They'd scavenge in the Eldest's City.

Nineteen, twenty.

It was his city, after all. If anyone had a right to scavenge, the Eldest did. Maybe they could make it to the next barony before the Dragon returned.

Twenty-four, twenty-five.

No use considering what he would do when he found them missing, or what he would do when he located them once more. Rose Red shook her head. She'd promised Leo that she would care for his family, and she'd think of something.

Twenty-nine, thirty—

"Where *are* they?" Rose Red growled. The queen startled at the sound of her voice, made some weak attempt to pull away, then sagged into still greater despair, so heavy was the poison in her lungs. Rose Red patted her hand compassionately. It wasn't right that the strong queen of Southlands was reduced to this state. Hateful, hateful monster!

Rose Red gently took the queen's arm and backed her up to the wall until she leaned against it, her shoulders slumped and her head bowed. "Wait here," Rose Red whispered. "I've got to find them. Wait here, and I'll be right back, see?"

The queen stared into the shadows over Rose Red's shoulder, but her face was not as blank as it had been. She looked as if she studied someone's face . . . only there was no one there. Rose Red shivered and patted Starflower's arm as though comforting a child. "Wait here," she repeated, slipping away.

She wanted to call for Daylily but feared the sound of her own voice echoing through those long passages. The hall down which Dame Fairlight lived was empty. Also the passage leading to the Baroness of Fernrise's chambers. The door to a lesser parlor was open, but when she looked inside, Rose Red saw no one. A spark caught her eye, and she turned. Could there be the remains of a fire glowing in the grate? No, it was empty. She must have imagined it.

Rose Red hastened on. She couldn't leave the poor queen in the darkness alone, but she must find Daylily and Foxbrush too. Why did she feel as though the House itself watched her progress? Why did she feel like a mouse fleeing the unseen owl? Her hands clutched the veil about her face as though it could protect her, and she hurried. Never before had she, a servant, made use of the main stairway, but she used it now in her haste, one hand pressing into the golden banister. Perhaps Foxbrush had wandered down to the main level before Daylily caught up with him? They certainly weren't in the east wing. She stood a moment at the bottom of the stairs, uncertain which way to turn. The whole House was an enormous maze; any turn she made was more likely to be wrong than right. And she couldn't leave the queen up there alone!

The creak of an opening door.

Under ordinary circumstances she would never have heard that soft sound. But in the silence of the Dragon's rule, it rang out like alarm bells. Rose Red darted down the hallway toward that sound. At the end of a narrow passage was a door she recognized. It opened on a spiral stair-case, a servants' stair that led up to the private rooms of the household members. Rose Red had used it a hundred times and more, coming to and from the prince's chambers in her daily tasks, often passing other servants as they went about their work. But she had never seen a member of the household near it.

Thus it struck Rose Red as odd to see Daylily and Foxbrush standing in the half-light gloom before that little door.

Neither moved as she approached, nor did they turn when she called to them. She slipped up behind them, speaking gently so as not to frighten them, and plucked at their sleeves. Still they did not respond but stood as statues. Daylily's hand was on the doorknob, and she had cracked it open. A terrible stench rolled through.

Rose Red looked around Foxbrush's arm and saw what it was they saw. "Silent Lady!" she breathed.

Pushing past Foxbrush so roughly that he fell into the wall, she slammed the door, and the whole house echoed with it. "How *dare* he?"

She grabbed Daylily's elbow and Foxbrush's wrist, dragging them back. "Come, come with me!" she said, too shaken to be gentle. "Back away now."

They moved as though drunk, staggering. Even Daylily. Rose Red could see how the poison had sunk into the deep places of her eyes; her face sagged with it. "Hen's teeth, hen's *teeth*!" Rose Red swore. How could she have let Daylily come here? Leo's betrothed, his lovely lady, and she had led her right into the Dragon's den! "I'll get you out," she said as she led them up the narrow passage. "I'll get you both out; Black Dogs take me if I don't!"

They were quite near the kitchens now, Rose Red realized. For a moment, she debated, hating to leave the queen upstairs and alone. But she dared not let these two alone again, not after . . . not after that. Taking a tight grip on their hands, she led them like two small children down the passage to the kitchens.

This passage should have been dark without candles. But the eerie half-light filtered through even here, so that the passage was no lighter and no darker than anywhere else in the house. The kitchen looked strange to Rose Red, full of silent people sitting exactly where she had left them. The Eldest sat nearest the door, his head buried in his hands. There were eighteen people, twenty altogether, now she had brought Daylily and Foxbrush. All were of noble birth, proudly dressed, from Southlands' finest families. All were reduced to quivering phantoms as they drew in more dragon poison with each breath.

She would free them. But she must find the queen first.

Rose Red sat first Daylily, then Foxbrush in chairs around one of the cutting tables. After a moment's hesitation, she carefully checked to be certain all the big carving knives and butcher's cleavers were stored where the poisoned ones would not see them. Affected as they were by the Dragon, Rose Red hesitated to trust them with any weaponry. At last, though she hated to let them out of her sight, Rose Red left them and hastened back to find the queen.

She did not have far to go. Queen Starflower had made her way down the great staircase. She was across the entrance hall when Rose Red found her, just putting her hand to the heavy front doors.

"Your Majesty!" Rose Red called and picked up her pace. "Your Majesty, wait!"

The queen did not hear her. She strained a moment, then the door gave way, swinging back and allowing the smoke in the courtyard to billow inside.

"Your Majesty!" Rose Red called again. She felt as though she were moving in a dream. Her feet refused to move as she told them. She reached out, but her arms were not long enough. "Don't go out there, not yet!"

Starflower turned and looked back over her shoulder. Her black eyes locked with Rose Red's; it was as if she could see right through the veils. Her lips moved, and her voice carried as though from far away.

"My dreams are dead."

By the time those words reached Rose Red's ears, the queen had already stepped over the threshold. "NO!" Rose Red cried.

A flash.

Like lightning but bigger; more like a meteor striking the earth. The Eldest's House shook to its foundations, and Rose Red was flung to the floor. She lay there with her arms over her head as the silence of a scream never uttered rang in her ears and heat consumed the world just beyond the doorway.

Then it was over. Rose Red uncurled and pushed herself to her feet. She staggered to the doorway, coughing in the smoke, waving it from her face. For an age, it seemed, she stood blinded on the threshold. Then at last the smoke cleared enough for her to see the melted stones that had once been the front steps.

Her nightmare incarnate stood in the courtyard, clothed in a man's shape.

"Welcome back, little princess," he said.

7

I'VE MISSED YOU."

Rose Red stood frozen on the threshold as her Dream drifted toward her like another cloud of smoke, across the destruction he had wreaked. "The last time we spoke hardly counted. No chance for intimate conversation with everyone screaming and running about the place. Hardly the reunion I had envisioned."

He reached out and slipped the veil from her face. She remained unmoving while his gaze crawled over her features.

"Princess," he said at last, "how sadly wasted you are here. So different from the child I knew in the mountains. You should have returned to me, and then I—"

"I'll never come back!" Rose Red snapped. She regained enough of herself to back away from him. But he followed her into the house, and his eyes gleamed red in its half-light. "You cain't make me come back," she said. Her voice was lost in the echoes of the great hall.

"Of course not," said he with a snarl. "After all, you have forgotten me and how once I was your only true friend. Cruel, cruel child, abandoning me for a mortal playmate! But see how my love for you continues despite your faithlessness?"

"You're despicable." She spoke with an effort, for his words besieged her senses, trying every possible weakness for an opportunity to break in and overwhelm her. "We were never friends."

"You have merely forgotten. Forgotten even the promise you made to return—"

"I made no promise!" Rose Red continued backing into the house, and he continued to follow.

"No promise?" His voice was unendingly sorrowful. The awful features, the black teeth, the sickly white skin, even the flames behind his eyes, melted away beneath that sorrow. "What about your promise to the mortal boy?"

Then his voice altered and became a horrible but perfect mimic of Prince Lionheart's: " 'Dearest girl, I will take comfort in knowing my parents have you yet.' "

Rose Red swore and turned away from the Dragon, hiding her face in her hands. But he drifted closer, like evening closing in around her. "What a fine job you've done with that promise of yours."

She pulled herself upright and glared in his face. Though all his features were still wrung with sorrow and regret, deep down in the depths of his eyes, she saw a smile.

Rose Red bared her teeth and slapped him.

Though her hand touched his face for only a moment, it burned all the way through her glove and on down through her skin, to the bone. Pain shot through her arm, up her neck, and into her head. But she was angry now.

"You killed her! You demon! Why did you go and do that? You have no quarrel with her. It was meanness; it was evil! Monster!" Rose Red knew she sounded like a child, screaming in his face. She didn't care. She clutched her burned hand to her chest and yelled so that her voice rang through the Eldest's House, disturbing the half-light and shadows. "I know who the real mountain monster was all along. You plague people's dreams, you plague their hearts, you leave them frightened upon their pillows in the small hours of darkness, and they're terrified to even live. No wonder they poured all that hatred on me. You *made* me an outcast. You did! If not for my old dad and Beana—"

Her voice broke there. An overwhelming loneliness swept across Rose Red, leaving her panting and empty as she glared up at the Dragon.

He handed her the veil. "Put this on, princess. You are not ready to walk without it in this place. Not until you let me kiss you."

"I ain't *never* goin' to let you kiss me." But her voice was a whisper, barely audible.

"You think not," said the Dragon. "However, I won the game." He leaned down. He was so tall that he had to bend nearly double to bring his face level with hers. Rose Red found herself desperately wishing for even the slim protection of her veil between them, and she twisted it in both hands.

"My darling," said he, "you are in my world now. I warned you, didn't I? 'Return to me, or I will come for you,' I said. Well, I've come for you now, and you are mine."

Rose Red stared into his black eyes, into the fires deep inside. She would scorch in them, she knew. With an effort, she turned away.

And the Name sprang to her mouth. She did not speak it, but it rested there on her tongue, ready. Its presence, even unspoken, filled her heart, relieved her spirit, and she breathed fresh air once more.

When she opened her eyes, the Dragon was gone.

She stood in the smoke of the hallway. The queen was dead. The House was haunted. The moment of peace was come and gone. But the memory of it lingered. Even as Rose Red knelt and covered her face with the veil to hide her weeping, she clung to that moment. She would not let herself think of her failure. She would not allow herself to imagine Leo's sorrow when he returned and learned of his mother's fate. There were others who still needed her—the Eldest, Foxbrush, Daylily, and the other sad captives waiting for her in the kitchen. She could not lead them out of the House. The Dragon would kill them; she knew that now. But she could care for them and feed them and do her best to relieve their suffering. For the Dragon's poison had no effect on her, at least, none that she could feel. So she would care for the prisoners, as much a prisoner as they, and wait for Leo's return.

For he would return and slay the Dragon. She knew he would.

At last Rose Red dried her tears and started back for the kitchen. At least she would not yet have to explain the queen's death to the others. In their poisoned state they would not comprehend.

The half-light never altered. When Rose Red entered the kitchen, it looked exactly as she had left it, dim and melancholy. The despair on the prisoners' faces was increased by the shadows settling into the hollows of their cheeks. She went to the Eldest first, gently taking his hand. He did not notice her. The tears had dried on his face, once so stern and strong, now withered into that of an old man. His eyes sought the window, though the smoke swirled too heavily against the glass to allow any view of the outside world. They were cut off from other worlds entirely, floating somewhere in a dark limbo.

Rose Red shuddered at this thought. She murmured comforting words to King Hawkeye that she did not think he heard, then moved on to the next prisoner. She came at length to Foxbrush, who sat bolt upright in his chair near the large kitchen fireplace. He looked strange to Rose Red with his hair unoiled and sticking up about his face. He bore a strong resemblance to his cousin, especially at this moment with his normally squinting eyes opened as wide as they would go, staring, staring. . . .

Staring at what? Rose Red turned to follow his gaze. One of the kitchen doors stood ajar, revealing a narrow passage that, Rose Red knew, eventually took one to a small breakfast room where the queen had liked to sit most mornings. Foxbrush stared at it with something between terror and rapt fascination.

"Sir Foxbrush," Rose Red whispered, touching his cheek with one finger. "You all right, there?"

He did not move. Rose Red poked him again and waved her hand before his eyes. Not even a blink. Rose Red gulped and turned back to the door. Perhaps *he* stood just beyond. Terrorizing these poor prisoners with his presence. As though his poisons weren't torment enough! She set her jaw and marched to the door, flinging it wide.

A half-lit passage, empty, lay beyond.

Rose Red narrowed her eyes at Foxbrush. "There ain't nothin' here, Sir Foxbrush," she said. "You're safe with me—Silent Lady!" She gasped and pressed a hand to her chest, whirling back to look down the hall.

For she realized that Daylily was not in the kitchen.

"Silent Lady shield us," Rose Red whispered, then hastened down the hall, one hand pressed against the wall to guide her in that awful half-light, her burned hand clutched to her chest as though she could somehow still her racing heart. Not Daylily too! Not her master's beautiful betrothed! He'd already lost his mother today . . . she could not allow him to lose his lady! She must find her. How could she have been such an idiot as to allow Daylily to accompany her here? She should have shown more will and stood up to her, should have disobeyed orders for the lady's sake. It wasn't in Rose Red's nature to disobey, but what excuse was that now? She should have known the poison would affect even the baron's daughter! For all her beauty, for all her strength, she was only mortal.

The breakfast room was empty, but the far door stood open. Rose Red went through it, paused a moment in the passage beyond, uncertain which direction Daylily would have taken. Then her heart sank to her stomach, and she thought she would be sick.

For she knew exactly where Daylily had gone.

She could not help it. Her pace slowed despite all her efforts to hurry. Fear grabbed her by the shoulders and struggled to hold her back. "I'm doin' what he wants," she told herself. "I shouldn't go; it's just what *he* wants me to do! I should go back, care for the others, give her up for lost. Leo will understand. Or if he don't . . ."

Even as she tried to convince herself, she knew she would not succeed. Though everything in her spirit warned her away, Rose Red continued doggedly forward until she came at last to that narrow pass where she had found Daylily and Foxbrush (was that only minutes ago? It felt like hours, or days) standing before a door that led to a servants' stair.

The door she had shut with such force.

The door that was now open again.

It gaped like jaws, and there was no stairway spiraling up. Instead, a tunnel lay beyond the door, a tunnel leading down, down, into darkness.

As Rose Red stood in that doorway, her hands clutching the frame, she thought she heard a trickle of water, a stream, deep inside.

It was the mouth of the mountain monster's cave. Here, in the Eldest's House. A stench like death rose up to meet her.

"Silent Lady," she whispered. "Silent Lady!"

She bowed her head and shuddered as she drew another long breath of that stench. Never, in all her life, had she been more alone than she was now, standing at Death's own door.

How long Rose Red stood no one could have said. But the only observer in that household, watching from the darkest shadows, knew full well what she would eventually do, no matter how long it took her to reach the decision. He knew; and when she passed through the doorway and vanished into the darkness of that cave, he smiled. Fire gleamed in his mouth.

PART FOUR

1

The Near World

Of all the kennel boys working for the Duke of Shippening in Capaneus City, one was most likely to be plucked from his regular duties and transferred to the serving staff should a position need filling. This had something to do with his appearance (which was pleasant in a boyish sort of way), much to do with his manners (which were better than the duke's), and something to do with his knowledge of a household servant's tasks, unusual in one who worked with dogs.

The first time he had volunteered to wait at table, the head butler had laughed a bitter sort of laugh. The head butler was a man of some taste and culture, well aware that his master the duke wouldn't have cared two straws whether a dog-boy served his ale or not. To what a state the Duchy of Shippening had fallen! No better than the days when barbarian thanes had roared drunkenly at table and thrown bones to the hounds underfoot.

But the lad had insisted on giving a demonstration of his abilities, and the butler was pleased to note that, though stiff and unnatural in his movements, he did indeed know the basic requirements of the work.

Thus Lionheart did not spend his entire life exercising the duke's hounds and cleaning out their kennels. Some evenings, he stood with his back to the wall in the duke's fine dining hall, assisting guests as needed.

One fine evening, Lionheart cleaned himself up after a day in the kennels, bending over a tiny basin and working without the aid of a mirror. His quarters, which he shared with three other men of the same occupation, were located behind the stables and beside the kennels, where the baying of the duke's hunting hounds could wake the dead at any hour of the day or night. It was not the ideal situation for sprucing up in preparation for housework. Not that the duke would notice if a serving boy's cravat was crooked. But the butler would.

Lionheart slicked down his hair with water and comb (which was intended for use on the hounds' coats, but he was in no position to complain). Pennies. That was all this job was worth . . . pennies. Barely enough to live on. So this was freedom, then. This was a life without expectations or restraints.

But a man must eat. To eat, he must work. To work, he must not be too proud. Especially when he was a dark-skinned foreigner in exile. Ultimately, this job at the kennels paid better than other work available in Capaneus City—he wasn't starved. But he would need money if he was to travel, if he was to learn.

If he was to discover how dragons may be slain.

Lionheart paused in the task of taming his hair, pressing his fingers into his scalp. He'd like to push that thought right out of his head. How could he hope to discover that secret? Trapped here, no better than a kenneled hound himself, working day in and day out just to feed himself. Already months had flown by, faster than he would have thought possible, and he had traveled no farther than Capaneus.

The Duchy of Shippening was separated from Southlands by the Chiara Bay and a thin isthmus. Lionheart had walked that isthmus, escaping the barriers of the Dragon's prison, and entered freedom. At least, the sort of freedom that is to be found in a city like Capaneus. The freedom to be mugged within moments of foolishly showing one's purse. The freedom to be beaten and left in a gutter. The freedom to crawl from the gutter again and beg for work wherever one could find it, thanking the Lights Above for the menial position of kennel boy for the duke.

Lionheart found himself more captive than ever: captive to his duty, equally captive to his inability to fulfill it.

Tell me what you want.

He didn't know what he wanted, but it wasn't this.

"Look out now, chappies." One of the kennel boys who shared the tiny room with Leo sprawled on his pallet bunk, lazily chewing a straw. He rolled over suddenly, spat out the straw, and pointed out the door. Leo turned to look where he indicated. "The duke's Fool has got out. Look at 'im! Strangest joke of a fellow you ever did see."

Lionheart had to agree. One rarely saw the poor Fool outside the duke's house. But there he was, wandering around the side of the stables and approaching the kennel, taking hesitant steps. His neck was long for his body, and it craned about as he looked here and there.

"Think he's gone and lost hisself?" asked one of the other kennel boys, just returned from running a pack and reeking of sweat and slobber. He wiped a dirty hand down his face, shaking his head. "He ain't supposed to leave the house, is he?"

"Well, go fetch him back, then," said the first boy.

"I ain't goin' near him! He's madder than a sack of starved ship rats."

"All the more reason to not let him near the dogs."

"*You* go catch him!"

Lionheart put up both hands. "It's all right, fellows. I'll get him."

He stepped from their shack of a room out into the yard. "Loons of a feather," one kennel boy said, and the other nodded and tapped his forehead.

Lionheart eyed the duke's Fool. Having rounded that side of the stables, the poor man had caught sight of the dog kennels, and these apparently frightened him. In any case, he'd pressed his back against the stable wall and closed his eyes, and his lips moved soundlessly. He certainly appeared mad, but Lionheart didn't, in that moment, fear him. Perhaps he should have. But since he'd stared down the Dragon's burning throat, one simple madman held little terror for him.

This Fool was a strange person, though. He was abnormally thin, too thin, really, to continue living. His jester's garb of brilliant colors sagged on his frame; yet his wrists, though tiny and more delicate than a woman's, were not emaciated and bony. He was an albino, whiter than snow, and rather beautiful in a way.

It was a wonder to see the man so near. Years ago, when Lionheart was a boy, the Duke of Shippening had sent this very same Fool to the Eldest's House to perform. What a marvel he'd been then, so merry in his brilliant colors, so strange with his white face and white hair. One would never have thought that he could be sad or frightened . . . though, in retrospect, Lionheart realized that he'd been quite mad. As a child, Lionheart had seen only the fun, heard only the laughter, and marveled at the feats and skills the madman had demonstrated.

Lionheart's fingers itched with remembrance of his own juggling days. Once upon a time, he'd thought to become a jester himself. He'd planned to run away from home, from the crown, from Southlands, and take up the merry life of a performer.

Well, he'd certainly run away now. But things never turned out like one envisioned as a child.

The Fool appeared unaware of Lionheart's approach. He continued murmuring to himself, and Lionheart realized as he neared that the Fool was speaking words, although not in a language Lionheart knew. Upon the few occasions he'd served at the duke's table, Lionheart had seen the Fool perform. But then his voice had been animated, and his eyes bright and lively as he bounded about the room. Now the voice was low, soft, and full of heartache.

"*Els jine aesda-o soran!*"

It wasn't gibberish. Lionheart thought that, with different ears, he might understand what the Fool said, even without knowledge of the language. It was more like music than language anyway. Like a wood thrush's song.

"*Aaade-o Ilmaan!*"

Lionheart licked his lips. The poor Fool, his face turned a little away, looked so distressed in his madness. Lionheart wondered what he could say to comfort him. This must be how his insanity took him sometimes, these wild words, this incomprehensible fear.

Something gleamed about the Fool's throat, an iron ring such as criminals wore when chained to a post. A necklace, maybe, but a strange one with that jester's motley.

Suddenly the Fool no longer spoke gibberish. Lionheart, who was now fairly near, distinctly heard him say in the same singsong voice, but in a language he knew, "If I but knew my fault!"

And here the Fool's eyes opened. They were very large and very wet, like clearest water. Shining but without color. They focused on Lionheart. There were never such sad eyes before in all the world.

"I blessed your name, O you who sit enthroned beyond the Highlands."

"Um," said Lionheart. "Are you supposed to be out here, old chap?"

The Fool stopped singing but did not shift those sorrowful eyes from Lionheart's face. At last he said in a voice as liquid as his eyes, "She has you in her hand."

Lionheart blinked. "Come again?"

"The Lady."

"What lady?"

"The Lady of Dreams." The Fool clenched fists with fingers abnormally long. Now that Lionheart really looked at them, he saw that each finger sported an extra joint. What a hideous mutation! "I pity you more than I pity myself."

"Um," said Lionheart again. He was uncertain of the approach one should take when addressing a madman. Was he likely to turn aggressive at any moment? He appeared docile, but those were the ones to watch for, weren't they? "I don't think you're supposed to be out here." He wondered if he dared take the poor Fool by the arm.

"No," said the Fool softly. "I'm not supposed to be out here in the world beyond. It is very hot. I will burn."

"Which means you should come back inside," Lionheart agreed. "You will sunburn with that fair skin of yours, won't you? Come." He beckoned gently. The madman gazed long at Lionheart's hand, then bowed his head and moved as directed, back around the corner of the stables. He started muttering to himself again in that strange tongue that, though beautiful, gave Lionheart the shivers. Lionheart tried to cover it up with soothing sounds such as, "There, there," which were entirely inadequate.

Suddenly the madman turned to Lionheart and said, "What has she promised you?"

"What do you mean?" Lionheart asked.

"The Lady. Death's sister. What has she promised to give you?"

Lionheart tried to smile but found it difficult. "I don't know what you're talking about. Let's get you inside—"

"What do you want more than anything in the world?"

It was impossible to brush off the compelling tone of the Fool's voice or to disregard the expression on his almost luminous face. Lionheart gulped and bowed his head to avoid that gaze. And suddenly he found himself saying what he had never intended to speak aloud.

"I want . . . freedom. But there is no freedom," he added quickly. He was trapped here in a menial job. He was free of all boundaries and expectations but remained captive. He could not even fulfill his task.

He could not kill the Dragon.

"I cannot give you freedom," said the Fool. "But neither can the Lady, though she will tell you that she can."

Lionheart smiled at the madman, meeting his gaze again. Poor, sad fellow! "I don't expect you or any lady to give me anything. I just want you to come back inside."

"If you will break my chains, I will grant you a wish."

The Fool grabbed Lionheart's hands with his long, many-jointed fingers. Lionheart felt how strong they were and, simultaneously, how weak. He was scared but tried not to show it. After all, the worst thing one could do with a madman was demonstrate fear, right? Rather like with dogs. Make them believe you are in charge, even if they're the ones with the teeth.

"It's not wise to go around granting people's wishes," Lionheart said, continuing to smile stiffly. "They might wish for something unhealthy."

"They always do."

"Besides, you have no chains." Lionheart's voice was calming despite its slight tremble. "Come, my friend."

"Do you not see my chains?"

The Fool reached up and grabbed the iron collar around his neck. It was not a chain; Lionheart could see the latch where it snapped together, and could see how easily it could be undone. The Fool could have plucked it off in an instant. Instead, he grimaced, hissing between his teeth, and dropped the collar, flexing his long fingers as though in pain. "Iron," he said. "Iron chains!"

Lionheart wished very much that he'd stayed away and let someone else deal with this creature. He wasn't as funny as one might expect from a jester. "Let's get you inside," he said again and firmly took the Fool's arm. His fingers wrapped all the way around the tiny bone, but Lionheart was surprised to feel strength in that arm. The Fool offered no protest as Lionheart led him back to the duke's house. "You have a performance tonight at supper, yes?"

"And tomorrow, another," said the Fool. "And tomorrow's morrow. And after and after and after."

The duke's house, despite the best efforts of the well-meaning butler, was in a constant state of disarray, suited to the duke himself. Lionheart brought the Fool to a back door but could convince no one to take him and put him where he belonged. Thus Lionheart found himself obliged to drag the poor idiot around the house with him for the next hour as he finished his own arrangements for that night's banquet. The duke was hosting a merchant from the Far East with the same courtesy (or lack thereof) with which he would have hosted a count of Beauclair, an earl of Milden, or a mere farmer of Parumvir. Social niceties meant nothing to the Duke of Shippening; just so long as he remained firmly at the top of the pecking order, he cared not who dined with him.

So Lionheart, wearing borrowed linens, stood along the wall, ready to wait at table. He'd stashed the Fool away in a nearby corridor, figuring that the poor man was as prepared as he could be for the night's performance. It bothered him as he stood at his post to think how unhappy the idiot was. But what could one expect from so deep-rooted a madness?

Strange, Lionheart thought. The Fool had not aged a day in the many years since he had visited Southlands.

The duke arrived, along with his guest, and settled comfortably into his chair. The duke was an enormous man with face and hands like a bear's, lacking only the teeth and claws. His clothing, though rich, was dirty and ill fitting, stretched tightly across his great frame. He treated his apparel with an abandon only the very rich can afford.

After seeing the duke drop food down his front and do nothing to clean it, Lionheart averted his eyes. An utter barbarian and, as far as Lionheart could discern, stupid to boot. Shippening was once a fine land with a fine history, the most powerful trade center on the Continent, governed by a Master of the Six Towers. One found it difficult to recall those glory days when observing its current master.

The eastern merchant was far more interesting, a stern and handsome man richly clad in silks (of which he took great care), with hair blacker than Lionheart's own, though his skin was pale. Lionheart guessed that he came from the Noorhitam Empire, though he might hail from Aja or any one of the kingdoms of the East. Watching him, Lionheart felt a sudden sorrow, recalling a boyhood declaration:

"When I'm a jester, I'm going to write my own songs. Better ones than Sir Eanrin's. Just wait. And I'll sing them for all the kings of the Continent."

"All of 'em?"

"And the emperors of the East!"

So much for that dream.

Lionheart deduced that this fine easterner thought little of the slovenly duke. The way he watched Shippening's master gave Lionheart the shivers . . . as though he were measuring him out for meat. Yet there was also a certain fear in the merchant's eyes, and with it, respect. This puzzled Lionheart. Though he worked for the man, he had yet to discover anything respectable about the Duke of Shippening.

"So," said Shippening, turning to his guest with his mouth full, "what do you think of our neighbors these days?"

"How means your lordship?" inquired the merchant. His accent was perfect, better than the duke's.

"Occupied, they say," the duke replied. "Enslaved by—get this—a *dragon*. Hence the smoke, see?"

Lionheart went cold.

The merchant nodded. "Do you doubt this tale?"

"I've no cause to doubt it. We ain't heard two words from our brown brothers these many months, and the smoke don't dissipate, now, does it? Seems farfetched, I'll grant you that . . . but who among us wants to venture in and verify the truth of the matter?"

It was all Lionheart could do to sit there and listen to the duke's laughter. His grip on his assigned amphora of wine tightened. But when the duke finished chuckling to himself, he said to the merchant, "I suppose you believe it all, don't you? Don't your people worship a dragon? Or some firebird or something?"

The merchant's face was a mask. "My land is vast and its people varied, stemming from many cultures. There are those who worship the Lady and her Dark Brother, and yes, one of his incarnations is that of a dragon."

The Lady. This distracted Lionheart momentarily from his thoughts of murdering the duke with a well-aimed swipe of an amphora. The Fool had mentioned a Lady too. Was she the same one the merchant spoke of now? Was she somehow associated with the Dragon?

For the Dragon was unbearably real. Perhaps this Lady was as well.

Half memories tugged at Lionheart's brain: memories of sleepless nights when bedroom drapes resembled a long-haired woman; memories of a voice and white eyes. But these were stranger even than the reality of the Dragon . . . or the much more pressing reality of the duke's objectionable existence.

"Where's my Fool?" the duke bellowed abruptly, slamming the table repeatedly with his fist. "Where is he?"

There was some scuffle. Lionheart wondered if he should abandon his post and fetch the poor madman himself, uncertain if anyone else knew where he was hiding. But a moment later, the albino in his brilliant costume stepped into the middle of the room.

He always wore a melancholy face while performing, but before, Lionheart had seen it as part of his act. This time, as he observed the Fool, he realized that the poor man was dying by inches. He could not laugh, even had he wished to.

"There you are!" the duke cried. "Sing us a song, will you? A good one for our eastern friend here. Perhaps something about dragons, since his folk are so fond of them."

"Your lordship," said the merchant, his voice sharp, "who is this person?"

"My idiot, of course," the duke replied. "Who'd you think? Sing for us, Fool!"

"Do you . . . how can you . . . ?" The merchant stared at the Fool, aghast, unable to finish his question. A new understanding seemed to settle in his brain, and the glances he now shot the duke's way were still more disgusted, yet more respectful as well.

The Fool opened his mouth and began to sing. But it wasn't the jolly, manic song of a jester. It was a song Lionheart had never heard before, melancholy and, he thought, old.

> *"I saw her standing on a hill,*
> *Her feet in swarthy shadows shod.*
> *The wind did wisp her hair*
> *And play its fingers there*
> *While the trees did bend their boughs,*
> *Did moan and bend their boughs.*
>
> *"She stood upon the shadowed hill*
> *And downward turned her glist'ning eye.*
> *She looked on Aiven great,*
> *Upon the closed gate,*
> *But saw the Final Water flow,*
> *The darkened water flow.*
>
> *"I saw her watching from the hill,*
> *Fair Aiven, burnt so red and sore*
> *Before the bleeding sun.*
> *So strong the spells were spun!*
> *The clouds could never stem the blood,*
> *Not catch nor stem the blood!*
>
> *"As she stood upon the hill,*
> *I saw within her searching eye,*
> *There formed a single tear.*

I tremble now in fear!
It fell upon her silver sword,
The pommel of her sword.

"A light upon that shadowed hill
Shone brightly from the deep'ning shade.
I knew me then the sword,
The fearsome Fireword.
The blade did shiver in her hand;
It trembled in her hand.

"She stood unmoving on the hill,
But whispers in her ear she heard.
Sweet voices called her name
And spoke no more of blame.
I would that she would answer them!
Will she not answer them?

"Yet as she stood upon the hill,
Unheeding all the whispered pleas,
A new voice spoke her name.
I know not whence it came.
She turned her face from burning Aiven,
Looked no more on Aiven.

"The trees alone stand on the hill,
For she has passed along her way.
The veil is o'er my eyes:
Who speaks of truth or lies?
For Fireword has gone from Aiven,
Borne away from Aiven."

Lionheart stood transfixed by the lunatic's voice. His mind filled with images of a land he had never seen but which appeared in his imagination as vividly as memories of Southlands. He saw a woman standing as described upon a hill above a burning estate. He saw her weeping, tears of sorrow, not remorse. Strangely, the image of her made him think of Rose Red. It was the first he'd thought of her in some time. The woman in his mind was not the little imp he knew and yet . . . and yet something about her brought Rose Red powerfully to mind.

Then he saw the sword, and it drove all other thoughts from him. He thought, *That is the sword that will slay dragons.*

The song ended.

Lionheart's head was light and reeling in the wake of the jester's voice. He gasped and nearly lost his grip on the amphora in his hand. But the duke spoke, and his growl brought Lionheart's swimming eyes back into focus.

"How dare you sing of such things in my house?"

The jester gazed at his master, his mouth open as though the last note of his song still lingered on his lips. Then he said, "You asked for a song."

The duke rose to his feet; his fingers closed threateningly about his carving knife. "You sing of cursed things, poison in my ears. *Fireword!*" He spat, and his eyes were bloodshot with fury. "You ghoul, you unholy monster!"

At a sign from their master, armed men strode from different corners of the room. The first one struck the Fool, and he dropped, howling in pain, though the blow had not been great. Each man wielded an iron rod, and when these struck the madman, he cried out as though branded.

Lionheart felt ill. The images of the song swirled in his mind, mingling with the duke's roar and the pathetic cries of the poor madman. No one moved to his aid. Everyone stared, horrified, either at the beating or at their own hands. Who dared cross the duke?

It was too much.

Lionheart leapt forward. He swung his amphora, and it struck one of the guards on the side of the face; then he swung back and hit another. Wine sloshed across the scene, spattering like red blood. Then Lionheart dropped his pitcher and wrested one of the iron bars from the first man. He was trained in swordplay, as these thugs apparently were not. He parried a blow, then jabbed his elbow deep into a man's stomach before striking another on top of the head. The duke shouted in the background, but Lionheart heard nothing in the frenzy of the moment.

He turned to the Fool, who was curled up in a ball of pain on the floor. Hardly knowing what he was doing, Lionheart knelt down and unsnapped the iron ring from about his neck.

What happened next was like a dream.

Suddenly there was no albino curled up on the floor . . . there was a towering giant, white and billowy, with streaming hair and eyes and fingers as long as zephyrs. It roared a great booming laugh and swept its horrible gaze across the screaming assembly. Its eyes locked with the duke's, and for a moment the white wind turned red.

The moment passed.

Two arms encircled Lionheart. He could not scream; he could not think. He was borne away through the door in a thunderous gale, his arms wrapped about his head and his eyes squeezed shut. This must be a nightmare; it could not be real!

He dared not open his eyes until the rush of wind and the pounding in his head stopped. He seemed to be standing on solid ground, so he carefully opened first one eye, then the other.

The eastern docks of Capaneus City spread about him. Nearby, sailors and dock crews were busily loading and unloading merchandise and readying sails and tack for lengthy voyages, but this portion of the quayside was quiet. Lionheart turned his head to gaze across the Chiara Bay. Haze lined the horizon where the mountains of Southlands should be visible. It was as though his kingdom had fallen off the edge of the world.

"I am free."

Lionheart turned back to stare at the one who had spoken. It was difficult to see that strange, fey creature, simultaneously visible and invisible, but huge no matter what.

"You set me free."

Its voice was that of the duke's Fool, yet also that of a rolling wind.

"Um," said Lionheart. "You're welcome."

"I will grant you a wish, if I may."

It was a sylph; the realization hit Lionheart like a thunderclap. A sylph—one of those airy creatures of which he'd heard stories as a child but had believed only existed in the metaphysical sense . . . like dragons. He swallowed, trying to maintain eye contact with the wafting thing so like and so different from the Fool bound by the duke.

"You are in danger now," said the sylph. "The duke will not forget what you have done in liberating me. Do you wish for safety?"

"Well," Lionheart said, struggling to speak, "I don't think so. I mean, I can manage the duke."

"So you believe."

"I'll leave Capaneus somehow. I'll get work. As a sailor."

"There is something you long for," said the sylph. "Something you seek. Tell me. Perhaps I may help you." Its voice, like gusting breezes, sounded impatient. Lionheart hated to keep it waiting. He thought of what he had seen just now across the Chiara Bay. The wall of smoke where his kingdom once lay.

"I need to know how to kill a dragon," he said.

The sylph's wafting face looked sad. "I must remain in your debt," it said. "That knowledge I may not impart to you."

Suddenly Lionheart found his arms full of brilliantly colored jester's motley, and a bell-covered hat plopped on his head. "Iubdan's beard!" he exclaimed. "What—"

"You said you longed for freedom," said the sylph. Its voice was more distant now, its face less visible. "This wish I cannot grant either. But perhaps these will help. You closely observed my work as Fool; you have a bright eye and a loud spirit. Take these, the symbols of my enslavement, and may they become the symbols of your freedom."

Gentle fingers brushed Lionheart's cheeks, like a summer breeze. "Flee the duke. Do not allow him to see you again. He is a powerful man, more powerful than you think. It is not every mortal who can bind one such as I."

Another breath of wind, this time like a kiss on Lionheart's forehead. "Go to Lunthea Maly and seek out the Hidden Temple of Ay-Ibunda. The oracle there . . . she will tell you what you wish to know."

The sylph was gone. Perhaps it had never existed.

Lionheart stood on the quayside of Capaneus, wondering how long he had been there. He looked down at the armload of bright fabrics and touched the hat on his head.

"Freedom," he whispered. "Why must it be so elusive?"

He started off at a trot down the docks.

2

The Netherworld

A WHOLE YEAR HAD PASSED since Rose Red vanished behind the gate.

Beana paced the circumference of the Eldest's grounds every day, seeking some way in. The days and nights blended into one another, and for some while she lost track of time entirely; it scarcely mattered in that ever-present gloom of smoke. But she woke from an uneasy sleep one day and realized that a year had gone by. And still, not a sign of her girl. Nor of any weakness in the Dragon's stronghold.

"Why don't you come?" she whispered, reaching out to touch the barred gates, straining her eyes to see inside the Eldest's courtyard. The Dragon's courtyard. But the smoke was too thick. For all Beana could see, the House might have completely vanished. "Why don't you come deliver these people?"

She listened for a reply but heard nothing. Beana bowed her head.

"Give her what she needs, my Lord. I beg you. Since I cannot help her, give her what she needs to walk your Path in safety."

When Beana spoke again, she sent her voice through the bars, deep into the swirling smoke, desperate for it to carry across distances greater than she could guess.

"Remember the Name, Rosie."

Beana had warned her of the Paths.

Warned may not be the right word. But when Rose Red was a little girl, she had taken Beana's words as a warning. The Paths were dangerous unless used with great care. They crisscrossed the entire world, and one could follow them across vast distances in a moment. But sometimes it wasn't a moment . . . sometimes it was a thousand years. One must choose a Path carefully.

Some Paths were good. One could follow these and be certain to reach the right destination in a right time. Others, however, were malevolent or controlled by those with malicious intent. It was best to avoid a Faerie Path unless one knew for certain who controlled it. With good intentions and a trusting heart, a body could step onto a Path, expecting a clear road through the wood, and end up instead in the depths of a swamp at the mercy of a will-o'-the-wisp, or at the gates of some dark tower to which travelers are lured, imprisoned, and never seen again.

"Most mortal folk can't see the Paths," Beana had explained, *"but they can stumble onto them just the same and end up in a terrible mess, dragged into the Halflight Realm or into the Far World beyond. They'll lead you through any place and time, sometimes all at once. Most who follow a Faerie Path never return.*

"This is why I'm showing you now, my Rosie. Learn to recognize which Paths are safe and which are not, which will lead you straight and true, and which are no better than snares. And my best advice to you: Don't use any of them!"

This Path was a trap if ever there was one. Rose Red recalled Leo's boyhood voice, speaking from across the years: *"In my book, there is an engraving of the Gateway to Death. It looks like that. Like a wolf's head."*

But this was the Path down which Daylily had wandered.

Rose Red passed through the door into the tunnel. It was like stepping off a cliff, that crossing into the Netherworld. This was the Dragon's Path, more dangerous than any she had encountered on the mountain . . . save the one she'd followed to the Monster's Cave. At the time, that Path had seemed harmless. But the moment Rose Red's feet crossed the threshold into the descending tunnel, she realized that this was, in fact, the very same Path she'd walked in the mountains. Only now she recognized it for what it was.

The Path to Death's world.

"Remember the Name, Rosie."

The voice touched Rose Red with more force than a mere memory just as she stepped through the doorway. She stopped as her hand let go of the supporting door frame and she stood fully in the darkness of that tunnel. She closed her eyes and pictured her goat, her comforter, her friend.

"But you're alone now," she whispered to herself, and her eyes flared open again. "Beana's gone. You're alone now, and you've got to be strong."

Rose Red walked blindly down that dark incline. She had never before encountered darkness so absolute. Always her eyes behind their veil could find some light and make use of it to guide her steps. There was no light here, however, no help for her. She must walk forward through that sickening stench, feeling out each step with a tentative toe. At first she was afraid to seek the wall of the tunnel for support, but at length she put out her hand. She nearly screamed at what she felt.

The familiar plaster and woodwork of the stairway.

In a flash of faint half-light, she saw that her feet were climbing spiral steps, and the closeness of the foul tunnel was replaced with the closeness of a passageway. This sensation roiled through her mind, and she quickly withdrew her hand. The darkness returned. Once more she stood in the cave. Once more she heard the trickle of water somewhere to her left.

Her mind revolted. Rose Red could either go mad or pretend she did not understand what was happening. She chose the latter and continued on her way, careful not to touch the walls again.

Even so, as she progressed, sometimes she could have sworn she still climbed the servants' stair. Only it was the longest in the world, like a stairway to the stars; either that or she climbed the same steps again and again, unable to progress. If anything, it was better in the depths of the tunnel. A nightmare seemed more bearable than a reality gone wrong.

The stench eventually either faded or she grew accustomed to it. The trickle of running water disappeared as well, and there was nothing but darkness around and uneven stones underfoot.

Then she saw a light ahead.

No more than a tiny pinprick, perhaps very far, perhaps very near; impossible to tell in that blackness. Like a star it shone in the depths of space, quite unlike dragon fire.

"Don't go near the light, princess."

The Dragon's voice hissed in her ear. For an instant she thought she must have died; but then her heart started to beat again and she managed to draw a breath.

"Avoid the light," he said. "Avoid it at all costs."

She kept walking.

"It's not worth it," he said.

"I . . . I'll go where I please." Her voice emerged in a tiny gasp. But Rose Red meant what she said.

The Dragon snarled, circling behind her. Then he spoke in her other ear. "You'll wish you hadn't. You'll only find sorrow. You'll only find regret."

"I'll find what I find," she replied and managed another step. And another. She knew he dogged her footsteps. She knew darkness fell into deeper darkness on either side of her. But she kept her eyes on that pinprick spark and moved toward it, sometimes down a rocky incline, sometimes up a spiral stair, always forward.

The Dragon's voice surrounded her. She felt him stalking her like a lion, disembodied yet potent.

"He killed his brother, killed him in his anger and his jealousy. He wanted to meet me, wanted to know the beauty of my kiss. But his brother would not let him. So he killed his brother and buried him here. Then in regret, he left a light upon the grave. How pathetic! As though such a light may atone for his sin."

Rose Red continued walking, her gaze fixed upon the glow. It was growing now, bolder and stronger. It cast shadows on the rocks around her, and occasionally on the rail of a stair.

"You know their names . . . the Brothers Ashiun."

She did not answer.

"They came across the Final Water to teach mortal man the cursed Sphere Songs. They doomed mortals to lives of slavery and taught them to fear the gift I offered."

"Good job on their part, I expect." Rose Red held her skirts in her hands, climbing the stair now. Her breath came in short gasps, partly because of fear, partly because of irritation.

"The younger brother longed for my kiss. He saw the hopelessness of his state, chained to a duty he could never fulfill. There could be no other alternative. There can be release only in my gift! His brother was different. His brother was favored by the Prince of Farthestshore, commissioned to carry a certain lantern. A blaze of white fire, princess. It will hurt your eyes. You must avoid it at all costs."

"I could try to care about what you're sayin'." Rose Red panted as she took another step and found the stairway gone and the rocks once more beneath her feet. Her head hurt with disorientation and she longed to close her eyes. But then she would have no light to guide her. "I could try to care, but I ain't sure it's worth the bother."

"But the younger was entrusted with a gift less fine, for he was less favored. Nothing more than a silver sword, a useless weapon . . ."

The Dragon's voice trailed off. Rose Red thought he might still be speaking, but she could no longer hear him as she neared that light.

She saw a grave.

The moment she recognized it for what it was, the cave gave way, and she stood on a vast, empty plain. No sky vaulted overhead, only emptiness. The light illuminated rolling gray hills, sparse with ugly growth. A lone wind drifted her way, tugging at her rags and her veil, billowing through the rough grasses that grew around the grave.

It was an old grave, she knew, though the turf looked newly turned. Something in the air told her that whoever dug this grave had come and gone long ages ago. But that one had done a neat job of it, even fixing a stone marker in place.

"*The stone is white,*" Beana had said, "*but you hardly see that for the brightness that shines upon it. A silver lantern of delicate work older than you can imagine. And within that lantern shines a wonder. Like a star, yet unlike as well.*"

Rose Red gazed at the lantern that sat, as her goat had told her, atop the marker. It was like a small, brilliant star she could hold in her hands. But the light was warmer than starlight, like a home fire upon a hearth for comfort, though of purer quality. A white light but full of colors like the sunset, just like Leo had once told her in his story long ago.

She could feel the Dragon trying to draw her back. His impotency in his own realm infuriated him, and the heat of that fury reached her even here, where he could not come. She approached the light, her ears stopped to his voice, alone on that empty plain save for the lantern and the grave.

The wind blew again, and it was cold. This she did not mind. She knelt at the grave. The letters in the stone were elegantly carved and foreign, and she doubted that she would have been able to read the writing even had she been taught as a child. They looked nothing like Southlands writing, but like something much, much older.

Suddenly, to her surprise, the markings on the stone shifted. As though dancing, they lifted and moved across the stone. They became images, like paintings come to life, yet not paintings either. Moods and expressions springing right into her head.

She read and understood.

> *Beyond the Final Water falling,*
> *The Songs of Spheres recalling.*
> *While you walk the Path to Death's own throne,*
> *You will walk with me.*

The wood thrush, her Imaginary Friend, sat on the handle of the lantern. *You know my song,* he sang, and she understood his words the same way she understood the strange writing. The music of his voice pierced her heart.

It has been with you from the time you were a babe. Falling from the sky, ringing through the mountains. Your father hummed it as he worked, and the trees surrounded you with their chorus. All sang my song to you.

Rose Red swallowed. Her own voice when she spoke was nothing but dirt and clay. "You still left me alone."

You are not alone, my child.

"You're no better than the Dragon," she said, standing and stepping away from the stone, from the lantern, from the bird. "You want me for yourself."

I want you for yourself. I want you to be everything you were intended to be before the worlds were formed. Everything this death-in-life has prevented you from becoming.

"You sound like the Dragon. He calls me a princess."

I call you my child.

She shook her head at him. "Both of you want something from me."

Yes, sang he. *We both want your love, your loyalty. And you cannot give it to both of us.*

"What if I don't want to give it at all?"

The bird's voice became sad, a trill of notes that might have broken her heart had she not set herself against him. But he replied, *I will never take something from you that you do not wish to give.*

She did not answer. She thought of the Dragon and his demands, and she shuddered. "I'm afraid of you," she whispered. "I'm afraid of giving you—or him—anything! What will be left of me if I do?"

Give me nothing, then, said the bird. *I will love you even so, though you break my heart.*

"I don't . . . I don't know if I can believe you."

You may, said he. *Will you accept a gift?*

Rose Red did not answer.

This Path you walk is perilous, and Death waits at its end. Those without hope will not survive. So please, my child, take this lantern. Take Asha in your hand and hold on to its light.

The light was so warm, so full of comfort. Rose Red remembered Beana's words: *"The folks who see the lantern, they take it with them as they walk the path. And the light guides them through the darkness, keeping at bay all the terrors of the Netherworld."*

As long as you carry Asha, sang the bird, *no monster of this realm may harm you. It is my gift, my protection.*

Hesitantly, she put out a hand. The bird spread his wings and flew from the handle even as her gloved fingers closed around it. *It is my protection,* he sang once more even as she lifted the light from the gravestone.

It remained in place. Simultaneously, it came away in her hand.

There were two lanterns now, only not really. Rather, the lantern remained unbound by time, so it was at once both in her hand and upon the stone. Either way, it was where it belonged.

Her Imaginary Friend was gone. But somehow, Rose Red no longer felt alone.

With the light held at arm's length before her, Rose Red continued on across the plain. Now and then when she blinked, the rolling, spurge-covered hills vanished, and she saw herself in a hallway of the Eldest's House, still dark with otherworldly gloom. It would seem she had climbed that endless stair at last. But the hall, when she glimpsed it, stretched ever on before her, and it was easier in a way to return to the plain.

The darkness shifted. Along the distant horizon a thin scarlet line like seeping blood appeared. The sun began to rise. Only it wasn't the sun Rose Red knew. It was like the Dragon's eye, red and boiling, and it peered at her from over the hills. A vast, ugly head, smoke pouring from its nostrils—or were those clouds? It was too horrible. Rose Red lifted up the silver lantern to shield her face.

The light in the lantern grew in potency, as though to combat that leering sun. Rose Red closed her eyes, then felt rather than saw a bolt of blinding light.

The words of the Dragon crashed down around her like fiery hail. "Take it from her! Destroy that light!"

The light of the lantern grew in potency, swallowing up the fire in its pure glow. It was all too terrible, and Rose Red screamed.

When she looked again the plain was gone, as was the boiling eye. She stood on a mountain. It was barren, stripped of all growth, naked rock beneath that empty expanse above. Rose Red, still clutching the lantern in both hands, turned to gaze at the half-lit range of mountains stretched about her. They were the Circle of Faces. In this place, the faces themselves were more clearly defined than ever; hollows became gaping mouths and eyes, landslides became hair, became tears, became teeth. The ugly faces and twisted bodies of ancient giants.

And this mountain upon which she stood . . . Rose Red looked up to its peak, black as pitch. This must be Bald Mountain.

The Place of the Teeth rose up before her.

Rose Red stared. She knew the story behind the Place of the Teeth, a secret hollow somewhere on the slopes of Bald Mountain to which no one ever ventured anymore. It was a site of sacrifice. Five stones like jagged teeth, carved from the natural rock, rose up from a smooth slab of stone, four of the teeth at the slab's corners, and one jutting from the middle. All were stained with blood, the middle one most of all. For here, in ancient days, the warlike elders had sacrificed ewe lambs to appease the Beast that was their god.

And here too it was that Maid Starflower had been bound and left under the cold light of the moon. Only there was no moon in this place.

No sooner had this thought crossed Rose Red's mind than she heard deep, guttural breathing. An instant later, an enormous black shape leapt onto the slab and paced around the central stone. It was like a wolf but, terribly, also like a man. His face was the face of the Monster Cave, only in flesh rather than rock. Blood matted his fur and dripped from his jaws.

"That cursed light," he snarled. His voice heaved, as though speech gave him pain. But his eyes gleamed in the glow of the lantern, glaring at Rose Red with hatred and despair. "Who dares bring that poison light and shine it in my eyes? Have you no compassion?"

Rose Red swallowed hard, her hand trembling so hard that she would have dropped the lantern had she not reached up hastily to grasp it in her other fist as well. "I ain't nobody," she gasped. "Nobody important."

The creature paced to the edge of the slab. He was bigger than a horse, with a ruff of shaggy fur like a mane about his face. But Rose Red realized that the blood in his coat was from many, many horrible wounds. Savage teeth had torn the flesh and left it gaping and bleeding.

"You . . . you're dead," she whispered. "Ain't you?"

He raised his enormous head and howled at the empty vault. The sound shattered through Rose Red's soul, and she crouched down upon the mountainside, holding the lantern before her face.

"They tore into me!" he bellowed. "My own! My own! She betrayed me, though I loved her. Yes, my love was all too violent, too terrible and great for her to comprehend. But she betrayed me, and they tore me to pieces."

The words trailed off into another long howl that rattled the Place of the Teeth like a chattering skull. But the howl too caused him pain. It ended abruptly in a snarl, and he bowed his head, panting and showing his teeth.

"I . . . I'm sorry," Rose Red managed, sitting upright at last. "It don't sound like you've had too great a time of it."

"Why," the creature gasped, "do you walk this Path? You are yet living."

"I'm lookin' for someone."

"Look elsewhere. Flee this place while you may."

Rose Red swallowed hard then set her jaw. "I cain't," she said. "The Dragon's taken someone I promised to protect."

"It's too late for that one," said the beast.

"No it ain't. She weren't dead neither, and he wouldn't dare kill her."

"How do you know this?"

"I just . . . know."

Here the creature looked her right in the eye. "If she's not dead, then she's been taken to the Village."

"Where's the Village?"

"You cannot go there. It is far down this Path, much too near the Black Water. You must go back." He growled out the last words, his chest heaving. His pain was so great.

Rose Red licked her lips and drew a long breath. Then, though she did not know why she did so, she put out a hand to the beast, stepping closer. He watched her, snarling, but made no move. She touched a wound at his shoulder. He shook his head sharply.

"Get that light out of my eyes! I beg you!"

She inspected the wound. "I maybe could mend this," she said gently. "If you'll let me try."

The look he gave her was agonized with regret. "There can be no mending for me. They tore me to pieces in the other world. I will remain torn to pieces in this one."

Rose Red put a hand in her pocket. Sure enough, her fingers found a needle and thread secreted there. She drew them from her pocket, set her lamp down at her feet, threaded the needle, then carefully parted the creature's coarse fur.

"Witch-fire!" the beast swore. "I told you, you cannot help me!"

"Hold still," she said. She slid the handle of her lantern up onto her elbow so that she could still hold it as she worked.

"Why would you help me? I ate them; I devoured them, the mortal insects! I enslaved them with fear and worship, made them offer me gifts upon this stone. And they hated me."

Her needle was sharp. She forced it through the torn flesh. She was glad her veil covered her face against that ghostly blood.

"They hated me, though I loved them, the little crawling things. They were ignorant and dirty; they needed my guidance."

"Liar," Rose Red said as she drew the thread tight.

"I did love them!" the wolf snarled. "In my way."

"No you didn't." Her eyes fixed upon her work so that she would not have to return the awful stare he turned upon her. "You're just sayin' that to make yourself feel better. You hated them and used them and disposed of them as you liked. I know who you are. I ain't so easily fooled as all that."

The beast roared. He broke away from her, yanking the needle and thread from her hand, and bounded back to the other end of the slab, where he crouched behind the central stone, as though frightened of her.

His breathing came hard, agonized and wretched. "Why do you help me, then?"

Rose Red put her hands on her hips. "If I only ever did for them what deserved it, I'd have little enough to do."

He stared at her, his gaze running over the folds of her veil and down her tiny frame. He could swallow her in a single gulp. But Rose Red slid the lantern back down from her elbow until she held it in her hand once more. The light glowed softly as she approached the monster, and it was he that trembled. She put out her free hand, feeling in his thick fur for her needle, but when she followed the thread back to the wound, she found that her stitches had all pulled out under his violent movements. Fresh blood oozed.

His voice, though that of a wolf, came as a sob. "You see, you cannot help. You and your cursed light. It hurts beyond bearing. I beg you to stop."

Rose Red paused, uncertain. Then she broke the end of her thread and put the dirtied needle back in her pocket. The wound was worse than ever. She could not fix it. "I . . . I'm sorry," she whispered. "I shouldn't have even tried."

The lantern light dimmed.

The monster raised his face, and the fixed snarl was almost a smile. "I told you as much. There is nothing you can do for those who are dead. Go back now."

She stepped away, clutching the lantern in both hands. "I've got to go on. You must let me pass, Wolf Lord."

He heaved himself to his feet, his eyes rolling with pain. "It's a fool's errand," he said. "Your friend cannot be recovered from the Village." He sniffed then, drawing in the scent of her, and when he finished, his eyes opened with a flash. "Or rather, your enemy."

Rose Red bowed her head. "She ain't my enemy. She's my mistress, and I promised to serve her."

"You hate her."

"I hate nobody."

"Dislike her thoroughly, then."

Rose Red did not answer.

The Wolf Lord shook his shaggy head wonderingly. "I will let you go. But you must leave something of your own behind with me. No one passes through to Death's realm without paying the toll."

"What do you want from me?"

"Your lantern."

She gasped. "No."

"That evil light is useless to you anyway. Did it help you to mend me? What makes you think it will help you win back this mistress you hate?"

"I cain't give it to you."

"Then you will not pass."

Rose Red ground her teeth, blinking fast. The image of a stairway in the Eldest's House flashed before her eyes. There were wolves carved into the banisters at the bottom step. Beautiful, polished wolves. "I . . . I'll give you one of my gloves instead."

The Wolf Lord growled, deep in the back of his throat. It was like a chuckle but harsher. "You need those, though. Don't you? They are part of the mask with which you shield yourself. Can you bear to strip even one away?"

Closing her eyes, Rose Red removed one of her ragged gloves. She took the damaged one from the hand she had burned when she slapped the Dragon. "Take it," she said. "But I cain't give you the lantern."

The Wolf Lord sighed then. "No, I did not think that you would. I am beyond the aid of its light, for I am dead." With a flash of white teeth, he darted forward and snapped the glove out of Rose Red's hand. It vanished.

"Very well," he said. "You continue this suicide. But don't tell anyone that I, the first god of the South Land, never warned you."

He was gone. As was the Place of the Teeth. The mountain, the whole range, disappeared.

Rose Red stood at the bottom step of the wide stair in the western wing of the Eldest's House. A chandelier creaked from the ceiling above her, and Rose Red shivered where she stood.

She hid her bare hand in the folds of her garment.

3

The Near World

"SHALL I BRING HIM IN, CAPTAIN?"

"Yes."

"He's a sullen one. Not trustworthy. Shall I bind him?"

"That will not be necessary."

Captain Sunan of the *Kulap Kanya* sat at a narrow desk in his cabin, keeping the ship's log. Today's entry noted, among other things, *Stowaway finally too much of a nuisance. Time to bring him in.*

Sunan always knew what went on on his ship, from the lookout in the crow's nest to the lowliest ship rat. His crew would swear on their mothers' graves that he possessed an intuitive sixth sense, if not a full-fledged mind-reading capability. They feared him, they respected him, and they were fiercely loyal to him.

Thus, when he boarded his ship after dining at the Duke of Shippening's, beckoned his first mate to his side, and said, "There is a stowaway in the hold. Pretend you do not know and leave him alone until I say otherwise. We sail at dawn," no one had questioned him. No one wondered how he knew about this stowaway whom no one else had spied; of course Captain Sunan would know. No one wondered why he did not have the wretch tossed over the side into the murky harbor along with the rest of the ship's trash; Captain Sunan always had his reasons.

And if he decided now, six days into the voyage, to drag the creature up to his cabin and (presumably) split him from stem to stern, Captain Sunan knew best.

Two weathered sailors dragged the stowaway suspended between them into Sunan's cabin and dropped him at the captain's feet. The brown foreigner barked a string of angry curses in Westerner. One of the sailors kicked him in the ribs. "Stand in the presence of your betters." The foreigner cursed again. Though the words were strange, the tone was unmistakably rude. The sailor kicked him again.

"Enough," said Captain Sunan. He rose. Sunan was a tall man and very thin, though, despite the thinness, he gave the impression of great strength. He dressed impeccably, even amid the rigors of a long sea voyage. He looked down at the stowaway, and his piercing gaze was worse than the sailor's kicks. The stowaway shut his mouth.

"Leave us," Sunan said. The sailors did not hesitate to obey, though they may have thought in the privacy of their minds that it was unwise to leave their captain alone with the foreigner. But if Sunan read minds as easily as they suspected, these were thoughts they dared not long entertain. They stood outside his cabin door, which clicked shut behind them.

Lionheart gathered himself up from before the captain's feet. The jester's garb was stuffed inside his server's shirt, though the colorful fabrics spilled out the front. He looked a fool, something the merchant captain could not fail to notice.

"Rise, boy," Sunan said, using the western tongue Lionheart knew. Lionheart hastened to obey. He stood as straight and tall as he could, calling into play all his princely bearing. But somehow, in the merchant's presence, he still felt as insignificant as the kennel hand he had been these last many months. Sunan took a seat at his desk again and regarded Lionheart as a king on his throne would regard a supplicant.

"Do you know," said Sunan, his voice just as comfortable in Westerner as it was in his native dialect, "the enemy you have made?"

"I beg your pardon, captain," Lionheart said, bowing quickly, "I meant no disrespect. I—"

"Not in myself," the captain said. He was the sort of man who, when he started speaking, caused other people to stop. It wasn't that he interrupted. Anything he had to say was certain to be more important than anyone else's thought, so how could that be called interrupting? "In the Duke of Shippening."

Lionheart gulped.

"That was a brave thing you did," Sunan continued. "Liberating a Faerie slave. Where I come from, it is a sin to keep such people captive. Perhaps your people do not believe the same."

This seemed like a question, so Lionheart dared reply. "I don't think my people have any particular views on the subject. We . . . we don't interact with people of other worlds. We don't usually believe in them . . . beyond superstition." He shuddered at the memory of the Dragon. "Until recently, that is."

"Strange," said Sunan. "Strange, for you live very close to the other worlds." His hands rested on the arms of his chair, his body like a carved statue. "It takes great power to keep hold of a Faerie slave." His black eyes were narrow as he regarded Lionheart. "Mortals cannot do so unless they are themselves very strong. Or allied with someone stronger. You have made yourself a terrible enemy."

In the silence that followed, Lionheart considered Sunan's face, trying to gauge whether he was supposed to respond. He said at length, "I am not afraid of the Duke of Shippening."

"You should be. He is not the buffoon he projects to the world. And his alliances are powerful, though even I cannot guess at them." Sunan's eye fixed on the brilliant-hued fabric escaping from beneath Lionheart's plain overshirt. Lionheart wished that he dared either stuff it back in or pull it completely out, but he did not move. He simply stood there looking like an idiot and hating his life.

His life which, now that he was a captive stowaway, stood a good chance of being abruptly ended.

Sunan said, "It was a foolish but brave act to liberate the duke's slave, and for this reason I have allowed you to hide on board the *Kulap*

Kanya and will bear you to safer lands. We will stop at many ports on our voyage back to the city of my emperor. You may disembark at the harbor of your choice."

Lionheart stood without breathing for a long moment. Then he managed, "You . . . you will give me passage?"

"I will. You have the word of a Pen-Chan, which is word you may trust."

Lionheart did not know what this meant exactly, but somehow he believed what the captain said. "I am trying to reach Lunthea Maly."

"The city of my emperor," said Sunan. "I will take you there."

"I seek Ay-Ibunda. This temple is in the city, yes?"

For the first time in the course of their conversation, Lionheart saw Captain Sunan's expression change, if only for a moment. But in that unmistakable moment, Lionheart saw a flash of fear, or dread. Then it was gone, and Sunan spoke in the same even tones. "The Hidden Temple. You will not find it."

"It is in the city, though, isn't it?"

"Lunthea Maly shelters the abode of the Mother's Mouth, yes."

"Then someone must know where it is. I'll find directions."

"No one may find the Hidden Temple of Ay-Ibunda," said Sunan. "No one knows where it hides save for Emperor Molthisok-Khemkhaeng Niran himself. And he will not tell you." Sunan rose suddenly and took one stride across his cabin, standing nose to nose with Lionheart. His gaze was nearly unbearable, and Lionheart only just managed to meet him eye to eye.

"You are not a serving boy," said the captain. "No one would mistake you for the person you have disguised yourself as. And you are not a man of Shippening. You hail from Southlands. The stink of dragon smoke lingers about you."

Lionheart said, "I hail from Southlands, yes."

"Who are you truly?"

"I will not tell you."

"What is your name?"

"I will not tell you."

"What has the Dragon promised you?"

"The Dragon has promised me nothing." Lionheart swallowed and almost immediately regretted his next words. "I am going to kill him."

Sunan drew a long breath. But his face did not alter as he stood mere inches from Lionheart. When next he spoke, his voice was low. "There are those among my people who worship the Lady and her Dark Brother. The Dragon."

Lionheart said nothing.

"But," Sunan continued, "I will, nonetheless, bear you to Lunthea Maly. You have liberated a Faerie from the Duke of Shippening's enslavement. Perhaps you will liberate others. But be forewarned, man of Southlands: Should you, by some miracle, find your way to Ay-Ibunda, and should you speak to the Mother's Mouth, you will be given what you ask. But the price at which it is given will be terrible."

Lionheart nodded. "I have been warned. Thank you."

"What will you call yourself now you have left behind all you know?"

"I am . . ." Lionheart paused a moment and licked his lips. "I am Leonard," he said. Then he smiled. "Leonard the Jester."

"You are Leonard the Fool," said Captain Sunan.

"Tell me what you want."

Lionheart opens his eyes and finds the night has grown very dark around him. The hammock in which he rests sways back and forth. But steady in the blackness above his face are two white eyes like beacons, gazing down upon him.

"Tell me, my darling."

"I want to find Ay-Ibunda," Lionheart said.

"Then you shall."

"I want to speak to the oracle."

"Then you shall."

"I want . . . I want to be a jester."

The darkness parts. Lionheart sees white teeth flash in a smile.

"Is that all, my child? Is that the deepest desire of your heart? To be free at last to become the person you have always wanted to be?"

Lionheart turns his gaze from hers. "I . . . I don't know. I need to find the temple. That's all I know."

"You shall. And you shall find it as a jester."

She vanishes.

Lionheart closes his eyes and sleeps once more.

Lunthea Maly, the Fragrant Flower of Noorhitam, was capital of the greatest empire in all the known world and home of his Imperial Majesty, Molthisok-Khemkhaeng Niran.

Who died.

People have a tendency to do so once they reach a certain age. Or, as in Emperor Molthisok-Khemkhaeng Niran's case, they reach a certain level of importance and acquire a certain number of enemies, which the emperor's brother-in-law insisted was the case.

But not to worry! Molthisok-Khemkhaeng Niran, though relatively young when he expired, had survived long enough to produce a male heir, the new Emperor Khemkhaeng-Niran Klahan.

Who was nine.

What a blessing it was, then, that the boy emperor had an uncle so loving to guide him in the way he should go, to gently take the reins of the empire from such tender young hands and steer it on a safe and true path until such a time as the young Klahan should be old enough to rule in his own right. Just like his father.

In the meanwhile, the boy emperor must be crowned.

"I want clowns," said the emperor.

"Imperial and Everlasting Glory," said his uncle, one Sepertin Naga, who looked rather like a snake with arms and a mustache, "you must take heed. The rites of your magnificent forefathers must be maintained, the holy words of the Sacred Cycle said in accordance with the passing of the spheres, and—"

"We never have clowns," said Emperor Khemkhaeng-Niran Klahan. "Not funny ones. The only clowns I've ever seen always teach a moral."

"Such is the role and duty of those who strive in the comedic arts, to instruct and enlighten their Sacred Father."

"Who?"

"You, most Glorious One."

"Oh. Yes."

The emperor was small even for his age, with a round, soft face. He looked frail as he sat cross-legged on a cushion in his schoolroom, contemplating the list of coronation regulations his uncle had spread on the floor before him. Sepertin Naga liked the look of that babyish face. It reminded him of his dear, departed sister. She had been a most pliable girl.

But there was a set to the emperor's jaw that his uncle failed to see. This jaw he had inherited from his father and a long line of emperors. Dynasties are not made of weak links. Young Klahan was certainly not about to be the breaking point in this chain of history.

And he knew what he wanted at his coronation.

"I want funny clowns. Clowns that do tricks. And sing amusing songs."

He turned his black eyes from the list of coronation regulations to his uncle's face. He was nine. He was his mother's son. He should be malleable as wet clay.

"As you wish, Light of Endless Noon," said Sepertin Naga through his teeth and backed out of the room, taking his list with him.

The Dark Brother devour all funny clowns!

But if clowns were required, clowns there must be. Sepertin Naga sent men to all corners of Lunthea Maly, searching the streets and inn yards, the docks and the alleys, bazaars and bandit dens, anywhere clowns might be found, and rounded them up. All of them, loaded in carts and wagons, were hauled up the central hill around which Lunthea Maly was built, at the very top of which sat Phak-Phimonphan, the great Temple of the Emperors, and just beneath it, the Aromatic Palace.

Somewhere, stuffed between a fire-eater and a contortionist, was a clown in outlandish Westerner's garb with strikingly brown skin and a strong accent. He'd been found in a back alley not far from the docks, performing a comical song for a crowd of peasants, who were at least as intrigued by his unusual garb as they were by anything he said.

"Is he funny?" a guard sent from the palace to collect performers asked one of the gathered peasants.

"You bet your eyes, he's funny. Just listen to him butchering the language. He's trying to speak Chhayan now. Listen to that!" The peasant dissolved into asthmatic laughter.

The guard, who was a Kitar and therefore didn't understand the Chhayan dialect, couldn't see what was so amusing about the foreign fellow other than his odd, bell-covered hat. But he was getting plenty of laughs. The guard shrugged his way through the crowd and placed a heavy hand on the clown's shoulders.

The clown yelped and started shouting in the common dialect of the city. "I say, old see you tomorrow in the corn cake! Let loose my monkey's eye! I love you! I love you!"

The peasants doubled over with laughter, though apparently the clown meant every word he said. The guard growled a curse. "What is your name, madman?" he demanded.

"What?" said the clown.

"Your name!"

"My name?" The clown smiled as understanding swept across his face. "My name is Leonard of the Tongue of Lightning. What is your name?"

"My name doesn't matter. You're coming with me." The guard yanked him through the crowd, but the clown wasn't ready to come quietly.

"I love you!" he shouted again, furiously this time.

"I don't care who you love; you're coming to the palace. By order of his Imperial Majesty, Emperor Khemkhaeng-Niran Klahan, Glorious Light of the—"

"Upward fly the lizard, same as everyone!" the clown shouted again, struggling to get free. "I have a cake!"

He was certainly passionate in his lunacy. And if the peasants found him amusing, perhaps his Illuminated Magnificence would as well. "Stop your insane babble and come with me."

So it was that Lionheart, a good three years after coming to Lunthea

Maly, found himself suddenly propelled from the status of street performer to that of imperial clown in one afternoon.

Coronation ceremonies are always a matter of pomp. In Noorhitam, pomp rose to an extreme unheard of in a country such as Southlands. Lionheart watched with open mouth as priests from all the temples in Lunthea Maly (the city sported no fewer than two hundred) chanted while dancers performed the sacred dances. A procession the size of an entire Southlands barony filed up the hill and through the gates, across the great open court of the Aromatic Palace. Incense, as pungent to Lionheart's nostrils as the expensive perfumes carted in Captain Sunan's merchant ship, hung in the air, heavy as the priests' chanting.

And over all this presided the boy emperor, his face as solemn as a statue.

Lionheart caught a glimpse of him now and then from his tucked-away corner with the other assembled clowns. Young Emperor Klahan looked so small upon the red and mother-of-pearl inlaid throne, the silken robes of his forefathers wrapped about his shoulders, the great pearl-studded crown upon his head. Everything was much too large for him, yet he bore it all with surprising poise for his age.

Lionheart's heart went out to the boy. He knew what it felt like to be born to a position of authority and never feel quite adequate, to hide behind the mask, letting them think you're prepared to manage the hundreds upon thousands of lives entrusted to your keeping. There was no room for boyhood in the face of such a task.

Though, a part of Lionheart whispered deep inside, there remained a marked difference between him and this boy. He had run away to play jester; young Klahan sat on his father's throne.

But he couldn't think that way. He was on a mission: He must discover how to kill the Dragon. The oracle of Ay-Ibunda must hold the secret . . . if anyone could see the oracle. Three years had slipped by, and though Lionheart had nearly killed himself studying the dialects of the city and befriending more than a handful of shady but knowledgeable characters, no one could give him a breath of word as to the temple's location.

"Only the emperor knows," they said.

Lionheart gazed up again at the child ruler of the Noorhitam Empire. Somehow, he doubted the little fellow had a clue.

It didn't matter. Lionheart adjusted the jester's hat on his head and smiled. Tonight, by the grace of the Lights Above, he'd have an opportunity to fulfill his childhood dream. He would perform buffoonery for an emperor.

You'll have your dream, my sweet, my Fool.

Trumpets sounded, gongs rang. Vows were taken and given, chants were sent dancing with incense to the heavens. And suddenly Lionheart found himself prodded between the shoulders, propelled out from his safe cubby into the very center of the open court. All the eyes of the lords and ladies of Noorhitam, as otherworldly to Lionheart as Faeries, looked down upon him. But Lionheart turned to the emperor, saw that solemn mouth set in a firm line, and decided that, while he may fail at everything else he turned his hand to in his life, tonight, he would make the emperor laugh.

Twirling his jester's hat, he swept a flourishing bow. But he was a clown, so of course he overbalanced and fell flat on his face, legs kicking the air.

Silence.

Lionheart, recovering himself, found he had broken into a cold sweat. He realized that what passed for comedy for peasants in an alley might be considered a mortal offense in the presence of a newly crowned emperor.

This, of course, was absolutely true upon most occasions, which was why poor young Khemkhaeng-Niran Klahan had never met any but the most moralistic of clowns. None dared perform to the full extent of his idiocy while the sovereign of many nations looked on. Lionheart felt that pressure now as he stood upright and bowed again, this time more respectfully. All his creative foolishness began to cramp up inside as his mind raced through his various routines, seeking out something that couldn't possibly be misconstrued as an insult to his Imperial Gloriousness.

There was nothing.

The boy emperor, whose face looked as though it had never, in all his tender years, cracked a smile, watched from his mother-of-pearl throne.

Lionheart flung wide his arms and exclaimed in a great voice, "BEHOLD! It is I, Leonard the Lightning Tongue! Who, I ask you, could compare to my wit, my singing, my brilliance of phrase?"

At least, that's what he thought he'd said. To the listening emperor, it sounded much more like, "ELEPHANT! My name is Leonard of the Tongue of Lightning! Why are the trees pink and dripping frogs?"

Young Klahan's mouth twitched.

"None, I tell you!" Lionheart declared, though the emperor heard, "The cheese fell!"

"Not even the great Sir Eanrin of Rudiobus can compare to the genius you will now hear."

Whatever the emperor heard this time, he raised his hand suddenly to hide his mouth. His uncle, standing close at hand, sneered deeply and gave a disapproving snort. Khemkhaeng-Niran Klahan ignored him.

And the jester burst into singing meaningless babble:

> *"With dicacity pawky, the Geestly Knout*
> *Would foiter his noggle and try*
> *To becket the Bywoner with his snout*
> *And louche the filiferous fly."*

He danced quite madly as he sang, like nothing the emperor had ever before seen. Dances in Noorhitam were stately affairs, rhythmic and slow, every movement laden with meaning. The jester danced and juggled with every limb flailing, his knees bending and feet kicking, his arms wide and wild. And his face twisted into expressions that Klahan couldn't wait to try sometime in the glass when no one was looking (should he ever be blessed with such a moment).

The jester ended with another flourish, declaring, "I eat you! I eat you all!" and blew kisses to the most elegant women in the crowd.

Emperor Khemkhaeng-Niran Klahan, master of the eastern world, burst out laughing.

Once the emperor laughed, of course, everyone must follow suit.

Soon the entire courtyard was booming with applause and laughter. Old men wiped tears from their cheeks, and beautiful women hid their faces behind their fans. Lionheart revolved slowly, waving and blowing more kisses, and if there were tears of relief in his eyes, they blended in so perfectly with the pouring sweat that no one could have noticed. The emperor had laughed. He was saved.

Now you'll have what you asked.

The already unusual evening became even more wonderful. Young Klahan rose from his throne and held up his hands so that all the assembly went silent. Lionheart turned and flung himself prostrate before the emperor.

A sweet, boyish voice declared, "You have pleased me greatly, Leonard of the Tongue of Lightning."

It took Lionheart a moment to work out his words. He was fairly certain they were favorable.

"Name any desire of your heart. So long as it is within my power to give, I shall bestow it upon you as a gift."

The assembly gasped. It was like a hurricane wind in reverse. Even the torches seemed to shudder in amazement at these great words spoken by the new emperor on the day of his coronation. The honor was incredible, unbelievable! Of course the Fool, if he had any brains at all, would know better than to accept this offer. He must declare that all he could wish for was fulfilled at the first sight of his Supreme Majesty, then crawl away quietly.

But this Fool was unlike anyone else. After all, had he not already proven his insanity?

As soon as Lionheart worked out what the emperor had said, he sat up. Then he sat awhile longer, desperately trying to figure out how to say what he wanted to say. This he dared not bungle.

"I want . . ." He closed his eyes for an instant, then opened them wide and finished simply with, "Ay-Ibunda."

No gasp. No whispers. Only dead silence.

Dead.

The emperor gazed down upon the jester, and in that dead moment

Lionheart wondered if the whole world had turned to stone. Then young Klahan spoke.

"No."

That was all. Two armed men approached Lionheart from either side, and he scrambled hastily to his feet and allowed them to escort him from the courtyard. The coronation celebration continued, but Lionheart was led through the various halls, expecting at any moment to find himself run through the heart for his insolence in speaking thus to the emperor. To his relief, they merely took him to the palace gates and flung him into the streets beyond.

He had performed for an emperor.

But he had failed Southlands.

Lionheart knelt in the dark street, so bleak and wretched after the beauty of the Aromatic Palace. He ground his teeth and clenched his fists and wished for all he was worth that the Dragon had swallowed him alive years ago.

4

The Netherworld

BEANA WAITED BY THE GATE. She rarely circled the grounds anymore. What was the use? The Dragon had sealed them off thoroughly.

"How long?" she whispered. "How long will you leave her to him?"

The silver song drifted across the distance: *I have not abandoned her. Or you.*

"It is so hard, this waiting!" The goat bleated and stamped her hooves. "Interminable!"

Trust me.

"I do," said Beana, bowing her head. "But his poisons thicken every day."

In the western wing of the Eldest's House was a long gallery in which all the kings and queens of Southlands were depicted in paint and preserved in gilded frames. Some of the depictions were nothing but fanciful notions. The Panther Master, for instance, who'd been Eldest of

Southlands in the time of the Wolf Lord. His portrait depicted him in robes of office that had not been officially accepted until several hundred years after his lifetime. Despite the fierce expression and the dramatic sweep of his arm, his face was one of those dull, everyman faces that could be anybody and nobody simultaneously.

Rose Red rather liked this portrait at the beginning of the gallery. She lifted the silver lantern, allowing its light to illuminate the work as the strange half-light could not. The artist had painted, beneath those rich and unhistorical robes, many wounds scarring the Panther Master's body. Vicious wounds he had received in another's place. Rose Red saw the delicate red lines that were almost unnoticeable beneath the gold and saffron cloths and the enormous panther fibula on his shoulder. But when the lantern light shone upon those scars, one could not help but see them. The Panther Master was a kind man, Rose Red thought, though the artist had painted him with a warrior's face. He was a good Eldest.

Suddenly, though she knew it must be a trick of the half-light, the Panther Master's painted gaze shifted and he looked directly down at her.

Rose Red gasped, hiding her exposed hand behind her back, and hurried on her way.

She proceeded down the gallery. For the moment, the House held sway, and she caught glimpses only now and then of the Netherworld into which it was slipping. In that world, she walked once more in a narrow tunnel, so narrow that it was difficult to breathe. Better to stay as much in the House as possible.

The eyes of the ancestors stared down from their frames upon the little chambermaid. She could feel their gazes following her, could swear that when she glanced at them she saw the eyes actually moving. She refused to look.

"Why are you coming for me?"

Rose Red stopped. Slowly, she lifted the Asha Lantern so that its beam might carry farther.

Down at the end of the gallery, she glimpsed through the gloom a person standing. Her skirts blended into the shadows, as did her long hair tumbling down from its usual pile of curls, its striking red melted away into twilight hues as though the color had never been. But when the lantern light fell upon her, her eyes were brilliantly blue in her white face, even from across the gallery.

"M'lady!" Rose Red gasped and started to run toward her. The moment she set her foot down, however, the gallery vanished, and she was once more in the tunnel, which constricted around her. She gasped, barely able to breathe. The more she pushed, the tighter the tunnel grew. So she held quite still and felt the stones, like muscles, relaxing. She could draw breath again, and her eyes sought the end of the tunnel.

It was a gallery once more. Daylily still stood there, her face as motionless as those in the portraits facing each other across the long gallery.

"You should let me die, goat girl," said the Lady of Middlecrescent. "I would if I were you."

Rose Red dared not take another step. "I'm goin' to find you, m'lady. I swear it! Don't give up and don't believe anythin' the Dragon tells you."

"If you should succeed," said Daylily, "you will one day wish you had not." Her mouth was hidden in shadows. Only her eyes were visible, as though peering through the slit of a veil.

"I promised Lionheart I'd care for his family. That means you too, m'lady." Rose Red set her jaw and, without thinking, held up her hand. The ungloved one.

Daylily closed her eyes and turned away. Only her black silhouette remained, just visible against the half-light.

"Wait!" Rose Red called.

"You should let me die, goat girl." Daylily's voice faded. "You should let me die. . . ."

"M'lady!" Rose Red stepped forward again. The tunnel returned, crushing her. If her body were not so sturdy, the rocks would have pulverized her bones to dust. She screamed in terror.

Then it was gone, and she stood at the far end of the gallery. Daylily was nowhere in sight.

Rose Red gasped and drew a long breath, exulting in the ability to breathe. But the next moment she coughed and sputtered. A terrible smell lingered in the air. Like the smell of a match just gone out, but multiplied a thousand times. It wasn't the smell of dragon smoke. More like the lingering smoke from a dead dragon's carcass. Rose Red gagged.

The gallery stretched behind her, the impersonal stares of the old kings and queens still following her progress. But before her, rather than the wall and following passage she knew she was supposed to find here, a great cliff stretched for miles upward into the darkness. Tufts of struggling vegetation grew from ledges, evil-looking plants, parasites sucking life from the very rocks to which they clung. If those were flowers growing from those stalks, they were not flowers that would bloom with new life. The jagged petals looked more like razors, the centers like evil faces. *Little witches,* Rose Red thought.

In the cliff, there was a door like the one that was supposed to be in the wall at the far end of the gallery. Except where the real door had been delicately carved with starflowers, this one was carved with replicas of the witch flowers on the rocks. Rose Red put her hand to the knob.

"Don't touch that."

The voice sounded like ashes with just the faintest hint of life still glowing in their depths. Rose Red turned. Someone materialized from the darkness on her right. A woman, or at least, what had once been a woman. She was tall and thin and walked as though she had been beautiful at one time and had yet to acknowledge that she was beautiful no longer. Her skin was burned black and gray all over, and the ends of her hair smoldered like dying matchsticks.

Rose Red knew what she was the moment she saw her. She could see in an instant that this woman was a dragon.

The woman approached. The evil smell came from her blackened skin. She stepped between Rose Red and the door, her head bowed so that Rose Red could not see her face. "Don't touch that," she repeated. "You don't know where it might lead."

"I have a fairly good idea," Rose Red said, though she retreated a few steps into the gallery. "Ain't many places Death's Path can lead, now, is there?"

"Only one end ultimately," said the woman. Her rasping voice sounded as though it pained her throat. "But you are yet living. Go back while you may."

"Another said as much, but he let me by eventually." Rose Red tried to put more courage in her voice than she felt.

The woman took a menacing step forward. Her eyes, like two lumps of coal, smoldered with remnant heat, hideous to behold. Her nose wrinkled as she sniffed, and her lips curled back in a sizzling snarl. Rose Red clutched her lantern tight.

"I smell him on you," the woman said.

Rose Red made no reply. The woman took another step toward her, her face wagging slowly back and forth. She was blind, Rose Red realized. But she sniffed again, and her snarl grew.

"I smell him," she growled. "The father of my sons."

"Oh," Rose Red whispered. "I know who you are now."

"Do you?" said the woman, drawing herself up to her full height. She stood at least seven feet tall. Her burned hair crumbled and fell from her scalp with every movement she made, yet somehow was always replaced with more burned hair. "Who am I, then?"

Rose Red did not like to say the name out loud.

"I am the firstborn," said the woman. "Most powerful, most glorious, most beautiful of all my Father's children. A dragon such as the worlds have never seen before or since. I was a glory!"

She was so hideous and so repulsive, her words fell more awfully from her lips. Rose Red adjusted her grip on the lantern and raised it so that its silver light fell on that ravaged face. But the woman could not see the glow of Asha. All hope had long since fled her blind eyes, leaving her in this dark place on Death's Path.

"I rivaled the Father himself in might and flame," said she. "I could not be bound. I could not be stopped by any who moved in the Near World or the Far. Again and again, their finest warriors sought to kill me. Yet though I was slain twice over, Death himself could not bind me. I returned stronger than before. At last I sought even to vanquish the Spheres in their dance in the sky. I could have swallowed Hymlumé herself!" She snarled again, looking far more like a dragon than a woman.

When she spoke once more, her voice was a pathetic whisper. "Thus my Father took my wings from me. In jealousy, he bound me to earth. A dragon trapped forever in the body of a woman."

Her blind eyes fixed on Rose Red. The girl felt as if her soul were exposed.

"But we can be strong, can't we, child? We are not so weak as they like to think."

The smell of her burned flesh was sickening. Rose Red wanted to turn away but could not, not even when the woman put out a trembling hand and almost, but not quite, touched her veil.

"Don't let them fool you, child," she hissed. "You are strong. You don't need them. Not the Prince. Nor my Father. You don't need anyone! You are alone and you always will be. So was I. But I became a goddess, did I not? Do not the worlds still tremble at the mention of my name?"

"You have no name," Rose Red whispered. "It was forgotten."

The woman stood as though frozen. Then she bowed her head, and her hand fell to her side. "Forgotten," she said. "Always, we are forgotten." She clenched her fists and, for just that instant, ghostly fire flickered in the corners of her mouth. "No, it cannot be so! I won't believe it! The Dragonwitch will live on forever in the nightmares of all worlds!"

"But *you* were forgotten," Rose Red said.

"I *am* the Dragonwitch. I need no other name, no other title."

Suddenly her hands gripped Rose Red's shoulders, pinching deep into her skin. It hurt. Rose Red screamed, as terrified by that horrible blind face so close to her own as she was wracked by the pain.

"Go back to the living world," the Dragonwitch said in a voice as hot as steam. "Go back and show them all who you truly are. Forget who you have been. You don't need any of them! Be beholden to no one!" She drew a long breath, then recoiled. She spat, and her hot spittle ate through a corner of Rose Red's veil.

"I smell the devotion on you. Evil stuff! It will enslave you, this willingness to serve others at cost to yourself. What do they care for you? Have they ever even *seen* you? Yet you care for them . . . for one in particular."

She flung Rose Red from her. The chambermaid screamed and lost her hold on the lantern, which rolled away in the darkness.

The light went out.

Rose Red lay in the half-light, worse than any darkness, for it did not conceal all but revealed only the horrifying shadows of the cliff, the witch flowers, and the looming Dragonwitch. She saw the long arms reaching out, feeling for her in the gloom. Rose Red pushed herself up and crawled away, her bare hand clutching at stones, feeling for a possible weapon. Where had the lantern gone?

"Love no one," said the Dragonwitch. "That is the first lesson you must learn if you will become the woman you might be. Love no one. Trust no one. Make them love you instead."

Rose Red tried not to breathe, afraid the sound might draw the Dragonwitch her way.

"You're alone now. You must be strong."

Rose Red could almost hear her own voice speaking, telling herself the same thing. Her own voice made far more horrible in the snarl of the creature's words.

"Love will betray you. Better to betray love first."

She did not know what the dead woman might do to her. She only knew that she did not want those burned hands touching her again.

Where was her lantern?

"You need no one. You need nothing."

The voice was seductive. It seared down into her heart to brand its message there.

"Stand alone, stand apart. Depend on nothing but your own strength."

Rose Red's bare fingers touched something cold and smooth.

"Then you too might become a queen, a goddess, as I did."

Rose Red grabbed the lantern's handle, and the world filled again with light. It poured through the silver filigree, casting shadows far away, filling Rose Red's heart with hope once more.

The Dragonwitch towered directly over her. The light shone into her ruined eyes, and she saw nothing. Nevertheless, she turned away, bowing her head and covering her face with her hands. And now, for the first time, Rose Red could see another strange aspect of her appearance. Though she was burned so badly that her features were scarcely discernable, she was also soaking wet.

"Leave this place," she said. Water streamed down her face like tears, but she cried no real tears. "I would if I were you."

Rose Red recalled the stories she had heard and shuddered. The Dragonwitch had not burned to death the third and final time: She had drowned.

Keeping the lantern between the Dragonwitch and herself, Rose Red got to her feet and moved toward the door. The light of the lantern cast images on the cliff wall . . . stars and moons and suns. Those images danced and changed as she moved, and became men, women, and children; they became birds and horses and trees; they became winds and waters, mountains and skies. All pictures made of light, moving through the darkness with hope and beauty.

The Dragonwitch saw none of it. She did not move until Rose Red stood at the little door in the cliffside and put her hand to the knob once more. Then she said, "You walk freely into Death's arms. Why?"

Rose Red made no answer. The poor, dead monster could not understand. She turned the knob and stepped through into the inky blackness beyond, taking the light with her. The door shut behind her.

5

THE NEAR WORLD

I T SHOULD NOT HAVE BEEN POSSIBLE to add insult to injury that night, but somehow the fates declared that it must be so.

Lionheart was just picking himself up from the street when a sharp voice at the gate demanded his attention. He brushed himself off and turned, with as much dignity as he could muster, to see a finely dressed man, a minister of some sort or perhaps merely a high-end servant, standing at the gate with, of all things, a peacock under his arm. He was saying something very fast, and Lionheart could catch only a word now and then. He stepped back up to the gate and tried to convey to the man that he didn't understand, and could he please speak more slowly?

"For you," said the man as though speaking to an idiot. "From the Imperial Glory, Khemkhaeng-Niran Klahan. For your performance."

Much to Lionheart's surprise, the peacock was plopped in his arms.

"I say!" he cried. The bird hissed at him, showing a gray tongue, and he nearly dropped it. "I really don't want this!"

"Your humble gratitude will be conveyed to the Imperial Glory."

"But . . . but what am I supposed to do with a dragon-eaten *peacock?*"

"And your wishes for his prosperous and eternal reign. Good night!" The gate slammed.

Lionheart looked at the peacock. The peacock looked at Lionheart.

"If you're not a stew by the end of the week, it won't be my fault," Lionheart said and rolled his eyes heavenward. "Why me?"

There was nothing for it, though. With the heavy bird under his arm, trailing its ridiculous tail behind, he set off down the hillside and into the lower streets of Lunthea Maly. He'd gone no more than a few yards before the peacock suddenly struggled wildly. Lionheart lost his hold, and it darted off down the road, screaming as it went in an all-too-human voice: *"HELP! HEEEEELP! HEEEEEELP!"*

If that didn't attract every thief and vagrant in the whole dragon-fired city, nothing would.

The following morning found jester and peacock sequestered away at the end of an alley in the room that Lionheart rented at exorbitant rates. The bird had decided to take his rickety bed, so he'd spent the night on the floor, staring at the ceiling.

What was he supposed to do now? The sylph had been very specific all those years ago. Find the oracle in Ay-Ibunda. *"She will tell you what you wish to know."*

But honestly, he reasoned with himself, what did a captive Faerie creature know?

Nevertheless, it was the only clue that had presented itself in the last several years of Lionheart's travels. During the voyage with Captain Sunan, he had visited port cities in the kingdoms of Aja and Dong Min and dozens more where the Noorhitam Empire began. In each city he had practiced his juggling and clownery for peasant crowds and done what he could to seek out the fortune-tellers and mystics, those who lived closer to the Far World than everyday folk. He found few. Those he did find could tell him nothing of how the Dragon might be destroyed . . . and some refused to answer at all but ordered him from their premises at once.

So he'd doggedly proceeded to Lunthea Maly as the sylph had said, there laboring to make ends meet and to find some word of the Hidden Temple. There were hundreds of temples in Lunthea Maly. He could have taken his pick! So why, of all the temples and oracles to be found in all the East, must he require Ay-Ibunda? Ay-Ibunda, which could be found only by the emperor.

The emperor, who had refused to aid Lionheart.

There was something sickening, after a long night of fretful turning on the hard floor, about waking up to the peacock's beady eyes glaring down at him from his own bed. *"Help,"* the bird said, more out of principle than with any real feeling.

"I wonder how much your feathers are worth?" Lionheart growled as he sat up. Every muscle in his neck and shoulders screamed ill usage. "I could sell them after I pluck you for stew."

The peacock hissed at him.

At that moment, there was a knock at the door. Lionheart never received visitors. He had made no friends in Lunthea Maly, since most people assumed he must be mad—and he felt inclined to agree with them more often than not. The only person who ever came knocking was his landlord, who showed up like clockwork once a week. But he never came at such an unholy hour of the morning. . . .

Lionheart slugged himself to the door and opened it, blinking like the undead in the face of the rising sun. A man in beautiful red and green garments stood there. How did anyone manage to look that fine when the day had scarcely begun? Lionheart, who was still wearing his jester's clothes from the night before, tugged at his shirt self-consciously. "Can I help you?" he asked in halting Noorhitamin.

"Leonard of the Tongue of Lightning?"

"Yes?"

"Yesterday evening at the great coronation of the century, the Imperial Glory, Khemkhaeng-Niran Klahan, bestowed his favor upon you in the form of a rare and reverenced bird like unto the incarnate image of the Mother as a Firebird, beautiful in plumage, graceful in deportment."

"Help!" said the peacock. It hopped down from the bed and strutted over to stand beside Lionheart's knees. The gorgeously clad gentleman

looked down upon it and bowed gravely. He would never have considered giving Lionheart that homage. The bird hissed at him too.

The man turned to Lionheart again. "The gift of the reverenced bird was offered in a symbolic nature."

Lionheart took a moment to try to translate this in his head. He responded with the Noorhitamin equivalent of "Huh?"

"You were not supposed to accept the bird."

Another moment. Then Lionheart flung up his hands and swore in every language he knew. "Fine! Take the bird too! Do I look like I mind?"

"Your veneration and devotion will be conveyed to the Imperial Glory. . . ."

"HELP! HELP!"

"And your prayers for his eternal and prosperous reign . . ."

Lionheart picked up the peacock, receiving several nasty pecks to his hands, shoved it and its wretched tail into the other man's arms, and slammed the door.

No stew tonight. And no profit from peacock plumes either. What wretched, wretched luck! He flung himself down on his bed and only then realized that the bird had used his blankets for more than sleeping. *"Dragon's teeth!"*

Another knock at the door. Probably the landlord, coming to charge for the disturbance. Lionheart, busily wiping off his jester's smock, stomped back to the door, muttering as he did so, "Dragons eat that wretched Imperial Glory and all his wretched Imperial Gloriousness! And all peacocks too—"

He opened the door and found himself looking down into the delicate face of the emperor.

At least, that was Lionheart's first thought. His second was that he must be mistaken. The little boy in front of him was dressed in peasant's rags, with mud smeared over his cheeks and his hair covered in a ratty old hood. He could be the emperor's doppelganger for sure, but certainly not the emperor himself.

Then the boy spoke, and all doubt was banished. "I have come to repay my debts, Leonard of the Tongue of Lightning."

He spoke in a smooth Westerner's dialect with only the slightest trace of an accent. This could be no beggar boy.

"I . . . wha—Your Majesty. Your *Imperial* Majesty!" Lionheart sputtered in Noorhitamin—or, what he thought was Noorhitamin—and bowed deeply. Then, on considering, he went down on his knees, prepared to prostrate himself as was considered right in the presence of the Imperial Glory.

But the emperor, trying to hide a smile, spoke hastily in Westerner, putting out his hand. "No, no, I am incognito! And perhaps it will be best if we speak your tongue when there is no one present. I will laugh otherwise."

Lionheart staggered up from his knees, his heart racing. Any moment he expected soldiers to leap out of the doorways down the alley and run him through for daring to speak to the emperor, to even look upon him in such a humble state. "You . . . Your Imperial—"

"Don't call me that," the Imperial Glory said rather sharply. "Klahan is enough. I have come to repay my debt, but we must go swiftly."

"Your . . . I beg your pardon, Your—Klahan. What debt?"

"I promised anything that was within my power to grant," said the boy. He backed away from Lionheart's doorway, looking carefully up and down the alley. It was quiet enough at this hour of the morning. The dregs that lived in this quarter were all passed out asleep and would be until evening. The emperor did not look concerned but wary. "We must go quickly," he said.

"Where?"

"Ay-Ibunda, of course."

Lionheart stared. For a long instant, his world froze, and he thought nothing. Then it rushed into motion again, and his mind was awhirl. At last! At last, he would get answers! He was out the door in a moment, scarcely remembering to lock it. (Not that it would do any good one way or another. One did these things out of principle, not practicality, in this part of Lunthea Maly.) The emperor was already moving, and swiftly for his age, back up the alley toward the street on the far end. Lionheart pelted after him, gasping as he went, "But I thought you refused!"

"Naturally," said the Imperial Glory. He spoke the word so gracefully.

Lionheart would probably have hated the boy had they met when the same age; everything about him was so carefully put together, every word spoken with such care. At age nine, it was not a manner that would win him friends among his peers.

It might win the respect of an empire.

"The location of the Hidden Temple of Ay-Ibunda may be known only by the master of the Noorhitam Empire. Should I be seen by all the assembly to give you access to that secret, I should have been forever stamped as weak. As too willing to give up those precious things that set the Imperial Glory apart from mere men. I would be dishonored in the eyes of my people."

He turned left at the street and started again at a brisk walk, weaving between the urchins and beggars who were already swarming the city. Lionheart had to be nimble on his feet to keep up. "Besides," the emperor said over his shoulder, "my uncle would have been furious."

"So why have you changed your mind?" Lionheart asked.

"I have not," said the emperor. "I always intended to bring you to the temple. I made you a promise, and it would dishonor me to go against my word when what you asked is within my power to grant."

"But . . ." Lionheart frowned. "But you said you would be dishonored if you granted my wish."

"In the eyes of my people." Khemkhaeng-Niran Klahan turned his grave black eyes upon Lionheart. Those eyes seemed far too old for that young face. "But I should be dishonored in my own eyes should I refuse."

No doubt about it. The boy Lionheart would have hated this child.

The exiled Lionheart, struggling to fulfill a quest that was, he knew deep in his heart, impossible, could not help but be grateful. And he was curious too. After all, if the emperor was willing to disguise himself and show up at his door at such an unmentionable hour, then Ay-Ibunda must, in fact, exist. Yet Lionheart could have sworn he had combed every street, every nook, every alley in the last several years, desperate to find it. As far as he could gather, it was not to be found. He still wasn't entirely convinced it was real.

Perhaps this strange child was leading him somewhere else entirely. This could be a trap. Lionheart cast the emperor sideways glances as they proceeded up one street, turned, and started down another. This one led past a market square where vendors were already setting up their wares, calling greetings and insults to each other, half of which Lionheart could understand (the insults especially).

"Have you been to the temple before?" he asked the boy.

"No," said the Imperial Glory.

Now, that was a surprise.

"Then . . . how do you know where it is?"

"The same way I knew where to find you." The boy gave him another of those enigmatic looks. "I am the Imperial Glory of Noorhitam. The Paths of my empire are open to me." He grinned mischievously. "But don't let my uncle know!"

As he didn't understand what this meant, Lionheart had no reply to offer. He followed the emperor, trying to tell himself that they were not crossing the same streets over again, that they weren't wandering in circles. The emperor was only a boy, after all. He could easily be mistaken—

There was no lurch. There was no flash of light. There was no discernable sensation. One moment they were walking up the market square, listening to the shouts of fruit sellers and fishmongers; the sun was swiftly climbing and shining hot upon the streets, baking those who moved about their lives.

The next, the world was shrouded in mist, and they stood at the gates of a temple.

Lionheart stopped and stared. The emperor proceeded to the gate. It was not an iron gate, merely wood. But somehow, Lionheart knew that no assailants could penetrate here. The posts were painted blood red, and above the doors were many words written in Noorhitamin characters, which Lionheart could not read. As he drew nearer, rather timidly behind the emperor, he saw that the left-hand post was carved like a dragon, and the right-hand, like some fantastic plumed bird.

The Imperial Glory raised his voice and spoke in Noorhitamin. "Open to me, Ay-Ibunda," he said. He sounded so young standing there before that great gate in the dark mist. Why should so powerful a portal open at the word of one so small?

But immediately the gates parted. Their hinges must have been perfect, the construction exquisite, for though they were enormous and exceedingly heavy, they swung out without a sound, parting the mist.

The boy emperor beckoned to Lionheart. "Come, clown," he said. "I will take you to the Mother's Mouth."

The emperor passed to the inner court, vanishing within the mist. Lionheart gulped and hastened after, thankful when he caught up enough to see the top of the Imperial Glory's hooded head. He cast a last glance back and saw to his surprise (and somewhat to his horror) that the gates had swung shut as silently as they had opened. He decided not to look again but focused on following the little emperor.

He heard humming.

Human tones, Lionheart decided after a moment. Low and rich and frightening. There was no melody in the sound, at least not in the sense that Lionheart thought of melody. But it was powerful and sounded as though it had been going on for hundreds of years.

Through the mist, Lionheart thought he caught glimpses of men in black robes, a few in white. They stood in clusters, and their heads were bowed, so he never saw their faces. This was a strange relief. The idea of anyone in this dark place looking at him gave Lionheart the shivers. There were statues in the gloom as well, huge statues which he only saw when he was about to run into them. But then he could make out the features of a tall man who was simultaneously a tall woman, wrought in black-and-white stone. Other statues were man-and-woman, but also dragon-and-bird. They were grotesque yet beautiful.

Lionheart hated them the moment he saw them.

The emperor led him across the courtyard, which was strangely long, and at last to the first door of the temple. Here he turned to Lionheart, a silken scarf in his hand. "I must blindfold you, Leonard of the Tongue of Lightning," he said. "Mortal eyes are not meant to see the inner halls of Ay-Ibunda."

"What of you?" Lionheart asked as the emperor fixed the blindfold in place. "Are you walking blind as well?"

"I am the Imperial Glory," said the emperor. "I am permitted to see what mere men may not."

But there was a tremble in the Imperial Glory's voice. Lionheart realized that the boy emperor was afraid. Mortally afraid, and desperately trying to conceal it. This knowledge did nothing to decrease Lionheart's respect for the child. In fact, he marveled at how steady young Klahan's hands were as they tied the scarf, then took hold of Lionheart and gently led him inside.

The smell was different here. It was more like a sensation of heat, followed very quickly by ice-cold. But he felt neither hot nor cold; he merely breathed it. The emperor led him down what must have been a long passage. Lionheart counted thirty steps. Then a left turn and fifteen steps; a right, and ten; another right, and fifteen . . . he lost track eventually. He wondered if the emperor was lost. After all, he had never been here before. But the Imperial Glory never hesitated; his grip on Lionheart's arm never slackened or tightened but remained comfortably firm.

They stopped.

"Here," said young Klahan, "you must go on alone if you wish to speak to the Mother's Mouth."

"I do," said Lionheart.

"She may require something of you. Have you anything to give?"

Lionheart had brought nothing with him, not even his bell-covered jester's hat. He frowned.

The emperor pressed something into his hand. Something tiny and round, no bigger than a pea. "Give her this," he said. "They are rare. She will like it. Now kneel, Leonard of the Tongue of Lightning."

Lionheart obeyed. The boy guided his hands so that they gripped the frame of a very low, open doorway. "You must crawl," Klahan said. "When you reach the end, set this at the feet of the Mother's Mouth and ask her what you would know of the Mother."

Lionheart nodded. Then, because he didn't know what else to say, he ducked his head through the doorway and started to crawl.

He expected this leg of his journey to take no more than a few moments. He was wrong. The low tunnel in which he found himself stretched on forever, and his knees and back were sore and protesting long before he felt empty space above his head again. He still wore the blindfold. The Imperial Glory had not told him whether or not he could remove it. But there didn't seem much use in keeping it on now, so he slid it down around his neck. It made no difference. Wherever he had crawled was a black void and he could not guess how high the roof might be. But he had come to the end of the tunnel, of this he was certain. When he put out his hands to either side, he could not reach the walls. He must be near the Mother's Mouth now. If he went just a little farther—

"Stop!"

He obeyed. His heart thudded into the pit of his stomach and stayed there for what seemed a long time. Then it began racing double time. Clutching the little something the emperor had given him tightly in his hand, Lionheart slowly reached out. "I . . . I bring a gift," he spoke in halting Noorhitamin.

Whoever was in the chamber with him began to speak. He did not understand the words. They sounded Noorhitamin but not a dialect he had ever before heard, not Pen-Chan, Chhayan, or Kitar. This was much older than any of those, more lyrical, though the voice that spoke them was old and unlovely.

"I'm sorry," Lionheart said. "I don't understand."

The voice stopped. When it began speaking again, more slowly this time, it continued in the same language in which it had begun. But strangely enough, Lionheart heard each word ringing through his head in his own tongue. The sensation made him sick inside.

"Have you a gift for the Mother's Mouth?" the voice asked. It was a woman's but so ancient as to be almost genderless now.

Lionheart extended the hand holding the tiny drop. He felt a wrinkled claw of a hand take his, and he placed the gift into that one's keeping and withdrew.

"Ah! A pearl!" said the voice. "I feel the smooth whiteness, like sea foam made solid. A gift of the water gods, beyond compare." Little clucking, smacking noises then, as though the speaker salivated. Had the oracle eaten the pearl? Lionheart shuddered.

"You have come to ask a question of the Mother, have you?"

"I have."

"You realize that when she answers, your life will forever change?"

"I hope so."

"Hope? Here?"

A light struck and flared. It nearly blinded Lionheart and he covered his face with his hands. When he looked again, he saw an ancient, wrinkled woman sitting cross-legged before him, smiling a hideous smile. She held a candle cupped in both hands, and the glow from it cast her face in awful shadows.

Her eyes were white. She was blind.

"There is no hope in this place," she said, her mouth speaking one set of words while Lionheart heard another. "There is no hope, only fulfillment." Those sightless eyes looked into the space above his head, and her smile grew, revealing bare gums. "Tell me what you want."

"Tell me what you want."

The white eyes before him are no longer blind. They are penetrating, staring at him from a smooth ebony face. The glow of the candle is gone. There is no light in this place, though Lionheart sees clearly.

He sees the Lady of Dreams Realized. She is beautiful. She is horrifying.

"Tell me what you want."

"Who are you?" he gasps.

"You know who I am."

And Lionheart knows this is true. He recognizes her from a hundred dreams, only he knows that he is not dreaming now.

"Tell me what you want."

Never in his life, not even when he gazed into the eyes of Death, has he been so frightened. But somehow he finds a voice and says, "I want . . . I want to know how to deliver Southlands from the Dragon."

She smiles. Her white hair flows about them both like storm clouds, and Lionheart feels as though he is being dragged toward her.

"That is secret knowledge, indeed. The secret of my brother's doom."

"You asked me what I want. I have told you."

"And I will give you your answer, my darling, but only if you tell me something first."

He has come this far. He knows this is his only chance. "What do you need to know?" he asks.

"Tell me what you want."

"*I just told you!*"

"*No, my child. That is not your dream, your secret dream most dear to your heart; that is merely your mission. Tell me your dream, Lionheart, for I am the Lady of Dreams Realized and I long to realize your dream for you.*

"*Do you wish to remain where you are? Free from the duties to which you were born, free to be the man you choose to be? Free to love whom you will, free to go where you please? Do you dream of freedom?*

"*Or do you wish to return? Do you long to fulfill the desires of your mother, of your father? Do you dream of being the prince you were born to be, of becoming the king? Will you marry as they have chosen for you and take up the burden of your forefathers? Will you be Eldest of Southlands?*

"*Tell me what you want.*"

Lionheart is suspended in blackness, enormous blackness without floor, ceiling, or walls. Perhaps he is falling; he cannot say. The weight of the choice pressures him from all sides while simultaneously tearing him in two. He knows the moment of decision has come. But he hates it. As though he must kill a piece of himself, sacrifice one man that the other might live.

In the end, there is only one choice he can make.

"*I will be Eldest of Southlands,*" *he says.*

"*So be it.*"

Lionheart blinked and saw the glowing candle once more. Then he saw the rest of the room as well. No longer did it seem a vast and unsearchable vacuum. It was nothing but a bare little room with a wooden floor, wooden walls, a straw pallet in one corner, and a basin in which something nasty reeked. A hermit's hovel would seem lavish in comparison. It was dark, dank, and disgusting, well suited to its occupant.

The Mother's Mouth gazed at him, the smile fixed on her ugly face.

"You have seen the Mother, yes?"

He shivered under her blind gaze. More than anything Lionheart wanted to crawl back out of that chamber as fast as possible. "I . . . I still have no answer to my question."

"I will give it," said the oracle. "The Mother has declared this wisdom unto me. Listen closely, mortal man! What you desire may be found when you have received a certain ring out of Oriana Palace in Parumvir. You will know this ring by two things: its stones, fire opals, as hot inside as a dragon's flame; and its giver, a princess who will fear you at first, but later will laugh."

"A ring?" Lionheart frowned. "How . . . forgive me, Mother's Mouth, but how will a ring help me kill a dragon?"

"Did you ask how to kill a dragon?"

"I . . . yes. I must deliver my kingdom."

"This is the Mother's answer. I have no other to give you." Her smile did not shift. The candle flickered and made it seem a snarl. "Find your ring, mortal. Find your ring, and your dream will be realized."

She blew out the candle.

The horror of being in the dark with that crone was too much. Lionheart backed out on his hands and knees, finally turning around and crawling as fast as he could. Much to his surprise, within moments he hit his head, and the little door swung open. He fell out into the passage beyond.

"Close your eyes!" cried the voice of the young emperor. Lionheart obeyed immediately. There was something about that boyish voice that compelled obedience despite his tender years. Lionheart lay in a pile on the temple floor, his eyes tightly shut. Small hands untied the knot of the blindfold behind his neck, then retied it across his eyes.

The Imperial Glory helped Lionheart to his feet. "Did you receive what you sought?" he asked as he led him back down the twisted, silent passages.

Lionheart did not know what to answer. At last he said, "I must make my way to Oriana Palace in Parumvir."

"Across the world?"

"Yes." Lionheart sighed. "Across the world."

6

THE NETHERWORLD

The moment Rose Red was through the door, she heard the Black Dogs howling.

It was too late to turn back. When she whirled around to put her hand on the latch, the lantern light showed her only a solid rock face. Frantically, she felt among the sharp stones. Surely the door could not have vanished! But it had.

The circle of lantern light was her whole world, and empty space extended forever all around her. There was no half-light in this place; here the blackness was almost solid. And somewhere out there the Black Dogs bellowed, hunters pursuing their prey with never-slackened bloodlust.

They pursued her now; she knew it. And those whom the Black Dogs chased, they always caught in the end, bearing that luckless soul away to Death. Unlike the Wolf Lord and the Dragonwitch, they were very much alive.

Rose Red began to tremble, her back pressed against the rocks of the cliff that stabbed like daggers. But her lantern still glowed, and the dogs were some way off.

"Move your feet, fool girl," she growled. "Move them!"

Slowly, she obeyed herself. Then faster. Not a run. No, she would not be chased. She would walk with purpose, keeping the light steady, and find what she found, whatever it may be.

The dogs bayed as one, and the voice was darkness.

Rose Red's hand shook, but the lantern yet glowed.

She heard a new sound: The gentle lap of water against a shore, rising and falling. Had she come to an ocean? The sound grew, so she knew she must be drawing near to it. Perhaps not an ocean, but certainly a large body of water. How was she supposed to cross? The Path led this way, she was certain, but it led to nowhere.

The Black Dogs cried again. Then they were upon her.

Fear was almost enough in and of itself to kill her when Rose Red saw their enormous bodies before her, blocking her path. They were too big to be measured. Sometimes she thought they were bigger than mountains, sometimes only the size of horses. Their baying deafened her so that she could not hear her own scream. She wanted to cover her ears, to curl up into a ball. She wanted them to swallow her and be done with it so that she would not have to endure this terror a moment longer.

But the lantern continued to shine, and the Black Dogs drew no closer.

Why didn't they finish her off? They skirted the lantern light, refusing to let its glow touch their shadowy bodies. When it even glinted in their red eyes, they turned away with hideous snarls.

Maybe she wasn't going to die. At this realization, Rose Red felt her heart slowly calm. It seemed like years, but at last she was breathing again and able to stand, shivering only slightly, and consider with a rational mind the problem before her.

They stood between her and her path. And though they did not like the lantern, they would not let her pass.

Walk forward, the thrush's silver voice sang in the deeper places of her mind. *They'll not harm you.*

When she stepped forward, they lunged.

They'll not harm you. Not while you hold the light.

In spite of this assurance, Rose Red could not help but stagger back.

Trust me, child. Trust me and walk before me.

"I . ᷁. I cain't," she breathed. They would drive her out. Maybe she would rather let them herd her from this dark realm where the living did not belong? She did not have to come here. It was what the Dragon wanted, wasn't it? Better to not give him his way.

Walk before me, child.

"I don't know you!" she growled. "Not anymore!" She took another step back.

Then the Dragon spoke.

"Throw them your glove."

That voice was more dreadful to her than even the baying of the Dogs. It came to her out of nowhere. But it came with heat and fire.

"Throw them your glove," said the Dragon. "They'll not stop till they have what they were sent for."

"Wh-what were they sent for?" Rose Red whispered, unable to hear her own voice above the Black Dogs' din.

"I sent them for your other glove, sweet princess," said the Dragon. "They'll not let you pass until you give it to them."

"Maybe I don't want to pass."

"Very well," said the Dragon. "Return to what's left of your promise to the prince. I'm sure I can make Lady Daylily very comfortable down here."

Rose Red swore. Then she looped the handle of the lantern over her arm and peeled her second ragged glove from her hand, this time with no hesitation. Her desperation to be rid of the Black Dogs and their midnight would have driven her to far greater extremes.

You needn't give in to him. Walk before me.

But there was no certainty that way. The Black Dogs growled and lunged, and her fear was far too great. Rose Red flung the glove with all her strength into the darkness beyond the lantern's glow.

The lantern dimmed.

There was a snarling, vicious noise as the creatures brawled like alley mongrels. The next moment, they were gone. The midnight faded into half-light.

Rose Red found that she stood on the shore of a vast black lake. She knew then that she had reached the depths of the Dragon's world. Her bare hands were cold as they gripped the handle of the dimmed lantern.

"The Lake of Endless Blackness." She named it, and knew the name was true. Only now the lake was no pond created by damming up a streamlet. It truly was a lake, too large for her to see across, and the water was as black as ink, even where the light shone upon it.

She had no boat. Was she supposed to swim? She put out a tentative foot, slipping a toe into the water. A dread like death overwhelmed her at that one touch, and she drew back with a stifled cry. "Silent Lady," she whispered like a prayer. "Silent Lady, shield me!"

But there was no Silent Lady here. Rose Red stood alone.

"You've always been alone," said the Dragon's voice, disembodied in the half-light. "You've always been alone but for me."

From the lake's black waters rose a mist that carried the poison of the Dragon. It whirled in elusive shapes, like the sound of a scream or the sensation of pain made visible. Ghostly hands dragged a small boat across the water to the shore where Rose Red stood. Thus was a crossing provided.

"I've got to go on now," she told herself. "I've come so far."

The boat creaked as its prow touched the shore. To all appearances, it was made of twigs . . . incredibly large twigs tied together with twine the thickness of a man's arm. Like one of Leo's toy boats but life-size. It sported one raggedy sail and a rudder, and it waited just for her.

Breathing many prayers to whomever might listen, Rose Red stepped onto the flimsy craft. The ghostly hands gave a last tug, and it moved away from the shore, carried by the waves out into open water. Rose Red held tight to the lantern with one hand, its dimming light her only comfort on that water. Her other hand gripped the rudder, for all the good it would do her.

The lake pulled her out to its depths.

Just as before, a vault of emptiness arched above her, not sky, just darkness. The lake water did not reflect that darkness but was, in and of itself, black. The only light came from the lantern, but Rose Red did not like to look at it for fear of seeing her own bare hand clutching the handle. She set her face ahead, surveying those unsearchable reaches, hoping to catch some sight of a distant shore.

How long she voyaged, she could not say. How could time be measured in this place? She felt very old and very young simultaneously. Like death and like birth.

Something flickered in the lantern light. Rose Red gazed forward and a little to her left and saw an enormous rock jutting from the lake. The little stick boat glided past it, and she saw that the rock was smooth and polished and gleaming, a pure gold stone. An altar. The sight of it made her sick, though she did not know why. She turned away and was glad when the boat sailed on and left the gold stone far behind her.

"You were always meant to be mine," the Dragon whispered from the emptiness.

Skeletons of other boats and even great ships littered the lake beneath her. Rose Red saw them the farther she got from the shore. The hulls, like bleached bones, shimmered with their own cold, hopeless light, very different from that in the Asha Lantern. Rose Red remembered the games she and Leo once played, making and sinking ship after ship on the Lake of Endless Blackness. How many of their own dreams had they built and destroyed with their own hands, leaving them to sink into oblivion? How many of their own and each other's?

"Leo," she whispered as she looked over the side of her small craft down at the broken ships below, "I'm so sorry." A tear slipped down her face behind her veil. "So far I've only failed you."

Stop striving, child, the silver voice said.

"Stop striving," said the Dragon. "Give in to me."

Walk before me.

"You were always meant to be mine."

I chose you before you were born.

"I want you."

I love you.

She shook her head, closing her eyes. "If you love me, why have you abandoned me? Why do you let me wander down this Path to Death?"

This is not his Path, child, said the silver voice, the voice of her wood thrush's song. *Though darkness surrounds you, and you walk to the very household of Death, you walk my Path, not his. I am with you always.*

"Don't believe a word of it, princess," said the Dragon. "Look around you! Could this world be anything but mine? I am Death-in-Life, and you have entered my domain. Your only chance is to turn to me. I am master here, and only I may help you."

"No!" she growled, her grip on the lantern and the rudder tightening. "I don't need you! None of you! I'll do this myself. I'll do this for Leo."

"That's right, my princess," whispered the Dragon. "Come to my arms."

Remember me, child.

Then, because she could not bear to hear those voices anymore, Rose Red burst out singing. Her voice was not beautiful. It was very ugly, in fact. But she sang loud and long, sending the words rolling across that black water, ringing from shore to shore. She sang the first song that came to her head, the song she had grown up listening to the mountains sing:

> *"Cold silence covers the distance,*
> *Stretches from shore to shore.*
> *I follow the dark Path you've set before my feet.*
> *Let me follow no more!"*

And answering her out of the empty vault above came the silver voice, stronger than her own:

> *Beyond the Final Water falling,*
> *The Songs of Spheres recalling.*
> *When you find you must pursue that lonely way,*
> *Won't you follow me?*

The light of the Asha Lantern flared to new and brighter life, and Rose Red felt her heart lifting.

At the same moment, she saw a red-gold glow flickering hot in the distance. She approached the far shore of the Lake of Endless Blackness.

Beana sat by the gates of the Eldest's House. She sat in her own form now. What was the use of disguises? Four years at least, perhaps a little more, had passed since last she'd glimpsed her charge. Deep inside, she knew she was despairing; and though she also knew this was wrong, at the moment, she did not care.

Very faintly, wafting through the dragon smoke, across the courtyard and out the gate against which her back was pressed, a voice reached Beana's ear.

Won't you follow me?

She was on her feet in a second just as the gates, at long last, swung open to her. "Light of Lumé!" she exclaimed. "It's about time!"

A shaggy goat pelted across the stone courtyard as fast as her cloven hooves could carry her, vanishing into the curtain of smoke.

7

The Near World

ORIANA PALACE SAT ON TOP OF A HILL overlooking the city of Sondhold by the sea. It was built in the time of King Abundiantus V of Parumvir, just outside the fringe of Goldstone Wood. This had been a daring move on the part of that king of old, for in those days Goldstone Wood was considered nothing short of an enchanted forest, a refuge for all manner of strange beings of the Far World. But the palace had been constructed nonetheless and, over the course of several hundred years, added on to until it was become a beautiful structure indeed, complete with a seven-tiered garden extending down the eastern side of the hill and ending where Goldstone Wood began.

King Fidel ruled the kingdom of Parumvir these days, holding court in Oriana. He was a well-liked king. Every third and fifth day of the week he opened the great Westgate to the common people so that they might bring petitions before him.

Southgate, however, was never opened to the common people. Certainly not on the first day of the week.

"Here! Here, what do you think you're doing?"

Two guards in heavy armor (which may or may not have added to their sour moods on that hot summer's day), who looked as though they were unused to actually working at this post, took hold of a brightly clad intruder as he sauntered without ceremony through Southgate into the gardens of Oriana.

"Oi!" cried the intruder, who was mad-looking in hideous, multi-colored raiment. "I say, sorry about that."

"Get out!" One of the guards pulled the idiot from the grip of the other guard and gave him a shove back through the gate.

The Fool shoved back. "Pardon me," he said. "I'll not leave just yet, thank you. I have a letter from—"

"Dragons eat your letter," the guard said and this time shoved harder, pushing him back beyond the wall. "Out!"

"Not until you hear me." The stranger shook himself free of the heavy hand and straightened his threadbare costume. "I am come from Amaury Palace, and I have a letter from King Grosveneur—"

"Sure you have," said the other guard. He was smaller than the first, his voice thin. "Away with you, lad." He made to shut the gate.

The Fool darted forward and caught it, and since he was stronger, pushed it back open and leapt inside. "I say, this is no way to treat guests!"

"We don't treat guests this way," the larger guard said. "Only tramps." He caught the Fool by the back of the neck, lifting him like a kitten by the scruff. The Fool kicked, catching the guard in the shin, and both guard and Fool howled in pain, pulling apart from each other and hopping about, the guard clutching his leg, the Fool clutching his foot. The smaller guard hooted with laughter, which earned him a knock in the side of the head from his fellow. Then they both turned to the idiot and lunged.

"Oi!" bellowed the Fool. "If you don't let me through, I'll be certain it gets back to your superior officer, and you'll wish you'd never—"

"Right. As though you'll be on chatting terms with my superior officer," the bigger one growled. "Listen, mister, we don't let just anyone come trampin' through here, and anyone who tells you otherwise—"

At that moment, movement among the bushes caught the Fool's gaze. A girl stood there, peering out from behind a bush. She wore a simple gown, and her hair was pulled back in a braid with strands escaping messily about her face. Her eyes were round with surprise, and when she saw the Fool looking at her she ducked back behind the shrubs. He could not tell if she was a lady of the palace or merely a servant, but it seemed worth a try.

"Lady!" he cried. He pulled and twisted, nearly breaking free again. "Fair lady! You seem of a gentle nature. Tell these blackguards to unhand me—*OW*!"

The smaller guard caught hold of his ear and gave it a vicious twist, knocking his bell-dripped hat off in the process. Then the big one picked him off his feet and tossed him out through the gate. The Fool rolled ungracefully in the dirt partway back downhill. With a cry of "And take your hat with you!" the guards slammed the gate with a final, ringing clang.

Lionheart—for it was he, somewhat thinner, paler, and more threadbare than last seen—picked himself up stiffly. He could feel bruises developing all over his body. How was it that he could face a dragon and live, yet couldn't get past two such bumblers? They watched him between the bars of the gate, so with great dignity he walked back up the hill. They stiffened and one put a hand to his sword, but Lionheart did not look at them. He picked up his jester's hat, which looked like a crushed flower. Shaking it out so that all the bells jingled, he placed it back on his head, tilting it at a rakish angle. Then he swept the guards a bow. "Farewell, great oafs of idiotic disposition," he said. "Until next we meet."

"Away with you!"

Lionheart hastened back down the hill.

He did not retrace his path down the western side of the hill into Sondhold. No, that would be to admit defeat. This was merely a regrouping to consider his next course of action. He'd already tried his luck at Westgate and been rebuffed. "Bring your petitions on the third and fifth days of the week," everyone said.

"I don't come with a petition! I come with a letter of recommendation from—"

But no one believed him.

One dead end after another. Lionheart cursed as he picked his way down the hill. Was he destined to spend another four years in Sondhold, just as he had in Lunthea Maly, desperately trying to gain access to the palace and being turned back at every portal? Performing at Beauclair had not proven this difficult. Amaury Palace was famed for its spectacles and entertainments, however, and a jester of any worth could easily find a place there. Not so in sober Parumvir.

Goldstone Wood grew up this side of the hill, and Lionheart found himself approaching its thick and untamed borders. The shade cast by the trees looked inviting. Any relief from this blistering heat would be welcome. Lionheart doubted any of the fabled monsters that purportedly lived within that shade would suddenly creep to this portion of the wood to devour one rejected jester. So he flopped down with his back against a tall, spreading maple at the edge of the forest, and took stock of his position.

Somehow he had to get into the palace and present his letter to the steward. King Grosveneur's seal would undoubtedly carry some weight, but not with idiots like those guards at the gate, who probably couldn't spoon porridge to their mouths without special instruction. Yet how could Lionheart get past them?

The weight of his problem, the heat of the day, and the long climb up the side of the mountain joined together in a force too great to withstand. Exhaustion worked its own persuasion, and he slept.

You know the Princess Varvare.

The voice sang into his mind while Lionheart lay between waking and sleeping.

She has gone from this world. Beyond reach of my voice.

He groaned and stirred, but his eyelids were too heavy with sleep to open. His body felt oddly paralyzed where he lay amid the roots of the maple tree. His mind felt paralyzed too, unable to drive out that voice that was not a voice, speaking without language.

My master grows impatient.

Lionheart muttered, "Dragons eat your master."

Then his eyes flew open and for the briefest moment he saw the Other. *When you see her, you will send her to me. I will wait in the Wilderlands.*

Lionheart woke in a cold sweat, still sitting up. His hands had torn up great handfuls of dirt, which he now released. Slowly his breathing calmed, and he crawled out from under the shade of the trees.

"Serves you right," he whispered, taking comfort in self derision. "Everyone knows you shouldn't nap in a Faerie Forest. Especially not so late in the day."

The sun was setting, and the day was cooler. Lionheart was just as much on the wrong side of the wall as he had ever been. He stood awhile, trying to shake off the nightmare. He remembered none of it—almost the moment he woke, the vision had fled his memory—but the sensation of fear lingered. To drive it off, he started walking along the wall of the palace gardens, trailing a hand against the stone blocks as he went.

Suddenly Lionheart turned and looked up the wall.

All he needed was a moment with a housekeeper or the steward, someone with brain enough to recognize King Grosveneur's seal. If he could just present himself at the palace and bypass those dragon-blasted guards, he did not doubt he would gain entrance.

He must gain entrance. He had a ring to find.

Resolve quickened him. He darted downhill until once more he reached the edge of the Wood, where the trees grew right up against the garden wall. As easily as he had once climbed the mountainside near Hill House, he scaled the trunk of a big oak and scooted along thick branches overhanging the wall. Gaining the wall itself, he looked down.

The sun was setting in earnest now, illuminating some of the world in a brilliant glow but casting the rest into deep shadows. In that awkward lighting, he found it difficult to guess how great the drop below him was, whether it was the same as on the far side, shorter, or longer. But there was nothing for it now. He took a deep breath and jumped.

And landed on top of someone who let out the most ear-splitting scream that ever shattered a man's eardrums.

They tumbled in the path, Lionheart ending up on top, squashing the slender person, who kept screaming for all she was worth. "Oh, hush!" he cried. "I'm so sorry! I beg you, please, quiet!"

Her screams increased, and he had no choice but to clamp a hand over her mouth. He still had not seen her face, but he could tell she was a young woman, hardly more than a girl. Poor thing, he must have terrified her; but then again, she wasn't increasing his peace of mind either.

She wriggled in his grasp, still screaming into his hand, though the sound was muffled. "I say!" he hissed between his teeth. "Really, I'm sorry. I had no idea you were down here. Terribly rude of me, I know, but I can't help making an entrance, it seems, no matter how I try."

He felt her relax a little in his grip as he spoke, and the screaming stopped. Hoping against hope that it had ended for good, he allowed her to sit up. "Are you quite calm?"

She nodded.

"All right, I'm going to let you go. Please—"

The moment he loosened his hold, she pulled free of him and leapt to her feet, whirling around to face him. In the last glow of the sunset he got his first good look at her. It was the maiden from the garden, her braid messier than ever, her eyes wide with terror.

She was, he noticed, quite pretty.

But she was drawing breath for another great bellow.

Without stopping to think, Lionheart flung himself on his hands and knees before her. He spread out his hands and cried in a voice of despair, "Please! Can you forgive this lowly worm, O gentlest of maidens, for his unforgivable rudeness, dropping in on you, so to speak? Will you forgive him or strike him dead with a dart from your eyes? Oh, strike, maiden, strike, for I deserve to die— No! Stay!"

She stared as he rose to his knees and covered his face with his hands, wailing, "I do not deserve such a death! Nay! It would be far too noble an end for so ignoble a creature as you see before you, to die from the glance of one so fair! No, name instead some other manner for my demise, and I shall run to do your bidding. Shall I cast myself from yon cliff?"

Leaping to his feet, he sprang over to a statue on a pedestal a few feet away. It was the figure of a king looking over his shoulder in stern scrutiny of the world. Lionheart clambered up onto the pedestal and put his arm around the stone king's waist. "She says I must die," he told it, indicating the girl with a sweep of his hand. She stood with her mouth open, hardly seeming to breathe. "Will you mourn for me?"

The stone king scowled. Lionheart turned and gazed with great melancholy across the garden, pressing a hand to his heart. "Farewell, sweet world! I pay the just price for my clumsiness, my vain shenanigans. My grandmother told me it would come to this. Oh, Granny, had I but listened to your sage counsel while I was yet in my cradle!"

He made as though to jump but paused and turned to the girl. "Farewell, sweet lady. Thus for thee I end a most illustrious career. The Siege of Rudiobus was hardly a greater tragedy, but then, Lady Gleamdren was not such a one as thee!"

He gathered for another spring, catching hold of the stone king's fist at the last moment. "I don't suppose my end could be put off until tomorrow, could it?"

The girl started to speak, but afraid it would turn into a scream, Lionheart interrupted with a hasty, "No! For you and your wounded dignity, I must perish at once. Go to, foul varlet! Meet thy doom!" With a cry, which he dared not make too loud, he flung himself from the pedestal, turned a series of neat somersaults, and stopped in the path just at the girl's feet, flattened like a swatted fly. He twitched once, then was still.

Silence followed.

He opened one eye and peered up at the girl, who was staring down at him. "Satisfied, m'lady?"

To his huge relief, a smile broke across the girl's face and she laughed out loud. At the sound of that laugh, Lionheart, for the first time in his life, fell in love.

It wasn't all that difficult, the whole falling in love business, Lionheart thought later on as he sat in a tiny room in the servants' wing of Oriana, darning his jester's motley. Inconvenient, to be sure, but not difficult.

The girl, it turned out, was a princess. Of course she was. He should have known the moment he set eyes on her that she could hardly be anything less. Princess Una of Parumvir, only daughter of King Fidel, out for a stroll on a fine summer evening, alone with her thoughts and a book of poetry.

And a fine opal ring gleaming on her finger.

Just like the oracle had said. Lionheart's face hardened into a scowl as he focused on his stitching. *"You will know this ring by two things: its stones, fire opals, as hot inside as a dragon's flame; and its giver, a princess who will fear you at first, but later will laugh."*

So the ring was found. That was well done, and about time, after months of weary travel.

But Una was a different matter altogether. Lionheart had never once considered, from the moment he crawled from the oracle's presence, that the princess in question would be so sweet, so pretty, so ready to laugh. She was nothing like Daylily. Certainly not as beautiful, but that was no great disadvantage on Una's part. Una laughed. Lionheart could not recall ever hearing Daylily laugh save in the most affected manner. What's more, Una thought he was funny.

There was something most appealing in that.

Don't forget your chosen dream.

Lionheart licked his lips and put a knot at the end of a seam. He snipped his thread, knotted it, and started another patch.

You will be Eldest of Southlands. You will deliver your people.

"I haven't forgotten," he growled.

Then take the ring, my darling, and be on your way.

"I can't just *take* something from her. She trusts me. She got me this job . . . didn't even ask to see my papers." He finished another seam and knotted his thread again. "I'm not going to betray that trust."

A snip and the thread dropped free. Lionheart, standing before a dusty little mirror, put his jester's jacket back on, buttoning it slowly as he regarded himself. He certainly didn't look a prince anymore. Neither did he look a boy. Five years of exile had passed, taking with them the last of his childhood. Lionheart gazed at a reflection he scarcely recognized; he gazed into a man's face.

Beneath a jester's hat.

"I don't even know who I am anymore."

What a wretched time to fall in love.

Don't forget your dream.

"Maybe my dream can grow," he said, tugged one last time on his shirt, picked up the lute he had been loaned for the evening, and stepped from the room.

He had a performance to give.

King Fidel, at his daughter's request, had agreed to take Lionheart— once more under the name of Leonard the Lightning Tongue—on trial. If he performed well tonight, he might find a place in Oriana, at least for the time being. That was a place he sorely needed if he was going to figure out a way to get that ring. A kind way, of course, nothing sly or underhanded. He wasn't going to hurt sweet Princess Una, not after she had done so much for him already.

He made his way from the servants' quarters down a twist of passages to the king's favorite after-dinner sitting room. The whole build and style of Oriana was so different from the Eldest's House. The walls were white, for one thing, the moldings much simpler, more discreet. But there was a richness to the simple lines of Oriana that appealed to Lionheart. He came to a hall of portraits, which he had glimpsed earlier that evening when Una led him through the palace.

One of the portraits had caught his eye. He stopped before it again.

It was a small piece in a very old style; a storytelling style intended to convey a certain truth of the tale without specific accuracy to the characters. There were three men with the same face, two of them chained together, the third one crowned. There was a woman in the center of the piece, and she wept beside a gold stone, an altar, on which lay a figure that was like a man and yet, horribly, like the Dragon.

Lionheart shivered when he saw that image. He knew it was the Dragon, knew it as surely as if it had been painted with scales and wings and flames. A bile of hatred rose in his throat.

"I'm going to kill you," he whispered to the painting.

Don't forget your dream, whispered the Lady in his head.

"I haven't forgotten," he said. "And I'm going to kill him."

Then he veiled his face in smiles and entered King Fidel's sitting room.

King Fidel, a middle-aged man with silver in his beard, looked up from a doze when Lionheart walked through the door. "Ah, yes," he said. "I'd almost forgotten. I asked you to entertain us tonight, didn't I?"

"Quite so, Your Majesty," Leonard replied. He bowed and backed into a quiet corner to tune the lute, glancing about the room as he did so. The king remained seated in his comfortable chair near the fire. At his feet sat the crown prince, Felix, a gangly young fellow who pretended to have no interest in a jester but who was obviously curious.

Across the room sat another prince; a visitor, Lionheart had been given to understand. One Aethelbald of Farthestshore. A suitor for the princess's hand. Lionheart spared him no more than a glance and decided, in that glance, that he didn't like the man.

He avoided looking at Princess Una, though he knew just where she sat. To his great pleasure, she rose, plopping a fluffy orange cat on the floor as she did so, and stepped over to greet him.

"I told you I'd get you a job, didn't I?" she whispered. Her smile was sweet. Inconveniently so.

"Don't count unhatched chickens," he whispered back. "Your father has declared little need for a full-time Fool, and I may yet find myself out on my ear."

What a bashful schoolboy he was acting. Look her in the eye and be a man!

"But I should not even have this opportunity were it not for you," Lionheart continued, smiling back at the girl. "I hope I can properly repay your kindness. He would not have given me a chance but to please you."

"It does please me," the princess said. "But make him laugh and you'll be hired on your own merit."

"I shall endeavor to oblige, m'lady."

"Una," King Fidel said around his pipe, "come sit by me and let the jester play."

Una obeyed. Lionheart quickly finished his tuning, stepped into the middle of the room, and struck a harsh minor chord. Then he was singing, a foolish jester's ditty he had written during his travels. It was grand to play it for an audience who understood the language. His voice was not beautiful, but he sang with enthusiasm and an expressive face, and soon had the princess, her brother, and her father laughing out loud. Even the quiet prince in the corner chuckled as Lionheart swept to a grandiose final chord.

"Excellent," King Fidel declared when the chord had faded away. "Sir Jester, we are glad indeed to have you among us. If you are half as skilled mopping floors as you are at spinning stories, we may just find ourselves at an agreement."

Mopping. Lionheart's face hardened, though he managed both a smile and a bow. Here he was, so near to his goal, and reduced to a household drudge.

He caught Una's eye. Her face was alight with laughter. In that moment, it made him sick. He excused himself with another bow and hastily exited the room. The lute slapped against his side as he went. The hall outside was dark with only a few of the candle sconces lit, illuminating some of the paintings. Lionheart marched to the end where that small painting rested and gazed once more upon that white face, that face he hated so.

My darling—

"Lionheart."

The sound of his own name startled Lionheart so badly, he thought his heart might stop. He whirled and saw someone approaching through the gloom of the hall. It was the Prince of Farthestshore, that man who visited Oriana to court Princess Una.

Lionheart swallowed, then bowed deeply. After all, he was only a jester and an extra mop. "I beg your pardon, Your Highness," he said in what he hoped was a cool voice. "May I help you?"

"Lionheart, I know who you are."

Lionheart straightened up and found himself gazing into the Prince of Farthestshore's eyes. They were kind eyes, though perhaps a little sad. But they gazed right down into his soul, and Lionheart did not like that.

"I . . . forgive me, Your Highness. I don't know what you're talking about." The Prince of Farthestshore would not break his gaze, and struggle though he might, Lionheart at last had to look away. "Maybe you've mistaken me for someone else," he said. "I am Leonard the Lightning Tongue, jester to kings and emperors."

"Yes, you are," said the Prince. "But you are also Prince Lionheart, exile of Southlands. And you seek to defeat the Dragon."

Lionheart felt his face paling. His whole body went cold. He licked his lips and tried to speak again. "You . . . you are mistaken—"

"No, prince, I am not." The Prince of Farthestshore's voice was gentle. It irked Lionheart no end. He wanted to run, to escape those kind eyes, to never again hear that voice. "Why," asked the Prince, "have you not returned to Southlands? Why have you not returned to face the Dragon?"

"I . . . I am from Southlands," Lionheart admitted. "But there's no use in facing the Dragon. He cannot be fought."

"Not if you do not face him," said the Prince. "And even then, there is only one way he can be defeated."

Lionheart thought of Una's ring. He'd seen it gleaming on her hand again as she clapped and applauded his performance. Strange that something so small, so insignificant should hold so much power. But the oracle had spoken, and Lionheart did not doubt her words. He remained silent.

The Prince of Farthestshore said, "You will have to die."

Lionheart shot a quick look at the Prince's face. Still those kind eyes burned into his. A thousand words rushed to his mouth. How dare this stranger come lecture him! Had he not suffered enough these last five years? The labor, the humiliation—and it only promised to continue. Did he need to have this upstart, who knew nothing of the trials Lionheart had experienced, telling him what to do? Speaking so blithely of things he couldn't possibly understand? Had *he* gone to the oracle in Lunthea Maly? Had *he* sought out hidden Ay-Ibunda? Had *he*, with his fine clothes and fine manners, any idea what it meant to suffer the Dragon's work?

And here he was, courting Princess Una, who by all rights should have been Lionheart's to pursue. If the world were fair, if the gods were just, he, Lionheart, should be here as a prince with a rich retinue to seek her hand. Yet here he was, a floor-scrubber and Fool, barely permitted to lay eyes upon her. In that moment, Lionheart believed he hated the Prince of Farthestshore.

"I can help you," said the Prince. "If you will follow me, I will help you defeat the Dragon."

Lionheart's face was as stone. "I don't know what you're talking about, good Prince," he said. "If I did, perhaps I could help you. I am nothing but a humble jester, however, and these things of which you speak are beyond my knowledge."

He bowed again and, though he knew it was unendingly rude, turned and marched down the hall, leaving the Prince standing beside the Dragon's crude portrait. His heart was racing so fast with fury and determination, he thought he might explode. He wished the Dragon was before him right now and that he was armed with a sword. He would hack the monster limb from limb with hardly a thought!

The Lady enfolded his mind in her arms.

He doesn't know what he's talking about. How could he possibly? You know what you're doing. You have a dream to follow.

"I know what I'm doing," Lionheart growled. He tore the jester's hat from his head and mangled it in both hands.

I will not let you die. I will see your dream fulfilled.

"I'll kill the monster yet. And I'll sit on the throne of my fathers. Silent Lady help me!"

She won't help you, sweet prince. I will.

8

THE NETHERWORLD

CHANDELIERS HUNG FROM THE DARKNESS, perhaps attached to a ceiling too high to be seen, perhaps suspended from shadows. They were gold and wrought in curious shapes, and held hundreds of black candles at a time.

The dragons moved below.

They entered the Hoard of their Father and gathered beautiful treasures. Gowns of purest silk from ages long past, crowns of purest gold that had belonged to kings and princes. One great dragon woman, whose fire burned more fiercely than that of all the rest, plunged both hands into a chest full of rubies and strung these through her long black hair.

Thus adorned, they filed back to the center of their Village, where the chandeliers glowed. The candlelight gleamed on their riches and their eyes. Beautiful yet unsmiling, they stood gazing out across the Dark Water. They had never seen this lake before. But this was the world of their Father, and he would shape it as he willed. They stared across the water, expecting something, though they knew not what.

"Dance," said their Father.

They turned, each taking a partner, and began to dance. There was no music here, but there was rhythm. They were graceful dancers, and though there were hundreds of them, each couple moved as though in a world of their own, like so many stars dancing their silent steps in the sky. Not one of the dragons looked into his or her partner's face. They were absorbed in themselves and could not bear to look at another.

The floor heated and writhed beneath their feet.

In the flow of the dance, a certain yellow-eyed dragon with a sallow face and lank hair came with his partner to the edge of the Dark Water. His empty eyes gazed out across the darkness and caught sight of something. He snarled and stopped the dance.

"That light!" he said. "The evil light!"

Other dancers stopped as well, the pause rippling across the whole dance floor until they all stood still once more.

Then the yellow-eyed monster snarled again. "Douse the light! Kill it!"

They were all roaring then, rushing down to the edge of the water—though careful not to touch it, for dragons do not like to get wet—stretching out their bejeweled fingers and arms as though they would pluck the silver light, which was like a white sun moving toward them across the surface of the lake, from its place and crush it into nothing. At first it was too distant for them to see what caused the glow so unlike the glow from their own chandeliers; they only knew they hated it.

It represented everything they had lost long ago.

The dragon with rubies in her hair pushed to the forefront, and it was she who first saw the person carrying the light. A tiny chambermaid, ragged and covered in a veil, trembling as she clutched the handle of a silver lantern. The ruby dragon gnashed her teeth, longing to devour the girl in a single bite.

And still Rose Red's boat drew nearer to that crowded shore. She could not tell faces apart, could not even discern man from woman, so united were they in their hatred. She saw claws and teeth; she saw jewels and crowns. She saw death in every pair of eyes.

Walk before me, child, sang the wood thrush.

She bowed her head over the lantern and held it before her face. "Stop!"

The Dragon's voice rolled across the mass of his children. Their roaring ceased. They parted ways, crowding into each other with only little snarls and snaps, creating a path through their midst. Down this the Father of Dragons walked, majestic in black robes, crowned in white fire. He paced to the edge of the Dark Water and waited as the narrow stick boat drew to shore.

"Princess," he said, "you have come to me."

His face was that which she had seen a hundred times and more in her mountain dreams. How strangely friendly and welcoming it seemed when compared to the faces of his swarming children. Rose Red peered through her veil at him and took comfort from his very familiarity.

Her lantern dimmed.

"Welcome to the Village of Dragons." The Dragon extended a hand to her as the prow of her little boat touched the shore. "Allow me to assist you."

"I'll assist myself," she snapped and jumped from the ship to the black rocks of the shoreline. Immediately, a wicked current took hold of the twig boat and dragged it out into the deeps. Rose Red looked over her shoulder and watched as her craft sank and vanished, joining the others at the lake's bottom. "Silent Lady," she whispered again and turned back to face the Dragon.

He smiled down at her. "You have not dressed properly for the occasion."

"And . . . and what occasion is that?" she managed. Her voice was small; the heavy breathing of hundreds of dragons threatened to drown it out.

"The occasion of your arrival, of course," the Dragon said. "We have all longed for you for years now. Have we not, my children?"

The dragons murmured and growled. There wasn't a trace of longing in their voices. One dragon somewhere in the crowd said, "That light! Rid us of that evil light! It hurts my eyes!"

The Dragon's lips drew back sharply, and Rose Red glimpsed black fangs where a moment before had been even white teeth. "Enough! Do not frighten the princess who will soon be your sister."

"Father." The voice that spoke was deep enough to belong to a man, but it came from the great red-clad dragon. She was tall and strong, but Rose Red had never seen a more heartbreaking face. Vengeance and fire had swallowed up all trace of womanliness. The rubies were like sparks and embers in the darkness of her hair. "Is this not one of the Veiled Folk? Is she not Vahe's lost one?"

"Indeed," the Dragon purred.

"Does he know you have her?"

"Do you think he would have tried nothing by now if he knew?"

The ruby-clothed woman laughed. There was fire in her mouth. "He hasn't long until the Night of Moonblood. He must be anxious."

"When have we known Vahe to be anything else?" The Dragon laughed as well. "He still has hope, after all these years. All these centuries. Hope is so beautiful, such a delicate flower! One must take a certain delight in watching how he nourishes it." He gazed at Rose Red's lantern as he spoke, and yet again, the light diminished.

"Is she the one, then?" the ruby-clothed woman continued. When she asked this question, a hush ran through the masses of dragons as they leaned in to hear what the Dragon might say. "Is she the one you seek?"

The Dragon's gaze did not leave the silver lantern. "That remains to be seen."

"She does not look as though she would have the fire in her."

"The fire has burned in stranger places."

The ruby-clothed woman was dissatisfied with this, and she stepped closer, inspecting Rose Red, making strange snuffling noises as though she were a hound sniffing out quarry. "What makes you think she is your Enemy's Beloved? She is so puny."

"Have you not noticed," said the Dragon, "the protections surrounding her? She reeks of him. See the Asha Lantern he gave her? And he set one of his knights to guard her."

"A Knight of Farthestshore?" The woman drew back from Rose Red. "Here?" She gnashed her teeth. "Where? I'll tear the flesh from his bones!"

"No, she is not here, my child," said the Dragon, his voice low and dark. "I would not let her through the gate. She'll not come this way again if I have anything to say about it."

Rose Red glared from the Dragon to the woman in rubies, not understanding a word that passed between them. Suddenly she stamped her foot.

"Here now! Don't you talk about me like I'm a hunk of meat or somethin'! I'm here with a purpose, and I mean to see it through. I ain't goin' to put up with any more of this nonsense."

The Dragon smiled down on her again. The black fangs were gone, and his face was remarkably handsome. Beautiful, even. "What makes you think you have a choice, my love?"

She quailed inside but forced herself to keep speaking, though her voice trembled. "I've come for m'lady. I know you have her down here. She doesn't belong to you, and I mean to fetch her back."

"She came of her own will," said the Dragon.

"Only 'cause you poisoned her!" Rose Red cried. Her fury at the Dragon rose, disguising some of her fear for the moment. "Only 'cause you tricked her. She ain't yours . . . she ain't dead yet, and I ain't goin' to let you keep her down here."

"But, darling, this isn't the Land of the Dead." The Dragon's voice was as smooth as the silken clothes he wore. "This is but one stopping place on that long road. Lady Daylily may remain here as long as she pleases and not die."

"She don't please to stay."

"That's what you think."

"Let me see her!" Rose Red cried. "Let me see her and talk to her! She'll want to come back with me, and you've got to let her go if she does." She held up the lantern, and the gathered dragons drew back, hissing like a pit of vipers.

But the Dragon stood firm. "I'll make you a deal, my sweet."

"No deals."

"If, after you speak to her, Lady Daylily wants to return with you to the World Above, I will let you both go. Otherwise, you both must stay. And I will kiss you."

"No deals!" Rose Red repeated. "I know better than to bargain with the likes of you."

"Princess," said the Dragon. "Shall we dance?"

Her free hand, the one not holding the lantern, was taken in his. He pulled her to him, one hand around her waist, and they were dancing. The other dragons danced around them, but she could not see them. She heard unreal music in her head, dizzyingly nightmarish. At first her surprise was so great that she did not think to struggle. By the time surprise faded, her feet were falling naturally into the rhythm of the song, and Rose Red could not think to break away.

The lantern dimmed to a mere glimmer.

"Your hand is so soft, princess," said the Dragon. "So beautiful."

"No . . ." Rose Red licked her lips behind her veil. "No it ain't."

"But it is. Have you looked at it?"

"No, and I . . . I ain't goin' to!"

"And you yourself," the Dragon continued, his eyes running over her from head to foot. "You are beautiful."

She realized that her servant's dress was gone, and she wore instead a rich gown of midnight hues, studded with jewels that snapped like sparks. The veil covering her face was soft indeed.

The Dragon was very handsome, his face that of an ardent suitor. They whirled beneath the brilliant chandeliers, and Rose Red glimpsed only here and there the world around her. The Village of Dragons. But, she realized with a pang, also the Great Hall of the Eldest. So, the Eldest's House was dragged still deeper into the Netherworld.

She gritted her teeth and scowled, though the Dragon could not see it behind her veil. "You look stupid in that getup," she said. "You look like a fop and fool! I know your real face. You cain't trick—" Her voice broke. Then she gasped, "Iubdan's beard!"

She no longer danced with the Dragon. It was Leo who held her in his arms.

"Rose Red," said Leo's voice, "I cannot thank you enough for all you have done for me."

She stared up at that face she knew so well. Those same dark eyes, those same boyish features. Only now he was grown into himself, manly in bearing, his face more handsome because of the trials he had endured. Rose Red could not breathe. "I-Is it really you?"

"Of course it is, Rosie," said he. "I've come back at last. Come back to face the Dragon only to find that you've done it already! You've saved my family, saved the kingdom. What a wonder you are, Rosie. Truly the best of friends. In fact . . ." His gaze pierced her veil, compelling and tender. "In fact, you are so much more than a friend to me. Won't you raise your veil?"

His hand reached up and touched the edge of it, lifting gently. "Raise your veil and let me kiss you," he said.

Rose Red felt the soft fabric moving, falling back from her face. She squeezed her eyes shut and wailed.

"NO!"

When she opened her eyes, the Dragon stood before her again. His mouth was set in a flat line, but after a long moment, he smiled a mirthless smile.

"Your secret is out, princess," he said. "You are in love with Prince Lionheart."

She stared at her feet, or at least at the edge of the long ball gown she still wore. A tear spotted its velvet bodice. "No I ain't," she said.

"Don't try to lie to me," said the Dragon. "I've known you for as long as you can remember. And I wanted you to love me."

"You're horrid," she said. "Where . . . where is Lady Daylily?"

"Prince Lionheart's lovely lady?"

"Where is she?"

"Your rival?"

"Hen's teeth, you demon, tell me where she is!" Rose Red raised her fist as though to pound the Dragon's chest. But she saw that cold smile on his face and turned away at the last moment. She pressed her knuckles to the side of her face and drew a long breath, like a sob.

The Dragon's hand took her own. "Come with me, little princess."

She was too weak, too exhausted by now to resist. She dropped the Asha Lantern, and it fell with a cold clatter on the stones and lay there, its light extinguished. As the Dragon led the girl away, the other dragons swarmed over the little lantern, fire dripping from their mouths, and when at last they parted, Asha was no more.

The Dragon led Rose Red across the Village, toward the edge of the chandelier light. Ahead, Rose Red saw a woman approaching, dressed in rich clothes. It took her a moment to realize that the woman was not Daylily; it was herself, reflected in a tall, black-framed mirror. The gown bared her shoulders after the fashion of Southlands; its midnight skirts billowed behind her like clouds. But her veil covered all her skin save for her ungloved hands.

Beautiful, golden hands.

She stopped before the mirror, gazing through the slit of her veil at that other veiled face.

"Lady Daylily can never rival you, princess," said the Dragon. "Not as you really are."

"You . . . you lie," she whispered.

"Remove the veil and see if I do. Remove the veil and see yourself for the first time."

"I don't want to see. I know what I am underneath."

"You know what they've told you. You don't know the truth. Look and see!"

Rose Red took the veil in both hands and pulled it from her head.

9

The Near World

He sees her in a dream, *dressed in silks and lace. The light veil that covers her face only just conceals the contours beneath. She is in his arms, and they dance to strange, dark music beneath a hundred brilliant chandeliers.*

They dance in the Hall of the Eldest, though nothing is recognizable in the vast, dimly lit room. Lionheart does not need familiar markers. He knows with the certainty that comes only in dreams exactly where he is.

"Rose Red," he hears his own voice say, "I cannot thank you enough for all you have done for me."

The veil gently wafts about her shoulders as she tilts her head to look up at him. He longs to see what is underneath. The world is hot around them, but in this place he is cool, and she is soft in his arms.

"I-Is it really you?" she whispers. Her voice is unmistakably Rose Red's, and yet nothing like the rough little country voice he knows so well. It is the voice of a princess. He smiles down at that soft veil.

"Of course it is, Rosie," he says. "I've come back at last. Come back to face

the Dragon." The words thrill in his heart. Is the time really come? His hand tightens about her waist, seeking her comfort and support. Lionheart never before realized how delicate she was beneath all those rags of hers. And what might lie behind that veil? "What a wonder you are, Rosie. Truly the best of friends. In fact . . ." He licks his lips, afraid of what her answer might be. "In fact, you are so much more than a friend to me. Won't you lift your veil?"

She says nothing. The heat from the chandeliers is almost unbearable.

His hand reaches out of its own accord, fingering the edge of her veil. "Lift your veil and let me kiss you," he whispers.

The world erupts in fire.

Lionheart woke with a start and wondered where he was. His face was covered in sweat, and the blankets were much too hot. He sat up in darkness, pushing the covers back and wiping his forehead, his breathing loud in that stillness. One small window above his bed was cracked open, and a soft breeze blew through.

Dreamlike voices rang in his head.

Leave him alone! He is mine!

He is the key to the princess's undoing. I will have my rights.

Touch him and you'll regret it, brother. He belongs to me!

Through the open window, a sudden burst of moonlight shone through. As it fell in a patch on Lionheart's blankets, the voices ended abruptly, as though severed. When they were gone, Lionheart doubted he had truly heard them.

He remembered where he was. Parumvir. Palace Oriana on the hill above the city of Sondhold. He had been hired to serve as jester and floor-scrubber and had, only a few hours before, given his first performance.

He hunched his shoulders and bowed his head, exhausted but too disturbed by the dream to go back to sleep. How awful the Great Hall of the House had looked! Beautiful but otherworldly.

And how strange that he should dream of Rose Red. Years had passed since he'd spared a thought for his childhood friend. Was she keeping her promise, watching over his family, those imprisoned in his father's house? He could only hope.

Hope, and return as soon as possible.

But first he had to get that ring. The oracle had spoken.

"Preeeowl?"

Lionheart startled at the unexpected sound, but the next moment, something large and fluffy hopped up onto the bed beside him and set up a thunderous purr. A big tomcat rubbed its head against his shoulder and flicked a tail in his nose.

"Dragons eat you," Lionheart growled. "How did you get in here?"

The cat's purring stopped. It put its nose right up to Lionheart's and hissed in no uncertain terms. Even by moonlight, Lionheart could see that the cat had no eyes. This handicap earned it no sympathy, however. Lionheart was a consummate cat hater. He tossed the creature from the bed, only just avoiding a severe scratch down his cheek.

"Rrrrrrrowl!" said the cat, and began pointedly grooming a paw. Then, with a suddenness that took Lionheart by surprise, it leapt across the room to the chair by the fireplace, where Lionheart had carefully folded and set his jester's garb for the night. Before he could make a move, the blind cat took his jester's hat between his teeth. Then it was out of the room like a shot, the way it must have entered, through the cracked window. Lionheart had just time to swear, but not enough to snatch the hat back before it disappeared with a forlorn jingle.

He leapt up and peered through the glass. His window looked out upon the kitchen gardens in the upper tier of Oriana's grounds. The cat sat in a patch of moonlight, grooming its tail. The hat lay beside it.

"Iubdan's beard!" Lionheart grabbed a pair of trousers, hauled them on with his nightshirt flapping down to his knees, and was out of the room in a moment. A few disoriented turns, and he managed to find his way out to the kitchen gardens. There the cat waited, still grooming its tail as though it hadn't another concern in the world. But when Lionheart approached, it perked its ears at him, hissed, and grabbed the hat. Lionheart darted forward but missed and landed hard on his knees, watching that plume of a tail dart off down the garden path. His hat jingled from the cat's mouth.

"You monster!" Lionheart cursed the beast and gave chase. The cat stopped and waited until he had almost caught him before dashing on again. The creature was a devil with a fluffy tail.

"I will return for you."

Lionheart pulled to a halt, his heart leaping to his throat. Someone else was in the gardens at this bizarre hour! Someone close. His hat momentarily forgotten, Lionheart sidestepped behind a shrub, taking shelter in its dark shadows. He peered through the branches and saw two figures farther down the way. The smaller one was a woman, but she stood with her back to him and he could not see her face. The other, he recognized in a moment: the Prince of Farthestshore.

The woman spoke, and her voice was harsh. "I . . . I don't want you to return!"

Una! Lionheart's fists clenched. She sounded distressed. Should he go to her? But one look at the Prince's face, which the moonlight revealed, and Lionheart held his peace and remained where he stood.

"Nevertheless," said the Prince, "I will come back for you."

Hate him!

The Lady's words hissed through his mind.

Hate him! Loathe him!

Lionheart had never before heard that icy voice so full of venom and fire. In that moment, it was almost indistinguishable from the Dragon's. He shivered and sweated where he stood.

"Please, Una," said the Prince of Farthestshore, "let me tend your hurts before I go. . . ."

Then Una was backing away from him up the path. Lionheart heard her voice, angry and fast, and he only just restrained himself from leaping out to her defense, though from what he would defend her he could not say.

Hate him, whispered the Lady.

"Go already, if you're going to!" Princess Una cried. The dismay in her voice could have broken hearts. Lionheart longed to comfort her. "I wish you'd gone ages ago! I wish . . . I wish you'd never come!"

Then she rushed up the path at a furious pace, her bedgown clutched in both fists. But the Prince of Farthestshore kept pace beside her, and

Lionheart heard him say clearly, "Una. I love you, Una. I will return to ask for your hand. In the meanwhile, please don't give your heart away."

Lionheart saw the expression on the princess's face as she passed so close to him. He saw the tears, the sorrow, and even the pain. Then she was gone up the path, and the Prince of Farthestshore stood alone in the moonlight, only a few feet from where Lionheart hid.

Hate! breathed the Lady. Her voice was very small now, as though afraid to be overheard.

"Preeeowl?" said the cat. It sat at Lionheart's feet and dropped the jester's hat. Lionheart gasped, and the Prince of Farthestshore turned and looked directly at him, his gaze piercing the shadows.

"Prince Lionheart," he said, "come out."

Lionheart stepped forward, aiming a kick at the cat as he went, which the creature dodged with ease. It scampered forward and twined itself about the Prince of Farthestshore's ankles, flicking its tail and purring smugly. The Prince gently pushed it away with one foot, though it came right back, still purring.

"Good . . . good evening, Your Highness," Lionheart said with a deep bow. "Pardon this disturbance, but the cat stole my hat." He reached out and picked it up, jangling it to emphasize the truth of his words. Why must he feel like a thief caught with his hand in the jewelry box? It wasn't his fault the cat had made free with his belongings! It wasn't his fault he'd overheard.

"Lionheart," said the Prince of Farthestshore, "it is time for me to go."

Lionheart blinked. "Um. Your Highness, my name is Leonard. I am not the person you seem to think I am."

"One of mine is threatened," said the Prince, never breaking Lionheart's gaze. "She is one of yours as well. I must return to Southlands and liberate her when she calls."

Lionheart licked his lips and took a step back, bowing again quickly. Return to Southlands! In that moment, how desperately he longed for his homeland.

"Come with me," said the Prince. His eyes were endlessly deep, and they bored into Lionheart's. Lionheart turned away. "Come with me, back to your kingdom. Together we can face the Dragon."

A raging desire to drop that wretched jester's hat and kick it to the moon filled Lionheart. To kick it all to the moon and follow this Prince back to his homeland. To finally, after all these long years, face the monster and reclaim his kingdom.

No! The Lady clutched at his mind. *Don't forget your dream! How will you fulfill your dream if you depend on this man? You* must *save Southlands. You, and you alone. Take the ring, as I told you, and you will learn how to rid Southlands of my brother's presence once and for all.*

Her voice was like daggers inside him. It pained him even to consider disobeying.

Take the ring, and don't listen to this man!

The Prince of Farthestshore extended his hand and spoke gently. "Come with me, prince. Now is the time."

Don't forget your dream. He is trying to take it from you!

Lionheart shook his head and continued backing away into the shadows. "No," he said. "I . . . I don't know what you're talking about. I am no prince. I am a humble jester. Do . . . do what you think you must, Your Highness, but I'll have no part of it."

The cat spat at him, its ears pinned back. "Peace," said the Prince, and the creature subsided. Then he spoke to Lionheart one last time. "It is your choice to make," he said. "You do not have to obey the one who haunts your dreams. Come with me."

Lionheart clutched the jester's hat tightly in both fists. "No!" he said.

Then he was running up the path, the same way Princess Una had run. He felt as though the Lady herself pursued at his heels, her voice filling his senses.

Remember your dream.

10

The Netherworld

THE GOAT FELT all the Dragon's powers seeking to drive her back. But his barriers had fallen the moment Rose Red sang the song on the Dark Water. Let him do his worst; there would be no keeping Beana from her charge now!

She barreled through the door and stopped a moment in the front hall, turning this way and that, her keen yellow eyes taking in more than what was readily apparent. She saw how much the Eldest's House had slipped into the Netherworld. She saw the Dragon's poisons climbing like ivy up the walls.

"Bah!" she bleated and trotted across the hall floor, her sharp hooves clattering on the marble. She followed her nose, followed the strongest of the awful stenches, and it took her to the doorway that should lead to a servants' stair but didn't.

Here she paused and dropped all traces of her goat disguise. "May my heart beat with courage," she whispered in song and in prayer. Then, bracing herself, she stepped through the portal into the darkness of Death's Path.

But the Path held no fear for her. The lady knight immediately recognized it for what it was. Although it passed through his domain, this Path did not belong to the Dragon. It belonged to her Master, and she could walk it with ease.

Her heart rose in her breast as she made long strides down into the darkness. One would have thought from the look on her face that she soared on eagle's wings. Following the silver light of the lantern, she hastened to the grave of the Brothers Ashiun and knelt a moment in respect to their memory. When she took the lantern from the stone, it yet remained in place to guide future travelers. Such was the power of that light.

The Asha Lantern's beam sliced through the half-light and gloom, across the far reaches of the Netherworld. The Wolf Lord did not try to cross her. The Dragonwitch trembled and hid her face. The Black Dogs turned tail and fled, dragging their Midnight behind them. The lady knight hastened down into Death's world.

She had passed this way before. This time she was not afraid.

⁓

The veil fell away and lay at Rose Red's feet. She looked into her own face, reflected back at her in startling clarity.

It was a face of unreal beauty.

Wide silver eyes set in a skin like warm gold. Thick black hair with glints of red fell in a tumble down below her shoulders, curling gently about a slender neck. Her lips were full and red. Her cheekbones were fine and distinct.

But above all, she glowed with a life that was more than life, which shone from every fiber of her being. Hers was a beauty beyond that of mortals. The words of the man she called father returned to her:

"My Rose Red, you are a Faerie child. Born different from everyone else, and that's why you look the way you do."

"Faerie child," she whispered.

"That's right, sweet princess," said the Dragon. He stood behind her, and his face was also beautiful, though not so beautiful as hers. "Now you know the truth. You're not what they have all feared. You're not the mountain monster. You are more lovely than their mortal eyes could bear to look upon. Thus your mortal father hid you in rags and veils; thus your guardian told you that you must never show your face. People would see at once that you are Faerie and not meant for their world."

"Faerie," she breathed. She touched her face with both hands, gently prodding the soft skin. How clear and sweet was her complexion. How radiant were her eyes. How unreal . . .

"You understand now what you may be, unveiled," said the Dragon. "Fairer than the fairest blossom. Thus you are named *Varvare*, the loveliest rose."

His hands were on her shoulders, lost in the thickness of her hair. Slowly he turned her from the mirror to face him. "They would have kept you captive, Princess Varvare. They would have kept you bound by lies. But I reveal who you truly are. Beyond rival. Beyond compare." His face was close to hers now. "Let me kiss you, my sweet."

Rose Red met him eye to eye.

"No," she said.

The Dragon vanished. So did the mirror, the chandeliers, the polished stone floor on which the dragons had danced. Rose Red found herself once more in her servant's dress, though the veil was gone from her face. Despair threatened to overwhelm her. Her lantern was gone, and the darkness, the potent smell of poison from every corner, grappled with her senses. She turned about, seeking some sign of her whereabouts. Was she yet in the Village of Dragons? Or had he transported her elsewhere by some dark art?

The Dragon's throne caught her eye.

It was a hideous creation, up on a black marble pedestal and carved like intertwining dragon skeletons, polished and dreadful. Bloodstained, it stank of death.

Seated on the pedestal, her feet dangling over the edge and her hands folded in her lap, was Lady Daylily.

"M'lady!" Rose Red cried and darted toward her. The pedestal was taller than she expected, and when she reached it she could not touch Daylily's feet as she stretched up her hands.

Daylily looked down at her, moving her feet slightly away. "So you've come," she said. "I told you not to."

"I'm here to fetch you home, m'lady," Rose Red said. "Please, come down!"

"Your veil is gone."

"I can catch you if you jump. I'm stronger than I look."

"It doesn't matter. I knew the secret behind your veil long ago."

"Hen's teeth," Rose Red muttered. She glanced about and saw a small stairway cut into the marble block. She hurried up and came around beside the Lady of Middlecrescent. "I don't know where he's gone off to, m'lady. But we'd best get while we can! I think I can find the way out of here. I've walked Faerie Paths before, though none like this."

Daylily's eyes were colder than stone when she turned her gaze on Rose Red. "The poison does not affect you, does it, goat girl."

Rose Red didn't know how to answer. It affected her, to be sure, but it did not shatter her inside the way she saw it shattering Daylily. "Please, m'lady," she said. "I've got to get you back. What would Leo do if you—"

"Leo? Ha!" Daylily's laugh was harsh. "Do you think Leo cares for me?" Her face twisted into such an expression of bitterness that Rose Red would not have recognized her. "I've watched my dreams die. Every one of them, burned to oblivion. I will never marry Prince Lionheart. I will never fulfill the expectations placed upon me. I wish—" Her eyes narrowed, and her hands twitched as though she might want to hide her face. But she did not. She stared into Rose Red's eyes, and the Lady of Middlecrescent was as unveiled as the chambermaid. "I wish you would go and let me die."

"You see what would happen were you mortal as she, princess."

The Dragon appeared before the pedestal, within reach of Daylily's feet. Rose Red clenched her jaw and, with strength her tiny frame should not possess, hauled the lady up and back, positioning herself between Daylily and the Dragon.

The Dragon smiled. "Everything would be so much easier were you a mortal child," he said. "The poisons would work faster on your brain. You'd have asked for my kiss ages ago!"

"I ain't askin' now."

"No, you are not." He folded his arms. His face was not beautiful now as it had been when they danced. It was ghastly white, and his eyes were black save in the depths of his pupils, where the fire glowed. "It would have been different, too, had I won Prince Lionheart in the game. But no. My sister must take him, manipulate him for her own pleasure." He snarled, and sparks shot between his teeth. "She's so selfish sometimes, I wonder how she can live with herself."

"I don't know what you're talkin' about," Rose Red said. She felt Daylily sagging behind her and turned just in time to catch the girl and hold her upright. She was not fainted, merely too worn out to stand anymore. Her spirit was broken, and her body failed as well. Rose Red gnashed her teeth in frustration and turned to the Dragon. "I only know that my good master has gone to find out how to kill you."

"I know."

"And when he returns, that's just what he's goin' to do. Then . . . then you'll be sorry."

The Dragon's snarl turned into another horrible smile. "He'll never fight me, Princess Varvare. Your puny mortal prince is destined for another fate. And he will never fight me."

Rose Red suddenly felt she could not hold Daylily. She knelt down, bringing the pale lady with her, and they crouched there before Death's Throne as the Dragon approached and climbed the stairs.

"Lionheart is destined to fulfill his dream," said he. "He will return to Southlands and reclaim his kingdom. He will marry Lady Daylily and make her his queen. Such has he dreamed, and such will my sister do for him. And where does that leave you, my darling? My treasure?"

Daylily curled into a tiny ball, her head pressed into Rose Red's chest. Rose Red wrapped both arms around her as though she could protect her. But her strength was running out. She'd given all she had, and it wasn't enough.

"He will forget you," said the Dragon. "He already has. Do you think he has once stopped to consider you in all these years? For it has been years, my sweet, years and years in the Near World while you have wandered in my realm. He's a different man now, and whatever you meant to him then, you mean no longer."

Her heart opened, and the poison flowed in. Rose Red could not stop it. It was like drowning. She felt the fear and anguish wash across her uncovered face, revealing everything to the Dragon's gaze. She wished for her veil, but it was gone.

The Dragon's smile grew. "My fumes work such beautiful marks upon your countenance, princess. I've never seen you more vulnerable. It enchants me."

He knelt down before her and the cowering Daylily. His long white hands reached out and cupped her face so gently, like a lover. Smoke poured from his mouth, and his eyes burned bright. He murmured, "There is no one left for you, child. I am all that you have. Will you allow me to kiss you now?"

She had no voice with which to speak, for her fear had struck her dumb. But her lips formed the word.

"No."

The fire in his eyes flared, and hot embers fell upon her face so that she screamed and crumpled over Daylily, covering the lady with her body. But the Dragon grabbed her wrists, burning her skin with his touch, and pulled Rose Red upright, forcing her to look at him.

She stared in horror, unable to tear away her gaze as his face lengthened and covered over with scales and his cloak became wings. His hands dropped hers and became great claws tearing the pedestal beneath him. As he grew, he backed onto the floor below, and soon towered over the throne, over Rose Red and Daylily. His flame burned through the darkness, revealing the highest crags of the cavern, miles above. One arm reached out and tore at the stalactites, and if Rose Red and her lady had not been crouched beneath the Dragon's body, they would have been crushed in debris.

Fire poured from his mouth onto the floor, surrounding the throne and the pedestal in a lake of flames. The smoke that rose from it was like a thousand ghostly faces howling in silent screams.

Then the Dragon whispered to her.

"You have a friend nowhere, princess. The Prince has dammed up the flow of his compassion against you. Even the knight he sent to guard you has fled my fire. No servant from his courts will stretch out a hand to help you. All heaven has abandoned you; you are alone. See the companions of your childhood from whom you once took comfort?"

The smoke took on flesh and blood, forming faces she knew: Lionheart, Beana, the man she called father. They turned and looked at her, one by one.

"What are they worth?" the Dragon said. "Cast-down child, see how the cowards spit upon you and hate you when you most need them! Behold!"

The effigies distorted into fierce masks, their arms raised against her, then vanished in heat and smoke. The Dragon dominated her view.

"You have no friend left in this world or the other. I have sent word throughout all regions, summoning every prince of darkness to set upon you this night, and we will spare no weapons. We will use all our infernal might to overwhelm you; and what will you do, forsaken one?"

His face, both dragon and human, was close to her own now, and his hot breath seared the skin from her cheeks. "Will you let me kiss you?"

Rose Red opened her mouth to answer.

But suddenly a white light shone so brilliantly that for a moment she thought her own fear had blinded her. Then she heard a voice calling through the smoke and flame:

"Rosie, child! Remember the Name!"

She shielded her face with her hands and saw a tall woman clad in brown and white, carrying the beautiful Asha Lantern. She walked through the flames as though they were not there and stood just beneath the Dragon's nose.

He looked down upon her, and the expression on his face was pure hatred. *"You!"* he bellowed, flames building up in his mouth.

But the woman spared no glance for him. Her eyes pierced Rose Red's. "The Name, child! Call upon the Name!"

With a voice that was hardly her own, Rose Red cried out:

"ESHKHAN! ESHKHAN, come to me!"

Protection surrounded her. It had always been there, but she had been unable to perceive it in the fire. Like silver water, like music rushing over her in a shield greater than stone, stronger than iron, the wood thrush sang:

Walk before me, child.

The Dragon shrieked. His wings beat the smoke and flames of the burning hall until they billowed to the sky.

But the birdsong surrounded her:

You are not abandoned.

"What have you done?" the Dragon roared. *"What have you done?"*

There was terror in his voice, more horrible than his fire. Rose Red crouched down with her arms over her head, unable to tear her gaze from the sight. He shrieked again, and the sound brought down the last standing pillars of the hall. Then he looked right at her, opened wide his mouth, and bellowed a great plume of fire.

But someone stood between her and the flame.

Her Prince. The Friend she'd once thought imaginary, now powerful and beautiful, unarmed before the Dragon's fury. Neither human nor Faerie, he was something altogether unique. Something wonderful and dreadful and worshipful. Rose Red covered her eyes, but her ears still heard.

"It is not my time!" The Dragon raged in the face of the Prince. "Your Beloved will be mine!"

The voice that spoke was as the silver voice of the thrush.

"Not this child," said the Prince. "You will not have her."

"I won the game! I won, and I must have my due!"

Flames spewed, roaring over the throne, the pedestal, the Prince, and Rose Red, in consuming death. But the Prince did not move. He stood over her and took the blast. The fire could not touch him, and his face was calm in the inferno.

"Away from this place now, Dragon," he said. "Release your hold and fly. What you seek is not here; you will never claim this child."

The Dragon bellowed volcanic ash. There was a crack as though worlds split one from another, and Rose Red felt her gut lurch, as if plunging in a terrible dream. She screamed.

Her Prince held her.

Her Imaginary Friend whom she had always known, who was more real than all else in this life. She had known him from the time she slept in her cradle and the wood thrush sang over her.

Exhausted, she rested in his arms, and he rocked her like a baby, the way the man she called father once had done. And the Prince sang softly the song she knew so well:

> *"Beyond the Final Water falling,*
> *The Songs of Spheres recalling.*
> *When all around you is the vastness of night,*
> *Won't you return to me?"*

She listened and felt the healing of his words upon her burned face and hands. When at last the song ended, Rose Red opened her eyes.

The Village of Dragons was gone. So was the Eldest's Hall. Rose Red rested in a place beyond them all, and while her eyes were unable to perceive a definite picture of this place, her other senses told her that it was beautiful beyond knowledge. She breathed a sigh and rested her head against the Prince's shoulder.

"Brave one," he said, "that battle is over."

"The . . . the Dragon?"

"He has released his hold on the Eldest's House and fled Southlands for the northern countries. He'll not return."

"How do you know?"

"You are not the one he seeks."

She studied his face. "Not your Beloved?" she whispered.

He smiled at her then. Her veil was still gone, she realized, and for a moment she shuddered and wanted to hide. But he smoothed a hand over her cheek and met her gaze. "You are beloved," he said. "You are my child."

She closed her eyes and felt two tears escaping. The relief of belonging, of being so loved, was too great in that moment to be borne. Then at last she managed to ask, "What of the one the Dragon seeks? The princess he mistook me for?"

The Prince shook his head, and sadness filled his face. "That one, I fear, has yet to suffer his work."

"But you will save her too?"

He nodded. "I will not leave her to his work."

Rose Red smiled, weary but peaceful. "All is well now, ain't it?"

The Prince gently stroked her cheek again. She then knew that she was wearing her real face, the face with which she was born. The knowledge saddened her but relieved her as well.

"All is well for the present," the Prince said. "But your story is not yet over. My child, you have much suffering ahead of you."

She gulped and licked her dry lips. Her heart hurt at his words. "You'll not protect me anymore?"

"I will always protect you," he replied. "But that does not mean you will not know pain." His eyes were tender and sad. "Will you let me kiss you?"

Without hesitation she nodded. He pressed his lips to her forehead, just as her father used to long ago. Only this was much softer and much stronger; the kiss itself was not only a gesture of affection but also a protection. Though she was tired and her limbs were weak as water, Rose Red felt a surge of courage at that kiss.

"I must return you now to the valley," he said. "No matter what happens, child, do not forget what I have said. I will always protect you. Just as I have always done."

She nodded. Bowing her head, she closed her eyes.

When Rose Red opened them again, the Prince was gone, and she lay amid the rubble of what had once been the Eldest's Great Hall.

11

The Near World

Five weeks.

In the grand scheme of things, five weeks were nothing when compared to five years. But as far as Lionheart was concerned, they were the five longest weeks of his life.

Each day he spent at Oriana scrubbing its many floors, he resented. Even the nights spent entertaining the royal family, he grew to dread. For though they meant the pleasure of seeing Princess Una applauding his antics—and often a stolen conversation or two with the girl—they meant as well the sight of that dragon-eaten ring glittering on her hand.

The ring he needed.

But Lionheart couldn't bear the idea of taking it from her. She liked him, he could tell. And he knew that he must be very much in love with her. Had he not fallen in love the moment he heard her laugh?

"And that's not something to be shrugged off," he muttered one day as he took a stroll down the garden path. He had finished his labors for the day and requested permission to practice his act for that night. He performed for King Fidel and his children at least three times a week and must have something new with which to entertain them each time. This required a certain amount of quiet and time to rehearse. Within the palace there were too many distractions, so he often took himself to the lower tiers of the garden, where it was unlikely he would bump into anyone.

On this day, his walk took him all the way to the bottom of the path, where the gardens ended suddenly at the edge of Goldstone Wood. Lionheart paused here, gazing into the long shadows cast by the trees. An enchanted wood, according to all the legends. Even Southlands had many a tale about Goldstone in the olden days.

With a glance to the right, to the left, and back up the path, Lionheart took the plunge into the Wood. It reminded him keenly of his boyhood days at Hill House. How long ago those seemed to him now! Bloodbiter's Wrath and the Lake of Endless Blackness, and all the various games he'd played with Rose Red. Monster hunters were they, brave and bold.

He shivered. Those monsters were never supposed to be real.

"I've got to get that ring," he muttered as his feet pursued a winding trail down into the forest. The trail was poorly marked, but Lionheart followed it as easily as he had once pursued the deer trails with Rose Red. "I've got to."

He came to a bridge. Just a few old wooden planks spanning a small mountain stream. Momentarily he considered crossing over. But something stopped him. He couldn't say what, exactly. Some sixth sense told him that it would be better to remain on this side, closer to the palace. After all, if he went too far, he might get lost.

He'd come all this way to practice, but for the moment he felt no desire to juggle or jig. Instead, he sat down with his back against an oak, watching the Wood beyond. The trees shifted in a summer wind, sending patterns of light and shadow skittering across the forest floor. The sight gave him a pang of longing for Hill House. For Southlands, for his family, and even, he realized, for Rose Red.

He buried his face in his hands, overwhelmed suddenly with the pain of homesickness. Perhaps he should have gone with the Prince of Farthestshore after all. Perhaps he should go even now, forget this wild goose chase.

Your dream!

"I hate dreams," he growled.

Crackling footsteps drew his attention. He looked up and saw that someone was coming down the trail from the palace. Someone muttering to herself and so completely focused on her own thoughts that she paid no attention to her surroundings. It was Princess Una.

His heart leapt, not unpleasantly. Then he saw the ring gleaming on her hand, and his heart lurched again.

Take it! said the Lady.

"Dragons eat you," he muttered.

The princess continued on her way, quite unaware of his presence, though she drew very near to him. He debated whether or not to call out to her, but then she was upon him, still hurrying, and kicked him.

"Ouch," he said. "That was my *foot*."

Princess Una screamed and clapped her hands to her face. Then she took a deep breath and cried, "Oh, Leonard! It's you!"

Lionheart rubbed his foot, which smarted from her kick, and offered her a small smile.

"Did I step on you?" she asked. Her pale face went bright red with embarrassment.

"No," Lionheart said. Then, remembering himself and his lowly position, he scrambled to his feet, dusting himself off and bowing deeply. "You kicked me. Hard. Like unto broke the bone!" The princess looked so distressed at this, however, that he had to take pity on her. "No, m'lady, you scarcely touched me." It was a bold-faced lie, but she looked relieved. "You appeared so set on your path, I feared if I didn't speak up, you might walk right on into the stream and drown without noticing."

"Without noticing you or without noticing drowning?"

"Both, probably." He grinned. "Do you come here often?"

The princess nodded but did not return his smile. Instead she folded her arms. "What are you doing here?"

Her words were sharp. Like a princess would speak to her lowest servant, should she deign to speak to him at all. Of course, that's what he was. Her lowliest floor-scrubber, of no consequence, who should not even look at, much less speak to, the Princess of Parumvir.

Lionheart replied with some bitterness. "You mean, of course, 'Don't you have a certain amount of mopping or sweeping, or some such menial task you could be attending to as we speak?' "

The princess's face crumpled a little. She looked truly hurt, and Lionheart winced at his own insensitivity. "I didn't—" she began, but he hastened on.

"But in fact, m'lady, this humble riffraff has already completed his quotient of demeaning labor for the morning and was given the afternoon off to practice his foolishness. And he needs the practice badly enough, for he is beginning to fear that he shall have to give up this brilliant career."

"What? Why?"

"Why? She asks me why?" Lionheart reached down, scooped up a handful of acorns, and started juggling. He disliked seeing that sad expression on her face. He would make her laugh again if it killed him. "Three times," he said, "three times I witnessed the princess yawn last night as I sang. Not once, not twice, but thrice! And yet m'lady asks me why."

"Don't be silly," Una said.

"Can't be helped. It's my job."

"But I didn't yawn when you sang, Leonard!"

"Then why did you cover your mouth with your handkerchief? I saw it with my own eyes!"

"I was trying to keep from laughing too hard!" Princess Una said. "I was. So you see, you must continue your brilliant career, jester. Where would my amusement come from if you abandoned it?"

Lionheart smiled at the way her eyes were circling, trying to follow the flying acorns. "Do I indeed amuse you, m'lady?"

"You amuse me vastly," she said. "Silly, how could I not be amused? Why, you've gone and tied bells to your elbows and knees. Just when I thought you couldn't look more ridiculous!"

"I am droll, though, am I not?" With that he tossed the acorns up in the air. They seemed to fly wildly, but with a few quick steps, Lionheart made certain that each one hit him smartly on the head, making a different pained face every time one struck.

Princess Una burst into that delightful laugh of hers. How bright and sweet she was, so free of all the heavy cares under which Lionheart labored. He loved her for her innocence and loved her for her laughter. Part of him wanted to throw off all pretense and tell her everything then and there . . . to reveal himself, his name, his quest.

Instead, he shook a fist at her. "You snicker at me, but I know that you are secretly jealous. 'Ah!' the lady sighs, 'if only *I* could wear bells upon my elbows, then my life should be complete!' "

"Heaven forbid," said the princess. "Oriana has room for only one Fool, I believe."

Lionheart's smile faded. "Especially so great a fool as I." He shook his head, as though he could somehow shake the gloom that held him. "And what brings you down here, Princess Una?" he asked.

She sighed. "Suitors."

He laughed. "You make it sound like the descending hordes. How many this time?"

"The Duke of Shippening."

A cold weight sank in his gut.

"Ah," he managed, his voice still light. But all the brightness of the world fled in that one instant. The duke? That cruel slave master dared haul his offensive carcass all the way up from Shippening to pay court to Una? True, he was rich. True, he was powerful. But . . .

Lionheart thought he would be sick. He remembered too vividly the last time he had seen the duke, more than four years ago. That old barbarian stuffing his face in front of his guests without a thought for common courtesy. And calling on his guards to beat the poor, enslaved Faerie. Lionheart's fists clenched. He would see himself hanged before he saw Princess Una in that dragon-kissed creature's hands.

But he said with the frivolity of a jester, "Comparable to a half dozen at least."

He turned from Una to hide the fury that gathered in his face and strode down to the plank bridge. He did not step onto it but climbed down the bank to the rocks alongside the stream instead, collecting pebbles.

Princess Una walked out onto the bridge and took a seat halfway across, dangling her dainty feet over the edge. Lionheart, always a gentleman, made a point not to look at her slim ankles peeking out beneath her skirt. "Have you ever," the princess asked, far more melancholy than he remembered hearing her before, "dreamed of one thing for so long, wanted nothing more than to have that dream fulfilled, only to find out that maybe it wasn't what you actually wanted all along?"

Lionheart found a few pebbles he liked and started juggling them. "I believe that's called growing up."

"But then," the princess continued, "you find yourself lost without your dream. Like half your heart is gone right along with it."

She twisted the opal ring on her finger. It caught Lionheart's eyes, though he tried not to look at it.

Your dream, said the Lady. *Take the ring!*

Lionheart tossed his juggling stones into the stream, perhaps with more vehemence than necessary. Then he spoke loudly, drowning out the Lady's voice. "Dreams are tricky business, m'lady. It's best to hold on to what you know, not what you want. Know your duty, know your path, and do everything you can to achieve what you have set out to do. Don't let dreams get in your way. Dreams will never accomplish the work of firm resolve."

Fine words, my sweet prince, said the Lady. *Now take what you need!*

Princess Una's eyes were very wide as she gazed at him, wisps of loose hair falling about her face. She was so delicate, so young. He could overpower her in a moment. "What have you resolved, Leonard, that you won't stop for dreams?"

He turned to stare out at the water flowing on down Goldstone Hill.

You could have it and be off in a moment. She cannot stop you.

"I am resolved," he said hoarsely, "to return home as soon as I may."

"Home? You mean Southlands?"

Kneeling to pick up another stone to check its weight, he nodded.

"Is it far away?" asked the princess.

"Very far, m'lady."

A long journey indeed, my sweet, and pointless without what you need. You asked, and I told you how you may deliver Southlands from the Dragon's hold. What good will that knowledge do you if you don't act upon it?

"Is it true, Leonard?" the princess asked softly. "Is it true what they say about . . . about your homeland?"

Lionheart swallowed. He tossed the new stone into the middle of the stream, still afraid to look at her, to look at that ring. "Maybe, maybe not. I don't know what they say."

"Did you escape before the rest of Southlands was imprisoned?"

Lionheart closed his eyes and took a deep breath before casting her a quick sidelong glance. "Does it really matter how or when I escaped, if escaped we must call it? I am here; my people are there. My friends. My family. So I will return."

"Can you do anything, though?" asked the princess. "Not in five years has anyone succeeded in crossing to Southlands alive. Don't you think you should stay away for now? What could you do by returning anyway?"

Lionheart felt her words like weights upon his shoulders. What could he do? Especially if he hadn't the courage to take from her what he required. In that moment, he hated himself.

But he hated the Lady more.

"Princess Una," he said, keeping his voice steady with an effort, "you are young and sweet. You can't know about such things. I may be only a Fool, but even a Fool must see his duty, and when he sees it, he must follow through. What else can he do and still consider himself a man? Perhaps I cannot help my people. Perhaps I will live long enough to see their destruction and then perish in the same fire. But nevertheless I will go." He turned away from her and kicked another stone into the passing water. "As soon as I can put together funds enough for the journey."

The princess regarded him quietly. She smiled a little. "Then I think you are a very brave Fool."

"If I were not a Fool, do you think I could be brave?"

He looked at her then, deep into those wide eyes of hers. How guileless she was, he thought. How unlike any girl he had ever met before, except . . . except Rose Red.

Rose Red, back when they were both children, and she did not know he was a prince. His one true friend, unconcerned with societal dictums. But that had all changed, of course, as soon as Rose Red learned the truth. And besides, she was nothing more than a mountain girl.

This girl was a princess and his equal. She did not know this, of course, and yet . . . and yet she talked to him as though they were on the same footing. She talked to Lionheart like a friend.

Take the ring!

But he didn't want to take the ring. He wanted to declare himself to her. To tell her his true name and purpose, to beg her not to receive the Duke of Shippening's suit. To ask her to wait for him until he had reclaimed his kingdom.

But instead Lionheart crossed his eyes and stuck out his tongue so that Una laughed that adorable laugh of hers and exclaimed, "Clown!"

"The things you call me," he said, sweeping another bow with a jangle of his bell-covered hat. "M'lady, the day lengthens. If I do not return you home soon, questions will be asked, and do you think this humble floor-scrubber will escape a kicking from his superiors for hindering a princess in her daily schedule?"

He offered his arm, and she accepted it, allowing him to lead her back up the hill, away from the Old Bridge. She didn't let go until they had reached the top tier of the garden, where they parted ways.

Foolish prince, the Lady hissed. *How do you expect me to fulfill your dreams if you will not obey me?*

But for the moment, Lionheart didn't care. His mind was full of Una. And the duke.

Shippening and his entourage arrived at Oriana five days later.

Lionheart saw him emerge from his carriage, enormous, full of self-importance. A great imbecile who didn't deserve to look at the princess, much less woo her.

The words of Captain Sunan of the *Kulap Kanya* returned to Lionheart even as he watched the duke enter King Fidel's household. *"He is not the buffoon he projects to the world. And his alliances are strong, though even I cannot guess at them."*

Lionheart clenched his fists. Buffoon or not, the Duke of Shippening should never have Princess Una.

The Fool was called upon to entertain the family that night. So Lionheart tuned his lute, adorned himself in jester's clothing, set the ridiculous hat on his head, and smiled. He would entertain all right. He was not afraid of Shippening.

After supper, the family retired to the primary sitting room. When Lionheart entered, he found Una seated across from Shippening, her hands folded and her face very still. What her thoughts were, Lionheart couldn't guess; but the duke's thoughts, as he lazily regarded Una between puffs on his pipe, were all too apparent. The man made Lionheart sick.

Princess Una looked up and smiled his way, but he ignored her. Setting his face into a grin, he struck a sour chord on his instrument.

"What-*ho*! A merry bunch you are tonight!" he cried, springing to the center of the room, making as much clatter and noise as he could. Shippening grunted and sat up, fixing his gaze upon the jester. Lionheart's smile grew. He knew the duke, too full of himself to recall a serving boy, would not remember him.

"Keep it down, jester," King Fidel said. "We're glad to see you, but must you *resound* so?"

"Resound? Your Majesty, I've hardly begun to peal!" He strummed another loud, discordant set of strings. "I've written a new song," he said. "Rather, rewritten an old one in honor of our esteemed guest."

The duke emptied his pipe onto the king's fine rug. His grin was greasy, and his eyes disappeared behind the creases of his face. "That's decent of you, Fool. I haven't heard a good song in ages."

"A *good* song I cannot promise," Lionheart said. "But such a song as it is, I give to you. 'The Sorry Fate of the Beastly Lout.' " Then he began to sing:

> "With audacity gawky, the Beastly Lout
> Would loiter and dawdle and maybe
> Try his luck wenching, casting about
> To court a most beauteous lady.

> "But to his dismay, he was made aware
> That his suit was unwelcome before her.
> Our poor Beastly Lout felt her pickling stare
> 'Cause his stories did certainly bore her.

"Ah, sad Beastly Lout, how he tried to be nice,
But his courting just could not amuse her right.
For, you see, his great noggin was covered in lice,
Which is hardly appealing in any light."

The Duke of Shippening barked a deep laugh. "Now, there's a song for you!" he boomed. "Bravo! Sing another, boy! And how about a round of something to lighten the mood? The rest of you are stiff as pokers!"

But Lionheart did not move. He cast a glance Una's way and saw how still she'd gone, though her younger brother was doubled up with silent laughter.

"Fool!" the duke cried. It was so like the voice he'd used to bully his enslaved jester all those years ago that it made Lionheart shudder. "Sing again, I tell you! Set that tongue of yours to work!"

"No," King Fidel said. Lionheart felt the king's gaze upon him. "I believe you are done here, jester. Good-bye."

Lionheart bowed and left the room.

"Why, Majesty," the duke cried, "I haven't been so amused in years! Is he hired on to you long term? If not—"

That was all Lionheart heard before the door shut, and even that much scarcely registered in his mind. What had he done? Gone and ruined his chances here in Oriana, that's what. A Fool? Try idiot, instead! He'd never get the ring now. He'd never return to Southlands. He'd never—

Someone was coming up behind him. He cast a glance back and realized that Princess Una followed him, though her head was down and she did not see him. Sudden resolve fixed itself in Lionheart's breast. It was now or never.

He stepped back, took her by the arm, and hastily towed her into a side corridor. Taking her by both arms, he made her face him, and suddenly found that he had no words.

The princess stared up at him. Then her face sank into an angry scowl. "What do you think you're doing?" she cried, pushing him away.

Lionheart could hardly think what to say as her words spilled out in an angry rush. At last he managed in a thick voice, as though he might choke on his own words, "You can't marry that lout."

"I don't intend to marry that lout!" she growled back. "I have no intention of marrying anyone, not that it is any of *your* business!"

"M'lady—"

"You've gone and gotten yourself discharged, you fool!"

"No!" Lionheart took Una's hands and pulled them away from her face. But she turned away, and there were tears on her cheek. He felt like a fiend to have made her cry. "M'lady," he said, "look at me. Please. I'm not a Fool."

"I don't know what else you call a commoner who insults a royal guest and gets himself—"

"No, Una," Lionheart said. He squeezed her hands in his. "I am not a Fool, not a jester. I am Prince Lionheart of Southlands."

12

SOUTHLANDS

Rose Red sat up, blinking slowly as she looked about at the destruction. At first, she did not recognize where she was. Then understanding came to her. The Eldest's Great Hall, torn to pieces, chunks of its walls and floor smoking and melted. The Dragon had done his work thoroughly.

As Rose Red got to her feet, swaying at first, she realized something more. True, the hall lay in ruins, and smoke still swirled heavily in the air. But that thick smell of poison was fading already.

The Dragon was gone.

"Bah!"

Rose Red turned and saw her nanny coming toward her, climbing through the rubble like the nimble mountain goat she was. For a moment, the memory of a tall woman bearing a silver lantern flashed across Rose Red's mind, but she shook that away. "Beana!" she cried, stumbled over a few broken stones, and wrapped her arms around the goat's shaggy neck. "Beana, you're alive!"

"That I am, girl," said the goat. Then she bleated again and nuzzled Rose Red's cheek. "Brave child!"

"Not really," Rose Red said, speaking into Beana's coarse coat. "I . . . Beana, I almost let him—"

"So would we all," said the goat. "There is only one who can stand up to that Monster in the end. Our strength must always give out at last, but his never will. You called him, just as you were supposed to, and all is well now. My brave child!"

Rose Red squeezed Beana one more time, then sat back. "Where's m'lady?"

She found Daylily half buried beneath rubble but unharmed. At first Rose Red thought she was unconscious, but Daylily was merely in a daze, as though she were mentally working through some complex problem, not newly rescued from Death's own doorstep. Rose Red helped her gently to her feet and shook her a little, saying, "M'lady, are you all right?"

Daylily blinked slowly at Rose Red. "You rescued me."

"Not me," Rose Red said. "It was the Prince what saved us. He sent the Dragon away."

Daylily closed her eyes and smiled. Only it was more of a sneer. "The prince left us long ago," she said, then went so quiet that Rose Red wondered if she had fainted while still upright.

"Best get her inside, out of this smoke," Beana said. "This way."

With the goat leading, Rose Red helped the baron's daughter across the ruins to a side door that led into the undamaged passages of the Eldest's House. As they went, she saw how changed everything was. The weird half-light was gone, replaced by murky but ordinary daylight. No more sensation of walking in two worlds at once. The Dragon had fled Southlands and released the palace back into its own realm, where it belonged.

Rose Red could have wept with relief.

"It's been five years, Rosie," Beana told her as they went.

"What?"

"Five years on the outside. At least! You vanished inside, and I waited five years until the way was opened for me to follow."

Rose Red's mind hurt at this notion. It had not seemed so long. What could have happened to Prince Lionheart during all that time?

But she'd not worry about that. Not right now. She held Daylily's arm around her neck and half carried the girl to the kitchens, where she had left the others in stone-faced stupors.

They were all still there, exactly where she'd left them, blinking and rubbing their eyes like those just awaking. The poison yet lingered in their faces, but they were conscious again, aware of themselves and their surroundings.

They were still frightened.

"Where is he?" one of them asked.

"Hush!" said another. "He'll hear you!"

"We've got to get out," said a third. "Eldest, can you stand?"

Rose Red entered with Daylily in time to see young Sir Foxbrush (who, no matter if five years had passed, still hadn't grown a beard) assisting the Eldest from his seat at the window. No one looked her way, so busy were they with their own thoughts.

Daylily glanced from Rose Red beside her to Foxbrush and back again. Then she cleared her throat and said sharply, "Foxbrush!"

His head came up, his attention fixed first upon her and then on Rose Red.

He screamed.

The next moment, he had grabbed a poker from the fireplace and charged at Rose Red, striking her across the face. Rose Red was so taken aback that she did not move to avoid the blow. It did not hurt, no matter how hard he hit, but it startled her, and she backed away, losing hold of Daylily. Foxbrush, roaring like a young warrior, swung at her again, this time catching her in the side.

"Please!" Rose Red cried. "Mercy, sir!"

"Out!" he cried. "Get out of here! Go, you devil! Monster!"

Beana bellowed like a bull and charged the young lord, butting him hard in the gut and sending him sprawling. The poker clanged across the floor as it flew from his hand. "Beana, no!" Rose Red cried, afraid that one of the others, who were grabbing weapons and approaching menacingly, would strike at her goat. She cast a desperate look at Daylily.

But the baron's daughter stood quietly, her gaze averted.

Rose Red grabbed Beana and, though she was hardly bigger than the goat herself, lifted the animal off her feet and ran from the kitchen. A kitchen knife struck the door close to her ear as she went. Once outside, she put the goat down and barked, "Run!"

The two of them fled while the newly liberated prisoners gave hot pursuit, shouting and brandishing whatever makeshift weapons they could find, furious in their terror. For although the Dragon was gone, his poisons lingered, and the frightened men and women must find some vent for their fear.

And Rose Red had forgotten that she no longer wore her veil.

13

The Near World

S HE BELIEVED HIM.

Light of Lumé be praised, Una believed him!

Lionheart may have been sacked. He may have been penniless. He may have been half a world away from his homeland. But as he made his way down Goldstone Hill that night, his heart exulted. He thought he might spread wings and fly all the way back to Southlands! For Una believed, and Una had given her trust.

She'd given him more than that.

Lionheart opened his hand to look at what nestled in his palm. Even in the darkness on the hillside, the white stones shone smooth and the opal fire inside gleamed.

He'd told her the whole story, of course. Everything, from the moment the Dragon arrived in Southlands and enslaved the whole country. He told her how he'd traveled to the Far East and learned how the monster could be defeated. He'd not revealed that little detail, of course. That was secret knowledge. Besides, he didn't want her to think he would take the ring from her.

And he wouldn't have. Even as he'd poured out his heart to her, Lionheart had known he could never do as the Lady asked. He would return to Southlands on his own and face the Dragon. But he'd do it without robbing Una.

Then, lo and behold! A miracle had happened. Just as he had turned to go, she'd called out to him again.

"Here," she'd said, twisting the ring off her finger and pressing it into his hands. *"It was my mother's. I don't know how much it is worth, but something close to a king's ransom, I should think. Use it for your journey and . . . and come back soon."*

Lionheart smiled as he remembered her words. Perhaps the storybooks weren't so farfetched after all? All those foolish songs of Sir Eanrin at which he had scoffed, those touting the virtues of true love and self-sacrifice . . . maybe they weren't the twaddle of an idiot? For Una loved him and had entrusted him with her ring. And he loved her, and would prove the hero he must be.

Don't forget your dream!

"You see," he whispered when the Lady's voice came to him. "I haven't forgotten! I've got what you sent me here for. I will kill the Dragon yet."

But, sweet prince, that is not your dream.

Lionheart closed his hand around the ring once more, frowning. "What . . . what do you mean?"

You dream of being prince once more. You said nothing of killing the Dragon.

"I . . . I did. I cannot be Eldest if I don't kill him."

You asked how you might deliver Southlands from the Dragon. You said nothing of killing him.

"I—" There on the empty road leading down from Oriana Palace, Lionheart stood still and pressed his fists to his temples. "I must kill . . . I must—"

"Well met, boy."

Lionheart's eyes flew open. He felt dizzy, disoriented, for the Lady's presence was heavy in his mind. Even so, he made out the dark figures surrounding him in an ever-closing circle.

He stood face-to-face with the Duke of Shippening.

"Beastly lout, eh?" said the duke, and his face twisted into an ugly smile. "Funny song, that."

Lionheart swallowed and shook his head, trying to focus. "It was a . . . a joke, Your Grace," he stammered. Then he bowed for good measure. "A jester's joke, no more. A Fool has to—"

While he was still doubled over in his bow, someone smacked him from behind, sending him sprawling at the duke's feet.

Shippening looked down from around his ample stomach. "I'm not what you take me for, boy," he said. Then he leaned over and grabbed Lionheart's shirtfront, hauling him up to stare into his face. The duke's breath was foul, and he spat when he spoke. "I am not the fool here." His smile vanished behind the deadliest expression Lionheart had ever seen. "What's more, I remember you. I don't forget a face."

He struck. Lionheart's head exploded with pain, driving even the Lady from his mind. The duke's voice was low and biting, like slow-working poison. "You stole my slave from me. You made a laughingstock of me before my guests and took from me a gift from my ally. A gift not easily reclaimed." He struck again, and his blow was like a hammer, jarring Lionheart's senses. A third blow, a fourth; then the duke dropped him. Lionheart lay where he fell, his mouth open in soundless agony.

"Take him," said the duke. "Bind him. We've got ourselves a journey tonight."

They followed one of the Paths.

Lionheart was blindfolded and trussed up like a hunting trophy slung between two broad men. But he felt the moment they stepped onto the Path. It brought back with painful clarity, even through the pounding of his head, that night on the mountain when he had lost himself in the darkness and wandered in a world not his own.

But there was no Rose Red to call to his aid now. Besides, his mouth was gagged.

He still clutched Una's ring in his hand, however, and he drew comfort from knowing it was there. Whatever else happened, he had what he'd come for. He'd just have to figure out the rest as he went.

Then the presence of the Dragon drove everything else from his mind.

Fire surrounded Lionheart everywhere, even deep inside himself. Fire and rage.

"Years I have wasted!" the Dragon's voice boomed like thunder. "Five years and more bound in this incarnate body, pursuing that little beast! She is not the one I seek. But I won the game!"

Then, to Lionheart's surprise—and somewhat to his horror—he heard the Duke of Shippening respond:

"Whatever, Dragon. I could not care less about your little games. Just tell me if I can gut this joker man here and now, or if I must wait a little longer?"

The blindfold was ripped from Lionheart's face, and he was tossed, still bound, to his knees. When he struggled upright, he found himself staring up at a being at least seven feet tall, with a face like a skull, skin stretched over the bone in a thin sheet. Black hair fell down his shoulders.

His was the face from the portrait in Oriana's hall. He was the Dragon.

Lionheart screamed inarticulately and hid his face in his bound hands. Poison filled the air; he breathed in lungsful. It boiled his blood.

"Come, Dragon," said the duke. "You told me to bring the wretch to you, and bring him I have, alive even, though I had ideas enough in another direction. Tell me, can I kill him now?"

The Dragon snarled and hissed, white lips drawing back across his long black teeth. "Prince Lionheart," he said. "We meet again."

"A prince, eh?" said the duke and kicked Lionheart in the side. "Thought he had too much snobbery about him by half. That don't make me like him any better, though. Is he the little brown prince of Southlands what's been missing all these years? Fancy that."

Lionheart could not hear the duke. His head pounded with poison. But he still clutched Una's ring.

"You were to be the key," said the Dragon to Lionheart while ignoring Shippening as one might an irritating housefly.

But the duke persisted. "He freed the slave you gave me. Bold as brass, took off the creature's collar and liberated it! By rights, he should have been put in a gibbet and left to starve years ago. I'm only asking to make up for lost time."

"Enough," said the Dragon, gnashing his teeth at the duke. "You've done your work, bringing him to me. Now cease your babble before I forget our alliance and have you for a late supper."

The duke opened his mouth, thought twice, and closed it. His face went red with impotent wrath.

The Dragon turned to Lionheart again. "You were to be the key to the princess's undoing. But she wasn't the one I sought!" He lunged. His hands went about Lionheart's neck, and his eyes burned the skin on Lionheart's face. "Where is she? Where is the Beloved of my Enemy? All the signs told me that you were the key, but the little goblin withstood me. So where is my rightful prey?"

Lionheart couldn't speak. He felt the life flowing from him, and for the moment, he did not care. Death would be better than this current existence, this fire in his veins that melted him from the inside out.

"Where is she?" the Dragon roared.

Suddenly the Lady was there. The ice of her coming was more painful than the fire, but she broke the Dragon's hold and stepped between him and the fainting prince. Even the duke screamed at the sight of her, and his men fell to their knees and hid their faces.

"What is going on here?" she demanded.

"You should have let me have him," the Dragon snarled. "He was supposed to be the key. If I'd had him, I could have convinced her to take my kiss."

"You were never going to convince her," his sister said. "You never won her in our game."

"If not her, then whom?"

The Lady smiled. "Ask the prince what he has in his hand."

The Dragon's eyes narrowed to fiery slits. "Why?"

"Ask him and see."

The Dragon turned on Lionheart, who had slumped to his side and lay with his knees curled up to his face. He could hardly breathe, the poison was so great. He closed his eyes, desperate not to see those looming specters.

"What do you have in your hand?"

Lionheart's fist tightened. *No!* They could take everything else. They could take his kingdom, his family, his identity. They could take his life. But Lumé help him, they would not take Una's ring! He'd worked too long and too hard. It was the key to the Dragon's undoing. It must be! The oracle had said . . .

"Lionheart, my darling," said the Lady, kneeling down beside him. "Show my brother what you hold."

He looked up into her terrible, empty eyes. "You . . . you said—"

"I said I would show you how to deliver Southlands from the Dragon. This is the only way. Show him what you have."

Closing his eyes, Lionheart uncurled his fingers.

The Dragon roared. "He holds the heart of a princess!"

"Not just any princess, my brother," said the Lady, turning to the Dragon once more. "That is the heart of Princess Una, Beloved of the Prince of Farthestshore. Your Enemy."

The Dragon's cloak billowed back in a sudden blast of heat. Lionheart screamed and closed his hand around Una's ring once more. He saw black wings and a great black body rising above him, towering as great as a mountain, and he thought he would melt in the heat. Red eyes filled his vision, and he looked once more into the face of Death.

"Give me her heart, Prince Lionheart," said the Dragon. The duke and his men fled, leaving Lionheart alone before the monster. "Give me her heart, and I will let you live."

"No!" Lionheart cried, raising his hands to shield his face from the heat, Una's ring still clutched in one of them.

The Dragon laughed, a terrible sound as hot as the flames flickering between his teeth. "Your life for her heart. That's the best I can offer you." The two red eyes lowered, and the awful mouth hovered just above the prince so that he thought he would be devoured then and there. He huddled down, helpless and quivering in the shadow of the beast.

The Lady was at his ear, speaking eagerly. "You must choose! Choose your dream!"

"It is an easy enough exchange," said the Dragon. "Then you may return to Southlands, reclaim your crown, rule your people. Only give me the heart of this princess, your love."

"No!" He could not hear his own voice.

"I will eat you now, little prince. And I will return to Southlands and burn it to ash. I will swallow your homeland in one mouthful and still be hungry for more! Only you can prevent it, Lionheart. Not by killing me. You cannot kill me. No sword you can wield will ever pierce my skin, little man! So save yourself and save your people, and give me the heart of this Una, for I have greater need of it than you do."

Lionheart thought the flesh would melt from his bones. Poison filled his soul.

"Choose your dream," urged the Lady. "Give my brother the girl's heart, for he played the game with me and won, and he must have it now. Give it to him!"

"Give it to me!"

Lionheart, lying on his face, his arms flung out before him, slowly opened his fist.

The ring rolled from his grasp and lay upon the stone ground.

"It's yours," he whispered. "Take it!"

The fire went.

The terror vanished.

Lionheart lay at the foot of Goldstone Hill, on the edge of the dark forest. He was alone.

Utterly alone.

PART FIVE

1

THE SOUND OF CONSTRUCTION followed Daylily everywhere she went in the Eldest's House. Without needing to be summoned, workers from all across Southlands had flocked to the home of their king following the Dragon's departure, desperate for work, equally desperate to see the glory and stability of their sovereign restored. It was a hopeless venture, but it gave them purpose and something on which to focus their minds other than that ever-pressing question:

Will the Dragon return? And when?

Daylily revealed nothing of her thoughts, but deep inside she despised those busy worker folk. As if their industry could ever wipe away the scars the Dragon had left upon the land during those five years of enslavement.

Five years! That thought hurt to contemplate. She'd not sensed the passing of time, at least not in years. She remembered the smoke; she remembered the poison. All too clearly Daylily remembered watching her dreams burn before her eyes time after time. She felt as though she had lived a thousand lifetimes and died a thousand deaths. But five years had escaped, unnoticed.

She remained at the Eldest's House at first because she was too weak to travel; later because she dared not return to her father's welcoming arms. When the baron sent messages requiring her presence in Middlecrescent, she used the king's seal to respond that *Lady Daylily is indispensable to the Eldest at this time*, etc. And so far, her father had enough problems of his own, resettling Middlecrescent, to come chasing after his wayward child.

Daylily could hide awhile longer.

She spent much of her time alone. She could not bear the fresh faces of those come to work on the House, so hopeful and so skittish all at once. They all bore some marks of the Dragon's work but were comparatively unscathed. What did they know of poison? What did they know of darkness? Little to nothing, otherwise they wouldn't bother to rebuild.

But none of these thoughts showed upon Lady Daylily's face. She sat at her bedroom window, watching the north road, and said nothing. They'd learn the futility of their actions in the end.

It was by thus quietly watching that Daylily became the first person at the House to spot Lionheart returning up the road.

She knew him instantly, though he was much too far away for her to discern his features. Something in the way he walked reminded her of the gawky boy she had once known. She was on her feet and out the door in a moment. Her movements were deliberate. She did not hasten down the hall or the stairway. Hastening gave one a sense of flight, or pursuit, so she always moved with a precise grace. By the time she reached the outer court, half the household knew of the prince's return, and a great shout had gone up among the staff, the construction crews, and those who had returned to dwell within their Eldest's walls.

Only a handful remained silent. These included the Eldest, Sir Foxbrush, and the nobles who had been imprisoned during those five years.

Daylily came to stand on the front steps beside the Eldest and near Sir Foxbrush (who rarely raised his somber gaze from his feet these days, though his hair was always perfectly oiled). The rubble of the Starflower Fountain had been mostly cleared out by now, so the view from the front steps across the courtyard to the gate was unobstructed. She saw the gates swing open, heard the shouts from the wall as guardsmen hailed their shabby prince.

She saw Lionheart walk through.

Not on horseback as he should have been, a triumphant hero returning to his homeland. Like a vagabond he came, shabby in dress and bearing. A beard covered half his face, like a mask.

But he was Lionheart, Prince of Southlands. And he was home.

The crowd grew but stayed back to give him a clear path across the courtyard to the steps where his father waited. Lionheart squared his shoulders as he neared, and Daylily watched his eyes darting about, resting first on the Eldest, then seeking familiar faces among the others gathered there. His gaze rested briefly on her before passing to Foxbrush and on.

Daylily set her mouth. He would not find the one he sought. She wondered if anyone had yet informed the prince of his mother's death.

The Eldest reached out to his son. Lionheart mounted the stairs, took his father's hands, and bowed over them.

"Welcome home," said the Eldest.

"Father," said Lionheart. His voice was changed, no longer boyish but deep. "I . . . I have ensured that the Dragon will not return to Southlands."

The Eldest said nothing for a long moment. His face was aged almost beyond recognition after years spent breathing in those poisons. His eyes were faded as well and not too quick at disguising his thoughts. But he smiled a sad smile and took his son in his arms, repeating only, "Welcome home."

A few hours later, Daylily's dream came true.

She had retired to the privacy of her chambers when the commotion became too tiresome. The means for celebration were pathetically reduced, and Daylily disliked watching the household desperately trying to behave as though there were some real reason for all this joy. So the prince had returned. Very well. Where was he during those five years when he'd been needed? But they wouldn't think about that now, would they. No, they'd save that for later, Daylily knew. And later would bring its price.

So she retired to her rooms and told her servant not to light a fire. She avoided fires, no matter how chilly her room might become at night, nor how dark. The smell made her sick. She wrapped a shawl about her shoulders and sat at the window instead.

Lionheart knocked at her door. She knew it must be he, though how she knew she could not say. Out of habit, she checked to make certain her hair was arranged and let the shawl drop from her shoulders down to her elbows. Then she said, "Come."

He was still shaggy with that wretched beard, though he'd changed into finer clothing. Ill-fitting clothing, to be sure. He'd outgrown all his own and there had been no time yet to fit him for others. But at least he was no longer dressed in the colorless sacking in which he'd arrived.

"Hullo, Daylily," he said. He carried a candle, for dusk was settling in. The light cast strange shadows on his face.

"Good evening, Lionheart," she said. She wondered briefly how she looked to him. The dragon poison had taken its toll upon her, leaving her thin and hollow cheeked. Her former beauty might never be reclaimed. She hoped the candlelight was gracious to her.

Not that it mattered. She knew that her dream was about to come true, and she dreaded the moment. After watching it burn and die so many times, the prospect of fulfillment was almost unbearable.

"Daylily, I was wondering," Lionheart said, shuffling his feet. For just that instant, her heart went out to him again. He looked so like the awkward Leo she once had known. Leo, who couldn't play a game of chess to save his life.

"Yes," she said quietly.

"I was wondering if . . . well, after all this . . . and I understand if you'd rather not." It was strange to hear that boyish stammering when his voice had grown so deep.

"What is it, Leo?" she asked.

The use of his childhood name brought his head up, and he smiled. The smile vanished quickly, but it had been there, a ghost of his former self. Daylily wondered at the amount of dragon poison she saw in his face. After all, Lionheart had been away; he had not suffered enslavement during those five years. Why should he bear the marks?

"Tell me what you want," she said.

He closed his eyes and drew a breath as though stung. When he looked at her again, there was a sharpness like thorns in his expression. But he said, "Daylily, will you marry me?"

So she would be the Eldest's wife after all. She would fulfill her father's expectations and Plan. She would prove herself in the eyes of Middlecrescent, in the eyes of the entire nation. Daylily had succeeded, as she set out to, in winning the heart and devotion of the crown prince.

"Yes," she said.

Lionheart stepped forward, leaned over, and kissed her, just once, before he backed away. She looked up at him, her eyes like a ghost's in the candlelight.

"Thank you," he said, turning to go. But he paused in her doorway and looked back.

"Daylily?"

"Yes?"

"I was wondering . . . do you know what became of Rose Red? The goat girl, remember?"

Daylily did not break his gaze. The candlelight reflected like opal fire in the depths of her eyes.

At last she said, "She disappeared."

"She promised that she'd come back and watch over my parents and those imprisoned here," Lionheart said. "Do you know if she did?"

"I believe so, yes."

"Do you know . . . did she survive?"

Daylily got to her feet and paced across the room. Fury suddenly thickened her voice to a menacing whisper. "She's not dead, Lionheart. She fled after the Dragon left. She lost that veil of hers, and we all saw her true face, and she fled. I don't know where she went. Followed the Dragon, perhaps? They were quite friendly, I'm given to understand. Last I saw her, she was very much alive and very much running for her life because she is no longer welcome in this land."

Lionheart's face hardened into stone. Daylily stood there, hissing up at him like an angry cat, her loveliness twisted so that he almost could not recognize her. His betrothed. Of all the damages he'd yet seen wreaked upon his homeland, somehow this was the worst.

"I think I know where she'd go," he said. He put a hand on Daylily's shoulder, gently but firmly. "And I'm going to fetch her back."

Daylily shook him off. But her normal calm had returned, falling over her features in a disguise. "Of course you are, Leo," she said. "Of course you are."

Lionheart left her. He did not see her sink to her knees. He did not see her weep. No one did. And when she finished, Daylily vowed it would never happen again.

She had her dream. And it was dust and ashes.

2

S o it was that Lionheart, within a few weeks of his return to Southlands, found himself once more climbing the mountainside above Hill House.

What a relief it was to have left his retinue behind and to once more be alone. During his long journey from Parumvir back to his homeland, he had many times wished so desperately for company. Anything to distract his mind from those memories of fire, of ice, of the Brother and Sister.

But once back in Southlands, Lionheart found that company was almost unbearable to him. Perhaps he imagined it, perhaps he did not . . . but everywhere he went, he thought he heard whispers behind his back.

"Did he face the Dragon?"

"I don't know."

"Did he defeat him? Are we saved?"

"Shhhh!"

For now, they treated him as a hero returned. And there was so much work to be done, so much lost that would take years of labor to reclaim!

They would have to trust their prince, to work alongside him, for the sake of his father, for the memory of his dead mother, for the renewing of the kingdom.

But today, he had other business to attend. Solitary business.

Bloodbiter's Wrath was much smaller and more flimsy than Lionheart remembered. But the beanpole felt right in his hand as he passed through the garden gate and on up the beaten path. He met no one on the way to the sapling tied with a red scarf. The sapling had grown since last he'd passed this direction. It was beginning to show signs of what it might be as a mature tree. But though its color had faded to a near-camouflaged brown, the scarf was still tied to the same branch. And the deer trail still twisted into the forest beyond.

Lionheart made the plunge. The air was so clean up here, smelling of dirt and roots and old leaves . . . hardly a trace of dragon smoke. Lionheart drew long breaths and felt once more the thrill of the hunt. Though, of course, this hunt was different from the first. For one thing, he knew what it was he hunted. And he knew, with a good measure of confidence, where he would find his quarry.

The Lake of Endless Blackness had long since vanished, taking its rickety dam along with it. But Lionheart knew its location better than he knew his own rooms back home. He stepped across the stream, using Bloodbiter's Wrath as a support, sticking it deep into the mud, and plopped down on the far bank. For some time, he simply sat there, inhaling the mountain air, allowing his mind to pursue memories, memories that, for once, filled him with neither shame nor dread. He recalled the first time he had encountered the veiled and wafting specter in the forest. He remembered his disgust when he realized she was nothing but a girl. He remembered stick-and-leaf ships sunk with acorns, and muddy adventures when the dam broke and was repaired. He remembered ambushing the postmaster's boy.

The postmaster's boy, who had seen a monster.

Lionheart bowed his head, trailing the beanpole back and forth in the stream, sometimes with, sometimes against the current. He remembered the first time he had seen the monster. When he raised his face again, there were tears in his beard.

"Rose Red," he said softly to the stream and the trees and anyone who might listen, "you said once that if I had any trouble, to sing out and you'd come. Well, I have plenty of trouble. And I need you. If you'll come."

"Bah!"

Lionheart startled and turned about where he sat. The goat stood behind him, chewing her cud and gazing at him through half-closed eyes.

"Hullo, Beana," he said. "I see you survived anyway." He got to his feet and approached the goat, one hand out to stroke her head. She dodged and gave him a look that can be seen only on an irate goat's face. Lionheart gave up. "If you're here, Rose Red's got to be close." He looked into the forest, though he knew it was useless. Rose Red would not be found unless she wanted to be.

"Please, Rosie," he said. "I'm . . . I'm lost. I need you."

He felt her behind him. How she came to be there, he didn't know, but he knew as surely as he breathed that she stood there.

"Don't look around, Leo," she said.

He gulped. Then he slowly started to turn. "Rosie—"

"No! Please!"

He stopped, licking his lips. "I know already," he said. "I know you're without your veil."

"I cain't—" Her voice was so small, more frightened than he'd ever heard it before. She hardly sounded like the spunky mountain-climbing companion he'd once known. "I cain't bear to have you see me like this."

"But, Rosie, I already saw," he said. "Remember? All those years ago, when you took me to the cave to show me the mountain monster?"

A sob behind him, very soft, but enough to break his heart. He clenched his fists and forced himself not to turn.

"I thought," she said, "you hated me then."

"No!" he said quickly. "How could you think that?"

"When you saw the monster, you were so angry."

Lionheart drew a long breath, choosing his words carefully before he spoke them. The memory of that night was too painful . . . all the more so now, after he'd faced the Dragon.

"Rosie," he said softly, "let me tell you why I was angry."

Another sob. Was her voice fading? Was she leaving him? He turned a desperate glance Beana's way, but the goat only gave him a sour glare and continued chewing her cud.

Then Rose Red spoke. "Because I'd misled you. Because I hadn't told you what I was. I hadn't told you that . . . that *I* was the monster."

Dropping Bloodbiter's Wrath, he turned around quickly and took her hand. For a moment, Lionheart stared into her unveiled eyes, and he thought for sure that he would end up on his back with his breath knocked out of him, never to see her again.

But she didn't move. She stood still, and neither of them breathed, each one taking in the other's appearance. She saw Lionheart's beard, that masking disguise. She saw the heaviness under his eyes, the lingering poison deep inside, and all the regret.

And he saw the goblin.

Wide, white-moon eyes, so enormous as to be horrible, set in a craggy rock of a face. Her scalp was bare save for a few sorry strands of coarse hair. Her upper lip, such as it was, twisted to reveal jutting teeth, some stumpy, some sharp. Her nose was flat to her face with wide, slitted nostrils. Her ears were huge, almost batlike. She was tiny and scrawny, but the hand Lionheart held could smash boulders without a thought.

But she didn't smash Lionheart.

Tears welled up in the huge eyes that were made to see in the depths of mines. They splashed down the crags of her cheeks.

Lionheart took the claw of her hand in both of his and squeezed gently. "No," he whispered. "That wasn't it at all. I already knew what you were . . . or, at least, I suspected. I wasn't the brightest of lads, but I wasn't a total fool. Not then. No, when I caught that glimpse of you reflected in the water, I wasn't surprised, wasn't even scared.

"I was angry because I saw myself."

He bowed his head, unable to meet her searching gaze. "Just for a moment," he said, "I saw my real face. And I realized that the mountain monster wasn't any one person, any one beast. It was me. It was Fox-brush. It was Leanbear and Redbird, all the people of the village who were so terrified. Because all that terror that they fixed upon you, all that hatred . . . it was really only what was coming from inside of them.

"And my desire to hunt the monster, to kill it . . . that was because

I knew, in my heart, that I was nothing but a coward. I am and always have been my own monster. My own worst enemy."

His voice broke. He dropped Rose Red's hand and covered his face.

You did what you had to do, whispered the Lady.

"Her heart for your life," said the memory of the Dragon. *"It is the only way."*

"Rose Red," Lionheart said, not even certain if she still stood before him, she was so silent. "Rose Red, I never fought the Dragon. I . . . I gave him what he wanted, and I fled. I haven't told anyone. As far as they know, I faced him after he left, faced him and killed him. I didn't. I made a bargain with him instead. Yes, I saved Southlands; the Dragon won't return. But I . . . never fought the monster."

To his surprise, he felt two spindly arms wrap around him. With a deep breath of relief, he hugged her back, and they stood there, prince and goblin, beside the quiet stream with only a goat for audience.

"It's all right, Leo," Rose Red said. "You're still my good, kind master. No matter what happens, I will serve you."

"Will you?" Lionheart asked, still holding her. "Even after what I did?"

"There ain't nothin' you can do that will turn me from you."

"It's been an adventure, to be sure," said the prince. His voice was heavy, burdened. "All this mess of ours, I mean. And there is yet so much to be done. I can't promise this will be a happy story, Rosie."

"Maybe it will have a happy ending," said she. "When everything's complete and come full circle. This part ain't so nice, but maybe somethin' good will come of it?" She gulped and stepped back to look up at the prince, for the moment forgetting what she was, not caring as his gaze moved across her face. "Remember, you have to read all the legends together to know for sure, and we don't know them all yet. There may be a story out there somewhere to make this one happy."

Leo nodded, and there was a trace of a smile behind his beard. "I'd like to know that story someday."

Rose Red turned away then. For no matter how deep or how sincerely she felt, there were some feelings not right for a servant to express to her master.

"Will you come back to my father's house, then?"

She nodded. The people of Southlands hated her. They wanted to kill her. But somehow, she would serve the prince even so.

Lionheart, as he had done those long years ago, took her hand and kissed it. "There was never such a one as you, Rose Red," he said. "Bless you a thousand times!"

So they started back down the mountain, Lionheart leading the way with his beanpole, Rose Red trailing behind with Beana. Perhaps it wasn't the joyous ending to the five long years for which one would have hoped. The hero did not return home triumphant from battle. The girl did not find comfort in the arms of her beloved. But the Dragon was gone, and rebuilding could begin. And they had each other for support. Dawn would find them on the road back to the Eldest's House, back to whatever new life the day could bring.

And the silver song of the wood thrush echoed through the mountains, calling:

Won't you return to me?

An Excerpt From the Next

TALES OF
GOLDSTONE WOOD

Moonblood

Timeless fantasy
that will keep you spellbound

PROLOGUE

THE UNICORN STOOD before the gates of Palace Var. It guarded the paths to and from Arpiar, watching them with eyes that burned through all tricks and disguises. The roses climbing the stone walls of Var cast their moonlit shadows upon the unicorn's back in dappled patterns. If a wind swelled, those patterns shifted, but the unicorn never moved.

The Queen of Arpiar could see the unicorn through a window in her chambers, where she lay upon her pillows. She turned her gaze away, closing her eyes.

"My queen," said her head woman. "The child lives. You have a daughter."

Across the darkened room, a newborn made no sound as gentle hands wrapped it in red and gold. When the babe had not cried at its birth, the queen had thought perhaps it was dead.

"A daughter," she whispered. Tears slipped down her cheek. "No."

Before she could dash traces of weeping from her face, her husband entered. Without a glance for his queen, he went to the cradle and looked inside. He smiled, and though his face was more beautiful than tongue could tell, the queen shuddered at the sight.

"A daughter!" Triumph filled the king's voice. He turned to the queen and laughed in her face. "A pretty daughter, my pretty bride. With blood as red as the red, red rose. Her name will be Varvare."

"Please," his wife spoke in a small voice. "Please, my lord."

"Please what, sweet Anahid?" The king laughed again and moved to the queen's bedside. He took her hand and, though she struggled against him, would not release his hold. "You'd think I was disappointed in you. On the contrary, beloved, I could not be better satisfied! You have proven more useful than I dared hope."

He dropped her hand and addressed himself to her head woman and the other attendants present. "See to it you care well for my darling Varvare. My perfect rose."

With those words he vanished from the chamber, though the shadow of his presence lingered long afterward.

Nevertheless, the moment he was out of sight, Queen Anahid rallied. She pushed upright on her cushions, turning once more to that sight out her window. The unicorn stood at its post near the roses, and it was hateful to her. But there was one path, she knew, that it did not guard.

"Bring me clothes and a cloak of midnight." She turned to her attendants, who stared at her. "At once."

They exchanged glances, but no one moved. In all the realm of Arpiar, not a soul could be found who loved the king. But neither was there a heart that did not sink with fear at the mention of his name. Thus the queen's servants remained frozen in place when she spoke. The queen stared at them with her great silver eyes, and they would not meet her gaze.

"Will no one serve their queen?" she asked.

They made no answer.

Straining so that a vein stood out on her forehead, Queen Anahid flung back the soiled blankets of her labor and rose from her bed. Her head woman gasped, "My queen!"

In that moment, the princess, who had made no more than a whimper since the time of her birth, gave a cry from her cradle. The piteous sound worked a magic of its own on the assembled servants. One leapt to the cradle and gently lifted the child. Another ran to the queen's side, and a third did as the queen had asked and brought her clean garments and a cloak as black as the night.

The queen was weak from her labor, but her strength returned in the face of need. She let her servants clothe her, then took and wrapped the deep cloak about her shoulders. "Give me the child," she said, turning to the youngest of her maids, who stood trembling near to hand, shushing the babe.

"My queen," her head woman spoke, "are you certain—"

"Do you doubt me?" The queen's eyes flashed. She took the baby, adjusting the scarlet and gold cloth that bound the tiny limbs tight. She tucked the warm bundle inside her cloak, close to her heart.

"Tell no one I have gone," she said, striding to the door. "Any of you who follow me does so at your own peril."

The blackness of her cloak shielded Queen Anahid and the princess as she made her way through the corridors of Palace Var, unseen save by the roses, which turned their faces away and said not a word. She slid from shadow to shadow. Woven enchantments whirled in endless grasping fingers everywhere she turned, but these Anahid had long ago learned to see and to elude.

But all paths from Arpiar led past the unicorn.

The queen stood in the darkness of the courtyard, breathing in the perfume of roses, gazing at the gate that stood between her and the empty landscape. She felt the tiny beating heart pressed against her own and gnashed her teeth. "Would that he had been devoured on the shores of the Dark Water!" Then, closing her eyes and bowing her head, she called out in the voice of her heart, a voice unheard in that world but which carried to worlds beyond.

"I swore I would never call upon you again."

An answer came across distances unimaginable and sang close to her ear in a voice of birdsong.

Yet I am always waiting for you, child.

"I ask nothing for myself, only for my daughter. She does not deserve the fate the king has purposed for her."

What would you have me do?

"Show me where I can take her. Show me where she may be safe."

Walk my Path, sang the silver voice.

There in the darkness of Arpiar, a way opened at the queen's feet. The one Path that the unicorn could not follow. Anahid stepped into it, full of both gratitude and shame, for she had vowed never to walk this way again. But she had no other choice. She followed the Path to the gate, pushed the bars aside, and stepped into the plains beyond.

The unicorn did not see her. She passed beneath its gaze, her heart beating like a war drum against the bundle on her breast, but the unicorn was blind to her passage.

Queen Anahid strode from Palace Var without a backward glance, her daughter held tight in her arms. As she went, the silver voice sang in her ear, and she found herself responding to the familiar, half-forgotten words:

> *Beyond the Final Water falling*
> *The Songs of Spheres recalling*
> *Won't you return to me?*

She followed the song across the hinterlands of Arpiar, speeding along the Path so quickly that she must have covered leagues in a stride. She came to a footbridge, just a few planks spanning from nowhere to nowhere. But when she crossed it, she stepped over the boundaries from her world into the Wood Between.

The unicorn felt the breach on the borders of Arpiar. It raised its head, and the bugle call of its warning shattered the stillness of the night. Anahid, even as she stood beneath the leafy canopy of the Wood, heard that sound across the worlds. She moaned with fear.

Do not be afraid. Follow me.

"It will find me!"

I will guide you. Follow me.

"Only for my daughter!" the queen cried. "Only for my daughter."

Her feet, in dainty slippers, sped along the Path as it wound through the Wood. She could feel the unicorn pursuing, though it could not see her. But the nearness of its presence filled Anahid with such dread, she nearly dropped her burden and fled. But no! Though she had come so far, she was still too close to Arpiar.

"Please," she whispered. The silence of the Wood oppressed her. "Please, show me somewhere safe."

Follow, sang the silver voice, and she raced after that sound. Her feet burned with each step. How long had it been since she'd followed this Path? Not since she was merely Maid Anahid, a lowly creature unworthy of a king's notice. She had not known then and did not know now where it would lead. She only knew the unicorn could not catch her.

It may have been days; it may have been minutes; for all she knew, it may have been centuries. But the Path ended at last, and once more the forest grew up around her. The queen stood with her heart in her throat, straining her senses for any sign of the unicorn. Panting from her exertion, she struggled to draw a deep breath and almost gagged.

"The Near World," she said. "I smell mortality everywhere. How can my daughter be safe here?"

Follow me, sang the silver voice.

"Will you not accept her into your Haven?"

Follow me.

She saw no choice but to obey. The trees thinned and ended not many yards distant, and though the undergrowth was difficult to navigate in the darkness, she broke through the forest at last. The ground was rocky and inclined steeply uphill, but after a few minutes' climb she could take stock of her surroundings. She stood at the bottom of a deep gorge filled from one end to the other with forest, twisting on around a bend beyond her sight. A trail that looked as though it had not been traveled in generations led up from the gorge to the high country above. And over her head, in fantastic, impossible beauty, arched a bridge, spanning the gorge, gleaming white in the moonlight. She recognized its Faerie craftsmanship and wondered that the world of mortal men should boast so beautiful a creation.

The climb up the trail was difficult, and the queen was near the end of her strength when at last she emerged upon the high country. This was not a land she knew, but it was far from Arpiar. She smelled roses, free blossoms unsullied by her husband's hand. And the moon that glowed above was no illusion. By its glow, she could discern the contours of an enormous garden or park. A king's grounds, she thought. A fit home for her daughter.

The unicorn sang from the Wilderlands below.

Anahid screamed at the sound and started to run but tripped on the uneven soil and staggered to her knees. The baby wailed.

"Why have you brought me to this place?" the queen demanded, though she did not speak aloud. "We are unprotected in the Near World. Even my husband's enchantments must fade. It will find her for sure!"

The Fallen One may not enter the Near World. It must remain in the Wood Between.

The unicorn sang again. But it did not call for the queen, so she could not understand the words. Her daughter ceased crying, and when Anahid looked at her, she was surprised to find two wide eyes blinking up at her. "Don't listen," she said, trying to cover the baby's ears.

She cannot hear its voice. Her ears are full of my song.

Anahid breathed in relief and got to her feet. She moved unsteadily across the terrain until she came to a rosebush, not far from the great bridge. Kneeling, the Queen of Arpiar placed her bundle there and stopped a moment to gaze into her child's face, watching it wrinkle and relax and wrinkle again as though uncertain whether or not to be afraid.

Sorrowfully, she watched the change spread across the little face as the enchantments of Arpiar frayed and fell away. She closed her eyes and placed a hand upon her daughter's heart.

"With all the love I have to give," she murmured, "though that is little enough." Then she closed her eyes and raised both her hands toward the moon, cupping them as though to offer or receive a benediction. "I cry you mercy, Lord, and beg your protections upon my child! Shield her within this land from my husband's gaze. So long as she dwells in this high country, let her escape the spells of Arpiar."

A flutter drew her attention, and she saw a bird with a white speckled breast land in the rosebush above the child. Its wings disturbed the roses so that they dropped great red petals upon the baby's face, the most delicate of veils.

Your child is safe in my protection, now and always.

"Do you promise?" said the queen.

I promise. I claim her as one of mine.

"Then I shall return to Arpiar glad."

You may stay, child. You are not bound to that world.

"I will return," she said.

Another voice disturbed the night, an old voice as rough as the earth, rugged with mortality. "Oi! Who's there?"

Anahid leapt to her feet, cast one last look at her daughter, then fled into the night. At the edge of the gorge, she turned, her enormous eyes watching from the darkness. She saw a stocky mortal man, a gardener perhaps, with gray beginning to dominate his beard, step off the Faerie bridge. He went to the rosebush and knelt. Anahid held her breath. She heard the sharp intake of breath, then the man exclaim, "Well now, ain't you a sight, wee little one! How'd you end up out here on so dark a night?"

I claim her as one of mine, sang the wood thrush to Anahid.

She watched the gardener lift her child, then bowed her head, unwilling to see more. The next moment, the queen vanished down the trail, swallowed up by the Wilderlands below.

The unicorn met her there.

PART ONE

THE PRINCE

1

THE PRINCE OF SOUTHLANDS WAS BEWITCHED.

Rumor of his bewitchment had been spreading like a plague through the kingdom ever since he was sixteen years old: how the prince had returned from a summer in the mountains, bringing with him a little demon child and installing her as a servant in his father's house.

Cheap chitchat, to be sure. But fun fare with which to scare the children on a cold winter's night. "Watch out that you put your muddy boots away where they belong, or the prince's demon will come fetch you!"

At first, nobody believed it. Nobody, that is, except the servants of the Eldest's House, who worked with the girl in question.

"She gives me the shivers!" said Mistress Deerfoot to Cook. "With those veils of hers, she looks like a ghost. What do you think she hides behind them?"

"Her devil's horns, of course. And her fangs."

"Go on!" Mistress Deerfoot slapped Cook's shoulder (for she was rather keen on him). "Do be serious!"

Cook shrugged and said no more, for the demon herself passed by just then, carrying a bucket of water. That bucket was large, with an iron handle, and when full probably weighed nearly as much as the girl herself. Her skinny arms did not look as though they could support such a load, yet she moved without apparent strain. Her face was so heavily veiled in linen that not even the gleam of her eyes showed.

She did not pause to look at Cook or Deerfoot but hastened on her way without a word or glance. When she vanished up a servants' stair, Deerfoot let out a breath she had not realized she held. "Coo-ee! Unnatural strength that one has. What can the prince be thinking to keep one like her around here?"

"He's bewitched," muttered Cook. Which was the only natural explanation.

So the demon girl remained at the Eldest's House. And it was she, said the people of Southlands, who called the Dragon down upon them.

Prince Lionheart stood before his mirror glass, gazing into a face he did not recognize. It was not the face of an ensorcelled man, he thought, despite the rumors he knew people whispered behind his back. It was the face of a man who would be king. A man who would be Eldest of Southlands.

It was the face of a man who had breathed deeply of dragon smoke.

The stench of those poisons lingered throughout Southlands, though in the months since the Dragon's departure it had faded to a mere breath. In the Eldest's House it remained the most prominent. And on dark nights when the moon was new, one smelled it strongest of all.

But life must go on. Five years of imprisonment under that monster had taken its toll on the people of the kingdom, but they must struggle forward somehow. And Prince Lionheart would struggle with them.

He adjusted his collar and selected a fibula shaped like a seated panther to pin to his shoulder. He never allowed his bevy of attendants to help him dress, rarely even permitted them into his chambers. He'd been five years on his own, five years in exile while the Dragon held his kingdom captive. During that time, he'd learned to button his own garments, and Lionheart would not have attendants bungling about him now.

Besides, their questioning faces unnerved them. Every last one of them, when they met his eyes, silently asked the same question:

"Did you fight the Dragon?"

His fingers slipped, and the point of the fibula drove into his thumb. "Iubdan's beard!" he cursed, chewing at the wound to stop the blood. The pin fell to the stone floor at his feet. Still cursing, Lionheart knelt to pick it up. He paused a moment to inspect it, for it was of intricate work and solid gold. The seated panther was the symbol of Southland's heir. When he became Eldest, he would replace it with a rampant panther.

"Did you fight the Dragon?"

He closed his hand around the brooch. "I did what I had to do," he said. "I had no other choice. I did what I thought best."

Of course you did.

This voice in his head might have been his own. But it was colder and deeper, and it was no memory.

Of course you did, my sweet darling. And now, with the Dragon gone, you will have your dream.

"My dream," muttered Lionheart as he looked into the mirror once more and fixed the fibula in its place.

He must make his way downstairs now to the half-constructed hall where a banquet was to be held that night. The scaffolds were pulled down for the week, and the signs of construction hidden behind streamers and paper lanterns. The Dragon had destroyed the Eldest's Hall before he left Southlands, but rebuilding was well underway. And though the winter wind blew cold through the gaps in the walls and roof, the banquet must, for tradition's sake, be held there, for this was the prince's wedding week.

A shadow passed over the sun.

Lady Daylily sat in her chambers, gazing at her face in a glass that revealed a young woman who was no longer as beautiful as she had once been. Not that her beauty was far faded. But the poison that yet lingered in her lungs pinched her features, sallowed her complexion, and left her once vibrant eyes filmed over as with dull ash. She was still lovely, to be sure. But she would never again be what she had been.

Her attendants bustled about her, laying out her gown, smoothing the long headdress as they pinned it to her hair, selecting furs to drape over her shoulders to protect her in the drafty Eldest's Hall. Daylily must be as elegant as human hands could make her this evening.

After all, the prince's wedding week was hers as well.

"Out."

The woman pinning the headdress into Daylily's curls paused. "My lady?"

"Out. Now." Daylily turned on her seat. Her face was a mask, revealing nothing. "All of you. I would be alone for a moment."

"My lady," said Dame Fairlight, her chief attendant, "the banquet—"

"I believe I have made myself clear."

The women exchanged glances, then, one by one, set aside their tasks and slipped from the room, closing the door behind them. Daylily sat like a stone some minutes before moving softly to her window. There she sat, gazing out across the Eldest's grounds.

Like a prisoner gazing on the boundaries of her prison.

Daylily's view extended over the southern part of the Eldest's lands, off into the parks and gardens that sprawled for acres. These, like Daylily, were no longer what they had once been, ravaged now by both the winter and the Dragon. Most of the shrubs and bushes had withered into dry sticks and would never bloom again, come either spring or frost. Only the rosebushes remained alive. But these had not bloomed for twenty years and more.

From her vantage point, Daylily saw all the way to where the grounds broke suddenly and plunged into a deep gorge. She saw the white gleam of Swan Bridge, which spanned the gorge in a graceful sweep. But she could not see the darkness of the Wilderlands, the thick forest that grew in the depths of the gulf.

For the briefest possible moment, Daylily thought she should like to throw on a cloak, slip from the House, make that long walk across the grounds to the gorge, and vanish forever into the Wilderlands.

It was a wild fancy, and she shook it away even as it flashed across her imagination. After all, she was Lady Daylily, daughter of the Baron of Middlecrescent, the most beautiful woman in the Eldest's court (despite the Dragon's work), beloved of all Southlands and bride of Prince Lionheart. Prince Lionheart, who would one day be Eldest, making her queen. It was her father's dearest wish. It was the purpose of her entire life.

But how bitter was its fulfillment! Daylily clutched her hands in her lap, refusing even a trace of emotion to cross her face, though there was no one to see. If only she had kept her heart in check. If only she had remained the icy and unreachable statue she must be in order to fulfill this role. If only she'd never permitted herself to love—

She shook her head sharply, refusing to admit that thought. No, better not to dwell on such things. Better to focus instead on the cold reality of her dream come true.

The Prince of Southlands would marry her. But he did not love her.

A movement near to hand caught her eye. Daylily dragged her gaze from the bridge and the gorge to a closer plot of ground. A small figure, stooped and thin, walked among the struggling remnants of the garden. A nanny goat followed behind her like a tame dog, nosing the shrubs for any sign of something edible, while the girl gathered what greenery she found into a bundle on her arm.

She wore a white linen veil that covered the whole of her face.

Daylily gnashed her teeth. In that instant, she looked like a dragon herself. "Rose Red," she muttered. "Witch's child. Demon."

She trembled with sudden cold when the shadow passed over the sun and fled swiftly across her face.

The day was cold, especially for Southlands, which was used to balmy weather even in winter. The goat snorted, and streams of white billowed from her nose. But Rose Red, bundled from head to toe in her veils, scarcely noticed the chill. She searched the shrubs of the one-time garden for any sign of life. Some rosebushes had miraculously escaped the Dragon's fire and, though withered, still managed to produce some green. Rose Red ran her hands through them, not noticing if the thorns caught at her gloves or pierced her sleeves. She put her nose up to the leaves, and they still smelled sweet.

It was difficult these days to find anything that could bring freshness to the poisoned chambers of the Eldest's House. But Rose Red cut stems as she could, gathering a great armload. She would spread these through her master's chambers while he was busy at the banquet tonight. Perhaps it would cheer him to return and find greenery among those gloomy shadows. Or perhaps he would not notice.

"Beana!" She turned suddenly on her goat, which had a large sprig of leaves sticking out of the corner of her mouth. "Don't eat that. You'll be sick."

"Bah!" said the goat, spattering leaves about her hooves. When Rose Red reached out to snatch the mouthful from her, she shook her horns and turned her tail on the girl.

"Beana, I need every bit I can find. There's precious little as it is without you snackin' on it! You don't behave yourself, and I'm puttin' you back in the pen where you belong."

The goat muttered and trotted several paces back up the path, still chewing. Rose Red turned back to her bush, parting the thin stems to better reach a patch of lingering growth.

She paused, taking a startled breath.

Deep within that tangle of brown and dying leaves, almost hidden by thorns, was a blossom. Pure white, almost too pure to be visible, as though made of light itself, but fragrant, extravagant even. It was like nothing the girl had ever seen.

But when she blinked, it was gone.

The goat, standing some distance from her now, turned suddenly and shivered. "Bah," she said and trotted quickly to Rose Red's side. "What do you have there?"

Rose Red backed away hastily. "Nothin' you need to see. You'd probably eat it anyway."

She moved on down the row of bushes as her goat stayed put, poking her nose into the tangled branches. Beana's yellow eyes narrowed, and she stamped a back hoof. "Rosie!" she bleated. "What did you see?"

"Nothin', Beana," Rose Red repeated without turning to the goat. Her arms were full by now, and she would need to put the stems in water soon if she hoped to keep them alive long enough for her master to see. "You're goin' to have to go back to your pen now."

"I don't want to go back to the pen."

"I'm sorry, but I cain't take you inside with me. Not so long as you insist on bein' . . . you know . . . a goat."

Beana blinked slowly. "And what else would I be, dear girl?"

Rose Red did not answer. Many things had changed for her during those five years with the Dragon, even more in the months following his departure. Everything she had known was gone. The man she called father was dead. Her home was destroyed beyond recall. Hen's teeth, her goat wasn't even a goat!

And dreams came to life and walked in the real world as living, fire-breathing nightmares.

Sometimes she did not think any of the events in her recent life could possibly have happened. The rest of the time, she simply pretended they had not. Best to focus on the tasks at hand. She must serve her master. And she must stay out of everyone else's sight as much as possible. Because they all believed it was she who brought the Dragon upon Southlands.

In a way, perhaps she had.

Rose Red sighed as she led the goat back to her pen, where other goats raised lazy eyes and bleated disinterested greetings.

"What was that heavy sound for?" Beana demanded.

Rose Red sighed again. "Sometimes I wish . . ."

"Yes?"

"Sometimes I wish we could go back to the way things were. To the mountain. We were lonely, sure. But we were happier then, weren't we? With old Dad to care for, and our cottage to keep, and no one to . . . to . . ."

She could not finish her thought. How could she bear to say it? No one to look at her like she was a monster slavering to eat their children. No one to startle in fright whenever she entered the room. No one to whisper about her when she'd gone.

She tugged at her veil, adjusting it so that it would not slip off, pulling out stray rose thorns and dropping them to the dirt. Beana's gaze was fixed upon her, and she did not like to meet it. She knew exactly what her goat was about to say.

"We can go back, Rosie."

Rose Red shook her head.

"We can," said the goat. "Your master will provide for our journey. He's said so before. He won't keep you here against your will. We can go back to the mountain. It was foolish to have let him talk us into returning in the first place. Have we really done him any good?"

Rose Red did not answer. She plucked thorns from the long stems, rubbing her hand over the smooth bumps left behind.

"He's more distant than ever, hardly the boy you once knew," the goat persisted. "You rarely see him, and when you do, you rarely speak. He's not your responsibility, sweet child. He never was. And it was wrong of him to place such a burden on you, asking you to come back to the lowlands. It's dangerous here."

Beana stopped herself. To continue would be to say too much. There were some dangers it was best to keep the girl unaware of.

To the goat's disappointment, Rose Red said nothing but opened the pen gate and ushered her pet inside. "Rosie?" said Beana as Rose Red closed and fixed the latch.

"I cain't leave him, Beana," said Rose Red. "He needs me. He came back and found me because he needs me. I know it's foolish to say it, even to think it but . . . but, Beana, I'm the only friend my master has. Though he rules the whole kingdom, he needs me still." She bowed her head, gazing at the bundle of green under her arm. "Yet there's little enough I can do for him."

The goat watched as the girl made her way back through the gardens to the Eldest's House. She felt helpless, and for a moment she cursed the shaggy coat and hooves she wore. "It's tearing her up," she muttered as she lost sight of the girl. "This marriage of the prince's. It's tearing her to pieces inside. Light of Lumé above, I wish we'd never met him!"

A shadow passed over the sun.

Beana shivered and looked up, squinting. That was no cloud. Perhaps a bird. But it must have been a large one, an eagle even, to make that shadow.

A moment later, she thought she caught a familiar scent on the wind. A scent of poison and of anger. But it vanished, and she told herself it was nothing more than the remnants of the Dragon's work.

After all, Beana had bigger things to worry about.

Festive music began to play as the guests of the Eldest arrived and filled the new hall to celebrate their prince and his bride to be. Women in gaudy colors danced with men in silken garments, and their smiles flashed as bright as their jewels, so determined were they to rejoice and forget the nightmare in which they had so recently lived.

Prince Lionheart met Lady Daylily at the door and gave her his arm as support when they entered. Each wore a smile that outshone all the paper lanterns, but they did not look at each other. A great cheer rose up from the assembly, drowning the music.

A burst of fire lit the Wilderlands for an instant. A few moments later, a dragon began to climb the gorge.

ABOUT THE AUTHOR

Anne Elisabeth Stengl makes her home in Raleigh, North Carolina, where she lives with her husband, Rohan, and a passel of cats. When she's not writing, she enjoys Shakespeare, opera, and tea, and studies piano, painting, and fencing. She studied illustration at Grace College and English literature at Campbell University. She is the author of *Heartless* and *Veiled Rose*.

More Epic Fantasy From
Anne Elisabeth Stengl

As Princess Una comes of age, she ignores the whispered warnings of an ancient evil approaching her lands. But when a foolish decision leaves her heart vulnerable to an enemy she thought was only a myth, what will Una risk to save her kingdom—and the man she's come to love?

Heartless
Tales of Goldstone Wood

"A clever debut from an author worth watching."
—Publishers Weekly